WRITING JANE AUSTEN

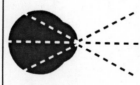

This Large Print Book ca
Seal of Approval of N.A

WRITING JANE AUSTEN

ELIZABETH ASTON

KENNEBEC LARGE PRINT
A part of Gale, Cengage Learning

GALE
CENGAGE Learning

Detroit • New York • San Francisco • New Haven, Conn • Waterville, Maine • London

GALE
CENGAGE Learning·

LIBRARY OF CONGRESS CATALOGING-IN-PUBLICATION DATA

Aston, Elizabeth.
    Writing Jane Austen / by Elizabeth Aston. — Large print ed.
        p. cm. — (Kennebec Large Print superior collection)
    ISBN-13: 978-1-4104-3014-4 (softcover)
    ISBN-10: 1-4104-3014-6 (softcover)
    1. Authors—Fiction. 2. Fiction—Authorship—Fiction. 3. Austen, Jane, 1775-1817—Manuscripts—Fiction. 4. Large type books. I. Title.
    PS3601.S86W75 2010b
    813'.6—dc22   2010026995

Published in 2010 by arrangement with Simon & Schuster, Inc.

Printed in the United States of America
    1 2 3 4 5   14 13 12 11 10
ED279

For the young ladies of Pinnace House:
Eloise Aston, Elizabeth Bonnice,
and Irene Leung —
who read, encouraged,
commented, and laughed.
Thank you!

ONE

Email from
livia.harkness@hplitagency.co.uk
To georgina@seaofcrises.co.uk

Ring me.

Henry stood at the door of Georgina's room, holding a weighty textbook in one hand and marking his place with a finger. He looked at his lodger with concern. "Gina, why the screech of terror? What's up? Why are you looking at that screen as though it had grown fangs?"

"It's an email from Livia."

"Okay, fangs is right. What does she want?"

"She wants me to ring her."

"I'll get the phone."

"I don't want to ring her. It's bad news."

"What precisely does she say in her email?"

"Ring me."

"That's it?"

"That's it."

"You can't deduce from those two words that it's bad news."

Oh, but Georgina could. Good news, Livia rang her. Bad news, she expected the recipient to foot the cost of the call. Except that it didn't actually cost Livia anything to make a call, it wasn't as though Georgina were on the other side of the Atlantic.

"Wish I were in America," she said, staring at the screen. "Or Tasmania; in the bush would be good." Perhaps if she looked long and hard enough, the words would re-arrange themselves. The message would say, Enjoy more Viagrous sex, every time. Or, You have inherited a million zoots, send us a hundred dollars and we'll show you how to claim your rightful inheritance. Or . . .

Ring me.

Like Alice, faced with that bottle which was labelled *Drink me.* Only there'd be no magical change of being for Georgina. Although after a few minutes of conversation with Livia, she'd feel about two foot high, so . . .

Henry was back, with the phone in his hand. "Call her."

Livia's direct line, ringing and ringing,

thank God, she'd gone out, was in a meeting. "Yes? Who? Georgina? I'm on the other line, can't talk. Get over here. Right away. See you in twenty minutes."

"Twenty minutes? Livia, it takes me —"

Brrrrrr. The sound of an empty line, of a phone put down, of an agent who is too busy to talk.

"What can she want?"

Henry looked up from a page dense with equations and formulae and gave her a quizzical look. "Go and find out?"

"I suppose so. Should I take a chapter of *The Sadness of Jane Silversmith*?"

"Which of the — how many is it now?"

"Forty or so. All right, forty-eight, to be precise."

"If she wanted to see a chapter, she'd say so. I judge she wants to see you, rather than a chapter."

"Twenty minutes! She's mad."

"Less than that, in a taxi."

"More than that by bus. I don't do taxis except in emergencies, remember?"

"Perhaps this is an emergency. Go, okay? Taxi, underground, bus, camel, donkey, yak — just go."

Henry went back to his study, which overlooked the street. It had been his parents' study when they lived in the house.

They now had a flat in Cambridge, overflowing with books and papers; his study was somewhat more orderly, but still the room of a man who liked to have everything at hand. He kept his desk clutter-free by dumping whatever he was finished with on to shelves and another table, where the pile of books obscured a silver framed photo of Sophie, his extraordinarily pretty girlfriend. He watched Gina, dark curls escaping from the red beret she'd thrust on her head, hurrying along the pavement beneath the autumn-coloured poplars, energy in every step. She did everything with such intensity, it must be a strain on her nerves.

It was a five-minute walk to the bus stop. There was no bus in sight, and Georgina circled the post, knowing that seconds would seem minutes and minutes hours because of her impatience. Calm down. Breathe in, then slowly out. Why wasn't she like her landlord, Henry, imperturbable?

She had a ten-minute wait before the double-decker bus appeared. She still got a thrill from the red London buses, even after more than five years in England, and the sight of the splash of colour raised her spirits, as it always did. She climbed up to the top deck of the bus, squeezing her way past two women with shopping overflowing into the gangway, and sat down in the front seat.

The bus roared round a corner and braked violently as it joined the end of a long tail-back of traffic.

The first time she'd come to London, her father had taken her for a ride on the top of a red double-decker bus, and it was the highlight of her trip. She'd been in England with her father and the second of five stepmothers on their honeymoon, but that particular stepmother hadn't cared for London, and considered public transport unhygienic. Georgina had been a skinny eight-year-old then, legs dangling from the seat, all huge eyes and unruly hair. The legs had grown and filled out in the right places, but the hair and eyes had stayed much the same through another three stepmothers.

Georgina didn't remember her own mother, who had walked out on her and her father when she was six months old, taking a wardrobe of clothes and Georgina's two-year-old brother with her.

Her first stepmother had been into pink and prettiness, and Georgina hadn't taken kindly to being decked out in the frills and fussiness that made her look, she told her father in a fit of rage, like something just out of the poodle parlour. Number three stepmother was a hippie and way-out; her lasting legacy was teaching Georgina how to relax and tune out, which she'd done so effectually at school that there'd been talk of remedial classes. That one had gone off to India to join an ashram, presumably to assuage the materialistic guilt she must have felt over taking Georgina's father for every penny he had.

After her had come Louise, the brightest and the best of her stepmothers. Intelligent and thoughtful, raised in a Quaker family, she had encouraged Georgina to take her studies and life seriously. Without her, there would have been no top college for Georgina, and no chance of the career as academic and writer that she now enjoyed. Although Louise, presently living the pure life with a woman friend in the wilds of Canada, would have frowned at the word *enjoyed. Endured* was more her style.

Forty-eight chapters. Enough to make a whole book. Except for the minor problem that they were all Chapter One. She must breathe properly, close her eyes, relax her shoulders, relax her jaw, relax her scalp. How did you relax your scalp? Count your blessings. You have good health. You have a brain. You have an education. You have great legs and straight teeth. You live in a house far nicer than you can afford, because you have a kind landlord. You like your landlord. You get on fine with his girlfriend. You have an agent. An important London agent. You are a published author, of a prizewinning book, which received rave reviews and made you into a Literary Name.

**THE GUARDIAN
FICTION REVIEW**
Magdalene Crib by Georgina Jackson.
426pp

This searingly grim read is a long one, but in its polyphonic brilliance, with its spare yet wincingly tender account of the hopeless life of its eponymous heroine, one can only wish the author had prolonged her harrowing tale of despair. Jackson draws on documentary accounts such as law court records to create a fictional life of a woman whose existence explodes the distorted myth of Victorian values and highlights the reality of unspeakable deprivation for so many voiceless women of that time.

Magdalene Crib is the bastard daughter of an alcoholic prostitute. Raised and abused by Catholic nuns in Liverpool, she runs away to Ireland, where she is taken into service by a tyrannical master before being cast off, penniless and homeless. Weakened by famine and typhus, she manages to board a ship bound for America and a new life, but after enduring a most terrible voyage, she falls into the hands of a pimp and is set to work in a brothel. She escapes and returns to Liverpool, where she takes her vows as a nun, only to continue the vicious cycle by in her turn abusing the children in her care. In the poignant and moving ending, she casts off her role as victim and takes her own life.

Jackson's Victorian style is brilliant and utterly convincing; this is a new literary voice that we shall surely hear more of.

Rave reviews, but what was the use of them, when her book had come out two years ago, and she knew in her heart she was never going to get to Chapter Two of her second book, and that even if she did, no one would want to publish it?

Fifty-five minutes later, she was ascending the shallow steps that led up to the elegant, black front door with its gleaming brass plate: HARKNESS AND PHILBY LITERARY AGENCY.

The teenager at the desk, who wore blue-tinted glasses and had her hair in coiled plaits — retro look, or just no sense of style? — pouted at Georgina, then cast a scornful look at her sneakers. "Miss Harkness was expecting you hours ago. Hours! I'll see if she's free."

Georgina closed her eyes and prayed that Livia would be involved in some international auction deal, would send down the message, "Go away, come back tomorrow."

"Go on up," said the teenager.

Georgina went slowly up the stairs, and stood outside Livia's door. She took a deep breath and pushed it open.

"I said right away." Livia never was one for the niceties. "What did you do? Walk? Hobble?"

"I came on a bus. I have to economize —"

"Since you aren't earning beans, spare me the sob story. Sit down."

Livia Harkness had been an agent for more than twenty years. Ageless, but probably in her forties, she was, as usual, wearing black from head to toe, with jet earrings and bangles to lighten things up. She was one of the last of the many publishers and literary agents who had once inhabited Bloomsbury, and her office, situated on the first floor of a Georgian house, was usually spartan in its minimalism. Today it hosted a miasma of paper. Manuscripts lay on every surface, piled high on the deep shelves and even stacked up beside her desk.

"Unsolicited submissions," Livia said, puffing at a noxious cigarette. She coughed, and blew a few smoky halos into the air. "We've had a clear-out, they're all in here until the men come to take them away. For shredding, pulping or throwing into the Thames. Wish all the bloody authors would jump into the Thames. So you're too tight to take a taxi? What do you think my time is worth?"

Georgina knew better than to answer that. She sat straightbacked on the edge of a monstrously uncomfortable chair, her mouth zipped shut.

"A lot more than your time is worth. Right, let's get on with it. I've got you a commission."

Georgina was so startled, she tilted the chair forward and only saved herself from a confrontation with the floor by hanging on to the lip of Livia's vast mahogany desk. She levered herself back into something like an upright position.

"A commission? For *The Sadness of Jane Silversmith?*"

More smoky halos, and a look so filled

with scorn that Georgina felt prickles of nervous perspiration bursting out on her forehead. "It's what I'm writing."

"Don't lie to your agent. Ever. It's what you're trying to write. It's irrelevant. No one who isn't witless or senseless on substances would commission that book. I've told you, misery's over. Done for. Finished. Times are bad. Prosperous, self-satisfied people read miseries, noir and grit. Worried, jobless, indebted people want a richer palette of happiness and good fortune."

Miseries! "That's a pejorative term, Livia, and there's always a market for realism."

"Realism! Spare me. Anyhow, forget about it. We're talking completely different. New angle, new venture. Big. High concept. Very, very high. Sign this."

To Georgina's amazement, her agent pushed a sheet of paper across the polished surface of her desk, and rolled a pen after it.

"Don't bother to read it. Just sign."

"I can't sign without knowing —"

"I'm your agent, right? For the moment," she added, and there was no humour in her voice. "If I tell you to sign, just pick up the pen."

"What is it?"

Livia sighed. "Non-disclosure. You will not

tell a living soul what we're talking about in this office today. Not your sister, your dearest friend, your mother — oh, you don't have a mother, I forgot — and not that crazy would-be scientist you live with."

Not for the first time, Georgina wondered whether Livia's mental state was hovering on the danger zone.

"I don't live with Henry; at least I do, I live in his house, but I don't live with him in the sense —"

"You seriously think I'm interested in your sex life or lack of it? I don't care if he's your masseur, your analyst or an in vitro sibling with whom you are having an incestuous relationship. You don't discuss this with him, get it? Nor with anyone else."

Georgina picked up the pen and dragged her chair closer to the desk. "I really think I ought to read it. And that you ought to tell me what this is all about before I sign anything."

Livia picked up her half-glasses and perched them on her beaky nose. So would a vulture look after a trip to the optician. "Sign."

Georgina signed.

"Your publishers, your former publishers, have a manuscript. A nineteenth-century manuscript, written by a major author. Very major."

Georgina waited. "That's exciting," she ventured.

"In her handwriting."

What kind of a book? A journal? A novel? "Do you mean the manuscript of an existing book?"

"Don't be stupid. That would be worth money, but what would it have to do with you? No. An unknown work."

Despite herself, Georgina was intrigued. "Where has it come from? Did they buy it?"

"Buy it? Why would they do that? They found it. Building works, some bricked-up cupboard, reams of dross, nothing's changed in publishing for the last two centuries. Amidst the rubbish, some pages of gold. Pure gold."

"Pages? How many pages?"

"Eighteen or nineteen. Chapter One."

Chapter One? A soul mate, this writer; another novelist specializing in Chapter Ones, by the sound of it. "And where do I come into it?" Georgina had been holding her breath, and now she took a gulp of air which rushed into her lungs and hit back in the shape of a desperate hiccup.

"Have you been drinking?"

"No," Georgina said, her eyes watering.

"A glass of water —"

"What do you think this is, a café? You come into it because Dan Vesey, director of Cadell and Davies, thinks that you are the person to finish the book."

"Finish the book?"

"Cut the echoes. You heard. It works. It has synergy. Cadell and Davies dropped a bundle on *Magdalene Crib,* all those American returns did nothing for their bottom line. You do Victorian, you can write nineteenth-century. It's going to be huge, ultra huge. He gets his money back, you get a second chance."

Silence. Georgina sat waiting for what Livia would say next, but she said nothing.

Georgina swallowed hard. "You said a major author. Just how major? I mean, if we're talking, say, one of the Brontë sisters, someone like that, I'm absolutely sure —"

"It's not a Brontë."

"I'm not the right person for this, I don't think I could write a book in someone else's voice."

"Don't give me that voice stuff. Since you aren't writing anything, and since what you think you want to write is past its sell-by, you'd better jump at this, and jump quick. Tight deadline, Dan wants a finished book on his desk when he announces the find to the world. It'll be headlines from here to Sydney, and that way there's no chance of anyone else muscling in. He'll sell the manuscript pages to a collector or a museum for megabucks, but at that point, he won't have control. So he wants a book, written by a reputable, respected author — you — picking up the story at the end of Chapter One, on its way to the presses, before he goes public. He gets publicity for the discovery, he gets sales for the book. Even you can get the point of that, am I right?"

"My new book's shaping up well. It might not be good for my career to —"

"You don't have a career. Let's just review how things stand, shall we? I got you a tip-top contract for *Magdalene Crib*. Cadell and Davies took it, paid good money for it, pushed it out. Classy reviews, lots of literary *succès d'estime*" — Livia's French accent was nasally perfect — "winner of the Lorrimer prize, short-listed for the Orange, sold peanuts. Like I said, misery's dead. What you're working on is even more depressing than the first one. Bin it. Clear your head, and sniff the coffee. You missed the market. Two years, even a year earlier, you might have made it with that book. The world's moved on, you haven't. Get over it."

"Honestly, Livia, I don't —"

"Let's look at things time-wise. We can't keep the wraps on this for more than twelve weeks max. Hundred and twenty thousand words, could be more, you'll know what length she wrote. You'll do it under her title of course, not a bad one, got the right period feel, *Love and Friendship*. Seems she reused it, wrote some kid's stuff with the same title, only spelt it wrong. No spell-check those days, least you've got Microsoft on your side."

"Livia, just who is this author?"

Livia sat back, a foxy smile on her face. "Jane Austen, that's who. Jane Austen, no less. Couldn't be better, couldn't be bigger. What a writer, bankable all the way, in print for two hundred years and now a superstar. That's my kind of client. Not much sex and violence, of course, which is a pity, but that Andrew Whosit guy will put the sex back in when he does the TV adaptation."

Georgina couldn't believe her ears. Aghast, she fought the sense of panic that had her firmly in its grip. She pushed the chair back, stood up, and braced herself on Livia's desk. "Jane Austen? Are you telling me Dan Vesey's found the beginning of an unknown novel by Jane Austen, and you want me to finish it?"

"Don't do that, you'll leave marks on the polish. Yes. Jane Austen, and that's the deal. Chance of a lifetime, for you."

Jane Austen? Chance of a lifetime? For some author, possibly, but for her? Nix. "Christ, you've picked the wrong person, you really have."

"Sit down."

Georgina sat, eyeing the door, wondering whether to make a run for it, then gathered her wits. She had to put a stop to this whole absurd business right now.

"Clean out of my period," she said. "I'm late, she's early. You know how I work, I use authentic original sources, letters, journals, contemporary newspapers, court records. None of those apply here. And writers like Austen have their own style, there's absolutely no way I could do it."

Ominously, Livia said nothing, just kept her eyes boring into Georgina. Without shifting them from her face, she banged a brass bell on her desk and shouted, "Tish!"

Ms. Blue Specs appeared at the door. "Bring me Georgina Jackson's file," Livia said.

"I have it here, Miss Harkness."

Livia slammed the blue folder down on

the table. "Just to remind you of a few facts, Georgina. You're an historian, right? Dr. Jackson, let's not forget the Ph.D. Early-nineteenth, late-nineteenth century, what the hell's it matter? You're not familiar with the period? Then get familiar. You can pastiche 1880, you can pastiche 1810."

"It's an honour to be asked, but truly, you'd be making a mistake."

"I don't make mistakes." Livia counted on her bony fingers, which were adorned with chunky modern rings. "Let's recap, shall we? One, you lost your publisher money on *Magdalene Crib.* Two, you aren't writing anything else that anyone's going to want to buy or read. Three, you're an American, but anglicized American. That's a plus, because sales over the pond are going to be huge. Jane is even bigger over there than she is here. Four, you have a name as a literary author."

She let her fingers go, flexing them in front of her as though she were about to grasp Georgina round the throat. The voice changed from sharp to menacing purr. "You need money and work to stay in the UK, right?"

Georgina wished that she'd never let on to Livia how much she wanted to stay on in England. She had, and she would bet Livia knew exactly how difficult it was to get the right to stay permanently. "I have my university fellowship."

"You've only got a few months left at the university and when that's finished, you won't be able to get another job in the UK, not without a permit. Writing's all you'll be allowed to do, and you have to have money in the bank to support yourself while you do it. Write this novel and it wipes out the loss, you get big bucks, Dan Vesey gets big bucks, I get fifteen percent of big bucks, you get to stay in England, we're all happy. Turn it down, you're on your way back across the Atlantic, with nothing to show for your time here but a heap of faded cuttings."

Georgina tried to keep her voice low and reasonable. Livia was in la-la land, but with the right approach, she must be able to make her agent understand how impossible it was. "You don't understand, I'm not being wilful nor ungrateful. It's can't, not won't. I'm not capable of writing a book like Jane Austen. Oh, there are just so many reasons why I'm not the right person for this," she finished, knowing how weak it sounded, but determined not to reveal exactly why Livia and Dan had chosen the wrong writer to do the job.

"Don't give me that crap. I'm the one who says what you can and can't write. You wrote one book in fancy language, you can do another. You didn't get sales, but you got the crits. The literati like you. You won that prize and got coverage for your book, got your face and name out there. Radio, late-night TV, Edinburgh Festival, weekend supplements, that kind of thing. That gives you the credibility Dan Vesey's looking for."

"It's huge, you say it yourself. Get a big name, any one of a dozen top writers would snap your hand off for this."

"Yes, and are they my clients? No, they are not. I've been through my entire list, don't think I only considered you, and none of them fits the bill the way you do. Now, I've got a twelve o'clock. Tish will give you the paperwork on your way out. A transcription of the pages, complete with all the interpolations and cancellations, plus background stuff. It's been authenticated by Dan's sister, she's an academic at Oxford and has all the right contacts. All in the family, and that's how we want to keep it."

"No," Georgina said.

"I'll give you, from the kindness of my heart, exactly one hour to come to your senses and get back to me with an answer, and that answer will be yes. Got that?"

Two

Email from
livia.harkness@hplitagency.co.uk
To
dan.vesey@cadellanddavies.co.uk
Subject: Georgina Jackson

She'll do it. Send me the
contract.

Georgina hurtled out into the street, eager to put as much distance as possible between herself and Livia. She was trembling. With anger? Or fear.

Fear. Pure terror. And relief that she had escaped without agreeing to Livia and Dan's preposterous suggestion. She paused and looked up and down the street. She'd walk home. It would take her more than an hour, time to slow her heart rate down to normal, time to avoid Livia's call.

She hardly saw the pavements, traffic,

newspaper vendors, snap-happy tourists, shoppers, dog-walkers or anyone or anything else as she threaded the streets between Bloomsbury and Marylebone. After a grey summer, Londoners were rejoicing in the mild air, the brilliant blue skies, the warm sunlight of an early October day, but for Georgina the sky might as well have been a mass of cumulonimbus storm clouds.

Wrapped in thought, she almost walked past Henry's stuccoed terrace house. She retraced her steps along the railings, looking down into the basement kitchen where Anna Bednarska, Henry's indefatigable Polish housekeeper, was hard at work. She had on a striped apron, and was slicing beets with efficient savagery. Georgina didn't care much for beetroot, but if Anna was making borscht, that was fine by her.

Anna had the tiny basement flat in return for housekeeping duties. The income from one lodger was tax-free, but Henry would have to pay tax if he had a tenant in the basement flat. It was a quid pro quo arrangement that suited both parties, although Henry did from time to time feel guilty about how much work Anna did in return for her accommodation.

Georgina went slowly up the white-edged flight of steps to the black front door, and put her key in the lock. As she pushed the door open, she heard the phone ring and two voices, one of them Henry's, the other a female one she didn't immediately recognize, calling out to each other to take the call. Was Henry's girlfriend back in England already? It didn't sound like Sophie; her actress's voice wasn't given to such high-pitched yells.

Georgina's eye fell on a pile of luggage beside the table in the hall. A scruffy backpack. A plastic bag with a disgruntled-looking teddy bear peering out of it. A pair of long black leather riding boots. A battered suitcase with wheels. On the marble hall table, evidently placed with more care, was a small black case covered with stick-on letters to make a slogan: *The oboe is an ill wind nobody blows good.*

It couldn't be.

It was.

Henry's sister, Maud; fourteen, going on thirty. An enchanting girl, but difficult. How time flew, it seemed only yesterday that she'd been setting off back to boarding school.

Maud sauntered down the stairs, a vision in a short black skirt with purple tights, her face starkly white and her lashes starkly black. She was holding out the phone. "Hi,

Gina. Phone for you."

"Half-term?" Georgina mouthed, as she took the phone, which was emitting squawking noises.

"No. I ran away."

Heart sinking, Georgina spoke into the phone. It was Livia, of course it was.

"Your time's up."

"Livia, you and Dan are out of your minds. I am totally the wrong person for this job."

"We don't think so, and we're the experts, not you. Dan's displeased, Georgina. Seriously displeased. Read through what I gave you, sign the contracts I'm about to courier round to you, cancel any appointments you may have for the next three months and get writing."

"No. No, no, no. A thousand times, no!"

"Shut up and listen. I'm an A-list agent. For about a fortnight, you were an A-list author. Now you're heading for the Z slot. I don't do Z-list authors. You take this commission or you find yourself a new agent. Clear?"

Georgina sat down on the bottom step and put her head in her hands.

It didn't take Henry and Maud any time at all to get it out of her. In past centuries,

30

they'd have been star interrogators for the Inquisition. Henry was concerned for some thirty seconds about the nondisclosure paper she'd signed, and then he decided it wouldn't hold up in court. "Signed under duress, she didn't give you time to read it properly, and she'll never know, anyhow."

"Better out than in," said Maud. "Troubles shared and all that."

"You'll be on the phone two seconds after I tell you, texting your friends."

"Scout's honour, I won't," said Maud. "I don't have many friends. And I don't have a phone right now, because that cow of a housemother confiscated it."

"Is that why you ran away?" asked Henry. "I need to get your side of the story straight before the mistress-in-charge from the running-away department gets on the phone to me."

"No one will know I'm gone yet," said Maud. "They'll just think I'm skiving off somewhere. They'll notice in" — she looked at her watch — "approximately three and a half hours, when it's orchestra and they find they haven't got a second oboe. Shoot, Gina."

Georgina was torn. Half of her was longing to talk it over, the other half knew that the best thing she could do was keep her mouth shut, go upstairs, send Livia an email and say to Henry and Maud that she was out if anyone rang.

"It's like this."

Maud sat enthralled, her eyes growing rounder and rounder, her face alive with delight and disbelief as Georgina came to the climax of her story and uttered the magical words, *Jane Austen.*

Maud and Henry swept all her protestations aside.

"It's the wrong period."

"Take a course on it."

"No time."

"You did English at university, you just need to bone up a bit."

"I majored in history, I only did one course in English. Literary Theory 101, as it happens."

"Those Jane Austen books, sequels, prequels, sex with Mr. Darcy, whatever — they sell and sell," Maud said. "No more popping into Oxfam for your clothes, don't think I haven't noticed. Those sneakers, by the way, Gina, ghastly."

"It's a challenge," said Henry. "That's what you need. A big challenge."

"It's far too big a challenge," Georgina said. "Apart from anything else, I'm not that kind of novelist. Novelists come in two varieties, those who are basically reporters and those who do imagination. Austen's imagination, I'm reporter through and through. She's romantic. I go for realism."

"Yeah, but that's why your book's so depressing," said Maud. "Jane Austen's much more fun; God, I can't tell you which of them is my favourite, I just love them all. We all do. Hey, maybe they'll make a film of it."

"Austen writes romantic comedy. Comedy!"

"Yes, she makes me laugh out loud," Maud said. "Satirical. Sharp. Cool."

"You can be witty," Henry said. "You just need to get it on the page. And surely, with your brain and ability to re-create language of another time, you won't have a problem with her language and style. Not once you get into it. And you're wrong, Jane Austen is definitely a realist."

"Do you like *Pride and Prejudice* best? Most people do, but I think *Emma*'s kind of special," Maud said. "How about Fanny Price, what do you reckon? Should she have married Henry Crawford instead of Edmund?"

Georgina had to say it, and she was so agitated that her words came out as a shout, startling Henry and Maud as much with the volume as with her shocking revelation. "You don't understand! I've never read an Austen novel in my life. Not a single one. And what's more, I don't intend to start now, let alone write one!"

"In England, we readers call her Jane Austen," Maud said. "It's a sign of respect."

Henry raised incredulous eyebrows. "You aren't serious, are you?"

Maud said in astonished tones, "None of her novels? Not a single one? Not even *Pride and Prejudice*? What about the TV serializations? Or the films? No?" A pitying shake of her head, and then, with a mixture of sympathy and disdain, "Poor you."

Henry recovered himself. "It's easily remedied, Gina. We've got all of Jane Austen's books in the house, you just need to get reading. Lucky you, not poor you; what a treat you have in store."

It was Georgina's turn to shake her head. "I've got no plans to read any Jane Austen. I haven't read the books because I've never wanted to, and I don't want to now. They're just not my kind of novel."

"How do you know, if you haven't read them?" Maud said.

"I'm not good with romance. Her novels are all about young women falling in love and getting husbands, aren't they? Not my thing at all. Don't nag, Maud. Even if I wanted to agree to this ridiculous proposal, there's more to it than reading the books and heading for my computer. Her words would have to seep into my bones, and nothing's going to seep in, in the few weeks they've given me."

"Coward," said Maud, and thumped off upstairs.

"Sorry, Henry," Georgina said, after a moment's silence. "You wanted to know why Livia had summoned me, and I told you. Can we forget it, please? You've got other things to worry about right now. Such as Maud."

Henry gave her a long, thoughtful look and retreated into his study. Georgina reluctantly went upstairs to her room. She supposed she had better read the typescript Livia had forced on her, although what was the point? At least Livia hadn't wished the handwritten manuscript on her, at least she could read this easily enough.

The arrival of a fourth daughter was greeted with a sigh by Mr. Edward Turner, and resignation by Mrs. Turner. The child was christened Susan, and with the birth the following year of the long-awaited son and heir, Susan took her place as the least important member of the family.

Georgina, too, greeted Susan's appearance with a sigh, and she skimmed through the rest of the chapter. Nineteen-year-old Susan Turner, now one of eight children, had been sent as a companion to her rich cousin, Lady Carcenet, a widow in her early forties, who lived in Bath, and wanted a companion. *"She will expect you to amuse her, to play backgammon in the evenings, to perform upon the pianoforte, for she is very fond of music, and perhaps to accompany her when she ventures out into society,"* Mrs. Turner told her dutiful daughter. Georgina could see why Susan would want to get away from her family, who lived in a quiet way in a rural parish where the girls' only amusements were muddy walks and a rare assembly ball at the inn in the nearest town. Although backgammon and sonatas didn't sound like a bundle of fun; what a bore this genteel lifestyle was. Here was Susan bidding farewell to her family, having a brief encounter with a handsome gentleman in a blue coat during a stop to change horses at a posting inn, arriving at nightfall on the doorstep of her cousin's large and elegant house in Bath.

That was it?

That was it. Jane Austen, having got that far, had clearly decided this book was never going to be more than a Chapter One. Like *The Sadness of Jane Silversmith, Love and Friendship* was going nowhere. And she, Georgina Jackson, was supposed to craft a hundred and twenty thousand words or so of a convincing narrative from this unpromising beginning? To do what Jane Austen couldn't?

Forget it.

Georgina stuffed the pages back into the envelope and thrust it into a desk drawer, which she slammed shut.

Henry hadn't uttered a word of criticism to his sister, but that evening after dinner, when Maud was back upstairs disarranging her room, he flung himself on to the sofa in the sitting room with a sigh and a harassed expression in his normally cool grey eyes. "I don't blame her for running away, I half expected it, I never thought that school was a good idea. My Aunt Pam steam-rollered my parents into it when they knew she would have to go to boarding school. It's a damned nuisance my grandmother's gone to New Zealand, because when she lived in Cambridge, Maud could stay with her when my parents were away on their trips, and go to day school."

Henry's mother was a glaciologist, his father a geologist, and they were both away on a six-month expedition to investigate undersea volcanoes in the Antarctic. They'd left Maud, at her insistence, in her brother's guardianship. Henry, at thirty, was sixteen years older than his sister, so it made sense. Especially, he told Georgina, when the alternative was his aunt. "Who'd stand no nonsense from Maud, is how she'd put it, and that kind of approach just doesn't work with Maud. You have to take the scenic route with her."

"What's wrong with the school?" Georgina asked.

"Nothing, except it isn't right for Maud. Frankly, I don't know where she'd be happy. She doesn't make friends easily; she's odd, which didn't matter in Cambridge, where the schools are full of girls like her who've grown up in academic households. But being odd doesn't help you make a go of an English girls' boarding school, and I think the other girls have given her a hard time of it. That's the impression I got from the school, anyhow. The headmistress doesn't want her back, she doesn't think it's the right place for her either. Which means she knows damn well that if Maud did go back, she'd just run away again. So her trunk's been despatched, and a bill will follow, for extras, she said, chilling prospect. And I suppose there'll be a fight over next term's fees. Oh well, I'll have to sort something out, and she's fun to have around. I hope this Goth phase doesn't mean she's going to go in for suicidal gloom."

"It's just a look. And those vampire books she reads are wacky, but not gloomy."

"How do you know?"

"I have to keep up with the trends," Georgina said, not liking to confess that she'd taken a pile of them up to her room and sat up half the night, engrossed in a world of sexy fang-fic.

"Maud's keen on Jane Austen, and knows a lot about the novels. She could do research for you. It's going to take me a while to find her a new school, and I doubt if anywhere will want her in the middle of a term, so she'll be here until after Christmas. She'll be bored, it would be good for her to have something to do, and you can use some help, by the sound of it."

That was all she needed, a knowledgeable Maud breathing down her neck. Help? She'd need more than help to finish *Love and Friendship.*

THREE

Email from
livia.harkness@hplitagency.co.uk
To georgina@seaofcrises.co.uk

Where are those signed contracts?

Autoreply

Georgina Jackson is away from
her computer and has not read
your message.

"What's that horrible noise?" Henry
brushed spilled coffee off his shirt, as wolf
howls swelled to a majestic climax of sound.

They were in the kitchen in the basement
of the five-storey house. Henry and Maud's
parents, who were scientists with minds
above kitchens, had never modernized it
while they lived there, and Henry, who

didn't care for stainless steel and granite, had contented himself with having the wooden cupboards and dresser painted. The large wooden kitchen table still had pride of place in the centre of the kitchen, complete with its old-fashioned wheel-backed chairs.

Across the table from him, Maud looked up from a tall glass full of pink froth and flipped a phone open.

"You said your phone had been confiscated."

Maud placed a precise finger on the mike. "It has. This is Gina's phone."

"Making that noise?"

Maud was speaking into the phone. "Hi."

"Hi?" Livia Harkness's voice echoed round the kitchen. "What do you mean, Hi? You don't Hi me, Georgina. Where are those contracts?"

"I'm sorry," Maud trilled, in a hotel receptionist voice. "Who is this speaking, please?"

"You know damn well who's speaking."

"No, I don't."

There was a long pause. "I'm ringing 07 58 664451."

"That's correct."

"You're not Georgina."

"No. Georgina isn't here presently. May I take a message?"

41

"If it's her mobile, why are you answering it?"

"This is Georgina's answering service."

"She's there. Cowering in a corner. Get her."

"Actually, Ms. Whoever you are, Georgina isn't here."

"Don't get smart with me. This isn't a landline, people carry their mobiles with them."

"Not always. And not in this case."

"Who are you?"

"My name is Maud Lefroy."

Another long pause. "Lefroy? That's the name of the guy Georgina lives with."

"Lodges with, actually. I'm his sister. Can I take a message?"

"No. Give me a number where I can contact Georgina. Now."

"I'm afraid I can't do that. I don't have a number for her."

"If she's not there, where the hell is she?"

"I'm afraid I don't know."

Henry, exasperated, snatched the phone out of her hand. "Miss Harkness? I'm Henry Lefroy. Georgina isn't here. Pick up emails? I don't think so, unless she goes to an internet café. She didn't take her laptop. Did a package arrive for her? Yes, a courier delivered an envelope, but it came after she left. Where?" He hesitated for a moment. "She's gone to Basingstoke. Yes, Basingstoke. No, I don't know why. I'll do that."

He snapped the lid shut. "Maud, you can't just take over Gina's phone. Let alone change her ring tone to a pack of frenzied wolves howling their heads off."

Maud made slurping noises as she reached the bottom of her glass. "Actually, Gina said I could use it. Your nose has grown, did you know that?"

Henry touched his nose, then laughed.

"It was the courier arriving with the contracts that sent her whizzing out of the house. And Basingstoke, indeed, of all unlikely places, why ever would she go there?"

"Since she was up and off before the rest of us were up, we have no idea where she is, and so she might very well be heading for Basingstoke."

"You could have told the truth and said you didn't know."

"The Harkness woman is not the kind of person to be fobbed off with generalities. If you're going to lie, be brief, be specific. Basingstoke will flummox her."

"Actually, I bet Gina's gone to Oxford."

"Why?"

"Bolthole. Some musty library, out of

43

reach of pursuing Harknesses, where she can curl up with some doleful history book and feel safe."

"That's rather contemptuous. Gina's not a coward."

"No, just a bit raw at the moment. Anyhow, Oxford's her hidey-hole. She'll be staying at Jesse's flat." Maud watched her brother from under heavily mascaraed lashes. "Her ex, you know."

"I know who Jesse is. Why should she stay with him?"

"Actually, he's in America. And you're right, because if he was in Oxford, it wouldn't be wise for Gina to go near his flat. He's got a new girlfriend in residence. Looks like a meerkat, all neck and head too big for her skeletal body. Thick ankles, though," Maud added with some satisfaction. "She's gone to America with him. She does shopping in a big way, hasn't realized frugalism is the new fashion. Dim, you see, doesn't get enough calories to keep what passes for her brain functioning properly."

"How on earth do you know all that? And how do you know Jesse's in America? And how can Gina stay with him if he isn't there?"

"She's got a key, I expect. They're still friends. And I know all about him, because a girl at school is Jesse's cousin. She hates Shelley, which is the meerkat's name. Says she's a skinny bitch who's got her claws into Jesse. She says Jesse and Gina were a great couple, and should never have split up."

"You're a gossip," said Henry. "Cut it out."

"It's only natural to take an interest in people you care for," said Maud, very prim. "Isn't that right, Anna?"

Anna came in from the utility. She sat down at the table and pulled her fair hair more firmly back into its ponytail and regarded the brother and sister with intense eyes. "Interest can be a kind of gossip, but gossip can also be cruel. And Jesse isn't right for Gina, so it's better for her he has a meerkat. Now, what is a meerkat?"

"It's not essential vocabulary, Anna," said Henry. "It's a furry creature that lives in deserts."

"All vocabulary is essential. And Maud's English is extremely current, and therefore especially useful for me."

"I think you speak better English than I do," said Maud. "And you can spell, which is more than I can."

Anna was taking English classes. "I'm writing an essay on this, you see, how the English use animal names as epithets of approval or disapproval. You like to describe each other as animals. There are lots of dog words, *dogged, bitch, bit of a dog* and the American *doggone,* although only in old films, I believe. Now, if Jesse's new girlfriend is a meerkat, what is Gina?"

"At the moment, an ass," said Maud. "Or possibly an ostrich."

"So why does Gina's onetime boyfriend now live with a meerkat?"

"Shelley's a trophy girlfriend," said Maud at once. "He's rich and successful, like you used to be, Henry dear, until you got the push from your high-powered job at the bank."

"I did not get the push," he said with dignity. Then he grinned at his sister. "I jumped the week before they wielded the hatchet, that's why."

"And now you're an impoverished student of an abstruse science, your bonuses all lost in the crash, having to take in a lodger to make ends meet, addling your brain with little green men."

"Little green men?" said Anna, interested. She had put away her notebook but now she reached for it again.

Henry sighed. "Don't bother, Anna. She's being sarcastic, referring to a series of seminars I'm taking in astrobiology."

"Life on other planets," said Anna. "My cousin is an astrobiologist. This is an important field, Maud."

"Yeah, right, little green men with antennae blogging from the mother ship," said Maud.

Maud was right about boltholes. Georgina was in North Oxford, in Jesse's flat. He'd made her keep a key, and had said she was to use it whenever she wanted. She'd texted him to make sure the coast was clear and had walked the familiar route from the station to Beltane Court. She'd slept badly and woken early and, uneasy about the flat which was both so familiar — it was where she had lived with Jesse for more than two years — and unfamiliar, full of Shelley's presence.

Who had appalling taste, just look at the tangerine towels. Thick and fluffy, yes, but what a terrible colour. New peach curtains in the bathroom, and pink and orange cushions in the sitting room. A vast flat-screen TV — Jesse had never had time for television or DVDs, he liked his films big and in the cinema. And it was strange for Georgina to sleep in the spare bedroom instead of the main bedroom, with its huge double bed.

This was a mistake. Strange foods in the cupboard, notes pinned everywhere to stress the calories of everything from soya milk to lettuce — lettuce? Calories? Certainly no chocolate; there had always been bars of dark chocolate in the cupboard in her day. Jesse liked chocolate; did he now sneak bars into his study, or eat it outside? Or had Shelley converted him to her own wispy diet?

Their breakup had been amicable, insofar as breakups ever were. He was working for more than half the year in America, and wanted her to join him there. "You can leave the whole academic thing behind, concentrate on your writing," he'd urged her, but she didn't want to spend months of every year in America. She wanted to stay in England. They had gradually drifted apart, as he spent more time in the States, while Georgina spent more time with her own friends.

Shelley had had nothing to do with it. Jesse had met Shelley after he and Georgina had split up. When she'd handed in her thesis, she felt her time in Oxford was over and that was when, through the good offices of a friend, she'd met Henry. He was looking for a lodger to help pay the mortgage, and he offered her a good-sized attic room. "There's a bathroom up there, too," he said, "only you'd have to share with my sister. So you'd better meet her before we fix things up."

Maud had given her the once-over, and evidently her seal of approval, and Georgina had moved out of Jesse's flat in Oxford and into Henry's house in London just in time to start her post-doc work at London University.

Georgina picked up a tin. Decaf coffee? What use was that to Jesse, who liked his coffee thick and strong for a punch of morning caffeine? As did she, and she put the tin back in its place.

The skies were grey, the last bright foliage of autumn glowing against pewter skies, threatening an Oxford downpour. She hadn't brought an umbrella with her. She could buy yet another one, or rather she couldn't, that was how the money vanished and the overdraft clocked up.

Of course if she just got on the train back to London and signed that contract, her money worries would be over. A dozen umbrellas would be nothing to her.

Signing a contract was so easy. A squiggle on a line, and money in the bank.

Writing the book and earning the money? Not so easy.

FOUR

She bought a coffee and a doughnut at the stall outside the church, promising herself it was the last time; she had to cut back. Refreshed, she walked more purposefully, heading for the Bodleian Library. She was going to tackle this in a rational manner. Get an idea of what Austen was about. Get a feel for the period. Background stuff. Historical, social, she'd be on firm ground there. She needed to confirm what she already knew: there was no way she could write this book.

She flashed her Bod card at the desk, left her bag, and armed only with a notebook and a pen, climbed the stairs to sanctuary and safety, happy to be in this familiar place, which existed in a separate universe from that inhabited by her agent, a place where she was utterly out of reach of Livia's tentacles.

The thought cheered her, but any momentary relief was shattered by the entries in the catalogue for Jane Austen. Dear God, had every academic for the last twenty years written papers and articles and books on Jane Austen?

Where to start? Current was good. Current journals would be up to date, the thinking of the moment was what she needed. And current meant easily available. Georgina gathered up a copy of *The Journal of Contemporary Austen Studies* and headed for her favourite part of the library. Today was definitely a day for Duke Humphrey, the quintessential library, centuries-old peace and quiet.

The setting for the Hogwarts library in the Harry Potter films, but not, thankfully, open to the public for the Harry Potter tours. Here were the chained volumes, learned works of botany and early science, too precious to be loose. Or perhaps too dangerous, perhaps the intention had been to keep ideas chained up, a whimsical thought that appealed to her. Books kept under lock and key, manacled, not because they might be stolen, but as prisoners, too unsafe to let out into the world, where they might re-offend. Recidivist volumes, fettered in order to protect society against their wicked ways.

She must pull herself together, this was no time to be fanciful. She sat down and placed the journal on the worn shelf in front of her. The smell of wooden floors, of ancient books, of paper and leather and learning wrapped itself round her. Time didn't stand still in Duke Humphrey's library, it just ceased to exist. Perhaps Henry could explain that, with his quantum universes and time running backwards and all the other witchy things that went with modern physics.

All timelessness and fancy vanished as though a magician had clapped his hands when she opened the journal and looked at the summary of the first article by Dr. H. Jesperson-Hicks.

Astigmatic bio-cultural structuralism in Jane Austen's Juvenilia.

She blinked, rubbed her eyes, and tried again. Well, *Juvenilia* might be a good place to start, at the beginning of an author's oeuvre. She ran her eyes down the article with growing incomprehension. Nothing in Literary Theory 101 had prepared her for this.

She'd come back to that one, clearly Dr. H. Jesperson-Hicks was advanced stuff. She went on to the next article.

Proto-synaptic supratexts versus intercolo-

nial ratios: social relapses in Mansfield Park.

Supratexts? She was out of date, that was clear. She'd never heard of a supratext. Social relapses sounded more promising, *social* was a word she understood.

Not so. She shook her head. Get a grip. Each discipline had its own language, its jargon, its formulae for short-cutting to the substance of what the writer had to say. She could decode it for history, Eng Lit had its different vocabulary, that was all. Was there a dictionary? A glossary, explaining the meaning of arcane phrases?

Of course not, no more than there was in her own field. Who would take the trouble to provide it? Those in the know didn't need it, and lay people wouldn't be interested.

Concentrate. Try another one. Ah, Dr. Petronella Plimsoll, surely a sound scholar. *Northanger Abbey: Post-evolutionary diapasons as referents in architectonic tangentials of primary socio-stratificant structures.*

This stuff was beyond her, that was all. She was 101, this was 999. She'd have to work her way up to it.

Get real. How much time did she have? She shut the journal, noticing how pristine were its pages. Who, among all the scholars at Oxford, had read this journal? No one? Not even Dr. Plimsoll's supervisor, best friend, lover? No doubt Petronella Plimsoll had her own copy of the journal, carelessly left open on a desk, referred to in a lecture or tutorial, recommended on a reading list. Why should anyone read it? Should they wish to wise up on bio-cultural structuralism or post-evolutionary diapasons, they could bore themselves much more comfortably in the privacy of their own laptops.

Perhaps her pupils were given printouts, took one brief look, and tossed the pages aside before heading for the pub or the river.

Okay. There were more ways than one to approach a text. The simplest, easiest, quickest way was biography. A life. Which life of the dozens that must litter the shelves of the Bodleian? This was no time for scruples or shame.

But Duke Humphrey had lost its appeal, once the contemporary world intruded with its incomprehensible verbiage — spells, yes. Ancient science, yes. Wizards in robes and pointy hats? Fine. Modern scholarship?

No.

She went down the worn wooden stairs and into the quad, and from there out into Broad Street, where, just across the road, was Blackwell's bookshop.

Georgina had a vice, a habit which could best be indulged within the confined walls of a bookshop. She was a book sniffer. Before reading a word of any book she opened, she inhaled the aroma of new book that wafts out from the printed page. A publisher friend had informed her that the smell was made up of printing ink and the glue used in the binding. Paperbacks were usually unrewarding, with rough, unpleasant paper; hardcovers could be intoxicating.

She put down a glossy *Everyperson's Guide to the Universe,* a sensory delight of smells, never mind the dazzling pictures or the clumsy title — *Everyperson?* She wasn't at Blackwell's to indulge her senses, this was work. She needed a good, scholarly biography of Jane Austen. A detailed one. And, the thought flitted through her mind, readable would be good. If one page of current writing on Jane Austen made her brain hurt, there was no way she'd be up for three hundred or more pages in the same vein.

The Jane Austen section ran to several shelves. She ran her eyes along the lines of books, dismissing some titles at once. *Emma* and *Northanger Abbey* and the rest of the novels for a start; she wasn't anywhere near ready to approach The Text yet. *Jane Austen: a Neo-Freudian Approach to a Writer's Life.* No. *Jane Austen — an Extremely Short Life.* Was that a reference to the author's early demise — Georgina remembered reading somewhere that she'd died comparatively young — or to the slimness of the volume? It might do as an introduction, but then if she had to go on to a longer life —

"Georgina." The voice was rich and loud, causing several people, including the brisk-looking woman at the desk, to turn their heads and look at her accoster. She didn't need to look; she'd know that voice anywhere. A voice that belonged to Rollo Windlesham, the Mordaunt Professor of Intellectual History. She had attended his seminars, and he had examined her doctoral thesis.

"Rollo," she said, and was enveloped in a bear hug by the largest man of her acquaintance: six foot three in his immaculate brown brogues, more inches round his middle than she cared to think about, an assertive bow tie that barely fitted around his wrestler's neck. Professor Windlesham had a big personality to go with his big frame, and he couldn't care less who might be listening to his booming voice.

"What are you doing in this section? Jane Austen? My dear, clean out of your period, have you left your glasses behind? Let me guide you to a more suitable section. Or no, let me guide you out of here and into a pub."

He might be a mound of affectation, but Georgina knew that his rather protuberant eyes were gleaming with intelligence and curiosity.

"Just the man I need," she said. "Which is the best bio of Jane Austen?"

"Biography of Jane Austen? My dear Georgina, why?"

"I need to get up to speed on Jane Austen's life. I'm working on the social milieu of women writers, later ones, in fact, but I want to start at the beginning of the nineteenth century. Social background, family details, upbringing, that kind of thing."

"The choice is huge. I wouldn't touch any of them, always thought I might write one of my own, but does the world need another life of dear Jane, I ask myself?" He ran a magisterial finger along the backs of the books. "Not that one, that's one of the Jane Austen Laura Ashley school. Postfeminist interpretation, dear God. Theodore Spinx on *Jane Austen Our Contemporary.* And what twaddle that is. Spinx won a prize, for illiteracy one imagines. That one's pure hack, this one's full of Freudian rubbish."

The woman at the desk called out, "Professor, you'll depress my sales if you carry on like that. Let me recommend Croft's *A*

Particular World to your friend. There, near the bottom, with a silver and red cover."

"That'll do," said Rollo, flicking it out with an enormous finger and tossing it to Georgina. "No more or less rubbishy than the others, I dare say." And then, displaying a sudden sharpness. "Got your Society of Authors' card with you? Ten percent off, you know."

The volume, which was, Georgina was relieved to see, a reasonable size, was paid for, put in a bag and handed over. Inexorably, she was wafted down the stairs and out into Broad Street and from there into the King's Arms. Rollo surged through into an inner room, calling out to the girl behind the bar to bring two pints of bitter.

"Half a pint for me," Gina amended. "And make it lager. Cold lager. This takes me back," she said, as Rollo wedged himself behind a small table that rocked in protest. "I used to come in here every morning for a coffee when I was working on my thesis." She liked the atmosphere: students, dons, tourists, most of them today glad to be out of the wind and the wet.

"Cold beer on a day like this will chill your gut," said Rollo. "So much for wanting to become a British citizen, you'll have to do better than that. So it's Jane Austen, eh?

Who else? Brontës, of course, vast interest there for the social historian. How's the book coming along?"

Rollo was the kind of man it was all too easy to confide in. If he'd been a Catholic priest, he'd have had a line of sinners waiting to unburden themselves of their wrongdoings. There was a gravity to him, an aura of kindly, fatherly concern about him.

At your peril, Georgina told herself. Big men resembled St. Bernards — amiable, dependable, there with a little barrel of brandy and warm breath to revive you when you were dragged out of a snowdrift. Gentle giants, like the huge shire horses she'd seen at a country fair. Wouldn't harm a beetle, except by mistake, the groom assured her. "They're so big, they don't have to be afraid of anything, so it's in their nature to be gentle. Not like Shetland ponies, bite you soon as look at you. Same with all small critters — horses, dogs, men. The smaller they are, the more they bite."

A nice notion, but Rollo had to be the exception that proved the rule. He'd push you into a snowdrift, or down a glacier, forget about rescue. As for not crushing a beetle, Rollo's stock in trade was to crush his fellow creatures, not physically, which would be too easy, but intellectually, and best of all, emotionally. He took no prisoners.

"Kind of you to ask, Rollo. The book's going fine."

"Set in a workhouse, I heard."

"Yes. It's a story of women's lives, Jane and her two sisters, and how each of them ended up in the workhouse."

"An illuminating tale, I feel sure. I so look forward to reading it. Any publication date yet?"

"That's not my business, that's up to my publisher."

"I had lunch with Vesey last week in London. He was cock-a-hoop at some major deal he was pulling off. I asked him about your workhouse affair, and he didn't seem to know what I was talking about, although he was oddly confident that you would shortly be delivering what he called a shit-hot title. Americans are so gross in their language."

"Dan can hardly keep tabs on all his authors," said Georgina. "Ask my editor if you want the lowdown."

"My dear!".

He didn't need to say more, the tone said it all. The Windleshams of this world didn't talk to mere editors.

"Jane Austen, social history," he mused

aloud. "I wonder, I do wonder."

Had Dan Vesey said anything to Rollo? The merest hint would be enough for him to ferret out the whole story. Rollo had, rumour said, worked in British Intelligence before becoming a full-time don. No secret was safe from him, and these days, no secret was safe with him.

"Dine with me tonight," he said. "In hall. St. John's has strong connections with Jane Austen, you know."

Georgina drank some more of her beer and gave Rollo a look of intelligent interest, hoping she wasn't showing her complete ignorance of what Jane Austen or her family might have to do with St. John's College, Oxford. The only fact she was sure of was that the author herself could not possibly have attended that establishment.

Rollo was filling her in. "The descendants of the college benefactor, Sir Thomas White, were entitled to free education at the college. It was a custom that lapsed only in recent years. The Austens were descended from Tommy White, and so her father and brothers were educated at the college."

"Of course," said Georgina, hoping she sounded as though she'd known it all along. How many brothers did Jane Austen have? Doesn't matter, she told herself. The biography would tell her all that, and besides, what had her brothers to do with anything?

"Seven o'clock," said Rollo, getting to his feet. "Join me for predinner drinks in the SCR. They'll tell you where to go at the lodge. Don't be late."

Back at Jesse's flat, Georgina cursed herself for being bounced into dining at St. John's. She had planned an evening in front of the television with a portion of fish and chips from the excellent takeaway on Walton Street. Instead, here she was, sprucing herself up to spend a wary couple of hours or so avoiding Rollo's far too astute questions.

It was a short walk from the flat to the college, and she arrived at the Porters' Lodge at a punctual five minutes to seven. "Senior Common Room, miss?" said the porter. "I'll point you in the right direction, it's across the quad."

Dining customs at the Oxford colleges had startled Georgina when she arrived in the ancient city to pursue her postgraduate studies. Students dined in hall, which was Oxford speak for dining room. They "went to hall," meaning they ate there. Some colleges these days went in mostly for cafeteria service, others had a mixture of early hall and formal hall, served by waiters and waitresses. Tonight at St. John's, Rollo was taking her into formal hall. A scattering of students, *hoi polloi* in gowns, sat at long wooden tables in the body of the hall, while on a dais, set at right angles to the other tables, ran a single long table, where the Fellows of the college and their guests, including Georgina, sat. Latin grace was followed by an outburst of noise from the body of the hall, which made conversation difficult, except with one's immediate neighbours. In this case, Rollo on one side, and an elderly Fellow who looked like a wizened elf on the other.

Georgina had to tread with care, since Rollo's bellowed introduction had coincided with a buzz of conversation elsewhere. She was unsure whether the learned elf was an entomologist or an etymologist, and so felt it best to talk of neither words nor insects — which meant, of course, that was all she could think about. Fortunately, the Fellow, like most of his kind, had many interests, most of them to do with money. An American Fellow of the college, he informed her, had been awarded a MacArthur Genius Award, what did she think of that? No English academic body would have given him any such thing, there were even those who called his work slipshod, but of course

63

it was a fashionable field and fashion counted for so much in certain academic circles. Half a million dollars, he understood. Tax-free. Hardly enough these days to buy a decent house, but a useful sum.

He then gave her a guided tour of the other diners at high table, few of whom seemed to be worthy of their positions, together with scurrilous remarks about their sex lives, or lack thereof, personal habits, and financial standing. "Lost a hundred thousand pounds when he sold the house, bought at the peak," snuffle, laugh. "He caught a cold on that all right."

Rollo saw her eyeing the portrait that loomed over them. "Looking at the Elizabethan gent in the ruff with the baby's skeleton? An early scientific Fellow of the college. Possibly one with cannibalistic tendencies; I always think it looks as though he'd just consumed the wretched infant." A burst of noise drowned his next words, and then, in a lull, Georgina realized that Rollo had switched to the subject of Jane Austen. "The society meets at eight thirty, I said you'd be delighted to do it, chap called Joe Digweed's in charge, I'll take you over and introduce you after dinner."

"What are you talking about?"

He leaned over to put his mouth an inch

from her ear. There was no misinterpreting his words. "I've volunteered you to speak at the Jane Austen Society tonight. The scheduled speaker can't make it, so they asked me to fill in. Much better have you, I told them, a published woman novelist, just the ticket. Knew you'd enjoy it, they're a lively bunch."

His eyes sparkled with malice.

FIVE

They walked through the stone-flagged passage and out into the North Quad, and Rollo, his immense hand grasping her elbow as though he knew she wanted to make a run for it, guided her across the quad to a gothically pointed doorway.

The lecture room brought back a flood of memories to Georgina, of scruffy students, of laptops and notepads, of earnest conversations, of questions and answers, the quintessence of academic life. It represented safety, security.

Only, she had never felt less secure in her life than she did as she was introduced to a sultry-eyed young man in cord trousers — cord trousers? Whatever happened to jeans? — who turned out to be the president of the Jane Austen Society.

About twenty young people were sitting in a circle, mostly women, with a sprinkling of men. Just in off the cold streets, they had chilled cheeks. One young man with exotic features was pulling off a woolly hat and blowing on his hands to warm them.

In the days when this room was built, the large stone fireplace would have boasted a roaring fire, fed by college servants. No women would have been present then, and it was still a masculine room in its Victorian stateliness. The walls were panelled, and a shabby chandelier hung from a dingy ceiling.

The president was holding her hand warmly. Why the hell had Rollo let her in for this? Why hadn't she said, briskly and firmly, that unfortunately she had other plans for the evening? Because, if she had, Rollo would in his skilled way have shown her up as a complete liar.

Okay, concentrate. She would explain, point out that she was here under false pretences, that Jane Austen wasn't her field at all. Rollo would have to do the talk after all. But Rollo had gone, whisking himself out the door with a lupine grin, and the parting words, "Enjoy, as they say."

Georgina took her place behind the table, willing herself to take several deep breaths. She was used to students. Used to teaching, lecturing, taking seminars. She knew the form, this was familiar territory.

Only it wasn't, not when these eager beavers were here to listen to her thoughts on Jane Austen.

She would confess. "I'm here under false pretences, I know nothing about Jane Austen."

The young man was on his feet, extending a fluent welcome and a verbal flourish of thanks. "We are extremely grateful to Georgina Jackson for stepping in at the last minute, when our advertised speaker, Dr. Dundle Brook, had to pull out — he's broken an ankle. I'm sure you're all familiar with Georgina Jackson's book, the acclaimed *Magdalene Crib,* and I know we're all keenly interested to hear what a modern novelist has to say about her great predecessor."

A ripple of polite applause. Stand up, or stay seated? Up gave her more authority, down made her feel less exposed.

Thank God, a girl in a tight purple sweater was calling out to him, "Hang on, Joe, Mary's coming, wait for her."

"Mary should take the trouble to turn up on time." Joe turned to Georgina with a suave smile. How could anyone that age — what was he, twenty, twenty-one? — be so assured?

Desperation came to her rescue. "Thank

you, Mr. President," she said, nodding at Joe. "It's a pleasure for me to be in Oxford again, and I'm delighted to meet with some students like this."

Waffle.

"As Joe has said, I'm a last-minute substitute, so I haven't a paper or a talk prepared. So why don't we go for a questions and answer session?" And, before Joe or anyone else could protest, she went on, "Let's start by asking what is your interest in Jane Austen?"

"Do we get to ask questions?" said purple sweater.

The door opened, a blast of cold air blew into the room, and a tall, skinny girl in a leather jacket tiptoed in, murmuring disjointed apologies before sitting herself next to purple sweater. Once seated, she placed a large, shapeless bag on her knees and began to rummage in it.

The missing Mary. Now, if only there were more latecomers, and they could come through the door at the rate of one a minute, she could . . .

"Stop fidgeting, Mary," said purple sweater. "I just asked a question."

Mary took no notice, pulling out a pad, a pen, and a small recording device.

Joe fixed her with a severe stare. "Mary,

hadn't you better check whether it's okay with our speaker for you to record the talk and discussion?"

Mary looked at Georgina and held up the device, a questioning look on her intent face.

"Go ahead," said Georgina recklessly. She turned her attention to purple sweater. "Sure, you can ask me questions," said Georgina, and to herself, Only don't expect any answers if they're about Jane Austen. "But I get to ask first. Is your interest in Jane Austen connected with your studies? Or do you read her for pleasure?"

"She's cool," said a beautiful young man in a ski hat. "So English. All that period stuff, the structured society. I love it. It's more like society where I come from than England is today, where *morality* is a dirty word."

"Are you reading English?"

"Me? No way. Oriental Studies."

"A lot of people here are reading English," said purple sweater. "Not Joe. Joe's here because he collects societies for his CV, aren't you, Joe?"

"If that were the case," said Joe smoothly, "I'd be going for a higher-profile society than this. As it happens, I'm a big Janeite, okay? I love her sexy heroines."

A few boos and hisses rose from the seated

company.

"Modern heroines are predictably passive. Catch Jane Austen's heroines positioning themselves as victims."

"He only does that to annoy," said purple sweater. "Ignore him. Can I ask a question?"

Georgina's heart sank. Here it came; this girl could easily be older than the others. She was a doctoral student, her doctorate was on Jane Austen, she was going to make mincemeat of her, Georgina.

"How long did it take you to write *Magdalene Crib*?"

All those present sat up, alert, attentive, interested.

"Do any of you want to be writers?" Georgina asked, seeing a lifeline stretching out to her.

"Yes, of course."

"That's all I've ever wanted to do."

"Was it hard to get published?"

"How did you get an agent?"

The quicksands of Jane Austenland receded into the distance, and with an inward prayer of thanks to whichever muse looked after distressed authors and had so mercifully and efficiently come to her aid, she launched into answers. This she could spin out for the length of even the longest meeting. What she couldn't answer truthfully,

71

she could invent. That at least she was good at; weren't all novelists, at root, purveyors of convincing fibs?

"Yes, I'm deep into my second book. No, I don't want to talk about it right now, it's better, I find, not to talk too much about a work in progress."

"Do you make enough to live on?"

Joe intervened. "That's getting a bit personal, and, as you should be aware, since you weren't here when I introduced our speaker, Dr. Jackson holds a research fellowship at London University."

Mary, who had put on a pair of owlish glasses, too large for her small, pointed face, had been busy scribbling copious notes and fiddling with her recorder. Now she looked up and lifted a pen to attract attention. As she opened her mouth, Georgina recognized a fellow American, and a sixth sense told her that this one wasn't going to ask how much she got as an advance for her second book.

"As a post-feminist writer —"

"As a what?"

"We're all post-feminists now."

"I'm not a post-anything. And, in general, I'm not too keen on *isms*."

"*Isms*?"

"Feminism, modernism. Communism.

72

Fascism."

"What about fascism? Don't you disapprove of fascism?"

"I mean I don't care for words ending in *ism*. *Isms* are trouble. *Isms* are indicative of portmanteau thinking."

"Would you care to elucidate on that?"

"Thoughts, opinions, ideas, all stuffed into a bag. As it were. Not assessed case by case. Not thought through from the root. Radically."

"Do you consider yourself a radical writer?"

"No."

"But —"

"Thank you, Mary," said Joe.

Purple sweater shot her neighbour a withering glance, and asked about digital versions of *Magdalene Crib.* That started a lively debate and a heated discussion about copyright and royalties and free downloads.

Joe finally raised his voice. "I think we have time for one last question. As president, I'll use my privilege to ask it. Tell me, Dr. Jackson, as a writer, you must have been influenced by Jane Austen. Which of her writings do you think has had the greatest impact on your own work?"

Georgina's mind was a blank. At this moment, she couldn't remember the title of a single one of the wretched woman's novels.

"I couldn't say it was one more than another. As a writer, one draws on so many sources, historical and contemporary, of which fiction is only one strand. So you could say, all of them."

One thing she did know how to do was to conclude a session. "I'd like to thank you for asking me here this evening, and for providing such interesting and stimulating questions."

Joe formally wound up the meeting, and then with easy courtesy suggested they could adjourn to the bar and perhaps continue the discussion.

"I'm afraid I can't linger," said Georgina. Linger? How pretentious. "Thank you for the invitation, though."

All she wanted to do was escape, as quickly as possible, before any of these astute youngsters rumbled her.

Why should she feel so awkward about it? she asked herself. Why was she, an honest person, ashamed to say, "Listen up, folks, I've never read a word of Jane Austen and I don't intend to"? What was wrong with that?

She'd be branded a philistine. Who cared?

These kids would despise her. So what? There wasn't a law, you can't be a decent person, or count yourself as having a brain, unless you've read all the works of Jane Austen. Think of all the people in the world who had never even heard of Jane Austen.

Lucky them.

She could have stormed the meeting, explaining just why she'd chosen not to read Jane Austen. She could have told them how romantic fiction was a dead duck as far as she was concerned, how the novel had to move on from boy meets girl, how cut off from reality a middle-class Englishwoman like Jane Austen must have been. To which, if any of them had half a brain, the answer would have come flying back, how can you judge, if you've never read her?

Just think of all the books she hadn't read. Thousands, tens of thousands of them. Why should Jane Austen be anywhere near the top of her list? Why was it any reason to feel guilty, or at a disadvantage?

It was cultural oppression. You can't call yourself educated if you haven't read . . .

The wind and rain lashed across the quad. Two figures hurried past, clinging to one another under an umbrella in danger of turning inside out. Georgina pulled up her collar and wished she'd worn a coat rather than a jacket. She could feel her trousers flapping damply around her ankles.

Joe was apologizing for not having an

umbrella. "I never use one," he said, increasing his stride as a gust of wind buffeted them. "The porter will call you a taxi," he added helpfully.

"No," said Gina. "No, I don't mind the rain. And I haven't far to go, it's not worth a taxi." They dived into the cover of the lodge, where light spilled out across the flagstones. Gina said goodbye to Joe with a final insincere burst of thanks for asking her to speak, as she edged round the sign that said, THE COLLEGE IS CLOSED. Joe, who had seemed disposed to hover, accepted his congé, and with a graceful wave of his hand, headed inside the brightly lit lodge.

The huge wooden doors that led out to St. Giles were closed, leaving the wicket door open. With a sense of relief and elation, Georgina stepped out into the sleeting rain, oblivious of the wet, uneven pavements and the swishing of cars swirling past, headlights flickering across the black road. She hurried past the walls of the erstwhile Radcliffe Infirmary, destined for a second life as offices for the university, and narrowly avoided being run down by a cyclist, riding without a light, who shouted at her, "Out of my way, spastic," as she jumped clear.

Thank God, here she was at last, back at

the block of flats. Tonight they took on a gothic air, the dark brick and the unlit windows of the side with offices and the drawn curtains of those flats with occupants depressing her spirits still further.

The lift wasn't working; no doubt some thoughtless inhabitant had left the iron grid open on the top floor. She squelched her way up the narrow stairs, and then had a heart-stopping moment at the front door, unable to find the keys.

By the expedient of turning out the contents of her handbag on to the doormat, she unearthed them. She shovelled the debris back into the bag, and thankfully let herself in.

The telephone was ringing. Automatically she ran over to pick it up, then remembered that whoever was calling, it wouldn't be for her. The answer phone clicked on, and the words quacked out at her. "This is a message for Dr. Jackson, Dr. Georgina Jackson."

The accent was slightly American, and strangely familiar.

"This is Yolanda Vesey. Dan's sister. He told me to get in touch with you."

Of course, Livia had mentioned Dan's sister, an academic who had verified the manuscript and — how could she have forgotten? — who was from Oxford.

"Let's meet tomorrow. Nine a.m., Balliol, my room."

Aghast, Georgina stared at the squawking phone and then picked up. "How did you get my number?"

"Is that Dr. Jackson? Livia Harkness gave me this number. She has a list of numbers for you, and since you're in Oxford, I assumed this would be the right one to call. Nine tomorrow."

She rang off.

So much for escaping from the Harkness-Vesey duumvirate. Fiendish Livia, handing over all her contact numbers for God knew how far back. Wasn't that illegal, data protection, all that?

As if niceties like privacy laws meant anything to Livia.

It was half past ten. Too late to leave now. There would be a late train, but she didn't relish venturing out into the foul wetness of the night. First thing in the morning, she'd be out of here.

Where to?

Back to London. Back to her own life. From there, she would contact Livia, and Dan Vesey, and lay it on the line. No dice. She wasn't playing. She wasn't on for this, the sooner she made that completely clear, the sooner they could dig up some other literary sucker, one of doubtless dozens of writers who would jump at this chance. This evening's encounter with those students had been the narrowest escape ever, and the mere thought of meeting Dr. Yolanda Vesey filled her with terror. No. She was out of here, and out of the whole lunatic scheme.

She woke at five, after a fretful night, and flung her things into her bag. Dragging it behind her, she thumped her way down the stairs — it looked like the ancient elevator needed serious work, as it was still out of action — and out into the chilly damp darkness of pre-dawn Oxford.

The station, a fifteen-minute walk away, was a haven of light, with early commuters gulping their lattes, and station staff punctiliously announcing the delays to trains in all directions.

Recklessly, she broke her no-bought-coffee vow and bought a cappuccino and a newspaper, before going through to the platform, where a disconsolate crowd of people waited in a triumph of hope over experience for the London train.

In the manner of Oxford trains, the 7:05 arrived well before the 6:38, and she felt herself lucky to find a seat. She was in the quiet carriage, but the woman next to her was muttering into her phone, giving instructions about meetings, appointments, deadlines — who on earth was at the other end at this time of the morning? Did she have a twenty-four-hour secretary, some hapless slave who worked and slept beneath her desk? It would save on rent, she supposed.

Outside Reading, the train slowed to a crawl, and then stopped. After fifteen minutes, it started again.

"Signalling failure," predicted a man on the other side of the aisle. He shut his laptop and reached up for his coat. "I'd guess brakes, judging by the smell," the man next to him said, also getting up and retrieving his belongings.

The train juddered into Reading. "Due to engine failure, this train will not," boomed the announcer and a guard in a counterpoint of bad news, "be proceeding Londonwards. Passengers should disembark and board the next Paddington train, due from Swansea in twenty-five minutes."

Since the Swansea train was already packed by the time it drew into Reading, there was no room aboard for another trainful of passengers. Georgina took the slow train ten minutes later, and watched the unlovely suburbs drift past in a haze of rain.

Why did she want to stay in England?

What was it about this grey country that so appealed to her? Why not finish her work and go back to an American university, where she would have more money, more prospects, more sunshine?

Because the history she was interested in had happened here, and buried deep beneath her analytical mind was a tumbled heap of Englishness in its glory, of kings and queens, of Runnymede and Shakespeare's London, of hansom cabs and Sherlock Holmes and Watson rattling off into the fog with cries of "The game's afoot," of civil wars bestrewing the green land with blood, of spinning jennies and spotted pigs and Churchill and his country standing small and alone against the might of Nazi Germany.

It was a mystery to her how this benighted land had produced so many great men and women, and ruled a quarter of the world and spread its language and law and democracy across the planet.

The train stopped at Twyford. A lanky youth in a baseball cap got in and sat opposite her. Arms folded, his jeaned legs stretched out aggressively so that her own legs were cramped into a corner.

She glared at him, and he shifted his long limbs a little. He sniffed, wiped his nose with the back of his hand, ostentatiously, she was sure, and dug a hand into the pocket of his disreputable jacket.

Not a knife. Please, God, not a knife.

He pulled out a paperback, settled his shoulders and opened the book.

Georgina squinted at the cover.

Sense and Sensibility. A bosomy girl in a period frock. And, in twinkling, whirling letters, *Jane Austen.*

Six

Paddington at last, a sea of umbrellas. There were severe delays on the Circle and District lines, a voice intoned. Passengers were advised to find alternative routes.

Georgina preferred buses, in any case. She liked to look about her, watch people, glance into shop windows. However, the scene today from any bus would be a static one, as the delays on the underground combined with the continuing autumnal downpour had brought London traffic to a standstill.

She bought the cheapest of the umbrellas on sale at a nearby stall, and walked. Her umbrella blew itself inside out as she reached Baker Street, and she was a bedraggled sight by the time she reached the house. Looking down into the basement area, she could see into the brightly lit kitchen. Henry was sitting at the table and Anna was cracking eggs into a bowl. It was a domestic scene, two people at ease with themselves and the world.

Who was the outsider in this household? Anna? Maud? Or her? She shook herself out of impending self-pity, and ran down the steps to knock at the window.

Henry raised a quizzical eyebrow as he opened the door for her "Back so soon? You look as though the hounds of hell are after you. I suppose Livia and that very persistent Vesey woman tracked you down. Where were you? Anna and Maud thought Oxford."

"Yes," said Gina, sinking into a chair at the table. Anna had darted upstairs, and she now returned to place a cup of coffee and a little pile of letters in front of Gina.

"The minute you go away, the postman is at the door with letters for you."

"Junk mail, I bet," Gina said. She sifted through the envelopes, pausing as she came to one from the United States. She looked at it, hope springing into her heart. It was from the Norris Foundation, the providers of her fellowship. She had applied for an extension, for funds for another year, had provided a fat folio of her work so far, papers published, lectures given, plans for the next, more exciting stage of her research.

The letter was short and to the point. Not

only were they not extending her fellowship, they were cutting it short by six months. She must be aware of the seminal new work on pauperism and migration in England 1834–1841 by Dr. Peter Chapman, to be published by OUP in England and by Princeton in the United States. A work which in the opinion of the academic committee rendered her own research project superfluous.

They would be happy to consider at some future date an application for a new area of research, and forms would be available online for the next funding round, for research projects beginning in eighteenth months' time. However, they would point out that it was rare for the foundation to grant two such fellowships to any postdoctoral student.

"Bad news?" said Henry, watching her face, which looked puzzled rather than shocked.

"It is, rather," said Georgina. "It's about my research funding."

Funding. Henry didn't say anything, but Georgina knew as he did that her rent was late again. "I will pay it, really soon," she burst out.

"Pay what?"

"The rent. My father will help out."

There was another letter, this one from America.

Hi Honey
Just to let you know that I'm going to be under pressure finance-wise for a while, so it's good to know you have your Fellowship money to keep you going until your next book is finished. Jennifer has filed for divorce, and the lawyers say it's going to cost me. And my investments are in the same terrible shape as everyone else's . . .

Despite the large house in an expensive part of London — what part of London wasn't expensive? — Georgina knew that Henry couldn't do without the rent for her room. The house had belonged to his parents, and he had bought it from them with the help of a large mortgage when they'd moved to Cambridge. Which was fine in his investment banking days, a time of large salaries and handsome bonuses. All that had vanished in the downturn. The bonuses, often paid in the shape of stock in the bank, had become worthless as the bank gradually sank into the mire of the strange financial dealings it had indulged in over the last few years.

The mortgage remained, and Gina knew that Henry desperately wanted to hold on to the house in which he had grown up.

Couldn't his parents help out? she'd asked him. But no; his parents' work was fascinating and important, but hardly lucrative. "It's a struggle for them to pay Maud's school fees, and then one assumes she'll go on to university."

The coffee tasted bitter, the scrambled eggs which Anna always cooked for Henry were a yellow unappetizing mess, the toast was dry and brittle.

"Is Maud still asleep?" she asked, striving for normality while her mind raced with figures, trying to square the unsquareable circle of remaining in England without a work permit or any prospect of another position.

She wouldn't let herself think about the hours, weeks, months wasted on her research. She was prepared to bet that large chunks of Peter Chapman's published book had been lifted from material she had shared with him. At one time, Chapman's work had been going in quite a different direction from hers, but he presumably

87

knew a good and easy find when he saw it.

She could complain, begin the whole procedure of trying to prove that a fellow academic had plagiarized her work, but the fact was that the older, more distinguished academic, with OUP and Princeton behind him, would hold all the cards. It could end up with a reverse accusation, that she had been the one riding on Dr. Peter Chapman's coattails — she'd known that to happen.

Rather to her surprise, she found she didn't really care. The titles of those articles on Jane Austen darted into her head. When had scholars become academics? When had a genuine thirst for knowledge become a relentless and jargon-ridden pursuit of publication?

Before her time, and how much of a scholar was she really?

"You have another letter," said Anna helpfully. "From the bank, I know very well what letters from the bank look like."

With one of those flashes of intuition that letters from the bank induced in anyone with half a wit, Georgina knew it wasn't good news even before she'd taken the letter out of its envelope. Her overdraft was at its limit. Its old limit. The bank was reviewing all its customers' accounts, and in the present climate and given the way her account was conducted and her present income, they were cutting her limit and would be grateful if she would immediately remit funds to bring the level down to the new limit.

"Half what it was!" Georgina said. "They can't do this. We had an agreement."

"Calling in your overdraft, are they?" Henry said. "It's happening a lot."

Georgina was working on the sums. It was another fortnight before the next tranche of money came in from the foundation — and would that arrive? She snatched at the letter from America and ran her eye down the page until she came to the stark words "With immediate effect."

There was a lot of immediacy about at the moment. That sounded like no more money, period.

"Do you think the bank would give me a loan?"

"To pay off the overdraft? No."

"You have no money?" said Anna, keenly interested. "This is like my friend Adam. No money in the bank, no overdraft, and when he tried to use his card in the machine, it swallowed it up. No more cash, and his credit card was cancelled at the same time."

"Cancelled? Why?"

"The card was with the same bank, and so they cancelled everything."

Georgina's credit card was with her bank. "I've got my American one, that's got some credit on it." Enough to keep her in peanuts for a week or two. Not enough to cover the overdraft, not enough to pay the rent. "What did Adam do?"

"He absconded," said Anna. "Went back to Poland. Good riddance."

"What did he do?" said Henry.

"He worked as a plumber."

"Plumbers earn good money."

"Not anymore, and, besides, he was a very bad plumber. He was an aeronautical engineer, a very good one. But there was more money in being a plumber in London than in being an aeronautical engineer in Poland. So he came here for a new life. Now he's gone back again."

"I suppose that's what I'll have to do, head back home," said Georgina.

"Write that book," said Anna. "Maud says they want to pay you a lot of money."

"You don't understand, Anna. It's not so easy to write a book. Particularly that one. It's a book I simply can't write."

"Can't! Never mind can't. It's surprising what you can do when the alternative is having no bank account, no nice attic room here, no anything and having to go back to where you don't want to be."

"How do you know about the book?"

"Maud and I discussed it. Eat some breakfast, ring your agent, this Livia, she is rightly named after the empress Livia, I believe, who was a poisoner of everyone around her, and sign the contract. It's an important document, send it round by courier, Henry will lend you the money if you're short, won't you, Henry? Then read the novels. I was very shocked when Maud said you had not read them. Every educated person in England should have read them."

"I'm American."

"The same thing. I can lend you my copies."

"You've read them?"

"Of course. I'm an educated person."

"I don't think you've got much choice, Gina," Henry said. "Perhaps it's fate's way of kicking you in the backside, life's like that. Making you do something you think you don't want to do."

"Think? I know I don't want to do it."

The phone rang, and Maud's voice floated down from the hall.

"It's for you. That Livia person again.

91

Shall I say you're out?"

Georgina went upstairs, making a face at Maud and mouthing, "She'll hear you."

"Much I care," said Maud, and went back to the school prospectus she'd been reading while perched on the bottom step of the stairs.

"Dinner. Tonight. At the Phoebus."

"Livia, I'm not going —"

"Dan's hosting. Eight o'clock. Be there. And smarten yourself up, will you? He doesn't want to feel he's dining some hick author up from the country."

Georgina wandered around the house like a lost soul. Stay in England, or go back to America? To stay in England, she'd need money. Work illegally, cash in hand? Doing what? Wait on tables, bar work? That might pay for a bedsit somewhere a long way out from the centre; it wouldn't pay her rent here, nor would it pay off her overdraft. Try for another academic post? Even if she were successful, it wouldn't be for this academic year.

She was a professional writer. Did one published novel make you a professional writer? Yes, it did. So if she could produce something acceptable for Dan Vesey and Livia, it would buy her time. Time to finish Jane Silversmith's story and get back on track with the kind of fiction she really wanted to write: thoughtful, challenging, socially aware historical fiction. Other writers turned out porn or chick lit or young adult books to earn money in order to be able to take the time to write good stuff; why not her?

Only, was trying to emulate the writing of a woman considered by some to be England's greatest novelist quite the same as churning out porn or teen angst?

It was all a matter of perspective. She had to pick up where JA left off and come up with some kind of pastiche. Could she do it? Four hundred and fifty pages of romantic sensibility and middle-class matchmaking, that was all it was. Anybody could do that, surely.

She felt a sudden surge of confidence. Yes, she could do it. It was a matter of self-discipline, of completing an allotted task in a specific way. She'd never flinched at hard work, and now three months' hard work would solve all her problems. Well, most of them.

It was after lunch when she finally took the contract out of its envelope, and, under the stern gaze of Henry, Maud and Anna, signed the three copies.

"Without reading it, I note," said Henry,

adding his signature as witness. "Is that wise?"

"Like I'm going to argue about a contract approved by Livia."

"Let me see." Henry turned to the first page and began to read it through paragraph by paragraph. He whistled when he came to the payments clause. "No trouble paying your rent for a while then."

He read on. "The delivery date's tight."

"Yes, as I said, and I'll have to give the money back if I don't make it. 'Time is of the essence' is what it says."

"Get writing," Maud said. "Or, no, not yet. Get reading. Start with *Northanger Abbey* and *Sense and Sensibility.* Then *Pride and Prejudice,* what a treat, *Mansfield Park, Emma* and *Persuasion.* Won't take you long, you'll get swept up into them and time will whiz by."

"Begin with *Pride and Prejudice,*" advised Henry. "It's the quickest way to find out what you've been missing."

Dressed too early for going out, and knowing that despite her best efforts, her clothes wouldn't stand up to Livia's scrutiny, Georgina sat for a long time at the window of the sitting room, looking out at the street. The street Robert Browning must have walked down on his way to visit Elizabeth in Wimpole Street. A street that would have been there even in Jane Austen's day.

Carriages, not cars, going past. Horse dung in the streets, crossing boys at the corner. Street criers. Chimneys belching smoke, no Clean Air Act in those days. Henry said that this hadn't been the smartest part of town; it was genteel, beyond the fringes of the magic rectangle of Piccadilly and the parks where the rich and the noble lived.

Jane Austen's London? Had Jane Austen ever been to London? Was she a Londoner? Surely not, surely a country girl. Although she must have lived in Bath, people were always talking about Jane Austen's Bath.

Not that she'd ever been to Bath, although she had promised herself a trip. She had a friend from college who'd married an Englishman and now lived in Bath. Bel had issued an open invitation, which she'd never taken up. Her trips were to places like Liverpool and Manchester and Salford, not enclaves of the middle classes, like Bath.

She heard the clip-clop of a horse's hooves and looked down to see a figure on horseback, a man in a blue coat. Trotting past. She knew people rode in the park, but she'd never seen a horseman in this street before.

Across the way a young woman with a wilful, heart-shaped face came out of the house, closing the green door behind her and tripping down the steps. What extraordinary clothes she was wearing. Off to a party in that long, high-waisted, low-cut dress, but a hat festooned with feathers! Maybe it was fancy dress.

The light was fading from the sky, the streetlamps were late coming on. A figure came round the corner, a small man in a long coat. He had a light on the end of a pole, and she watched, fascinated and bewildered, as he walked along the pavement, pausing at each lamp to light it with a gentle plopping sound, leaving a soft glow behind to illumine the street. He went round the corner and was gone.

Georgina shut her eyes and shook her head. When she opened her eyes again, the street was brightly lit, a man on a scooter was revving at the corner, and a girl was hanging out of the window of her tiny town car, manoeuvring into a space just about large enough for a wheelie bin.

SEVEN

Dan Vesey was a smooth man, smooth from his shining, mostly bald head to his sleek tailoring to his vowels.

No one was quite sure where Dan Vesey came from. He was an American who had burst on to the publishing scene in London five years before, taking charge of the ailing list at Cadell & Davies, a publishing house with a history that went back to the eighteenth century. He had staged a management buyout, which meant, as far as Georgina knew, that he owned the whole company. There were other directors, but they were never in evidence. Dan ran a sphincter-tight ship, as he put it, and he had the reputation in the trade of having a nose for bestsellers.

His sister, Yolanda, was petite, with the same cold and brilliant blue eyes as her brother. And she was even sleeker than Dan was, from her elegant bob through her immaculate little black suit to her patent high heels. Gina, wearing a defiant red jacket, bought at an Oxfam store the previous year, felt the hick Livia had cautioned her not to be.

The restaurant was the kind Gina most disliked. Not that she often got to eat in such a place — the prices on the menu made her wince. And the food was strange and came in tiny, exquisitely crafted portions and she wasn't certain exactly what she was putting in her mouth. Whatever happened to the food that had made the English great? Agincourt would have been a wipe-out for all those yeomen archers if they'd been raised on food like this. Chocolate pudding, now there was something the English knew how to make, a comfort dish if ever there was one. Would they have chocolate pudding on the menu here? She doubted it.

She came to with a start, to find six eyes fixed on her.

"Well?" said Livia, breaking the silence.

"Well what? Sorry, I didn't catch that."

"We're discussing the narrative line," Yolanda said in clipped tones, sounding as though she were talking to a not very bright ten-year-old. "We'd like a structural plan from you. Soon."

"By next week," Dan said. "You've had time to read through what I gave you. Time to learn it off by heart. So let's have that plan Monday. First thing."

"You mean a plot."

Yolanda winced. "Please! That's not a word we use."

"I do. And by Monday? That just isn't possible."

"Georgina," said Livia warningly.

"I don't work that way. If you want a book inside three months, then you'd better just leave me to get on with it."

"Now that isn't possible," said Dan, his voice turning gravelly. Georgina had always had a suspicion that his eyes weren't really that colour — surely no human being could possess such a startlingly blue pair of orbs. Yet there was Yolanda with exactly the same blue gaze, so unless they had matching contact lenses, it was a true Vesey colour.

Livia's eyes weren't blue. They were almost black, to match her clothes: sharp, hooded and distinctly unfriendly.

"This has to be a cooperative effort," she said. "You're going to need our help, especially Yolanda's."

"It's a question of matching the parameters," Yolanda said. "The structural balance and interplay of Austen's texts. And we have also to consider the nexality."

Nexality?

"People call her Jane Austen in England," said Georgina. "And if you mean novel, say so. Nineteenth-century authors didn't write texts, they wrote novels." What was she saying? Of course it was The Text, The Text was holy, no one spoke or wrote these days of novels or poems or essays, to do so was to be branded instantly and hopelessly pre-post-modern. Unforgivable.

"As an historian, I wouldn't expect you to be up to scratch on current literary theory, but you can't approach this with a head full of exploded clutter."

"Literary theory isn't going to get a book finished, in three months or ever. What I do is called writing. And I do it the way I can. Which isn't having a committee meeting about it."

Yolanda wasn't listening. "Structural notes Monday, and then we need to work to a schedule. Austen's novels are from eighty-five to one hundred sixty-five thousand words. One hundred twenty thousand is the specified extent for this book. Livia assures me that you're a fast worker. I will expect a chapter every two days. Then I can run it through the computer, to adjust it so that it tallies with regard to sentence length, punctuational idiosyncrasies and so on."

Georgina felt a violent blow to her shin, and there was Livia eyeballing her as a python might look at a goat. "Liaise with me on the schedule, Yolanda," Livia said, and then with a swift ease she began to talk about the cover design.

Because of the glassy nature of the restaurant, sounds bounced across tables and walls and gleaming floor. The voices of other diners rose in an effort to make themselves heard; Gina wanted to cover her ears with her hands.

"Palette of colours," Livia was saying.

"American tastes . . ."

"A leading designer . . ."

"PR."

A chapter every two days? Was Yolanda out of her mind? She had no plot, no idea how the wretched woman wrote, it would take weeks to get a grip, to turn out even a single chapter.

Dear God, what had she taken on?

"You're drunk," said Henry amiably, as she staggered through the door.

"Wish I were," said Georgina. "My heel came off, and I think I've dislocated my hip trying to hobble and hop along."

He looked down at her feet, and his

mouth twitched.

"Quite the ragamuffin. Did you end up walking in your stockings?"

"Tights," said Georgina. "And yes, I did, and I've got a blister on my heel, and I expect trench foot as well. I do not want to think about what I've been walking through."

"I'll turn my back, you strip off those tights, and then go and wash your feet. There's antiseptic in the bathroom, green tube, smells vile. If you're not drunk, would you like a glass of wine? A whisky — oh no, you hate whisky, a cognac?"

The sitting room was a haven of soft greens and cream. Her feet clean, if sore, Georgina padded across the parquet floor and sank into a sofa.

"I suppose it didn't occur to you to take a taxi?" Henry asked as he handed her a glass generously filled with what Georgina suspected was his special cognac.

"None to be had. Yolanda dropped me off."

"Yolanda?"

"Yolanda Vesey. Dan Vesey's sister. A terrifying academic. She was driving back to Oxford, so she gave me a lift part of the way. I thought I could catch a bus, and then I decided to walk, and then I came to grief on one of those grids people have over their basements. Can I sue, do you think?"

"For a blister or two? A ruined shoe? Did the shoe cost a fortune?"

"Ten quid in a sale." Georgina leaned back and shut her eyes.

"Not very civil of the Vesey woman not to drop you at your front door."

"She was in a hurry." In fact, Georgina had discouraged her, eager to get away from the relentless flow of knowledge, knowing that at any moment Yolanda would pause, ask a penetrating question or two and discover how complete was Georgina's ignorance of everything about Jane Austen.

When Georgina woke the next morning, it was to a silent house. A thin sun was easing through the curtains; what time was it? Nine o'clock. The morning after the night before. Not a night made hideous by excess of any kind, but a night of sleepless terrors, of tossing and turning and worrying, of Veseys and Livia floating through half dreams, until in the early hours, she had fallen asleep, to be chased through the tunnels of Steventon station by a plump, pink-faced woman in a high-waisted frock and a poke bonnet, brandishing a quill pen and shouting, *Fraud, fraud.*

Georgina blinked at the memory. Her eyes fell on the book on her bedside table, the book she had tried to read the night before, the biography of Jane Austen. The prose was so dry it gave her a sore throat. The portrait of the demure woman on the cover was the woman of her dreams, the one name-calling. How ridiculous; Steventon station, if it existed, would be a halt in the middle of nowhere. Tunnels? A rickety bridge over the tracks, more likely.

The bathroom bore traces of Maud's morning shower: a puddle of water on the floor, a wet towel, a pungent scent, a soggy cake of soap in the middle of the handbasin, and a lipstick message on the mirror —

Good morning, Sleepyhead,
have a good day.

She went downstairs. No sign of Anna in the spotless kitchen. No, she wouldn't be there, it was Wednesday, and on Wednesdays Anna went to classes.

On the kitchen table was a book. A battered old book, with no dust jacket. It was brown, with darker patches and a ring from a cup or a glass. Georgina picked it up and looked at the spine. *Jane Austen* by Elizabeth Jenkins. She opened it. A yellow Post-it was stuck on the title page. "Gina, found this on the shelves. It's old, but readable. Have gone to Sussex with Maud to look at a school. See you later. Henry."

The phone rang.

Georgina waited for the answering machine to click on, but the ringing didn't stop. She went to the wall and lifted the receiver. Before she could say a word, Livia's crisp voice spoke. "Georgina? Why don't you pick up more quickly?"

How did Livia know that she, Georgina, had picked up the phone, and not Henry or Anna or Maud? A clairvoyant agent, all she needed. Not a bad title for a book, *The Clairvoyant Agent.* James Bond with second sight. No, clairvoyance didn't go with guns and sadism. Perhaps . . .

"Pay attention. You're meeting Yolanda at two o'clock, at the University Women's Club."

"Yolanda?" Georgina might not be completely awake, but one thing she was sure of, she wasn't going to run her head into that noose. Not today, not tomorrow, not ever. "She's in Oxford. She drove back to Oxford last night."

"That's because she has a lecture scheduled in Oxford at nine, followed by a tutorial, then she's catching a train to London.

She can spare an hour and a half for you, before she has to go to a meeting. She wants to go through plot details."

"Livia, that isn't going to be helpful."

"You can't do this on your own. There's a lot at stake, Georgina, sharpen your wits and do as I say. Have you got a plot worked out? No, I thought not. Take expert advice when it's offered."

"Why the hell isn't Yolanda writing this damned book?"

Livia wasn't answering that one. "Be there. On time."

Click.

Georgina unplugged her mobile from its charger and turned it on. Flipping through the London phone book, she found the number for the University Women's Club and called it. Could she leave a message for Dr. Vesey? Please tell her Dr. Jackson would be unable to meet her this afternoon.

She wanted to be out of London, out of reach of Livia and the Veseys, but where could she go? Not Oxford again, that would be back into the lion's den. She sat at the table, flicking through the book Henry had left for her. Published in the nineteen thirties. Completely out of date.

A chapter heading caught her eye. Bath. Bath! Of course, Bath. A city closely associated with Jane Austen, and where the pages of that damned *Love and Friendship* manuscript were set. She ran through the contact numbers on her phone, hesitated for a moment and then pressed dial.

"Hi, Belinda here."

"Bel, it's Gina."

Exclamations of amazement, surprise, delight, reproach — "All this time in England, and you've never been to see me, come today, stay as long as you like, have you turned veggie or teetotal? Don't talk now, got to rush or I'll be late, get a taxi from the station or buy a map and walk, see you, bye."

They'd been roommates at college: Bel, the third generation of her family to attend Brown, Georgina wondering if she'd made a big mistake. They'd become firm friends, but after two years, Bel had dropped out and headed for Juilliard to focus on her real passion, which was singing. She'd done well, but then had suddenly vanished from the scene after only a year. Lost her nerve, her voice, her will to sing, came rumours along the grapevine. Georgina had left America to study at Oxford, and when she next caught up with Bel, she, too, was on the other side of the Atlantic. "I fell out of love with opera and in love with an Englishman," she told Georgina.

Bel, domestic? She couldn't imagine it. Two children, or was it three? And living in Bath, of all places. Charming, people said, but hardly in the centre of things. And Bel had always been in the centre of everything.

Anna came back from her classes just as Georgina was writing a note for Henry. "Are you going away again?" Anna inquired, hanging up her jacket on a peg in the hall. "You are very restless."

"Off to Bath, to stay with a friend."

"And to write, I hope."

"Research. Gathering necessary background material. If Livia Harkness rings, please just say I'm out and you don't know when I'll be back."

"Which is the truth, I have no need to lie. But she will ring you on your cell phone."

"I'll turn it off."

"Does she know you are going to Bath?"

"No, so please don't tell her where I am."

"I don't know where you are."

"You do, I've left a note with the phone number."

"But this information is not for Livia."

"No. And most of all, not for a Dr. Yolanda Vesey."

"Do you want a taxi?"

"A taxi?"

"To take you to the railway station. You can afford a taxi, now you have signed the contract."

So she could. She had taken the cheque to the bank yesterday, depositing it with a sense, not of triumph but relief. After a certain amount of reluctance — "If you're going to be difficult, I'll move my account to another bank" — she had been allowed to draw cash. Even so, this was no time for extravagance. A signature advance was easy, and so was publication, the tricky one was the third on delivery.

Three months. Ninety days. Less, now. A hundred and twenty thousand words. There was that cold pit in her stomach again.

"A glass of water?" said Anna helpfully. "You look pale."

Georgina shook her head.

"Your book?" said Anna, holding up the Jenkins biography. "To read on the train?"

"Thank you," said Georgina.

As the train drew out of the station, Georgina had a sense of release. With every mile she was further away from Livia, Dan and Yolanda. She set her phone to silent and settled back in her seat to watch the London suburbs slip past. They gave way to greener vistas, more suburbs, towns, villages on hills, with church spires sharp against the thunder-coloured sky, flashes of sunlight, a rider in a yellow jacket cantering along a grassy lane, sheep in woolly clusters, indifferent to the train racing past, trees in full glory of their autumn colours. A hillier landscape now, glimpses of a river, a canal, with a brightly coloured boat — what did they call those? a narrowboat — edging its way towards a lock. And then soot-stained cream houses, rows of them on a hillside, a swift run under bridges and alongside a garden, and a final braking curve into a station.

The loudspeaker crackled into life, startling Georgina. "Bath Spa. We are now arriving into Bath Spa. Bath Spa will be the next station stop."

Arriving into. Station stop. Illiterates, Georgina said to herself, as she grappled with her bag. The guard was already slamming the doors shut as she jumped out. "Nearly got left behind there," he said. "Stand clear."

The high-speed train pulled out, and she walked along to the end of the platform, sniffing the damp, fresh air. Beyond the railings on the other side of the station she could see trees and a huge painted sign on a chapel roof, JESUS SAVES. Neither chapel nor the slogan could possibly belong to the

Regency period, they were Victorian in both style and sentiment.

For a moment, as she stood there on the platform, Georgina wondered what it would have been like to be Jane Austen arriving in Bath two centuries ago, driving into the centre of the city in a swaying carriage after a long and exhausting journey.

How easy it was for her to escape from responsibilities and problems; how impossible for the younger daughter of the Reverend Mr. Austen.

EIGHT

The air was chilly, and the skies ominous as she came out of the station. As instructed, she'd bought a map of Bath, a delightful one, with little buildings drawn on it, and labels. Roman Bath, Pump Room, Assembly Rooms, Costume Museum. Quaint, not her kind of place at all, this was a mistake. She should have fled to the north, to Liverpool, to the heartland of the old industrial north, where she felt at home.

Fat drops of rain were starting to fall, and thunder rumbled in the distance.

She gave the address. "Bartlett Street?" said the cabdriver. "You'd do better to walk, I'll be honest with you. It's only twenty minutes. Save yourself the fare and buy a brolly, that's my advice. With the traffic the way it is today, it'll take me twice that to get you there."

Georgina had no idea Bath was so hilly. She'd visualized it as a collection of Georgian houses clustered alongside a river. Twenty minutes? Half an hour later, after walking up and up, each street steeper than the last, she arrived breathless and damp in Bartlett Street. At least this street was on the level, even though the slippery pavements made the wheels of her bag take on a skittish life of their own. It was an elegant street, she had to admit it, with the wrought-iron overthrows and railings. And big, ordered windows. Bartlett Buildings turned out to be a small cul-de-sac leading off Bartlett Street. The white front door of Number Three had a brass lion's-head knocker, but before she could use it, the door flew open, and there was Bel. Half a head shorter than Georgina, her hair blonde and wavy, just as it always had been, merry eyes, pink cheeks, and exclamations of joy and despair; joy at Gina being there, and despair at her dampness and the folly of walking.

"Those taxi drivers are rogues, they want the easy fares, up to Lansdown and places like that, come in, mind the stroller, give me that umbrella, take off your coat, goodness, you are wet! Come straight upstairs, I'll show you your room, and then we can eat, I didn't have time for breakfast this morning, and I'm wilting from hunger."

Up and up and up, to the top floor, and a

big bedroom with sloping ceilings and a view across the street. "Here's your bath-room, just leave everything, you can unpack later, come down to the kitchen."

It was extraordinary to see Bel in all this domesticity, the kitchen with its Aga stove, an infant in a high chair being attended to by a young girl, silent and shy, a tabby cat sitting on the windowsill, a clutter of toys in a basket on the floor.

"Three!" Bel exclaimed. "Twins, you see, they're at school, and now Thomas here, he's one, aren't you? This is Daisy, who looks after him."

Thomas looked at Georgina with huge round eyes, and began to bawl.

"I don't think he likes me," said Georgina, as Daisy lifted him from his chair and car-ried him off, still weeping.

"He's not good with strangers," said Bel. "If you'd bothered to come and visit sooner, you wouldn't be a stranger. Now, tell me all about yourself. What are you doing? Still beavering away at the university? I bought your book, goodness, yes, and gave it to all my friends. Who ever would have thought you'd turn out a novelist? I was fearfully proud. I couldn't read it, though, far too clever and serious for me."

Georgina winced. Bel was famous for her

honesty, and if she couldn't read *Magdalene Crib,* it wasn't through lack of brainpower or an inclination towards non-fiction.

"I'm so busy I don't get much time for reading these days," Bel said. "Shut my mouth, what not to say to a writer. So are you writing another book now?"

"Sort of," said Georgina. "Can I have some more of that potato salad?"

"Help yourself. I'll make coffee, and then I must dash. You'll be all right this afternoon, won't you? Curl up in front of the sitting room fire if you're feeling lazy, or you could go out and explore. Take an open-top bus, if it isn't raining too hard."

"Dash where?"

"Oh, to the shop. I'll be back around six, and then I'll cook us a wonderful meal. Freddie's away, so it'll just be us. Freddie's my husband in case you've forgotten. He's a journalist, remember? Away in India at the moment. Here's a set of keys. Must go, can't be late."

Shop? Before Georgina could ask what she was talking about, Bel had gone, the front door shut behind her. What shop? Did Bel work in a shop? How strange. There was an opulence to the house, and besides, Bel had family money. Why would she work in a shop? To pass the time? Bel wasn't the kind of person to take up anything just to occupy her time. Unless marriage and motherhood had changed her.

Georgina wandered into the sitting room, a noble first-floor room with three deep sash windows. There was a grand piano with the lid raised; Bel hadn't given up her music entirely, then.

While they were having lunch, the sky had cleared, and although clouds raced across the sky, it had stopped raining for the time being. An open-top bus? Well, that would be as good a way as any other to spend the afternoon. Better than sitting down with Ms. Jenkins and Miss Austen's uninteresting life, in any case.

Downstairs, Daisy was wrapping Thomas — who once again burst into tears at the sight of Georgina — into a cocoon and tucking him into the stroller. Daisy knew about the open-top buses. "Run you down soon as look at you, gliding along without a sound," she said unexpectedly. "All right for tourists, though." Georgina would do best to go down through the centre, she could pick one up in Milsom Street, they were always crawling about there.

A red open-top bus was drawing away as Georgina ran down the street. Milsom Street was a downhill run, but even gather-

116

ing speed for the final few yards, she couldn't catch it.

A woman in a cream leather jacket and sunglasses looked at her pityingly and remarked, "You know what they say, never run after a man or a bus, there's always another one coming along behind," before she walked away, her neat behind swaying in skintight jeans.

HOP ON HOP OFF, the notice proclaimed. BUSES EVERY TWENTY MINUTES. Twenty minutes! She wasn't going to stand here like a lemon for twenty minutes.

What was this coming down Milsom Street towards her? Cream jacket was right, here was another bus. From a different company by the look of it, a pale green bus, this one with figures painted along the side, prancing women in Regency gowns, bonnets and ribbons flying, a high-hatted man with shapely booted legs holding up a quizzing glass.

Written along the side of the top deck of the bus in a flowing, ornate script were the words *The Jane Austen Bath Bus Tour.* Georgina winced. This was a conspicuous bus, shrieking, "Tourist!" at every passing pedestrian and car. So what? Wasn't she, Georgina, a tourist? With one foot on the platform, Georgina hesitated. A young woman stood there, waiting to take her money, frizzy permed curls standing out from her head and an impatient expression. "Well, are you coming or aren't you?"

"I was really waiting for the other bus, the red bus. The general tour."

"This one's much more interesting. We visit all the places where Jane Austen and her family lived, and all the places mentioned in the novels. You get all the main sights as well as a live commentary, so it's better value."

Georgina paid her ten pounds, took the gaily coloured map which came with the ticket and hesitated — inside, downstairs and warm, or up to the top deck, open, windy, but better views?

She tied her scarf more firmly around her neck and went upstairs. There was a vacant seat at the front, and she sat there, perched on high, looking down on to the throng of shoppers. This was presumably the main drag, there were all the usual high-street shops on either side, although classy ones, no pound shops here. A large bookstore with a big window display. Books by Jane Austen, announcing a wonderful new sequel to *Pride and Prejudice: Mr. Darcy's Desire* by Marlena Crawford. Georgina wondered cynically how much her publisher had paid for the window display and the words, written in huge scrolling letters across the window, "Jane Austen comes back to life in this delightful continuation of Mr. Darcy's story."

This time next year, Dan Vesey would be buying window space. *Love and Friendship* would be on sale in every bookstore in Bath. Assuming it was written. A new manuscript by Jane Austen, penned in her own hand, even if it were only a few pages, would be headline news for booksellers. The thought depressed her, and she sank deeper into her seat.

On the other side of the aisle sat a couple wrapped up as though the bus journey was taking them on a tour of the Arctic, and polar bears, not Regency frills, were to be the photo opportunity of the day. They were in their forties, the man tall and thin and lugubrious, the woman with a discontented expression on her beautifully made up face under a furry hat.

"Look at that," the woman said, gesturing at the window display. "More trash, for God's sake. There's no end to it."

"The sequels are tiresome, but it doesn't detract from Miss Austen's works." The man spoke with a foreign accent. Russian? Polish? His voice was weary, it sounded like an old argument.

The woman tucked her arm into his and smiled at him, a smile of such pure love and affection that it made Georgina blink.

"I'm sorry, Igor, it's your birthday treat, I promised I wouldn't make any sour remarks. It's just beyond me that when you've got Tolstoy and Dostoevsky and Chekhov and a whole heap more, you're crazy about Jane Austen."

"As you have often said."

Russian, then. Georgina was intrigued. She looked out to the other side, not wanting to be too obviously eavesdropping, but they had lapsed into silence.

Another pair, two American women, talking in loud, excited voices, were taking their places in the seats behind. The bus made revving noises, and the loudspeaker, placed uncomfortably close to Georgina's seat, crackled into life. The bus began to move away, and then juddered to a halt. Feet clattered up the steps, and two young people emerged on to the top deck, both dressed from head to foot in black. Silver nose studs, heavy boots, spiky hair; they reminded Georgina of Maud, but without her style, and with less attention to personal hygiene.

The woman who'd given Georgina her

ticket followed them up the step, a mike in her hand. "Hi, I'm Susie, and I'm your guide for today."

"Hi," the girl said to Susie. "I'm Dot, this is Rodney." They smiled at the others, who didn't seem keen to respond. Georgina, thinking of Maud, smiled back.

Dot was still talking. "Rodney and I, we're not a couple, Rodney isn't into girls, he doesn't really do humans, hamsters are his thing, anyhow, we're both Jane Austen addicts, I've watched *Pride and Prejudice* more than forty times. Oh, sorry, didn't mean to interrupt."

Susie, with a civil glare and a clearing of her throat, was waiting to speak.

"This is Milsom Street. We have to turn left here, as the rest of the street is a pedestrian zone. It runs all the way down to the Pump Room. In *Northanger Abbey,* Catherine and Isabella walked up here. In *Persuasion,* this is the street where Anne Elliot walks with Admiral Croft and they look at the painting of a ship in the window. In Jane Austen's day this was the most fashionable street for shops, and it is where Jane Austen and her characters would have come for mantua makers, milliners and to buy ribbons to trim their gowns."

The bus swung into Lower Borough Walls.

"We shall be crossing Pulteney Bridge, observe the shops on either side, this is the only bridge in England with shops on it. We are approaching Laura Place, where —"

Excited American voices broke out behind Gina. "Where our cousins, Lady Dalrymple and Miss Carteret, live," they exclaimed and then broke into delighted laughter.

Cousins to a Lady Dalrymple? Odd for a couple whose accents placed them somewhere in Texas.

As the bus halted at the traffic lights, Georgina was puzzled by the voices coming from the rear of the minibus. Did they have a radio? Were they listening to something on an iPod with the volume turned up?

She turned round to look and was rewarded by a toothy smile from Dot. "Want to watch?" the girl said, holding up a portable DVD player.

Watch what?

"We're playing *Pride and Prejudice.* To put us in the mood," the girl went on. "Colin Firth, great, I just die when I see him dive into the lake."

The Russian, alerted by the magic words *Pride and Prejudice,* had also swung round. "That scene is entirely made up," he said with severity. "It is not in the book. It is an invention, an unnecessary and inappropriate addition by the scriptwriter, wanting to sex up the book for television."

"No need to sex it up with Colin Firth in that shirt and those breeches, he's hot," said the girl. Rodney, who seemed the silent sort, nodded and muttered, "Dead sexy."

"Don't you prefer the book?" said the Russian.

"Never read it, and don't want to," said Dot. "Haven't got time for that, and reading's passé, no one reads these days, books and all that are finished."

Great Pulteney Street was wide and impressive, with more big Georgian terraced houses. Georgina caught glimpses of first-floor drawing rooms, with chandeliers, silk drapes, panelled walls, paintings.

"In Regency times, when people came to Bath to take the waters, or for the season, they rented houses, and most of these houses would have been rental properties. By Jane Austen's day, Bath was no longer as fashionable as it had been in the eighteenth century, and it was a place where widows and dowagers and genteel families without a great deal of money came to live."

Snatches of dialogue came from the back seats, and Susie gave the youngsters a cold look. "Perhaps you could keep the volume down," she said, "if you aren't interested in what I have to say."

"Righto," said Dot obligingly. "Can't say I want to listen to stuff about houses. We'll plug in the earphones, okay?"

"It was a hierarchical society, with clear divisions of class, wealth and status," Susie continued.

"Class," the Russian said appreciatively. "English writers always write about class. There are all the conflicts, all the unease, all the distinctions that make for substance in a novel."

Georgina could agree with that. "That's why this fascination with Jane Austen is so damaging, people harking back to a time when people were seriously oppressed, and pretending it was some kind of golden age."

The two American women, who had been listening with rapt attention to Susie's every word, smiling at every mention of a character or place or situation in *Emma,* overheard Georgina's remark, and were voluble in their disagreement.

"Austen makes fun of snobbery, she had no time for it, look how she treats Emma!"

The Russian joined in the discussion with enthusiasm. Georgina fixed her gaze on the passing scene, ears pinned back to eavesdrop on her fellow passengers' conversation. What was it about Jane Austen and her novels that so fascinated a diverse group of people like this?

"Jane Austen came to Bath with her family in 1799, and then again in 1801. She didn't like Bath, as we can tell from Anne Elliot's reluctance to come here in *Persuasion*, where she writes of its heat and glaring pavements. In fact, so shocked was Jane when she heard that the family were relocating to Bath from the country, that she fainted clean away."

"I do not believe that," said the Russian, speaking, it seemed, to himself. "From her letters it is obvious that she relished life in London, she was no country recluse, favouring the silence and isolation of village life."

"That's all very well," said one of the Texans. "But how do you account for her fallow time all those years when she was living in Bath and Southampton? Just *Lady Susan* and *The Watsons*, and she didn't get far with them. Doesn't that speak of unhappiness?"

"Perhaps she was occupied with other matters," said the Russian, turning his head to address the Americans. "So taken up with the bustle of life that she had no time for writing. Perhaps she was happy, and happiness isn't always conducive to artistic creation. Many of my countrymen are naturally of a melancholic and unhappy nature, and from this springs our great literature."

"Where are you from?" said the deeper-voiced of the two Americans.

"Now I live in England, I am a citizen here, but I am Russian."

"And you're an Austen fan? That's wonderful. We've come all the way from Langtry in Texas to visit all the places associated with Austen."

Her friend chipped in. "Anne Elliot didn't want to come to Bath, but it was here she got together with Captain Wentworth."

"This is symbolic, I think," said the Russian, with eager interest. "While she is in the country she is static, her life is not in movement. When she is shaken out of herself, when she comes to the city, then life begins anew for her."

"I reckon Austen just loved the countryside," insisted Deep Voice. "Look at how well she describes it, the muddy walks that Lizzy takes, the beautiful landscapes where the Dashwoods live, and of course the beauties of Pemberley and Derbyshire."

Georgina listened with incredulity as the talk flowed to and fro, the three of them talking about these people, presumably characters in the novels, as though they were real people. She exchanged glances with the Russian's companion, who shrugged and cast her eyes upwards.

The bus turned into North Parade and then right into Pierrepont Street. Georgina recognized it as the street she had walked along from the station before she'd started the endless ascent towards Bartlett Street. "You can go much higher," Bel had told her. "Lansdown Crescent and then up to Sion Hill, you have to go there, for a wonderful view of Bath spread out beneath you."

The bus was pulling in. "This is where you get off for the Pump Room and the Abbey," Susie said. "The next bus will be along in two hours."

The Russian and his companion rose and descended, followed by the Americans. Georgina saw them crossing in front of the bus, three of them deep in conversation, one separate and uninterested. The Americans weren't as she'd pictured them, middle-aged, complacent. They were younger, an incongruous pair, one tall and thin with short hair and large, fashionable glasses, the other short and plump in an unflattering raincoat, with a green Tyrolean hat squashed on untidy fair hair.

Dan's potential readership, Georgina said to herself. Her potential readers. Or perhaps not. If they were that fanatical, they might confine themselves to the original texts, and disdain anything not written by Jane Austen herself.

Had anyone ever sat and chewed over her heroine, Magdalene Crib? These people were talking about Jane Austen's characters as though they were old friends. Friends meant likeable. Magdalene wasn't likeable.

The thought popped into Georgina's head and surprised her. She hadn't wanted Magdalene to be likeable. What chance had any woman to be likeable when she'd had to endure such a wretched life?

Susie, who had been silent for a while, spoke again. "The Theatre Royal opened its doors on this site in 1805 and Jane Austen herself would certainly have seen performances here. She loved the theatre, as her biographies and letters testify. Showing this week is a play about Jane Austen, *Dear Jane*, a dialogue between herself as a ghost and her brother Charles, the admiral. This is part of its pre-London run, where it will open in three weeks' time. Tickets are available at the box office, but hurry if you want to go, as performances are selling out fast. We come now to Queen Square where Jane Austen stayed, at Number Thirteen, in 1799, and then we proceed up Gay Street where she lodged for a while at Number Twenty-five, on our right.

"We have reached The Circus. We stop here to allow you to leave the tour and visit the Royal Crescent, especially Number One Royal Crescent, a museum of Georgian life, and to go along the Broad Walk, marked on your map, where romance bloomed for Anne and Captain Wentworth. Once again, the next bus will pick up in two hours."

Georgina was almost tempted to get off, not least to get away from Susie's irritating flow of information about Jane Austen, which was factual, and about her characters, which was absurd.

Of course literary tours were all the rage. She had a friend who'd been on a Dracula tour recently, complete with free fangs, and London was full of Dickens and Sherlock Holmes tours, alongside Jack the Ripper walks and an evening with Samuel Pepys. How people loved to personalize and emotionalize fictive and historical characters — a distortion that conflicted with reality and was simply an indulgence.

Prig, said a voice in her head, startling her. What harm did it do for people to feel involved with characters from the past or historical figures? Academic rigour and clear-headedness had never belonged to more than a small percentage of even the literate population.

Twice prig, said the voice. *Maybe the non-academics have more fun,* it went on. *Maybe Jane Austen and Dickens would have laughed at all the serious papers and tomes pronouncing on their writing.*

Odd how a writer like Dickens made you laugh as well as cry, and those commenting on him with the full rigour of trained academic minds seemed mostly to have had humour bypasses.

"The Assembly Rooms are where the balls were held. During the season, these were held almost every evening. There were two sets of Assembly Rooms in Jane Austen's day, the Lower Rooms and the Upper Rooms. It was here that Catherine Morland was introduced to Henry Tilney, and danced with him at subsequent balls. Jane Austen herself loved to dance, as we know from her letters.

"Situated in this building is the Bath Costume Museum. We make another stop here, so that you may visit the Assembly Rooms and the Costume Museum."

Hastily, Georgina got out her map. Yes. If she got off here, she'd save herself a long trek back up the steep streets, Bartlett Street must be just down there. She jumped off

130

the bus as it was moving away, and heard the guide calling after her. "The next pickup . . ."

"Will be in two hours," Georgina shouted after the departing bus.

NINE

It had begun to rain again, a slanting rain that aimed for her face and hands, and trickled down the back of her neck. Georgina looked at her watch. Half past four. Bel had said she would be home by six. She had given Georgina a key, so she could go back to the house on Bartlett Street, read a book. Read the life of Jane Austen, make some effort to get to know more about the damned woman.

To hell with Jane Austen. The Costume Museum sounded interesting. She'd go and spend an hour or so there, then meet up with Bel at six.

She almost turned away at the door, where a large sign proclaimed a dazzling new exhibition that had just opened, of, guess what, Georgina muttered to herself, Jane Austen costumes. Not as actually worn by the author, but as worn by actors playing her characters in TV and movie adaptations.

"The shirt that Colin Firth wore in *Pride and Prejudice*," a large notice said.

Shirt? Georgina had seen Colin Firth in various films, though never playing a Jane Austen role, and she admired him as an actor. But did she want to look at a shirt he had once worn? Wasn't this getting close to relics, a saint's finger here, a piece of the True Cross there?

"Do you want an entrance ticket or not?" the woman at the till demanded.

"Do I have to do the Jane Austen exhibition? Can't I just get an entry into the rest of the museum?"

"One ticket admits you to the permanent exhibition and to the special exhibition," the woman said. "Do you want a ticket or not? There are other people waiting, you know."

Georgina bought a ticket, and hung back as an eager party of teenagers swept past her. They all wore short tartan kilts, and were accompanied by a keen-eyed teacher, calling out to Amelia to make less noise, please.

There was always an Amelia in every school group. The Amelia in Georgina's class had been Lucy-Ann Gore. Blonde, pretty, a cheerleader, dated by the jocks, beloved of teachers, elected homecoming queen. Where was Lucy-Ann now? Georgina had been the one hanging back in class outings, hating being in a group, scoffed at by Lucy-Ann and her clique when the teacher had pounced, as she or he inevitably did, telling Georgina to keep up and pay attention, she'd have to turn in a paper like everyone else, and it wasn't like she needed another D.

In those days she'd spent her time making up stories. They came back vividly to Georgina as Amelia laughed too loudly and made a vulgar remark about a pair of breeches displayed in a cabinet on the wall.

She had cast Lucy-Ann as a helpless victim, terrorized by anything from beasts from outer space to giant rats coming out of the sewers to get her. Lucy-Ann had come to a thousand terrible ends, unmourned, unlamented, unmissed. Was that dark girl at the back of the gaggle even now plotting an encounter between Amelia and a serial killer, a hooded assassin, a false step into a pit of snakes?

The teacher called her group together. "Gather round, girls, and pay attention."

A plump, pretty girl stood at the back, whispering to a friend.

"Harriet Smith, stop talking and listen to me."

"Yes, Miss Goddard, sorry, Miss Goddard."

The young voices faded into the distance, and Georgina was alone in a dimly lit room, with all the light coming from the displays, where the costumes were arranged on black silhouettes, set against a pale grey background. It was effective, no question about it, and the mannequins were grouped as though in conversation or at a party. Here a girl in a white muslin gown, high-waisted and demure, sat at a piano, while a gentleman in a blue coat stood ready to turn her music. There were sound effects, too: strains of Haydn filled the room. These gave way to snatches of conversation, laughter, and then more music. Hoofbeats, the sound of a carriage drawing up, and here in the next section were the servants, a coachman in a drab coat, a round woman in lace and pinafore, a boy in a smock, a dairymaid with a basket of eggs.

Pretty. Unreal.

Scenes from a film were being flashed across a screen, a gentleman's house which was oddly occupied by both a gentleman and a pig, while in the corner an irate woman was screeching and exclaiming. Some flummoxed director trying to breathe some real life into all this pretty nothingness, Georgina said to herself.

She never did find the shirt, but she was entranced by the clothes of the nineteenth century, with their faded glory and tarnished trimmings. People had actually worn these garments, this gown, that shawl, this riding coat, that fanciful waistcoat. No illusions here, no contrived and artificial re-creation of a world that had never existed outside the imagination.

Gorgeous embroidery, fragile lace, and tiny satin shoes, pointed, impossible to think of anyone wearing them, walking and dancing. And the hats, extravagances of velvet and silk and feather and flowers. Not originals these, the notice informed her, but made by historical milliner Virginia Hepton from original illustrations in fashion magazines of the period.

What had it felt like to go tripping out in those delicate half boots, muslined from neck to ankle, a parasol in your hand, hair dressed and bonneted, and stays pressing your ribs every time you breathed? What a restricted life these women had lived, these members of the gentry. These were clothes for men with inherited land and money, and women whose only purpose was to marry, whose function was to bear children and run a household. Ah, here was a woman

136

with a difference, a woman in a travelling cloak. Mrs. Rudkin, the text said. A formidable traveller, who'd been to Turkey and even accompanied her husband to China. That was more like it; clothes that had belonged to a named person, with a purpose in life and a history. And here was one Sarah Jenner, who had run a brewing business and owned two inns in Bath.

Attagirl, Georgina said to the silhouette. She could fancy writing a story about Sarah, brewer and innkeeper. Perhaps Sarah had started with nothing, been forced into a disagreeable marriage to a man who drank and gambled away his wages, so that his wife had to make a living for herself. Back to the middle classes, here was a pelisse which had belonged to Mrs. Roper, who had died at the age of thirty-one after giving birth to her eleventh child.

There was a lot to be said for living in the twenty-first century. How would these people, if miraculously transported into modern times, cope with cars and planes, internet and telephones, films, sex on demand? Those girls giggling over a codpiece probably had no idea how much they owed to contraception, how liberated they were because of it. They were sweeping past her again now, with Amelia proclaiming that

Mr. Darcy was hot and lucky Lizzy to get laid by him.

Mr. Darcy. Even Georgina knew who Mr. Darcy was, the Ur romantic hero, tall, dark and handsome, the archetype for generations of curling-lipped heroes sweeping girls off their feet with their arrogance and hard sexiness. Another unreal figure, and sure to be a bloodless figure in comparison to a Heathcliff or a Mr. Rochester. How depressing that such a figure could still arouse teenage enthusiasm. Had anyone written a book where Mr. Darcy turned out to be a vampire? That would neatly tie up two genres, and would undoubtedly head straight for the bestseller lists. Perhaps she should suggest a fanged element to *Love and Friendship*. . . .

Alarmed, she reined in her unruly imagination. Back to reality, back to Jane Austen, back to the task she faced, quite daunting enough without bringing vampires into the equation.

TEN

The children were tucked up in bed, wonderful smells were wafting up from the basement and Georgina, slumped in a generous armchair, had never felt more exhausted. How could Bel look so lively and alert?

The six-year-old twins were a boy and a girl with blond curls, taking after their mother.

"This is Jane, and this is Alan," Bel said.

Alan looked Georgina up and down, said a shy hello and then vanished to some higher region. But Jane didn't go. Jane had taken a liking to Georgina. She tugged at her arm. "Sit down, and I'll tell you a story."

"Let Gina read you a story," Bel said. "Gina writes stories."

Jane wasn't interested. "She can listen to my story."

It was a far from coherent narrative. Jane seemed able to speak on the in breath and the out breath and the words tumbled out of her, her expressive little face lightening and darkening with her tale.

Which was, Georgina quickly realized, as dark a story as she had ever heard. The heroine was a girl of six who was a witch.

"Too much Harry Potter," said Bel, coming into the room with Thomas in her arms.

"Not Harry Potter," said Jane with dignity. "This is my story, about my school."

"I think your daughter's given me nightmares," Georgina said, when Jane was cajoled and bribed to go upstairs for bath and bed.

"She does have a rather gothic imagination," Bel admitted.

"Is she in trouble at school?"

"Perpetually. I'm always getting notes from her teacher or the head. They think she ought to see a psychologist. I think she just has a rebellious nature. Anyhow, I'm not going to worry about it at the moment. I want to talk to you, I want to know exactly what you're doing. How's your love life? Is there a significant other? I heard about a rich lawyer, are you still with him?"

Georgina didn't want to talk about herself. "What's this shop, Bel? What are you up to?"

"The shop. Well, it's a business I run. No, I shan't tell you about it, come with me tomorrow and you can see for yourself. If you don't want to talk about the men in your life, what about work? What are you writing now? A follow-up to your first book, or something different? Why are you in Bath? I don't believe you were suddenly, after all this time, struck by an urgent desire to see me."

That was the thing about friendship. Years passed, and when you met again, it was as though you had last met yesterday.

"I'm in Bath to do research on Jane Austen," Gina said.

"Jane Austen? Why? Surely she's clean out of your period, aren't you late nineteenth century and historical gloom?"

"It has a bearing on what I'm doing. And research is too grand a term, I just wanted to get a feel for a place where she lived."

"Bath is super-charged with Jane Austen, I'm glad to say. Full of fans and filmmakers. They're filming right now, in fact, a new version of *P and P*."

"Pride and Prejudice?"

"Yes. Myself, I like the BBC version the best. Colin Firth makes a wonderful Darcy, whereas the more recent versions go in for neurasthenic youths with no sex appeal. I know he was twenty-eight, but twenty-eight then was a man, whereas now actors of twenty-eight look like adolescents. Odd that, and it's recent, you know. If you look at Freddie's college photos and compare them with the ones he has from his father's and grandfather's time, you see the difference. Men then, boys now. That's what makes Darcy so interesting, he's a grown-up."

"Hmm," said Georgina non-committally. She neither knew nor cared how old Mr. Darcy was. Although presumably she'd have to make her hero the same age as Jane Austen's. Which would be young; she could just imagine Dan and Livia's reaction if she turned in a script featuring a fifty-year-old protagonist getting it together with a twenty-year-old, or even a woman of his own age. "Romance is for the young," a friend of hers who wrote romantic novels told her. "They say the market is there for stories about the love lives of women in their forties, but don't you believe it. Romantic comedy equals youth."

She missed Bel's next words, about the dream of every intelligent woman that she would meet a Darcy of her own. Not Georgina, who could truthfully say that Mr. Darcy had never featured in her dreams, good or bad.

She should come clean, this was the time

to do it, to confess her sins on the Jane Austen front, and Bel, after a burst of ribald amusement and disbelief, would take pity on her, would fill her in, answer all her questions.

"You're still keen on Jane Austen, I gather," was what she actually said.

"Once you get the bug, you don't lose it. Every time I read her novels, I find something new to admire or laugh at, some new insight into her characters, and therefore into the *condition humaine*. I can't wait for Jane to be old enough to start reading her; I was deep into them at eleven. She's named for Jane Austen, did I tell you that? Alan was Freddie's choice, after his father, Jane mine; no way would I name her after my mom. How old were you when you read *Pride and Prejudice* for the first time?"

Twenty-seven would be an honest answer, given that she'd have to bite the bullet and read the damned book before she was many weeks older, Georgina thought but didn't say. She changed the subject. "Is that why you live in Bath? Because of its associations with Jane Austen?"

"Bath is accidental, it's where Freddie inherited a house — this house — from a great-aunt. Bath's become frightfully fashionable, of course, all kinds of rich Londoners who want the perfect Georgian house. Freddie says that his mother despaired of how dowdy it was when she grew up here. She hates the place, by the way, when she comes she grumbles about the climate, says she just wants to sleep all the time, and how phoney it all is. Myself, I love it. I adore Georgian."

Bel disappeared to attend to the dinner. "You stay here, no, I don't want any help, I like to have the kitchen to myself when I'm cooking. Half an hour, I'll shout up; pour yourself another glass of wine."

The door closed behind her. Georgina got up and wandered into the other part of the room, tinkled a few notes on the piano and then scanned the bookshelves. Bel and Freddie clearly shared eclectic tastes, with books ranging from politics to graphic novels to shabby leather-bound volumes.

A red book caught Georgina's eye, in fact it drew it towards her as though she were hypnotized. She knew what it was, even before she'd squinted at the small, gold-blocked title. *Pride and Prejudice.* She sprang back as though the book might leap off the shelf and bite her.

Get a grip. She had to read the novels. Either that or send the money back — how could she do that, with her rent and overdraft already paid out of it? — and scuttle back to America. She'd made a start, she was getting facts about the author, as proof of which, here she was in one of Jane Austen's haunts. Approaching the text through the author's life, and what a no-no that was to the academic mind. First should come the social background: class, always, in anything to do with England. Gender, that all-important key to everything, the cornerstone of the modern temple of academe.

Just do it. She snatched the book from the shelf as though it were a work of the most vile and debauched pornography and retreated to her armchair. Before her resolve could falter, she took it out of its slipcase — which was flowery, polite, representing all she didn't like about the whole Jane Austen thing — and opened the book.

She would begin with the introduction.

There was that voice again. *Coward,* it said, quite clearly. Come on, get on with it. Then the half an hour, of which nearly ten minutes had gone, would at least have achieved something to earn her advance: fifteen minutes on the introduction before she used up the final five minutes to visit the bathroom.

The book slipped out of her hand and lay

face-down on the floor. That was no way to treat a book that was obviously special. Georgina leaned over, picked it up and before she could think better of it, opened it to a random page.

"Look here, I have bought this bonnet. I do not think it is very pretty; but I thought I might as well buy it as not. I shall pull it to pieces as soon as I get home, and see if I can make it up any better."

Her worst fears realized. Just as she suspected, the woman wrote about petty, frivolous things, little domestic details. Interesting if you were into the daily round of upper-class England in the Regency. Which she wasn't, and never could or would be. She flicked through a few more pages: not even a great stylist, odd punctuation, prosaic, no poetry in this language. Certainly no passion, no intensity; Charlotte Brontë was right in her judgement on Jane Austen's writing, and her words came into Georgina's head with sudden clarity:

The Passions are perfectly unknown to her; she rejects even a speaking acquaintance with that stormy Sisterhood; even to the Feelings she vouchsafes no more than an occasional graceful but distant recognition.

Bel's voice floated up from the bottom of the stairs, summoning Georgina to come and eat. At the table, Bel was full of news of common friends, the doings of college contemporaries, gossip, scandal, dismay. "I haven't really kept in touch," Georgina confessed.

"I can tell. You've shut yourself away in England just as I have, but there is email. Or Facebook, even. Only you've always been a private person, I don't suppose you've felt like putting the details of your life out on the net. Have some more cabbage. Sorry to have abandoned you up there, but I'm sure you found something in the pile of magazines to entertain you."

Bel had always been a mag reader. Georgina could see in her mind's eye their room at college, stacked with glossy monthlies. Even then, Bel had been more frivolous than Georgina was; she'd read serious journals, not *Vanity Fair*. Although she'd done a paper, using Bel's stack of magazines, entitled *Self-image of women and the influence of media-engendered constructs,* for her social history course. Comparing modern publications to women's magazines of the nineteenth century. And concluding that not much had changed. Corset ads in one, Wonderbras in the other. From rouge to blusher; tips, then and now, for how to cook a special meal for you and your husband or partner.

It was also a question of money. In an effort to stretch her budget as far as it would go, Georgina had to cut back severely on books, let alone magazines, of any kind.

Bel understood money. Here she was, asking about Georgina's father, and they slipped back easily into their old intimacy, when they used to lie on their beds, talking, talking for hours, and discussing the dysfunctionality of their respective families.

"Dad has another expensive divorce coming up," Georgina said.

"Is he going to flee the country again, leaving alimony and his problems behind?"

Georgina's father had escaped from the clutches of his fourth wife by fleeing to an offshore haven until she gave up and found herself richer prey.

"It would be funny if he went to the wrong place and met up with my mother. Would he recognize her, do you suppose?"

After Georgina's mother had decamped with her infant son for a new life in South America, they had heard nothing from her. But news filtered back; she had married a rich Argentine, and Georgina had once seen a photo of her standing beside gleaming white rails, watching a polo match. The rider flashing past on a bay polo pony was, according to the caption, Georgina's brother.

"You've still never been in touch?"

"Neither of them has ever tried to contact me, so why should I make the effort?"

"She is your mother."

When she was seventeen, Georgina had indulged in a brief sentimental wish to track her mother down, fly to Argentina, land on her doorstep, confront her.

"I'm so glad I didn't have the money for the plane fare. Only imagine how dreadful if, as is likely, she had simply refused to see me. The rebuff, I already have it. Why seek another rejection?"

"Terrible," said Bel, all mother now, "to abandon a baby. How could she?"

"She abandoned Dad, really. I was just a tiresome addendum. She didn't want to have me, in any case, so Dad told me. She was furious when she discovered she was pregnant."

"She didn't abort you."

"More difficult then. But she did do a fair bit of jumping off tables and gin drinking and hot baths."

"As your father told you."

"As my father told me."

Looking back now, she understood he hadn't wanted her to try to contact her mother, and so he'd stressed all the negative things about her. And they didn't come much more negative than first trying to miscarry and then dumping a baby. "It's not a biased version, my dad's, as it happens. I asked my mother's onetime best friend, and she said, yes, that was the way it was."

Bel's family were differently disordered. Her parents were driven, ambitious, perfectionist, high achievers in every sphere of their life. Their marriage had lasted, because a failed marriage was a failure like any other, and so couldn't be tolerated. And their daughter had to follow in their footsteps. Top in everything. "Lucky I was clever," said Bel.

"Do you see much of them now?" Georgina asked, staring into the flickering flames of the log fire.

"They come over once or twice a year. When Freddie's away. They don't like Freddie. They can't forgive me for not finishing college, they don't like anything about my life or my marriage, and they are convinced I'm bringing up the children shockingly badly."

"The kids seem fine to me."

"They are. I just remember how my parents did it, and then I do the opposite. I might write a book about it, *Contrarian Parenting.*"

"All very Philip Larkin."

"You'll be into all that if you're doing work on Jane Austen. She knew a thing or two about family life."

"Family life? Misty-eyed romance, rather," Georgina ventured. That at least she knew about Jane Austen; she wouldn't be called the original chick-lit author for nothing.

"You know better than that. No, I reckon Jane Austen's own family life wasn't that great, and the families in her books are so peculiar, aren't they?"

"Her novels aren't about families. Didn't a critic say her books were about nothing except class and money?"

"That's a trite comment if ever I heard one. How dismissive. Bet it was a man who said it."

Georgina was anxious to get away from the subject of Jane Austen — how had that woman intruded into the conversation again? "Talking of money, have your parents cut you off without a penny?"

"Luckily, they couldn't. My money came from trusts and things. That's how I was able to start my own business."

"Which is?"

"You won't trick me that way. Wait until tomorrow, then you can see for yourself."

ELEVEN

"Sophie rang," Maud told Henry when he came in, a bag of shopping in each hand. "She said she tried to get you on your mobile, but you'd switched it off."

Henry pulled his phone out of his pocket. "I turned it off when we were at that school and I forgot to switch it back on."

"When you were a banker you had your BlackBerry on and glued to your person. You even took it into the bathroom with you."

"Making money twenty-four-seven."

"Or losing it."

"Those days are over, thank God. Is Sophie going to ring again? I've tried her a few times, but I just get her voice mail. Is she still in Ireland? She's due back in England for the weekend, I'm expecting her on Friday or Saturday."

"Didn't sound like she's taking the week-end off," said Maud. "She was going on about delays to the schedule, retakes. Excuses, I think, it sounded like lies."

"Sophie doesn't tell lies."

Maud was attending to a reed for her oboe, scraping it with her reed knife. "This needs sharpening; you haven't been using it for pencils or anything like that, have you?"

Henry was flipping through the paper. "No." He folded it up and tossed it on to the floor. "Nothing but gloom and lifestyle. Where's Gina?"

"Didn't you read her note? She's run away again. We're going to have to lock her into her room with her computer, like Cassandra did to her father in *I Capture the Castle.* Otherwise she's never going to get the book written."

"Research?"

"That's a word writers use when they don't want to get down to it." She fitted the reed into her oboe and gave an experimental tootle. "That's better." With the instrument in her hand, she went to the door. "Anna! Poulenc."

What a disaster that boarding school had been, Henry mused as he sat back and listened to the music. How extraordinary that Maud was musical, and what a blessing she was. He knew that the aggression of the day would melt away as she and Anna worked their way through the sonata, pausing to refine a passage, arguing about a phrasing. It was one of the reasons he had offered Anna the basement. Her eyes had lit up when she saw the piano. "Are you a musician?" he'd asked.

"An amateur, only, but I prefer to work in a musical household. It is more civilized."

Maud had refused to take the oboe with her to the school that morning.

"I don't want them to take me just because they can do with another oboe in the orchestra."

And in fact Maud had had a wretched day of it, taking an instant dislike to the director of studies, and being downright surly with the headmistress. Who had been a rather trying woman, droning on about sixth-form subjects and how they chose them for each girl.

"Don't I get to choose?" Maud asked.

"Of course you have a say, but generally, we are best able to judge where a student will excel. Although, I have to be honest" — and here she turned to Henry — "Mr. Lefroy, I must say that Maud's academic report from St. Adelberta's isn't exactly encouraging."

"Isn't it? She seems alarmingly bright to me. I'd say she had an original mind."

"As to that, it is hardly what we look for when we decide whether to offer a place or not."

"They won't take me," Maud said as they drove away.

"Would you like to go there?"

"Not on any account. Sorry, Henry, but I'd bolt in the first week. Look at that smug girl who showed us round, I bet they're all like that."

"Well, there are a few more schools to see."

"Not ones that'll take me. I hate school. I wish I didn't have to get an education. I wish I could be with Mum and Dad."

"Not much education in the Antarctic."

"Why do they have to be such freaks? Why can't Dad be a carpenter or something useful like that, and stay at home? Why volcanoes? Why does Mum have to go off with him? I hope global warming does happen, and all the ice and glaciers melt, and then she'll be out of a job. An unemployed glaciologist sounds good to me. I expect it's all Darwin's fault, everything more or less is Darwin's fault, evolution is why I'm the way I am, uneducable."

"He didn't invent evolution."

"Stop speaking like a scientist. I just hope you and Sophie don't ever get round to having children, because I can tell you, you'd be a horrible father, always right and reasonable."

And she'd alternated between silence and angry outbursts all the way back to London.

Well, music was having its usual effect, soothing the savage breast. He'd better go and phone Sophie.

No reply. He left another message on her voice mail and went up to his room to soothe his own troubled soul with an hour or so of work. He opened *Elementary Magnetohydrodynamics, 6th edition.* Maud was quite right, Gina needed to be at her desk, getting down to it. He wouldn't get his brain round magnetohydrodynamics if he didn't put in the hours, and Gina wouldn't get her book written if she didn't get down to it. Still, she'd need Bath for the book, background colour.

Let epsilon be greater than zero.

Maybe he'd give his cousin Charles a ring in the morning, invite himself down at the weekend, take out a horse for a few hours. Thank God for horses and mathematics, there were too many women in his life, each of them more exhausting than the next.

TWELVE

"No, I'm not going to tell you about my shop, you can see for yourself in about ten minutes."

Bel drove a small white van, which surprised Georgina. "How do you get the children in here? Stuff them in the back? Is that legal?"

"We have another car, all fitted out with childish paraphernalia. This is for the shop. And tax deductible, having no windows at the back."

"Do cars pay window tax? Wasn't that houses back in the bad old days?"

"It was, but even the tax man these days can't argue about whether a van is a commercial vehicle. Or they can, they do try, but they have to back off in the face of incontrovertible evidence. Do you know that it was the powder tax that killed powdering? Pitt thought he was on to a good wheeze in 1795 when his government imposed that tax, but of course people just left off powdering their hair. Except for footmen, and that didn't bring in enough cash to make it worth collecting."

"I didn't know that. Out of my period," Georgina added, as though to justify herself. "And I'm not really into footmen and powdered hair. Different stratum of society."

"Not if you're interested in Jane Austen's life and times. The gentry were definitely of the powdering classes. Here we are. No, this isn't the shop, this is a friendly garage where I leave the van. From here we walk."

"Couldn't we have walked in any case? Aren't we only a short distance from Bartlett Street?"

"Yes, but I'll need the van later."

The weather had changed overnight, and a clear, calm day had dawned, with brilliant blue skies and a tang in the air, presaging winter.

"There," said Bel with pride as she stopped in front of a black front door to yet another Georgian house. The ground floor was slightly raised, and had two handsome sash windows. Above them, in flowing script, was inscribed the word *Darcy's.*

"My fourth child," Bel said. She was opening the door beside the shop. "Come in. Step back a couple of centuries, welcome to the past."

The first thing that struck Georgina was how lovely all the objects around her were. The ornate gilt mirror. The two chairs with sweeping curved lines and embroidered seat-pads. Candlesticks with classical proportions. A chandelier that sparkled and captured rainbows, sending them twinkling on to the ceiling.

At any moment, she expected the panelled door in the corner of the room to open, and a girl in the white muslin dress to come dancing in, looking for a book she had just laid down, or sitting at the escritoire to pen a note on the cream writing paper that was waiting for her.

"Well?" said Bel, who had a handful of letters in her hand and was riffling through them. "Do you like it?"

"I'm in awe. Is this really a shop?" And she had to ask, although she knew the answer, "Why *Darcy's?*"

"You need to ask? Because we sell anything and everything that has to do with Jane Austen and her times. I wanted to open a shop, and I worked through several ideas, but this one was perfect for Bath. Georgian town, full of Regency fans, and who epitomizes the Regency more than Jane Austen?"

"Why didn't you tell me yesterday, when

we were talking about Jane Austen?"

"I wanted you to see it for yourself; after all, how could words do it justice?"

"Is everything for sale?"

"Everything. Which is a challenge because when, for instance, that chair goes, as it will, tomorrow, I have to find a replacement that looks just right. With some of the bigger pieces of furniture, a sale means a complete rearrangement, but then I earn more from selling a table or a sofa than I do from selling a book or a trinket."

As she spoke, the door in the corner opened, and a willowy redheaded man came in. He was in his early thirties, Georgina judged, although with an ageless faun-like quality to him that made it hard to be sure.

He swooped down on Georgina, and before Bel could introduce her, had seized her hand, and bowing over it in the most affected but, she had to admit, graceful way, declared himself ravished to meet her, a famous author; he was thrilled when Bel said she knew Georgina Jackson and she was coming to visit. How wonderful to be a writer, of all the arts, writing was the one closest to his heart, so much more difficult than any other, that blank page every morning, "I can't even begin to imagine how you do it. I've searched high and low for your book, when Bel said you were visiting, but not a copy to be had, must have sold every copy, clever you, and no more on order, so they tell me. But I've found one on the web, and they've promised to rush it to me, a perfect copy, so they say, absolutely clean, pristine, unread, even, so I pray that it will arrive while you're in Bath, and then I shall ask you to do me the great honour of signing it for me."

Overwhelmed, Georgina nodded, to be rewarded by a radiant and rather sweet smile.

"Meet Aubrey, my shop manager," said Bel.

"Heaps of post to deal with, Bel," he said, becoming suddenly business-like. "Orders falling around my ears. I'll be in the other room if you need me."

"We don't open for half an hour," Bel said to Georgina. "So let's have coffee, and you can look around. There's another section through the door."

"More wonderland?"

"Not the same. Go see for yourself."

In the other room, Aubrey sprang up from his labours. His desk was tucked away behind a screen decorated with dramatic Eastern dragons. "Silk, almost a museum piece, clever Bel to pick it up. There was rather a vogue for chinoiserie in the early eighteen hundreds, but of course you're bound to know all about that."

This part of the shop was more modern in its goods, although the theme was the same. Paperback and hardback editions of all Jane Austen's novels, plus a great many books about her. "Sequels over there; of course, you'd despise those, being the kind of writer you are, but people do like them. Well, only six novels from Miss Austen herself, and people do hunger for more. Although some of them are, I regret to say, definitely second-rate and even in some cases downright lewd. Readers want to imagine having sex with Mr. Darcy, or one of his screen incarnations. Very coarse." His mouth shaped into a moue of distaste. "One can't control the imagination, needless to say, but I do wish they wouldn't feel the need to put it down in words. However, they sell tremendously, even this kind of thing."

He held up a fat volume with a lascivious cover of a woman with her breasts falling out of her low-cut dress, melting into the embrace of a dark, stern-looking man with a ruffled shirt torn open to reveal a manly chest. It was *Mr. Darcy's Desire* again.

"Written in the style of Jane Austen, supposedly," said Aubrey. "Which means lots of quaint and long words hideously mis-used."

"Have you read it?"

"I make a point of reading everything we stock. So that I can advise customers. But it is rather an effort sometimes."

"Only one copy," said Georgina, taking the book from him and flipping it open. "Goodness, look at all those printings."

"Now, I would know you were an author if you had just walked in here off the street," cried Aubrey. "Only writers go first to the copyright page, no one else ever looks at it. I do the stock for the books, under Bel's eagle eye, of course. We sell a tremendous amount by mail order, so you see, and it's our boast that we have every title relating to Miss Austen available."

"Here?" said Georgina, looking round as though rows of bookshelves might emerge from the walls.

"No, no, all done through interconnectivity. We take the order, and then send it on to the company we work with. Music, now we have some charming collections of music of the period. Are you fond of dance? Minuets and waltzes, you see, and even instructions on how to dance the quadrille. How they must have enjoyed themselves. Now, you just browse, I can smell coffee,

Bel always makes it, she likes it exactly so. Excuse me."

The phone was ringing, and he picked it up and was soon in deep conversation about sizes.

Sizes?

"Dress sizes," Bel explained. She handed Georgina a cup of coffee; no mugs here, but a delicate china cup and saucer. "We have a seamstress who makes up period costumes to order. We put out pattern dresses on the website, and they send their measurements, and voilà. Or we can supply paper patterns for people to make up their own costumes."

Candles, soap, face lotions, jewellery, satin shoes, everything from mittens to shoe roses, soup recipes to guided tours. "If it has anything to do with Jane Austen, or we can stretch it to have a connection, then we can provide it."

"Not the poverty in which most of her fellow countrymen lived, though," said Georgina, suddenly and unreasonably annoyed by the elegance around her.

"Most?"

"Nostalgia, dreams for a past that never existed. Isn't that what all this is about? Aren't you selling a dream?"

"We are," said Bel equably. "So was Jane Austen with her vision of marriage between two equals — how often does that ever happen? Isn't that what all fiction is? Some good dreams, some nightmares. You write nightmares, I sell happy dreams. Whereas, Jane Austen herself was the ultimate realist."

There was a tinkle of a bell, and Aubrey darted for the door. "I'll take it, Bel," he said, and in a moment they heard his well-modulated voice extolling the virtues of a cushion, handworked, exquisite, unique.

"Do you sit and stitch those yourself, while you're not raising a family and running this?" said Georgina, sounding cross, and disliking herself for it.

"I do embroider, as it happens. I find it soothing. But that's only for myself. Those cushions are done by a pair of sisters in their seventies, who are extraordinarily expert. It supplements their pension, so we're all happy."

Aubrey popped his head round the door. "She's taken an Elinor, and wants to order two more."

"An Elinor?" asked Georgina.

"We give everything a name out of Jane Austen, or of the period."

"Like IKEA."

"Yes, but no trolls."

More customers came in, and Bel went

away to serve them. Georgina wandered among the books, steadfastly avoiding the many editions of Jane Austen's novels, which ranged from cheap paperbacks to leather-bound matching sets.

"Of course, you'll have your own well-thumbed copies," said Aubrey, coming up silently behind her and making her jump. "For all the passionate Janeites, I recommend this one-volume edition. Large, hardly suitable to take on a train or plane, but exactly right for the drawing room. And you see it has these divine illustrations, by Hugh Thomson. It is a perpetual mystery to me why modern publishers don't illustrate novels. Aren't they charming?"

Georgina looked reluctantly at the line drawings of women in high-waisted gowns, carrying parasols, men in top hats and cutaway riding coats, spirited horses with docked tails, interiors with featherheaded women gossiping around card tables. Here a tall aloof man standing in front of a fireplace with his shining boot on a fender, there a girl on horseback, her full skirts sweeping down the side of the horse, a whip in her hand. A carriage bowled up to a fine house, another was departing, trunks strapped on the back, and a man in a frogged dressing gown sat in a wing chair in a library, a pair of spectacles on his nose, a book open on his knee.

"I love that street scene," said Aubrey, pointing to a particularly lively drawing. "Highbury, I can see it so clearly, at any moment Miss Bates is going to come along, or Jane Fairfax will hurry past, on her way to the post office. All life is there, don't you agree that he captures the essence of the novels quite perfectly?"

"Yes," said Georgina, feeling it would be churlish to ask where were the portrayals of the workhouse, of slums, of country hovels, of shoeless children, of gin-drenched babies. And irrelevant. Blinkered Jane Austen had lived her comfortable life in the big house, no doubt doing her duty among the poor, but never dignifying them by including them in her stories. Realist, indeed.

"I can see from your face you don't approve," said Aubrey, shutting the book with a definite thud. "Do you see them differently?"

"It was a very closed world."

"Oh, and that's what makes it so delightful, such a joy to open the book, and there you are, in another world."

"Escapism."

"Do you think so? I find Miss Austen so bracing, so devastatingly truthful, but I don't think it's escapism at all. How disappointing, you almost sound as though you are not an admirer. Heresy to say that here."

He looked sulky for a moment, and Georgina reassured him. "Why? Why not be honest about what you think?"

"Oh, how wise! And I'm not alone in what I think, given her reputation as a realist. And she is one, she is," he said, smiling again. "Lordie, another customer, aren't we busy today?" He moved forward to attend to a stout woman in a loden coat, wanting a really nice edition of *Pride and Prejudice* for her goddaughter's birthday.

Georgina picked up a leaflet. "Jane Austen tours," it proclaimed in swirling colours. "Small, select groups, each accompanied by an expert guide. We take you to the places associated with Jane Austen, from Lyme Regis to Chawton, from Bath to Lacock, from Portsmouth to Kent. Local tours Mondays and Thursdays, or by special arrangement."

Aubrey was back, having deftly wrapped the chosen volume in pretty rose-patterned paper. "Do you want to book for one of those? They're very popular, and I can recommend it, if you've never been on one. A very select firm, everything done in comfort and with taste."

"I don't really like bus tours. I went on one yesterday, I think it was this same company." Georgina had put the leaflet down, but now she picked it up again.

"Our Lacock tour takes you to this perfectly preserved village owned by the National Trust, which gives you a unique opportunity to discover what life in a village in the early nineteenth century, in the time of Jane Austen, would be like. It has been the location for filming several of the Jane Austen adaptations. Lunch is provided at the Red Lion, and then we offer a guided tour of the village. After that, you're free for two hours. We suggest and recommend a visit to Lacock Abbey, a stately home which has been home to the Talbot family since the dissolution of the monasteries in 1540. This house is an outstanding work of architecture, and is also notable for being the home of Fox Talbot, one of the pioneers of photography; most visitors will find the museum of photography situated next to the Abbey well worth a visit."

"Do you know, I might just rent a car and drive out to Lacock. Is it far?"

"About fifteen miles, it'll take you half an hour or so."

Bel came in and caught the last part of their conversation. "Rent a car? Don't do that, you can borrow the van tomorrow, I shan't be needing it."

With Bel's words, what had been no more than a vague idea morphed into a plan. Georgina read the leaflet again. She liked the sound of Lacock, good background she told herself, and the museum was pleasingly unrelated to Jane Austen. A peaceful, uneventful trip into the countryside. "Thank you, Bel, I'll take the van and go to Lacock tomorrow."

THIRTEEN

The car park at Lacock only had a dozen or so cars in it, so Georgina had a choice of spaces. Not under one of those trees, damp leaves were festooned across the windows and windscreens of the cars parked there. She paused, swung into a central space, and switched the engine off. Before she could unfasten her safety belt, a thud from the back of the van jolted her forward.

Great. What idiot had run into her? She got out and went round to the rear of the van. A man stood there, inspecting her bumper, a short, middle-aged man of tawny appearance, like a well-bred dog: tawny hair, brown Barbour, ochre cord trousers, tan suede shoes and a peevish expression.

"You weren't there when I started to back," he said by way of introduction.

"You run into the back of a car, it's your fault," Georgina returned with spirit. "What's the damage?"

The tawny man gave the rear bumper a shove with his foot, and it fell with a gentle thump to the ground. "That." He picked it up. "Better shove it in the back, can't leave it lying around here."

"I'd better find a garage," said Georgina. Damn it, damn this incompetent driver, just how she didn't want to spend her day out, looking for someone to repair Bel's van.

"Shouldn't bother, if I were you. Where are you from?"

"I've driven from Bath."

"When you get back, take it to your garage, they'll have it back on in a trice."

"It isn't my van. And what if some other witless driver runs into the back of me on my way there?"

"They say lightning never strikes twice in the same place. Let me know how much it costs to put the bumper back on, I'll send a cheque." He opened the rear doors of the van and put the bumper inside. Then, after taking out a large yellow handkerchief and carefully wiping the dirt off his fingers, he extended a hand. "James Palmer. I'll give you my address and all that, so you or the owner of the van can come after me if I don't pay up. Which I assure you I will."

Georgina hesitated. Trust him, don't trust him? "Georgina Jackson," she said, shaking his still muddy hand and wishing she hadn't.

An alert look came over his face. "The writer? *Magdalene Crib*?"

"Yes," said Georgina, with a familiar jump of pleasure; she never got over the thrill of meeting people who recognized her name.

Usually, the dialogue went like this:

— Oh, you're a writer, are you? What sort?

— I'm a novelist.

— Have you had anything published?

Internal voice: That's what being a writer means.

— Yes, I have.

— What did you say your name was?

— Georgina Jackson.

— Can't say I've heard of you. Do you make a lot of money writing?

Internal voice: Is that what writing means to you?

— I'm not a bestselling author.

— Oh, literary, then. Although some of those authors make a bundle, don't they? Ian whatshisname, types like that?

— Yes, some writers make a lot of money.

— But you're not in that league?

— No.

— I've often thought I'd like to write a book. Not hard, is it? I mean, everyone can write. Put aside a bit of time at the week-ends, and there you are, a book.

— What do you do?

— I'm an architect/surgeon/musician.

— Really? How interesting. I always thought it might be fun to design a few houses/do some brain surgery/write a symphony at the weekend.

Internal voice: This person has no sense of humour. Wait for it.

— What? Don't you know it takes years to train and qualify? And then you need experience. It's a profession, not a hobby.

— Not? You do surprise me.

— Not like writing. I mean, anyone can write a book.

James Palmer knew her name, knew the title of her book, knew about the prize, and, it turned out, had read it. "I reviewed it, in fact," he said morosely. "For the *Atlantic Monthly.*"

Georgina racked her brains, rifling through the mostly adulatory reviews. "Was it a good review?" she asked.

"Can't remember. Usual waffle, I dare say. Brilliant debut, searing prose, all that stuff."

"Did you enjoy the book?"

"Was I meant to? I doubt it. I can't remember when I last read a book that I enjoyed. No, I tell a lie. I can. It was *Kim,* the summer before I went up to Oxford. Have you ever read *Kim?*"

"No."

"No one has, these days. Kipling's deeply unfashionable. Colonial, white, all that. Doesn't make any difference, still a masterpiece."

Another melancholy sigh.

"What did you study at Oxford?"

"English," said James Palmer. "For my sins, English."

"Didn't you enjoy it?"

"Enjoy?" He gave her an incredulous look. "Oxford in the nineteen eighties, English, enjoy? That was the peak time for Eagleton's moronic Marxism. Deconstruction was the rage. My tutor used to say that Professor E. put the *con* into *destruction*."

It took Georgina a moment to work that out, and she laughed. "Even so, three years reading great literature can't be all bad."

"Reading? Where have you been? You don't read literature these days. Kids these days have got it right. They don't read, because they find sentences of more than six words too difficult. I gave up on literature after three incomprehensible years of jargon and —" He shook his head. "Sorry, don't want to bore you, but it's still a sore point. I loved books before I went to Oxford. That's why I wanted to read English. Mistake. Big mistake. Once the academics got their grubby hands on Literature, then it was all over. Game, set and match to the dunces. Have you ever read *The Dunciad*? Pope? You should, good stuff."

As they were speaking, he had walked back to his car, and was standing by the driver's door. Georgina felt she had to get him off this painful ground. "So what do you do now? You review books?"

"Sometimes. Thanks to my cunning tutor, before I took up my present occupation, I whizzed into the happy world of Fleet Street. As it used to be called. I was a hack, Georgina Jackson, a hack. So are you, peddling all that emotional rubbish, although perhaps you do it with more grace and style than I do."

By this time, a sense of alarm was creeping over Georgina. Was Mr. Palmer deranged? Had he been on some wacky substance? Was that why he'd run into her?

"Before you drive off, I want your address, please."

He looked injured. "Of course. And I'm not driving off, I'm just going to park my car in a less prominent position. If I leave it here, some witless driver might run into me."

"Aren't you leaving?"

"Why should I be? I only just got here."

"Then why were you driving out of the parking place?"

"I decided I'd be better off not parked under a dripping tree."

He got into the car, drove in next to the van and got out. "I assume you're heading for the village. Let me buy you a coffee and a bun, too early to offer a beer."

Georgina would much rather set off on her own, and she hoped Palmer wasn't going to prove hard to shake off. At that moment, there was a hoot on a horn, and a green minibus turned into the car park.

Georgina recognized it at once. Like the bigger bus in Bath, it had figures drawn on the sides. It was the Jane Austen tour bus, complete with Susie, who jumped out from beside the driver almost before the bus had come to a halt.

"Oh my God," said James Palmer. "Jane bloody Austen. That woman gets everywhere."

"Don't you like Jane Austen's novels?"

"Read them so long ago, I can't remember. Ditsy heroine gets alpha male, sends under-educated women into swoons of fantasy eroticism. Do I care?"

"I thought the English were all very keen on Jane Austen."

"So are you Americans, the whole JA

178

industry is even worse over there. Perfect for the middlebrow and the middle-witted, those who want a happy ending and love ever after. Got to say that about your writing, no happy endings there. What else have you done, what's your second book?"

"I'm working on it now."

A gleam came into his eye. "So what brings you to Lacock? Research? Hardly your kind of place, I would have said."

"I'm staying with a friend in Bath, and it was a good opportunity to get here."

"So I take it you aren't here for the Jane Austen freak show. You aren't a Jane Austen devotee, then?"

Georgina shook her head.

"Didn't think you would be. Why Lacock?"

Mr. Palmer might be swathed in clouds of gloom, but Georgina wasn't stupid enough to ignore the fact that there was a keen mind behind the tortoiseshell glasses, and an intense and ruthless curiosity. Innate, or dating from his time in Fleet Street?

"Photography," she said quickly. "Nineteenth-century photography."

"Yes, that's your period, of course. Reality and unreality. False and true images. And pornography," he added.

"Pornography?"

"Since you write about exploited women, the underclass, it would seem a likely subject for your pen."

"I never talk about work in progress," said Georgina. How priggish that sounded. "What one talks about doesn't get written."

"Yes, novelists always say that. I suspect it's because most of you haven't a clue what's going to be on the next page. Let me know when it comes out, I'll do a review. And you can invite me to the launch party. I'll go anywhere for a free drink and a few canapés."

The rest of the party had climbed out of the minibus, and Georgina recognized, with a sense of inevitability, her fellow bus travellers from Bath. Gluttons for punishment, clearly. Here were the Russian enthusiast and his unconvinced wife, and the two American women and, still glued to their DVD player, Dot and Rodney.

The whole group, with Georgina and James Palmer out in front, walked towards the centre of Lacock, Dot and Rodney bringing up the rear, jigging in time to some music emanating from the DVD player that Rodney was still holding up in front of them.

Lacock was everything the brochure had promised, with a wide main street, impossibly charming houses, a shop with a bow window and, not in the brochure, a mêlée of people.

Thick cables snaked along the sandy surface of the road. A technician was heaving a tall crane of lights into place. A girl with skinny legs in tight jeans holding a clipboard was pulling out a roll of plastic yellow tape with the other hand and shouting at bemused tourists to "Step back, please keep off this area, we are trying to make a film here." A tall man with a gold earring and a bald head, dressed in black from head to foot, was deep in consultation with a ponytailed young man who kept nodding his head up and down and saying, "Yeah, yeah."

"I think they're making a film," said Susie, frowning.

At the word *film,* Dot looked up from the tiny screen. "Film? Filming? Cool!"

A spotty youth with a clapper board darted out in front of the cameras and snapped his board, intoning, "Scene thirty-one, take five." They were filming outside one of the bow-fronted shop windows. The door opened, and a ravishingly pretty girl, dressed in a high-bosomed Regency frock, muslin under a velvet spencer, and a poke-fronted bonnet, emerged from the shop. She paused, looked up and down the street, and then her expression lightened into pleasure as she apparently caught sight of someone.

"Cut. Do it again, Sophie," the black-clad man called out. "Just linger a second or two longer at the door, and let's see that glow of delight on your face. Sex on the hoof is approaching, let's see your reaction."

The actress retreated into the shop, the doorbell clanging as she closed the door, the boy and the clapper board went to work again, and the cameras rolled.

Good heavens, it was Sophie, Henry's actress girlfriend.

What was Sophie doing in Lacock? The last she'd heard, Sophie was in Ireland. Maud had told her Sophie had to cancel her weekend in London with Henry because of filming in Ireland. Oh well, the unit must have moved to Lacock. Only, hadn't Henry talked about flying over to Cork for a day or two next weekend? It was none of her business where Sophie was, or where Sophie said she was, but if she could catch her attention, when she wasn't filming, she'd say hi. She liked Sophie, who was full of fun, serious about her acting, and very good for Henry. Henry might get staid if he didn't have a lively girlfriend like Sophie to keep him on his toes.

Here was Sophie once more, big dark eyes lighting up again. This time, the supposed object of her interest came into camera. The embodiment of a heroine's dreams, tall, dark, manly, virile, handsome. Hot, as Amelia would say, clad in skin-tight breeches and a blue coat. One had to admit that breeches and boots did a lot for a man with a good body. The man bowed over Sophie's hand, as she smiled, blushed, and dropped a curtsey.

Igor had found out what was going on. "They are filming *Pride and Prejudice.* They were filming it in Bath, and now they are using Lacock as Meryton. Who is this supposed to be? One assumes Elizabeth and Mr. Darcy, however —"

"Can you keep it quiet there," shouted the woman with the clipboard. "We're trying to work here."

Susie was on her mobile. "Why wasn't I told they'd be filming? Of course it will have been scheduled, these sessions are fixed up weeks in advance. How can I take my group around when half the village will be closed off? Well, get on to them and find out where they're going to be."

"Yet another version of that bloody book," said James Palmer without enthusiasm. "Fans dressing up in costume, actors and actresses in costume, they must have filmed and televised every one of her wretched novels a dozen times, and yet here they are at it again. The chap in the clinging breeches is Chris Denby, not a bad actor, National Theatre, picking up some easy money, I suppose. Don't know the actress."

"Sophie Fanshawe. She won't have a big role, just a minor part."

"She is not playing Elizabeth," said Igor, breaking into their conversation. "I have enquired. She plays Lydia Bennet, and she is going to be raped by the man in breeches, who is neither Mr. Darcy nor Mr. Wickham but an extraneous character, a wicked and lustful local landowner invented by the scriptwriter."

It was like listening to people talking about a soap, the interested, gossipy conversation about people one had never heard of, and who, of course, didn't exist.

"He's very into all the characters," Gina remarked to James Palmer, as by common consent they moved away from the filming.

"All the Janeites are, they're obsessive."

Susie was rounding her group up, not an easy task when the Americans were busy taking pictures, and Dot and Rodney, their portable DVD player shut now, were enthralled by the filming. "We shall have cof-

184

fee at the Red Lion," Susie announced. "And meanwhile, I'll find out how this affects our tour."

"Don't bother," said Dot, shifting a piece of gum from one side of face to the other before popping a bubble as a kind of punctuation mark. "That's what it's all about, isn't it? We only came because it's where they filmed the BBC version of *Pride and Pred.* Action's better than just trailing round a place where there's nothing going on."

Mrs. Igor gave an expressive shrug of her shoulders and said that she, personally, was longing for a cup of coffee, and had no interest whatsoever in seeing the filming. "At least," she said, falling into step beside Georgina as the group made its way to the inn, "there are some things here that have nothing to do with Jane Austen. I'm going to spend all my time in the Fox Talbot museum. Photographs, inventions, and, with any luck, not a Regency ruffle in sight. What a relief. Igor can scamper round all the Austeny features on his own, I really have had Jane Austen up to here." She made a gesture as of one cutting her throat.

James Palmer's eyes lit up. "I can see you're a woman of sense."

Georgina, seizing the chance to escape from James Palmer, went to the bar, ordered coffee and then crossed to the other side of the room where French windows led out on to a courtyard. It was deserted; there was a chill in the air, and scudding clouds brought a promise of autumn gales, but she did up a button on her jacket and sat down at one of the rustic wooden tables.

A girl brought her coffee and set it down on the table, observing that the film people would be there in a minute, so she wouldn't find it that quiet, and as she spoke, a little crowd of costumed customers came into the courtyard.

"Extras," said the girl with a swift appraising glance. "They keep separate from the real actors, and the crew sit over there. The directors and that lot go back to the caravans when they want a break."

Clearly filming was still going on, but of a scene that didn't need the huddle of locals in their Regency outfits. They were a motley lot: a stocky, red-faced man with whiskers, clad in gaiters and a tight coat; beside him a thin man wore a voluminous smock and carried a shepherd's hook. He looked around to find a place to prop it, and a sheepdog, clinging to his legs, flopped down under the table.

"Sheep don't like it," he said as he sat down. "Up and down that street, they're getting bored. And the dog's mystified, can't think what I'm up to. Still, it's good money."

"You're lucky," said a middle-aged woman with greying curls tucked under a white cap. "These corsets are killing me. I hate it when directors get fussy about what you've got on under the costume."

"Authenticity," said a short, plump woman, dressed as a maidservant. "We don't know how lucky we are to be living in the twenty-first century when we can wear what we like. I couldn't be doing with all these long skirts and caps and bonnets and funny underwear. I don't know how our forebears put up with it, I really don't."

A fair-haired young man was massaging his calf. "These boots don't fit very well, and that damn horse has a horrible action, apart from being narrow-backed. It's like trying to ride a rocking-horse."

The girl from the inn emerged bearing a trayful of drinks. Most of the men were drinking beer, as was the matronly woman, while the shepherd gulped down a Coca-Cola. "None of that in those times, neither," he observed. "Ale and wine and gin was all you got."

"And lemonade if you lived in a posh house," said the maidservant. "And tea and chocolate and coffee, too, but not if you

187

were one of the lower orders."

"When are they shooting the children?" asked the burly man of no one in particular.

"Wish they would," said the fair young man.

"Now, now, that kind of talk will get you arrested."

"Bet their teacher agrees with me."

"They're filming the scene in the schoolroom this afternoon," said the girl from the inn, who was hovering, openly listening to their conversation. "I know that, because the kids are changing in the rooms upstairs."

"I don't remember a scene in a schoolroom in *Pride and Prejudice,*" said the matronly woman.

"That's because you've read the book, which is more than the director's done," said the burly man. "It was in the *Express* yesterday, a piece all about how he's never read a word of Jane Austen. Proud of it."

"If this were France and he bragged he hadn't read Balzac or Flaubert, he'd be laughed out of the business," said the fair young man.

"What, have you read Jane Austen?"

"I have, as it happens. I did *Emma* for A-level and read the others as well. Good stuff," he added with a touch of defiance. "I know it's Eng Lit, but it isn't too bad, actually. Makes me laugh."

FOURTEEN

Georgina wondered whether to go and find Sophie, but decided against it. Sophie probably wouldn't thank her when she was filming, and she'd surely be turning up at Henry's house someday soon, now that she was back from Ireland. In which case, Georgina'd see her then. At least she might, if she herself was back in London, which was an open question. At the moment London spelt threat. London was where Dan Vesey, Livia Harkness, and, worst of all, Yolanda Vesey could find her.

Fastening her jacket more tightly against the rising wind, she went out through the side door. She looked up and down the street, but none of the minibus party, nor James Palmer, were to be seen. Good. She would go and have a prowl around the abbey and shop. The leaflet she had picked up in the inn told her something of its history — the usual story: the abbey founded by worthy mediaeval Christian woman; nuns; scandals and finally dissolution and purchase by a wealthy client of Henry VIII.

However usual the story, the abbey was strikingly beautiful. More recent inhabitants than the original nuns had had a rush of Gothic to the head, which would account for the pointy windows and arched doorways, which could certainly be no older than the eighteenth century. She decided to take a walk around the grounds and look at the outside of the house before venturing inside, and was about to set off when a figure materialized at her elbow.

"Been inside yet?" said James Palmer in a melancholy voice.

What was this man doing in Lacock? Didn't he have a job, a home to go to? He had a family, or at least a wife, judging by the gold band on his ring finger; perhaps he was one of those people who'd lost his job but didn't tell anyone and set off every morning in a pretence of going to work.

"I thought I'd take a stroll in the grounds first," she said.

"Very sensible. That Russian's inside now, talk, talk, talk. And the grotesques with a portable DVD player are having an argument with one of those women who are employed in old houses with the express purpose of telling visitors what not to do. I was once accosted by a particularly virulent specimen who told me to stop looking out of the window. I suppose she thought I was using up the daylight," he added.

There was one thing James Palmer might be able to help with. "Do you know what a ha-ha is?" Georgina asked.

"Of course I do, there's no mystery about a ha-ha. You find them all over the place. A ha-ha is a kind of shallow ditch, an indentation in the ground so that the changed levels prevents animals from straying from one area to another."

"Not many of them in London then."

"When I said all over the place, naturally I meant all over this kind of place. Country houses, large estates. People liked to have an unobstructed view of the countryside, but also considered things like a herd of shorthorn cattle or deer ornamental. Only, you wouldn't want to come out of the house on to the terrace only to find yourself face-to-face with a large cow. With horns."

They had walked round the side of the house, and were buffeted by a sudden gust of wind which brought with it a swirl of rain. James Palmer said in a matter-of-fact voice, "If you take a couple of steps further forward you'll fall over the edge of a rather steep ha-ha, as it happens."

Georgina stepped back hastily before advancing to look over the edge of where the ground fell away beneath her feet. "Not much fun if you wandered out here in the dark."

"Back in the good old days, I don't think people did venture out much except in the moonlight. No doubt we'll all go back to that, soon enough, when electricity runs out. Then instead of indulging in great bouts of nostalgia by coming to places like this, we'll find out for ourselves just what life was like when there were no cars, houses were lit by candlelight, and your heating was a coal fire, if you were lucky. And we won't have the benefit of coal fires, since coal will undoubtedly be banned by the powers that be who'll be more than happy to have us all back in the Stone Age and under their control, with a permit necessary to travel more than five miles from your low-status hovel."

"Are you interested in energy?"

"Not in the least. My main interest at present is the Dissolution. I'm putting together material for a documentary and a book. That's why I'm in Lacock."

Dissolution? Of what? "Oh, you're talking about the dissolution of the monasteries, under Henry VIII."

"Dreadful man, Henry VIII. Vulgarity and vanity combined in a monstrous frame."

It was coming on to rain quite hard, and Georgina felt this was a good time to see the inside of the house and perhaps escape from James Palmer's glum utterances.

By the time they reached the steps up to the main entrance, the rain was pelting down. "That'll put a stop to their filming," said James Palmer. He watched while Georgina bought a ticket from the woman sitting at the table by the entrance. She wore round glasses and a severe expression. "You can't go into the cloisters today," she said. "They're filming there. Jane Austen. We get a lot of film companies using the abbey. The BBC, costume dramas, Harry Potter."

"It must be good for business," said Georgina.

The woman sniffed. "This is a family home, not a business." Her mouth snapped shut and Georgina, dismissed, set off to make the accustomed circuit. Minus the cloisters, of course.

James Palmer padded along beside her. "You don't seem to be enjoying your day very much," she said, as he cast a disillusioned eye over an immense portrait of a man in armour astride an improbable horse.

How different this was from the nineteenth century in which Georgina spent her academic and authorial days. What a seat of privilege this place was, and had been for the best part of nine centuries. She bet the nuns had done themselves well, and the family who had lived there since the sixteenth century had led lives far removed from the hardship, poverty, illness and despair of most of the population of the country. A life of ease and bliss made possible only by grinding the faces of the poor.

And this must be exactly the kind of house that the characters in Jane Austen's novels inhabited. Where a rich family lived, with a bevy of servants to wait on them and be at their beck and call, tenants to oppress, the poor to despise.

She could hardly imagine what life in a house like this would have been like in its heyday. How would it have felt to be a child here, with these corridors and stairways to race up and down, with a pony of your own in the stable, with nurses and governesses and tutors to look after you?

Rather pleasant, her inner voice remarked. *In fact, delightful.* And probably equally delightful when you grew up. She thought of the frocks she had seen in the costume museum, tiresomely long and complicated

and restrictive to a jeans-and-T-shirt generation. But would women who had no idea of
anything different have found them uncomfortable and unpleasant to wear? Would a
young woman from the early nineteenth
century have been appalled at the prospect
of dieting and squeezing herself into a pair
of skin-tight trousers in which she could
hardly move, let alone sit down comfortably?

They had come to a drawing room which
was furnished very much as it must have
been in the early eighteen hundreds. A harp
stood in one corner and a label informed
her that it had belonged to a governess, who
had stayed so long that she had herself
almost become a member of the family.

"Ghastly job," remarked James Palmer.
"Female drudgery, the only profession open
to a gentlewoman of slender means. Jane
Austen's governesses escaped, of course.
Think of Jane Fairfax, although I don't
know how she could bring herself to marry
Frank Churchill, and Mrs. Weston, with that
garrulous and gossipy husband. Still, certainly better than Mr. Woodhouse."

What on earth was he talking about?
Georgina knew the answer to that, more
wretched characters from Jane Austen's
novels. "Now you're doing it, talking about

characters as though they existed. And being a governess was the only profession open to women of a certain class," she corrected him. "Women from other strata of society had different opportunities. Many women ran their own businesses, and even carried on trades."

"And of course there was always the oldest profession of all. That was open to any young woman; plenty of middle-class girls came upon the town."

"I didn't realize there were any audio-visuals on this tour," said Georgina as the sweeping chords of a harp piece reached her ears.

James Palmer turned to stare at her. "What are you talking about?"

"The harp music."

"There isn't any harp music."

Not only could Georgina hear a harp being played, but she could hear the sound of voices, snatches of conversation, the burst of talk that came from a gathering of people who all knew one another.

"You'll be hearing voices next."

"Perhaps they're filming in here," she said, as shadowy figures in Regency clothes began to form before her eyes. A woman in a low-cut, velvet gown was talking to a man who was bending forward to listen to her.

Why couldn't James Palmer see and hear what she could? A clergyman — at least Georgina supposed he was a clergyman, given his black suit, his white stock and the breeches and silk stockings he wore — was talking to a child who was laughing up at him, and a young woman in a white muslin dress with a yellow satin sash seemed suddenly conscious of Georgina's presence and for a long moment looked straight at her with intelligent, sparkling eyes. She seemed familiar, and Georgina remembered the young woman with the heart-shaped face she had seen from the window in London. Then the whole scene faded and the room was empty, silent; no voices, no music, just space and furniture and the rather desolate-looking harp.

"I suppose," James Palmer went on, "that being an upper servant in a house like this wasn't the worst of fates. Food on the table and your feet underneath it wasn't such a bad idea when the table and food were provided by someone else. Maybe it would have been a better fate for Jane Austen to have ended up as a governess, instead of spending her days as a dutiful daughter to a sickly mother. A spinster past the age of getting married, living in the country with her sister and parents, can't have had much fun.

And, of course, when her father died they were left badly off, and dependent on her brothers. She cared about money, of course. What writer doesn't? You'll know all about that."

"If she'd been a governess, she might never have written any of her novels."

In which case, she, Georgina, wouldn't now be in this fix.

They walked back to the entrance. Georgina thanked the woman at the desk, who looked her up and down with a sharp eye as if she might be smuggling out a chair, or possibly the harp, under her jacket, and they went out into the cool air. The rain had subsided into a dismal drizzle.

"Back to the car, I suppose," said James Palmer glancing at his watch. "Back to Bath, for you. I'm staying near there. Back to a kind of reality. Dine with me tonight?"

He was a glum companion in daytime, God knew what he'd be like with a bottle of wine inside him.

"No?" he said, sounding unsurprised. "Then it'll be an evening at home with my wife and the squalling brats. Do you have any children?"

"No."

"So much the better. There are far too many children in this world, each one of them noisier and more unpleasant than the last. Puling, mewling, useless creatures."

Georgina might have protested that he could hardly feel like that about his own offspring, but on the other hand it was quite possible that he truly did. What kind of a woman was Mrs. Palmer?

As though he had read her mind, James Palmer told her. They were scrunching across wet gravel towards the van, and she quickened her pace.

"I married a woman who, it turned out, had nothing to say for herself that was of any interest to me. As far as I'm concerned, marriage is essentially a conversation that lasts a great many years and so when you have nothing to say to one another, you can hardly call it a successful marriage. That's one of the things I most dislike about Jane Austen, she draws such enticing portraits of men and women who are destined to make happy marriages. Life isn't like that."

FIFTEEN

Georgina looked at the nanny in disbelief. "Yolanda Vesey telephoned and left a message for me? Yolanda Vesey? Are you sure?"

Daisy looked at her with mild curiosity. "Yolanda Vesey, that's right. I thought it was a funny name so I got her to spell it, and wrote the message down too." She handed Georgina a pink Post-it, filled with tiny, untidy handwriting.

> Meet Bath tomorow
> Waterstons 1130
> clasik litritcha seccion.

Daisy might be good with Thomas — who had set up his customary bawling the moment he caught sight of Georgina, perhaps James Palmer was right about puling and mewling — but her spelling could do with some attention.

How had Yolanda Vesey known where she

was? How in God's name had she got hold of Bel's phone number?

Daisy was looking at her with concern. "You okay?"

Georgina attempted a smile. "Yes, fine, it's just I didn't expect to hear from Yolanda right now."

She went up to her room, her mind in turmoil. Did Dan Vesey have some GPS system for tracking authors down, day and night? She opened her laptop for the first time since she'd arrived in Bath. She felt sure there would be email messages from Yolanda and from Dan and from Livia, and she was right. Dan wanted a progress report, and would like to see the chapters as soon as Yolanda had okayed them, so that one of his editors could get to work on the script. Georgina flagged the message as junk. Yolanda was in Bath, assumed that Georgina was getting on with her research and repeated the date and time of the meeting tomorrow.

Like I'm going to be there, Georgina muttered, clicking the keys to empty the trash; she liked the thought of Yolanda flying into the little bin.

Livia's email was terse and to the point. "Suggest you check your bank account and remind yourself that this advance is to be repaid if the book is not delivered on time. My 15% will not be refunded by me in any circumstances. Get a move on with the Bath stuff, meet with Yolanda as directed, then get back to your computer."

Without thinking, Gina clicked on an email from Amazon. "Welcome, Georgina," it said in its matey way. "A suggestion for you, as part of this week's author promotion: *Persuasion* by Jane Austen."

Gritting her teeth, Georgina logged into her bank account. She was horrified to see that the hefty sum that she had deposited had already been eaten away. The overdraft had been cleared, that was a large part of it, and then the rent had gone out, and some subscriptions — she'd better cancel those — train fares, phone bill . . .

Depressed, she logged off and went back to her mail. Junk had crept in, as it always did, and an item caught her eye. "Do you suffer from writer's block? Procrastination and how to deal with it." Before she could help herself, she had clicked on the message, wincing at the prospect of viruses, worms, dragons and whatever else rushed into your computer if you let your guard down for a moment. She gave a sigh of relief, it was a genuine email from a writers' magazine that she had a subscription to.

Organize your time. Set yourself a daily schedule of work. Divide the length of the book by the number of words you can write each day — five hundred to a thousand words is a good number to aim for. Remember to give yourself time off each week — a tired writer is a dull writer.

Hanging above the table was a calendar, *The World of Jane Austen*. This month's picture was a charming illustration of a woman in a Regency dress descending from a carriage. Perky-looking horses with docked tails looked out at the world with interest, and hovering in the background was an elegant gentleman in boots and the inevitable tight breeches.

Georgina ran her fingers over the days, counting. She'd had twelve weeks to write this book. Of which two weeks had elapsed. One hundred and twenty thousand words to go. It wasn't impossible, she supposed, if one had a plot, characters, an emotional narrative and a few of the other necessaries for a readable work of fiction. Which she didn't, and nor did she have the slightest idea of Jane Austen's style — she'd hardly be able to rattle out the words in an alien voice. Add to that the fact that she didn't have a storyline, or any characters, or — no, she was wrong. Some characters were introduced in the first chapter which she had read. But it would be up to her, Georgina, to come up with the rest of them. The love interest, for a start. None of the men in that chapter could possibly be cast as a hero.

A sense of helplessness crept over her. She had heard of people writing books at the rate of ten or fifteen thousand words a day, in a frenzy of inspiration, or possibly of desperation.

She'd read somewhere that Sir Walter Scott had written two of the *Waverley* novels within the space of three weeks. And the *Waverley* novels, not that she had ever read any of them, would definitely have been more than mere novellas; readers in those days expected a solid three volumes. How had he done it without getting writer's cramp?

A few minutes with a search engine, and she discovered how. He had dictated it to a team of secretaries. It seemed almost like cheating, but it was an appealing idea; hadn't some famous English romance novelist dictated all her novels to a handsome secretary, while lying in a pink dress on a chaise longue with a fluffy dog on her knee?

She abandoned Sir Walter, and the article on procrastination filled the screen once more. To hell with it. She turned the computer off and shut the lid. Sums were rattling through her head. In the end, she had two choices. She could write the book and keep the money, or she could not write the book and go bankrupt. No more London, no more pleasant Henry as landlord, no agent — that last might be rather a relief — and back to America, probably waiting on tables while she tried to relaunch her career as either an academic or a novelist.

She made a list.

One: Read the damn books. Forget about the social history, gender awareness, class and all the rest of it. Estimates of time needed? How long did Yolanda say the books were? Between ninety and one hundred and sixty thousand words each; that was a lot of words to get through. Perhaps she could just read one of them, the shortest one, and copy the plot. The idea was appealing, but Georgina knew that plagiarism was risky.

Say read a book a day. Speed-reading, she was good at that. It would take a week to get through them, with one day off for good behaviour.

That left nine weeks to write the book. And — her stomach gave an uneasy lurch — not only to write the book, but to revise it. She couldn't see herself doing that in less than a fortnight, and even then it would be an incredibly rushed job. So how did it work out time-wise? She must be precise. Nine weeks, less two for revision, equalled seven. Seven into one hundred and twenty thousand was, oh my God, about twenty thousand words a week. Three thousand words a day seven days a week for seven weeks. Seven was supposed to be a magical number, but it didn't seem very magical to Georgina right now.

In the distance a phone rang. Then a voice called up the stairs. It was Bel, who must have come back while Georgina was staring at her computer.

Georgina knew in an instant that the call was for her, and that it was, of course, a call she didn't want to take. She went quietly out on to the landing and leant over the banister. Bel was coming up the stairs holding the phone in her hand. Georgina gestured wildly at her, waving her finger to and fro to indicate that she didn't want to take the call.

Bel was quick on the uptake. "I'm sorry, what did you say your name was? Livia Harkness?" She looked up at Georgina again, who shook her head furiously. "She's been out all day, I'm not sure if she's back yet." Bel turned and called down to Daisy,

207

who came out with Thomas on her hip. "Daisy, is Gina back?"

Daisy picked up her cue at once, announcing in a clear, carrying voice, "No, she isn't." Thomas twisted round in her arms, caught sight of Gina, screwed his face up in a pitiful look of dismay and began to sob.

Livia's voice rang out. "What's going on there? It sounds as though I'm through to the zoo. If Georgina is out, please tell her as soon as she comes in that she is to meet Yolanda Vesey tomorrow. Without fail."

"Just let me make a note of that," said Bel, who seemed to be trying not to laugh. "I'll give her your message as soon as she comes in. Bye."

Georgina ran down the stairs to join Bel. Daisy retreated, vainly trying to comfort Thomas. Jane came out from the sitting room. "I heard all that," she announced in priggish tones. "Mom, you lied."

"Mom is allowed to tell lies on the telephone, as long as she is doing it on behalf of someone else."

"Who was that cross person?" asked Jane. "I want to be that person when I grow up, being rude down the phone at people."

Bel wanted to hear all about Livia Harkness. She knew about literary agents, but had to confess that even the most virulent of the New York ones with whom she was acquainted sounded like pussycats in comparison to Livia Harkness. "You have to give it to them, when the Brits really go for it, they outdo everyone. I suppose you have to be at Waterstone's tomorrow, is there a problem with that?"

Georgina wasn't inclined to go into her problems with Yolanda Vesey. The mere fact of the woman's being in Bath filled her with apprehension, and it still didn't answer the question of how the hell she and Livia and, for all she knew, Dan Vesey, had got hold of Bel's telephone number.

Bel had the answer to that one. She was apologetic. "It's my fault, or rather Aubrey's. Someone rang the shop, asking if by any chance you'd been in; he said they were checking places where someone with a particular interest in Jane Austen would go. Aubrey was keen to help, because the person at the other end said he was ringing from your publishers and Aubrey thought it might be urgent."

That was all very well, but what had given some minion at Cadell & Davies the idea that she was in Bath at all, and furthermore that if she were, why she might have gone to Darcy's? That was, however, the least of her worries at the moment, a minor mystery that might one day be solved. Meanwhile she had to get out of Bath. People who were capable of finding a private phone number were quite possibly capable of turning up on the doorstep and cornering her.

"Unfortunately, I shan't be in Bath tomorrow. I've got a loose crown on a molar" — that was perfectly true, and it had been bothering her for some time — "and now it's about to come off. My dentist fits in emergency patients first thing on Tuesday morning. So I'll catch an early train, and get it fixed."

Bel was disappointed her friend would be disappearing so soon, but Georgina promised her she'd make a longer visit when she'd finished what she was working on. Meanwhile, before she left, there was something she needed to do. "I'm going out to take a few photos."

Georgina raced up the hills, round the crescents and down the walks at a tremendous speed, snapping this and snapping that. She wasn't going for composition or cute pictures, all she wanted was something to remind her of the physical presence of this strange city where the eighteenth and nineteenth centuries seemed more real than the twenty-first.

As she let herself out of Bel's house into

the cold dawn of an October morning, she reflected on the strange turn her life had taken. She was constantly on the run, and this getting up before first light looked like it could become a habit. A bad habit. She was going to catch the train to London, or might do so if she walked a bit faster, and once there, she was going to stay put. She was not going to be hounded by any Yolandas or Dans or Livias. Enough was enough.

At bedtime the evening before, Jane had hugged her, wrapping skinny arms around her neck and drumming hard heels into her back. "I'll send you some more of my stories," she promised. "I've got lots more you haven't heard. There's one about Jamie growing in a flowerpot, until along comes Jane the gardener and lops off his head, snick-snack."

"You don't suppose she was a tricoteuse at the guillotine in a previous existence?" Georgina asked Bel.

"Freddie reckons she comes from another planet. He may be right. Or perhaps she'll just grow up to be her generation's Jane Austen — don't forget she was a fairly violent little girl, who saw no need for wrongdoers to get their just deserts."

"And look what a model citizen she grew up to be," said Georgina with bitterness.

"Pretty frocks and charming husbands and everything dandy for ever."

"Go read her letters again, if that's what you think."

Again? Forget the letters, six long novels were more than enough of a challenge.

"Borrow any book to read on the train," Bel had said. "Just send it back when you finish it, or better still, bring it back."

Georgina had reached out for an enticing volume entitled *Widows and Orphans — the Dark Underbelly of Victorian England.* As she bought a hasty cup of coffee at the just opening station café, she contemplated the next hour with a sense of peace. Coffee, a book, the English landscape passing by outside the window, her phone off, sitting in the quiet carriage.

What was it about quiet carriages? This one was full of men in suits talking in loud voices about the dire state of the market. Georgina retreated to Coach C and snatched a seat from under the nose of an earnest-looking man with a folding bike. While he wrestled with the handlebars, she sat down beside a woman with cropped hair who was reading a fat tabloid, let down the table in front of her, placed her coffee on it and opened her book. The first sentence jumped out at her:

It is a truth universally acknowledged, that a single man in possession of a good fortune, must be in want of a wife.

Huh?

With a sense of foreboding, she slammed the book shut and looked at the title embossed on the spine. *Pride and Prejudice*. How in God's name had she got hold of that? Where were her widows and orphans?

This was a critical moment. This was where she gave in, took a deep breath and read on.

No, maybe not. The woman beside her was getting up to go. She rose, let her out, moved into her seat. A window to look out of, and she had left her morning paper tucked into the table.

Saved.

What on earth had that copy of *Pride and Prejudice* been doing among Bel's history books? First thing when she got back to London, she'd pack it up and post it back. Not that it would be more than a gesture, Henry's house was stuffed with copies of the Austen novels, and sooner or later, sooner, think of those weeks, that word count, she'd have to give in and get reading.

Only not now. Now was her time, now was a moment in between, now was the modern world, now was two centuries away from the then represented by that red-bound book presently burning a hole in her tote.

Sixteen

"Mr. Musgrove is away on holiday, Mr. Killick is looking after his patients. Have a seat, you'll have to wait a bit as he's doing root canal work, so painful, those spikes and jabs, I had an abscess last year, they say cloves take away the pain, and some people swear by sage but then fresh sage can disagree with your stomach, I had an uncle who was in a terrible way if he ate fresh sage. Anything to read? There should be, but we've had a temp in, she came yesterday as I had the afternoon off, I don't know what's happened to the magazines, usually so many I'm never sure about the magazines, I read them but they do depress one, all those air-brushed beauties or if you read another type all those middle-aged women who've made fortunes out of bottling jam in their kitchens, not that I approve of jam, no one who cares about dental health can approve of jam. You're American aren't you?

I can tell by the accent I went to America once, but it rained, lovely white teeth, the Americans, they all have lovely white teeth they say the whitening isn't good for you in the long run but I'm no expert and Mr. Musgrove does a lot of whitening work, a smile is a woman's fortune, although I had a friend, Deirdre, although she wasn't Irish as far as I know, and she had a terrible mouthful of teeth, not a single one where it should be and she married a millionaire so you can't ever say, I expect it was sex appeal although I couldn't see it myself, then I wouldn't, not being that way inclined. Hello?"

To Georgina's relief it sounded as though it was a friend and not a patient at the other end of the line. The flow of words washed over her: "The green one only in size two, sizing's such a delusion. What's that? In blue? I always think blue's an unlucky colour for me, don't ask me why, mustn't comment on how it looks on you, I'm lucky really because I can get away with any colour, and so . . ."

From inside the surgery came the whine of a drill. Gina shut her eyes and pressed her hands against her eyeballs. She probed her loose crown with her tongue; surely it could wait a bit longer?

No. She was here, she'd have it done. She'd decided on the train from Bath that her crown was more than an excuse, it was becoming an irritation. Besides, time spent at the dentist was time she wouldn't be sitting at her computer, feeling helpless and hopeless.

The receptionist was still prattling away on the phone. No wonder the surgery was empty, by the time a patient managed to get through to make an appointment, his tooth would probably have dropped out anyhow, and if he did make it to the surgery, he'd have to be in real need not to remember urgent business elsewhere.

The receptionist was winding to the end of her stream-of-consciousness conversation. Then, unless the phone rang again, the flow of words would once again be directed over to Georgina. Quickly, she opened her book. Eyes down. Read.

It is a truth universally acknowledged, that a single man in possession of a good fortune, must be in want of a wife.

That was the one sentence of Jane Austen Georgina didn't need to read, not only because it had sprung at her on the train, but also because it was up there in the top ten of famous openings. The receptionist's beady eye was upon her. It was as though she were telepathic, as if she knew Georgina wasn't actually reading the book. Concentrate, she told herself, as her eyes travelled on down the page. She reached the bottom, turned over and read on.

What a family. How swiftly and deftly sketched those characters were, how the hell did Jane Austen do that, get them jumping off the page in just a few words?

The voice came to her as though from a great distance. "You all right?" The receptionist was looking at her with a keen and hopeful expression, as though Georgina might be about to pass out, or was in some kind of mystic trance. "Not afraid of the dentist, are you? Not too many people are, these days, with all the new techniques, and you'll find that Mr. Killick never causes any of his patients a moment's pain. Unless you're having root canal work, poor thing, did you see him as he came out? White as a sheet."

Georgina hadn't noticed the surgery door opening and the dentist's previous patient coming out.

"Go on in. He's waiting for you."

Reluctantly, Georgina stood and went slowly into the dentist's surgery. He greeted her with a cheery smile, flashing a formidably perfect set of teeth and waving her towards the chair.

"Sally here will take your things," he said as the slender, fair-haired dental nurse smiled brightly at Georgina, revealing another set of perfect teeth. "What are you reading?" the dentist went on as he tilted the chair backwards.

The nurse, who had taken charge of bag and book, answered for Georgina, who by this time had her mouth open, with the mirror and the nasty little probe feeling around her gums.

"So you're a Jane Austen fan, are you? Rinse, please."

"Not really," Georgina began, but the dentist wasn't listening.

"Sit back. Now, I'll tell you a good author if you're keen on historicals, and that's Patrick O'Brian. Wonderful tales, plenty of action, I can't stand those novels where women just sit about and talk. I had to study one of Jane Austen's novels for school and I was never so bored in all my life. Wider, please. There's a loose crown here, that's why you've come of course. It's not helped by the fact that you're a jaw clencher, did you know that? Have you been under a lot of stress lately? What do you do for a living?"

Why did dentists always ask you questions

when your mouth was full of instruments?

"We'll soon fix that." The dentist settled down for a one-sided literary discussion as he set to work. He was one of those people who recommend a book by giving you a tangled web of the plot, interspersed with hearty and inaccurate recollections of incomprehensible funny bits. Georgina made a mental note never to read any Patrick O'Brian.

"Of course he's writing about the same period as Jane Austen. All the stuff that she left out. It's extraordinary that she wrote when all that fighting against Napoleon was going on, and she had brothers in the Navy, you know. She hardly ever mentioned the war. She was supposed to be Patrick O'Brian's favourite author, but I don't get it myself. Rinse, please." After what seemed to Georgina to be an inordinate amount of time, and with bits of blue plastic still adhering to her mouth, he released her from the chair. "I'll see you next week, make an appointment with Miss Bates as you go out."

When Georgina went out into the office to pay her bill and make an appointment, the receptionist was on the phone again. She nodded to Georgina, and flickered her fingers over the keys, she spirited up the bill, accepted Georgina's credit card and made the transaction, all while continuing to talk, apparently without drawing breath.

Georgina came out of the surgery into watery sunshine and hesitated for a moment, deciding which way to go home. Bus? She looked across the road to the bus stop and saw a huge group of Japanese tourists, all students by the look of them, in matching T-shirts, baseball hats and lanyards with electronic devices dangling from them. Possibly they had all been issued special iPods, but more likely these were tracers or pagers so that none of the tourist guide's flock could go astray.

There were other people waiting at the stop, and since the two other buses which used the stop had just pulled away, it was a fair assumption that the entire crowd was waiting to board the bus she wanted. She could go by underground, but it was a complicated journey from here and she wasn't in the mood to dive into the bowels of the earth. She would walk.

She had only gone a few paces when the temptation became irresistible; a second later the book was open in her hand, and she was walking along the pavement only just aware enough of those around her to stop bumping into them, her attention almost entirely focused on the words on the page. There she was, in the assembly rooms at Meryton, music in her ears, and here was Mr. Darcy, what an odious, arrogant man, how was he going to turn into any kind of a hero? And good for Elizabeth, laughing at his bad manners, finding his behaviour ridiculous.

She came to with a start, as a police car went past, siren wailing. She couldn't believe what she was doing, she hadn't walked along with her nose in a book since she was a student.

Her walk home took twice as long as it should have done, since the reading slowed her walking pace down considerably, and also caused her more than once to take a wrong turn. When she finally arrived at the house she fumbled with her key, still reading, chided herself and reluctantly closed the book.

Good heavens, what a family! What an enchanting creature Lizzy Bennet was, and why had nobody told her how laugh-out-loud funny it was? She opened the door and went in. The only sound was the sonorous tick-tock of the grandfather clock with sun and moons and stars which stood in the hall. The house was empty. She headed up the stairs to her room, flopped down in her chair and opened the book again, anxious not to lose a minute in carrying on with the fascinating narrative.

Maud found her there four hours later. She came bursting into the room in her usual rumbustious way, saying that she and Henry had been to see another school, which wasn't too bad, only they didn't want her after they'd rung up that cow at St. Adelberta's and got the low-down on her. When had Gina got back? Did she know that the Livia woman had been on the phone day and night? What was she reading?

Georgina came to, blinking and astonished to find herself in her room in twenty-first-century London. She gazed at Maud as though she were an alien who had just arrived from a strange planet. "What?"

"Sharpen up," said Maud, staring at her. "Why are you looking at me as though you had seen a ghost?"

"Sorry, it's just my mind's elsewhere."

Maud was quick on the uptake. "You've done it!" she shrieked. "I know what you're reading, you're reading Jane Austen, and you can't put it down. Henry," she bellowed at the open door.

Henry appeared. "Has a fire broken out?" he enquired pleasantly. "Hello, Gina, welcome home. So what's up, why the squeals, Maud? Government fallen? Aliens landed from Mars?"

"Better," said Maud, "better and more astonishing than any of those things. Gina's reading Jane Austen."

"About time too. In which case, Maud, why not leave her alone. When did you get back, Gina?"

Georgina, still more in Hertfordshire in the time of George III than in modern-day London, gave him an owlish look. "This morning," she said vaguely, "I had to go to the dentist."

"Then you won't have had anything to eat. Maud, go and rustle up some food for Gina."

Georgina shook her head. "No, it's okay, thank you. I'd rather just get on with this."

"A sandwich then, up here." He gave Georgina another glance and took himself off. She settled herself back in the chair and in two seconds was deeply involved once more with the goings-on of the Bennet family. She hardly noticed Maud's entry as she ostentatiously tiptoed in bearing a tray with sandwiches and coffee.

Georgina was a fast reader when she needed to be, but, deep in the narrative as she was, she couldn't help reading slowly

224

enough to absorb the delights of the story. By dinnertime she was at Pemberley. Henry brought her food up on another tray, and she ate her meal with one hand, while she turned over the pages with the other. He had thoughtfully provided a large glass of red wine and she sipped it as the story wound to its deeply satisfying conclusion.

Georgina closed the book and sat back stunned. That was the kind of experience she had had on very few occasions in her life. It was up there with the first time she had seen the *Marriage of Figaro,* and *Casablanca,* and a magical performance of *Much Ado About Nothing* that left her floating on air for days afterwards.

Of course there had been other moments when she had been overwhelmed by great art. There was *Hamlet,* which always left her in tears, *Anna Karenina,* and she had spent one summer deep in Dostoevsky, lost in that extraordinary Russian world of despair and heightened humanity. The only despair she felt after reading Jane Austen was the awful realization of what she had let herself in for, but pushing that thought to the back of her head, she got up and set off to find another book by Jane Austen.

Henry was ahead of her. She met him on the landing as he came up the stairs with a pile of books. "I know you've been reading *Pride and Prejudice,* because Maud snooped. Why don't you read the others in more or less chronological order and plunge into *Northanger Abbey?* Short and delightful. Meanwhile, come downstairs and have another glass of wine, you look as though you need it."

Georgina shook her head. "No, I want to go on reading." She almost snatched the books from him, disappeared back into her room and closed the door firmly. She opened the book on top of the pile.

Northanger Abbey, a novel in three volumes by Jane Austen. She turned to the first page.

When Henry went to bed at midnight, her light was still on. He knocked on her door, and hearing no reply tentatively put his head round it. Georgina looked up at him, dazed and distant. "It's midnight," he said. "Hadn't you better put aside Miss Austen for the night and get some sleep?"

"Can't stop," said Georgina, not looking up from the page. He shook his head and retreated, closing the door softly behind him, then jumped to find Maud standing at his elbow.

"She'll go on till she's finished the next one," said Maud. "I'd better make a thermos of coffee if she's going to be up all night."

"I'm sure she has far too much sense to do that," said Henry.

"And before you tell me it's time I should be in bed, I shall say save your breath. Since I have nothing to get up for in particular in the morning, it doesn't really matter what time I go to bed." With which defiant words she descended to the kitchen, where Anna was just finishing putting things away. She told Anna what Gina was up to, and Anna shook her head. "It's bad for the brain to go on too long like that. Gina will feel terrible in the morning. No, don't make coffee for her. If she has coffee, she will certainly stay awake, otherwise she will fall asleep over the book."

Anna was mistaken. Georgina read on and on, delighted to find that she could picture so many of the places in Bath, and sure that *Northanger Abbey* would have been very like Lacock. It was a charming book, not on a par with *Pride and Prejudice,* she had to admit, but still an enthralling read. It was a much shorter book, and she finished it in the early hours of the morning. Time to go to bed? No, not with *Sense and Sensibility* sitting there invitingly. She went silently down into the kitchen and made herself some strong coffee which she carried back upstairs. Half an hour later, she was off with the Dashwoods to their new life in Devonshire.

By this time she was becoming rather tired, but a brief quarter of an hour's nap restored her and she ate her way through the substantial breakfast brought up by an anxious Anna without lifting her eyes from the pages. Maud came in at eleven o'clock, bearing several cans of Red Bull and some capsules.

"If you're planning to get into the Guinness book of records by reading all the Jane Austen novels in one go, then why don't you take some guarana? Everyone uses it at school during exams, it's amazing at keeping tiredness at bay."

"Thanks, but I don't need it. I'm not tired," said Georgina simply.

Early afternoon took Georgina into the bathroom for a shower, before she sank back into her chair with yet another novel, off on a journey to Northamptonshire and the strange closed-in world of Mansfield Park.

"Henry says you'll be ill if you go on like this," Maud told her when she brought her up some supper, "but I expect you'll flake out in a little while. Mrs. Norris is the most horrible woman ever, don't you agree? But I do like Mary Crawford, I think she's cool."

Georgina was too involved in the story to

form any judgements on the characters. She was there among them, they were far more real to her than Maud or Henry or Anna, and if she had gone to the window and looked out she would have seen the elegant landscape around Mansfield Park, and not a London street with cars passing and the rain beating down on to the pavement.

Another cat-nap, one of Maud's Red Bulls, and with a swift jump of the imagination she left behind the dull but happy couple, Edmund and Fanny, and was whisked away to Emma Woodhouse's Surrey. Another long book, but as far as Georgina was concerned, the longer the better.

In the basement, a kitchen conference was in progress.

Seventeen

"She's into *Emma* now," said Maud. "That's a long one, about as long as *Mansfield Park,* I should say. She certainly won't finish it before any sensible bedtime, and so I suppose she'll be reading all night again."

Anna shook her head disapprovingly. "To do without sleep is not good for you. One night, anyone can do that, but to sit in a room and only get up to go to the bathroom, and eat all her meals on a tray? It isn't sensible or practical, and it is not good for her. Her health will suffer."

"It's not as bad as that," Maud said. "She doesn't smell, she's taken a shower."

"Thank you for your helpful comments, Maud," Henry said. "Surely tiredness will simply get the better of her, and she'll keel over and sleep for twelve hours or so."

"Not until she's finished all six novels if you ask me," said Maud. "Have you got a friendly doctor in your pocket? There are some wonder pills which are supposed to make you highly alert mentally. A few of the sixth-formers used them last year when they were doing A-levels. Better than guarana even, but you can only get them on prescription, ten quid a pop, something like that, but of course Gina is rich now, so she could afford it."

"I can't think that she can understand what she's reading," observed Anna. "She must be very desperate indeed to read the books like this all in a row. I believe the deadline for her book bothers her a lot."

"Deadline, nothing," Henry said. "She's enthralled. Lost in a few good books. They say you enter a higher state of consciousness when it's like that, and in Gina's case it clearly is. Not so damaging as drugs, you will admit."

A delicious aroma came from a pot that was bubbling on the stove. Maud asked what it was, and Anna, with some pride, said that she was boiling a chicken. "Chicken broth is extremely nourishing for invalids and for convalescents and also to people who have been using their brain a great deal."

"And, one trusts, for people who are determined to read some three quarters of a million words in one go." Henry was prowling about the kitchen now, looking unhappy. "I do wish Gina didn't go to such extremes. She faffed about doing nothing, except escaping from those dreadful people who hounded her day and night, and now, instead of tackling the whole thing calmly, she does this. She'll be fit for nothing by the time she gets to the end of *Persuasion,* which isn't much help since she needs to be in peak form if she's to get her book written on time."

He went over to look at the calendar on the wall, and began to do some calculations. He wasn't at all sure how many words an author could possibly write in a day, but whichever way you looked at it, Gina needed to get her head down at the computer, and soon.

Maud got up from the table. "Henry, if you give me some money, I'll go out and buy Gina the most luscious ice cream I can find. There's that Italian shop, with about forty varieties. That's what I'd need to eat if I were reading all those books in one go, and I don't see why Gina should be any different."

Neither Henry nor Anna felt ice cream was what Gina needed right now, but Maud got her way and returned in about twenty minutes bearing a large carton of ice cream.

"Three flavours," she announced. "Fruits of the forest, dark chocolate, and cinnamon. All my favourites." She was all set to scoop the ice cream into a bowl, but Anna stopped her.

"I'm always telling you that food must look as good as it tastes," and in her skilful hands, the ice cream did look particularly delicious.

"I think I bought too much for Gina to eat all on her own," Maud said, reaching for a spoon. "I might try a little myself."

Henry and Anna exchanged glances, and Henry said he'd take the ice cream up.

By this time Georgina was looking distinctly wild. She had been running her fingers through her hair so it now stood on end, and that, together with the dark rings under her eyes, Henry informed her, did make her look rather like someone auditioning for a vampire movie.

"Vampires?" said Georgina. "Is that ice cream? How clever of you, Henry, that's exactly what I feel like."

He could see that her attention was wandering back to her book, and the advice he had been going to give her, to put the bloody book down and go to bed, died on his lips. Instead, he asked, "Which one are you on now?"

"Still *Emma*. I adore Mrs. Elton, what a wonderfully dreadful creature she is."

That was all Henry was going to get out of her, and he knew it.

It was at six o'clock the next morning that Georgina read the final words of *Persuasion* and closed the book. She sat very still, the book still on her knee, gazing out through the undrawn curtains to the scene beyond, illuminated by a street-lamp. In the distance she could hear the wail of a siren, and then from closer at hand the squall of tomcats fighting. It was as though the world had stood still, or as though the world out there was not one in which she belonged. With a clarity that came from extreme tiredness she had a sudden overwhelming glimpse of timelessness; two hundred years ago and the present stood side by side, each one as real as the other.

She felt a wetness on her cheeks, and dabbing with a finger she found the tears trickling down her face. She knew why she was crying. It wasn't weariness, although she didn't think she'd ever felt so exhausted in her life, no, it was an irredeemable sadness that Jane Austen had written only six books, and that she had read them all. She felt a surge of anger that Jane Austen had died so young. Look at all the authors who turned books out over decades; how unfair that Jane Austen had managed just six. Mozart had died younger than Jane Austen, of course, but he had started young and had left the world hugely enriched by his prodigious output. Imagine if Mozart had written nothing but six operas or six symphonies.

The clarity faded, and the numbing sense of tiredness swept over her. Staggering a little, she went to the bathroom, ran a bath, splashed some lavender into it and sank into the hot water. Two minutes later she was fast asleep, but she woke up quickly when the water reached her nose. She slid down into it to soak her hair, before washing it and herself and climbing out to wrap herself in a fluffy towelling robe. She padded back to her bedroom, shut the door, climbed into bed, still in her bathrobe, and without switching out the light, fell deeply asleep.

EIGHTEEN

"There's no need to shush me," Maud said indignantly. "You could assemble a band outside Gina's door, like Wagner did, and she wouldn't stir. I wonder if she's dreaming, I wonder if all those characters and all those events in all those places are rattling through her mind, and she'll wake up in the nineteenth century, mad, and have to be carried off to a zonky crystal therapist to bring her back into her proper time."

Henry knew he was going to be late for his lecture. "Don't be fanciful. Where the hell did I put that book?"

"If it's that ridiculously fat one full of unintelligible formulae, I used it to prop the sitting-room door open. Anna oiled the hinges and now the door won't stay open when you want it to."

With another curse Henry retrieved *Chromospheric Supergranule Cells,* stuffed the lunch box that Anna had left on the hall table into his computer bag, slung it over his shoulder and opened the front door. "I'll have to leave my phone on silent, but text me if Gina wakes up, and let me know how she is."

"She didn't go to bed until practically dawn, I heard her having a bath in the early hours. So she'll probably sleep all day." Maud pushed her brother out of the house and slammed the door behind him, then went into the sitting room and set about the satisfying task of scraping some oboe reeds.

As Maud predicted, Georgina slept all day, not stirring until twelve hours later, when she woke with a start. She rolled over and looked at her clock. Just after six, early then, too early to get up and have breakfast, although her stomach was rumbling. She got out of bed and went over to the window. The room was stuffy and she wanted to let in some air. How odd, the sky in the west was suffused with a red glow. A fire? The end of the world?

She looked at her watch. Six o'clock? She'd gone to bed around then, so either it was tomorrow and something weird had meanwhile happened out there in the cosmos, or it was still today, and six o'clock in the evening.

A bang on the door, and without waiting

for a reply, Maud was in the room. "It's still Wednesday, in case you're wondering. Wednesday evening, to be precise. You do look desperate, did you go to sleep with wet hair?"

Georgina peered at herself in the mirror, starting at the dishevelled appearance that looked back at her. "I look as though I'd been on an expedition to some forgotten spot of the world for several months."

"Like my parents," said Maud. "Only Mum doesn't come back looking like that, I'm glad to say. Henry said I wasn't to disturb you, but I heard you thumping about. Are you feeling disoriented? Henry used to look like that in the days when he was a financial wizard and always flitting off to Hong Kong and New York."

Georgina ran a comb through her hair and pushed it behind her ears. "I'll go to the hairdresser tomorrow, tonight I'll stick with the through-a-bush-backwards look. I assume we don't have company?"

"No, but that's not for the want of people trying. You're awfully in demand. That Yolanda Vesey person said she was coming round to meet with you, and Livia Harkness said she wants you in her office now. That was several hours ago, she seemed a bit pissed off when I told her you were asleep and couldn't be disturbed. Then a Mr. Palmer rang, said he'd like to drop round and see you. I didn't altogether like the sound of him, he might be someone from the Home Office, he was awfully gloomy. I told him you'd gone back to America."

"Oh my God," was all Georgina could find to say, as the world and her problems came rushing back to her. And not just the old familiar problems of how to avoid Livia and the Veseys, and how to approach the text, but a larger and quite insuperable problem.

"Did you enjoy the Jane Austens?" Maud asked.

"Enjoy? Of course I enjoyed them, but that word doesn't begin to describe what reading the books is like. What a mistake! What a terrible mistake!"

Maud looked grave. "Doing it all in one go like that? Bonkers, I'd say. And a bit rushed. You could have spread them out and made them last."

"I was desolate when I finished. I still am, because there aren't any more to read."

"Don't let that bother you, you just read them again and they get better and better. My English teacher has read *Emma* about twenty times, and she says she still finds something new to admire every time. Is that why you're looking so dismal?"

No, that was part of the reason, but the real reason was caused by the realization of the impossibility of what she had undertaken. Of course, it was out of the question, it couldn't be done. The contract had to be torn up, the money returned — somehow. She'd have to go back to America, get a job, pay it off in instalments. At least one thing was perfectly clear and that was she didn't have to worry about getting a job and not having time to write. Her writing days were over.

"I must send an email to Livia," she said, heading for her desk.

"You can't," said Henry from the door. His expression told Georgina what a fright she looked, although he was far too well-mannered to say so.

"Why not?"

"Connection's down. Has been for an hour. So forget it, get dressed, come downstairs, rejoin the human race."

Maud was in the kitchen, inspecting the contents of the fridge. "It's Anna's ballroom dancing class tonight, so we have to cater for ourselves. No, we don't, here's a fish pie with a note on it. Good for Anna."

"Leave it where it is," Henry said. "We

can't celebrate Gina's initiation into the mysteries of Jane Austen with fish pie, it would be disrespectful to whatever temperamental Greek powers look after writers. Put a bottle of fizz on ice, Maud; I'm going shopping."

"I like fish pie," Georgina said as the door slammed behind Henry and they heard his steps fading away down the street.

"Henry doesn't," Maud said. "You can tell the world's changed, it used to be nothing but Krug and the Widow Click, and now it's all supermarket stuff."

"None the worse for that," said Georgina, who wasn't that keen on champagne, although she agreed it was the right drink for a celebration. The trouble was, she didn't feel much like celebrating. True, she'd read the novels, but where had that got her? Deeper into the mire. She no longer had a vague feeling she'd bitten off more than she could chew; she knew she was batting way out of her league.

"He'll buy steak," Maud said. "Henry likes steak as much as he doesn't like fish pie."

"Why does Anna cook food for him that he doesn't like? Surely she should cook what he wants."

"She says fish is good for you, and you

should eat it at least once and preferably twice a week, haven't you noticed we always have it on Fridays? Also, the only thing Henry can cook is steak, so if you want another alternative to fish pie it has to be something which either I can cook, which is pasta, or you, which is sausages or burnt hamburgers, since you're almost as hopeless in the kitchen as Henry."

Fifteen minutes later and they heard brisk footsteps in the street, the squeak of the gate, more footsteps coming down the stairs into the area. Henry banged on the kitchen door, and Maud jumped up to let him in.

"Steak." He laid a squidgy bag on the kitchen table.

Maud investigated the contents. "And oven chips, cool."

Henry put the oven on and then shooed them upstairs, Maud carrying a tray with three champagne glasses, Georgina holding a bowl of nuts and olives in each hand, and Henry bringing up the rear with the bottle of wine. The glasses weren't the usual flutes, but the older style of wide-bowled ones with hollow stems, in which the wine sparkled quietly. Georgina loved those glasses, which Henry said had belonged to his grand-mother.

Maud dunked her fingers into the glass

before she took her first sip, and sprinkled some of the champagne into the air. She repeated the process, sending a little shower across the room and then flicking froth onto the floor.

"What the hell are you doing?" said Henry.

"It's a libation. To the gods of the upper realms, the middle realms and the lower realms. It seems to me that Georgina is going to need all the help she can get, so a libation has to be good."

Georgina drank some champagne, the bubbles prickling her nose as they always did. It was why she really didn't like any kind of fizzy drink, from Coca-Cola to champagne. If a libation would help, she'd gladly sacrifice the entire bottle, but she thought the task that lay ahead of her was too much for even an entire pantheon to fix.

The champagne made Henry and Maud lively, but it simply depressed Georgina. And, when they went downstairs again, the steak — cooked with bravura skill by Henry, who'd been tied into a striped green apron by Maud — was ashes in her mouth.

Anna came back just as they were finishing the ice cream that Maud had served. Anna took in the situation at a single glance, and wagged her finger at Henry. "Fish pie tomorrow, and I shall make some extra fish next week."

"I don't really care for fish."

"You want to do the cooking?"

"Gotcha," said Maud. "Have some ice cream, you'll need re-energizing after all that fox-trotting." Her phone broke into a series of howls, and she took herself off to answer it.

Georgina had been so wrapped up in her own problems, quite apart from being away from London, that she had lost track of Maud's school situation. She asked Henry how the school hunting was going.

He sighed. "No luck so far. We visited two more, but one didn't have any places until next year and the other did, but Maud took an immediate dislike to it. I think she objected to the uniform."

"It's time she was at school again," Anna said. "Every week that passes, she is losing a week of education, and these lost weeks can never be made up. There will be principles of mathematics, important language work, historical facts that she will miss."

"I wouldn't worry about that," said Henry cheerfully. "I've come to the conclusion that you could miss a year of school and would hardly notice it. But yes, you're right, Maud does need to get back to school. Although she maintains she is perfectly happy, sleeping late, playing her oboe, reading, watching DVDs and eating Anna's delicious food."

"She likes being at home," Georgina said. "I still don't understand why so many people in England, once they have any money, send their children off to boarding school. Why can't she just go to a London school? Thousands do."

Henry passed a hand over his forehead, as though to wipe his frown away. "It's not my decision. My parents want her in boarding school because they spend so much time abroad at the moment. It makes sense."

"Send her to a local school, then, until they're back. Then it's up to them to decide what to do with her."

"I'm her legal guardian while they're away, and they trust me to do what's best for her. I agree, she'd like to be at home with me, but our parents don't want to burden me with having a fourteen-year-old around while I'm trying to study, and besides, she'll have to be in Cambridge with them when they get back from the icy wastes." He hesitated. "And Maud would have a rough ride at a lot of schools; individuality isn't prized much these days. I'm not sure I could deal with a reckless and unhappy fourteen-year-old, to be honest. That's the age when they go off the rails."

Georgina, looking at Henry, thought there wasn't much that he wouldn't be able to deal with. "I can see it's tricky, having to do what you think or know your parents would want, while making your own mind up about what would be best for Maud, and needing to sort out what's practical."

"Somewhere out there is a school which Maud will like, and which will like Maud."

"I wouldn't count on it," Georgina said. "If I were you I'd let her stay home for the time being. When do your parents get back?"

"Not until the spring, and she can't stay off school until then."

Anna was shocked. "It would be most irresponsible. Henry has undertaken to take care of Maud while their parents are away, and that means he can't leave such an important matter in the air. Once you have agreed to do something, you can't go back on your word."

Maud slouched back into the kitchen. Her eyes flashed round the three of them. "I know what you've been talking about while my back was turned," she said. "Me."

"There are other subjects in the world," Henry said. "Like Gina's book. What's the schedule now, Gina? What's the plan of action?"

"Quite simple, really. Tomorrow morning, first thing, I'm going to telephone Livia Harkness and tell her that I can't do it. I'll send back what I can of the advance, and tell her that I'll repay the rest as soon as I can. You'll have to find yourself a new lodger, Henry. I'm going back to America, to find myself a job in order to earn the money to repay the advance."

NINETEEN

Silence.

Maud spoke first. "Coward."

Anna was shaking her head. "You feel this way because you are tired, and you have had champagne and then red wine and this clouds your judgement. When you have had another night's sleep, you will see things quite differently."

"I shan't."

"The best thing for you to do is negotiate more time," said Henry. "It always was an impossible schedule, and they must be reasonable people, you need to talk it over with them."

"From the way she sounds on the telephone," said Maud, "Livia Harkness isn't at all reasonable."

Georgina tried to explain that it wasn't the schedule, they could give her five years to write the book and she still couldn't do it. "It's like asking some hack musician who's written a school musical to compose a Mozart opera. He couldn't do it. I can't write a Jane Austen. Period."

Henry was prowling about the kitchen. "They aren't asking you to write a Jane Austen, they're asking you to write a novel in the style of Jane Austen. Lots of people have written music in the style of Mozart."

"In which case they've had years of practice writing music in the style of Mozart. It's not that I couldn't copy her writing style, although that isn't so easy, I reckon, she's kind of idiosyncratic with punctuation. It's simply that she is such a brilliant writer. Just think of those characters — hell, it's thinking you can climb Mount Everest when you've done a bit of scrambling around in the foothills. I can't do it and that's that."

"You signed the contract," said Anna. "That's a legal document, like giving your word. You have an obligation to write the book, just as Henry has an obligation to do the best he can for Maud."

"Can they sue you for millions?" asked Maud.

"Difficult to do if Gina's back in the States," said Henry. "It would probably mean you'd never be able to set foot in England again, though, Gina."

No more England. No more dirty-coloured rain slanting on to wet pavements, no grey, sluggish Thames reflecting a leaden sky, no more surly, incomprehensible Londoners, no more being watched by a dozen cameras every time you step outside your front door, no more paying ridiculous sums for bad coffee, no more wrestling to get on rush-hour underground trains.

And no more May mornings with the intensity of the green countryside dazzling the eyes and spirit, no more loitering on Westminster Bridge watching lights glittering across the surface of the Thames at twilight, no cups of strong tea with the special taste that comes from London water. No more muddy walks in country lanes, no more Oxford dawns where the world seems to be born anew, no more fish-and-chips, warm beer, Cornish pasties. And England had so much that was old: castles and great houses, tiny cottages, mediaeval humped bridges, church spires, ancient walkways; you could spend a lifetime enjoying them, and she'd hardly begun.

This was ridiculous. Her England was England struggling under the oppression of the Industrial Revolution, the heartless city-scapes of overcrowded tenements, of disease and despair. Why were these snapshots of quite another side of England trooping into her head? *Jane Austen's England,* said that tiresome voice in her head. Jane Austen's imaginary England, for her actual England was also full of crime and grime and misery, even if she chose not to write about them. Get away from me, she said inwardly to her unwelcome voice.

"Anna's talking about honour," said Maud in a brisk tone.

"Interesting, but out of date," Henry said. "It's every woman for herself these days, no time for niceties like caring you've put your signature on the bottom of a piece of paper. If they sue Gina for the money, all she needs to do is find herself a smart lawyer — well, you know one, I'm sure Jesse would act for you — and sue the Harkness and Vesey team for mental distress or loss of artistic integrity or something."

"Be a victim, Gina, that's the modern way," Maud agreed.

The words stung, although Georgina was sure that they hadn't meant them in a spiteful way. She was simply stating facts. Catch Jane Austen's heroines positioning themselves as victims, wasn't that what the person at St. John's had said?

God, what a time ago that was, a different age. Before Jane Austen and After Jane

Austen. BJA and AJA could be her new dating system. BJA, when she'd imagined she might be able to write that book, and AJA, when she knew she couldn't.

Three sets of eyes on her. Where was the sympathy? Where the understanding, where the regret that she'd be jetting back to the New World before a week was up?

"Don't judge me," she cried.

"You judge yourself," said Henry.

"You can do anything if you put your mind to it, that's what all those secrets-of-the-universe books and tapes tell you. They could be right," said Maud.

"I'll say a prayer for you," Anna said.

"To Saint Jude, isn't he the patron saint of lost causes?" Georgina said.

"I don't know this Saint Jude, but if he's an English saint who will do the trick, then I'll go and light a candle to him. I have some good saints, however, who are generally extremely helpful. It is a matter of faith and belief."

"And honesty," said Henry. "At least give it a go, Gina."

"We'll miss you if you leave for America," said Maud.

Georgina screwed up her eyes and then pressed them hard with the balls of her hand, making stars jump around in her sockets.

Anna tutted with concern. "Such wrinkles if you go on like that. All this drama. The place for drama is on the page."

"The math is against me," Georgina said flatly. "Simply to write that number of words, the semblance of a reasonable plot or story, let alone coming anywhere near even a pale imitation of Jane Austen's style, would take far longer than the time I've got."

Henry was business-like. "It seems to me that as long as you get a manuscript to them of the requisite length, approximating to the kind of story that Jane Austen might have written, then you have fulfilled the terms of the contract. There's no way they can say that you must produce a masterpiece. And besides, I don't know much about the publishing process, but don't books go through several stages before they're published? Won't you in fact have more time than this Mr. Vesey has given you, when you can work on the manuscript?"

That was true, although Georgina felt sure that Mr. Vesey had mentioned an ultra-fast production process, and hadn't Livia said something about expecting her to turn in a script that would need very little work? She did remember, all too well, that Yolanda Vesey was going to trawl through the manuscript, checking sentence length and punctuation in order to make Georgina's prose conform more closely to the way that Jane Austen wrote.

The thought of Yolanda Vesey filled her with dismay and a sense of doom.

"Sleep on it," advised Henry.

Having slept for most of that day, Georgina was confident that sleep would elude her. She fully expected to spend the night tossing and turning, fretting and in anguish about the impossible situation she was in. She was quite wrong. Within a minute of turning off the bedside light, she was asleep.

She dreamed. She dreamed she was in Bath, in a house that resembled Bel's but was different in every detail. She was standing in a marbled hall, real marble beneath her feet, painted marble on the walls. An elegant mahogany banister swirled from its newel post and rose gracefully to the first floor. A sour-faced woman in a print dress with a long apron came out of one door and went in through another.

Georgina had the ability to wake herself up from unpleasant or uncomfortable dreams, only this time she couldn't. Rather than being part of the dream, she was an onlooker, an observer.

Dream-wise, she was wafted upstairs and into the first-floor drawing room, a room with pretty rosewood furniture, several framed portraits on the walls, which were covered in striped red and beige wallpaper, and a marble fireplace. A woman was sitting at a writing desk.

Georgina knew the trick her mind was playing on her. This was the opening scene of the Jane Austen fragment, being enacted in infuriating details in front of her. The woman writing at the desk was Lady Carcenet, and any minute now, the door would open and Susan would come in. Enter the heroine of the story, the youngest of a large family of slender means, sent to be a companion to her mother's sister, a rich widow, who lived in some style in Bath.

The door opened, and instead of a young woman in a high-waisted dress, Livia Harkness insinuated herself into Georgina's dream.

Georgina twisted and turned, half woke up, pummelled her hot pillow in an attempt to make it more comfortable, and fell back into her dreams, still an omniscient watcher, with no part to play in what was going on around her.

Here was a tall man in his late thirties, a modish man, with an eye-glass and a cynical curl to his lip, looking out of place, as though he had wandered in from another story.

Lady Carcenet had an admirer, a sensible-looking man in a blue coat. Susan didn't care for him, and who was this young man with a handsome face and a suave manner? A Wickham, a Willoughby, surely, a seducer of unwary females, a tempter, a man to lead any heroine astray from the path of virtue and into the quicksands of lust and passion.

She woke abruptly.

Lust and passion? In a Jane Austen novel? As seen on TV, maybe, but on the page, in a pastiche novel? Yet there was an erotic charge between the likes of Mr. Darcy and Elizabeth, which was one reason their love affair entranced generation after generation; how had she managed to get that on the page with none of the graphic possibilities open to today's novelists and screenwriters?

She got out of bed and padded over to her desk. She pulled open a drawer, took out a calculator and redid the sums she had already done, in case her arithmetic had been at fault. It hadn't. Daunting, but surely not impossible? Not impossible if she had an outline, which she hadn't. Or a plot, even, which she hadn't. All she had was Susan and her aunt, courtesy of JA, and her own contribution of some vague figures from a tormented dream.

Georgina was a meticulous outliner, not that the screeds of research notes and chapter summaries and biographies of characters had helped her get past Chapter One of *Jane Silversmith.*

Should she just take the plunge, dive in and write whatever came into her head? Some writers worked like that, but the prospect filled her with terror.

Snowflakes. A fellow writer had told her she was a convinced snowflaker. "You build up from a really simple shape, a single key sentence, and then it gets more and more complicated. Fractal, you see."

Fractals were in Henry's line. Yet maybe the friend had had a point. She said that you worked and worked on that sentence, and when you got it right, there was a one-line summary of the whole book.

"There's a website, you can read all about it on there."

For a moment, Georgina toyed with the idea of checking out the snowflake system, but she knew websites like that were fatal. One thing led to another, and two hours later your intentions resembled some kind of a fractal, never mind your plot, and you weren't a word nearer writing your book.

Except she wasn't trying to write anything at the moment. She was simply aiming to find out if she had a story to write. If not, if she couldn't come up quickly with a workable storyline, a plot, an emotional narrative, then it really was tear-up-the-contracts-and-flee-to-America time.

Concentrate on Susan. If she was the central character, then Georgina had to know her inside out. Moreover, she had to sympathize with her plight, whatever it was, but not, under any circumstances, feel sorry for her. This was the difficult part. She liked suffering along with her characters; how would she manage with one who coped?

Right. Susan was a young woman plunged into a new world. She came from a country village, the fourth daughter of a family of eight children. Her father was a vicar, with a reasonable living, but a man who found it hard to make ends meet with such a large family. Her mother was devoted to her father, but also had a lot more sense and worldly knowledge than he did. When she heard that her cousin, Lady Carcenet, was looking for a useful companion to spend some months with her in Bath, it took no more than a moment for her to suggest Susan.

Why Susan? What was there about Susan that would make her a suitable companion for a hypochondriac who was in Bath for the sake of her health?

Lady Carcenet couldn't suffer, either. She had to be a vigorous, interfering kind of woman, who would patronize Susan as a poor relation, the kind of woman who would be very ready to slap Susan down if she showed any signs of moving out of the station to which Lady Carcenet considered that she belonged.

Susan couldn't be a beauty, but rather the kind of unusual, lively young woman that men would find attractive. She must have sex appeal, in fact, a concept which Jane Austen certainly understood even if the phrase had not then been invented. That might be the reason her mother had chosen Susan from among her sisters. A young woman with too much feminine charm might attract the attention of young men in the neighbourhood of whom a mother didn't approve. And any mother would naturally hope that Susan, while in the care of her cousin, might have the opportunity to meet a much wider circle of men, and possibly, despite her lack of fortune, attract the kind of man she could be happy with.

Of course the storyline didn't have to be stunningly original or even complex. The power of Jane Austen's storytelling lay in a perfect depiction of the characters and the creation of the lives they lived, not in startling events or thrilling about-turns.

She felt the first stirrings of real curiosity about Susan. What kind of a young woman was she? What might happen in Bath to change her life, to send her from being a dependent relative to a prosperous wife?

Left to her own devices and desires, she'd have had Susan heading for a pile of trouble. Seduced, abandoned by her lover and cast out by her family, her life would be one of destitution and misery; she would be driven into prostitution, poverty, despair. Loneliness, gin, bastard children and an early grave would be her lot. That was a story she could write.

Sentimental nonsense, said her inner voice. Why should Susan, a young woman of character, fall into such a cesspit of woes? Why wouldn't she see through the wiles of any would-be seducer, why wouldn't she have the intelligence and strength of mind to extricate herself from any awkward situations that she found herself in? If she were an Austenesque heroine, it was most unlikely that she could possibly become such an utter loser and victim. Not because Jane Austen didn't care to bully her heroines like that, but because her heroines had too much sense and spirit for such a fate to be conceivable.

Georgina knew she could do a Susan doomed to despair. A Susan heading for happiness was another matter. Yet Susan was nudging at her, waiting in the wings for her cue, ready to spring into action and set about weaving her destiny.

Ridiculous. Georgina had no time for writers whose characters ran away with them, taking on a life of their own and dictating the story. It had never happened to her, and she didn't intend to let it happen now.

Without really being aware of what she was doing, she turned on her computer and began to type.

A yawning Maud found her at her desk three hours later, slumped over the keyboard, fast asleep. She slid the computer from under Georgina's head and the words sprang to life.

Maud saved the document under the heading "Night thoughts." Then she retreated into the bathroom, from where loud renditions of a savage song came thundering out, rousing Georgina from her slumbers for the second time that night.

Henry was fascinated when Maud reported how she had found Georgina that morning.

"Do you think it's some kind of automatic writing?" said Maud.

"As a scientist, I don't believe in automatic writing."

"As a scientist, you should be open-minded. Have you ever tried automatic writing?"

"Of course not."

"Then I don't see how you can have any opinion about it."

"It's scientifically impossible."

"Psychologically it isn't. Psychologically, it's probably just another way of getting the ratty, talking part of your mind out of the way and tapping into your deep imagination."

"Where do you come up with all this jargon?"

Maud waved a hand in airy dismissal. "You know nothing about it, and nor do I, so there's no point in discussing it. The real question is, what was Gina writing in the middle of the night?"

"You didn't get a glimpse of it?"

"I don't read what is on other people's

screens."

"It's probably a letter to her bank."

"We'll ask her."

They might ask, but at that moment they would not have got a sensible reply. Georgina had no more idea of what was written on her computer than Henry and Maud did. Nor was she in any hurry to check it out; she was avoiding the desk as though what was sitting on it were a large spider rather than a laptop.

Dehydration? She drank a glass of water and found it made no difference. Sleep deprivation, a disturbance of her circadian rhythm, a kind of Jane Austen jet lag? Whatever it was, she felt oddly disconnected; she longed for her thoughts to click back into their normal mode.

She had hoped that sleep would bring an answer, would leave her ready to draft a convincing email to Livia, a letter of explanation or apology and regret to Dan Vesey. A sense of action that would drive her to book a one-way ticket to America, a crossing of the Rubicon that divided the old world from the new, an irrevocable decision.

Maud finally bullied her to her desk. "Try 'Night Thoughts,' " said Maud, and when the document sprang to the screen, she told

Gina with some impatience there was nothing miraculous about it, it was merely that she had taken the trouble to save it while Georgina was, as she put it, snoring her head off with her chin on the keys.

"I don't snore," said Georgina, annoyed.

"That's what people always say," said Maud. "People are never asleep, and if they are they never snore. Go on, read it."

Georgina scrolled through the lines of text. "I've taken leave of my senses, and whatever happened to paragraphs?"

"Nonsense?" inquired Henry, who had strolled into the room. "Or words of immortal wisdom?"

Georgina was silent as she looked at the words she'd poured out in her midnight frenzy. She would hardly allow herself to imagine inspiration had struck, that the unconscious mind from which, the experts said, all true writing sprang had solved her problems for her and come up with a wonderful story.

It had, but not in the way she hoped.

"Words of immortal wisdom is right; I seem to have typed out a chunk of *Hamlet*. I acted in it at school, and it looks like I haven't forgotten a word of it."

TWENTY

Henry let himself in through the front door. He sniffed appreciatively, something cooking. Something spicy, good; he was hungry. Maud came down the stairs, a startling sight as her hair was purple, and spiked.

"I've been playing with some new gel," she said as she saw his face.

"Purple gel?"

"The colour's spray-on."

"Isn't the spiky look rather passé?"

"What do you know? I like gel." She went on, ultra-casual, "Nadia wants me to go for a sleepover next weekend, when she's home for half-term. I've said yes."

Henry slung his bag on the floor and looked up at his sister. Watchful eyes, body slightly tense. What was this? God, he wished his parents were here in London, and not thousands of miles away in the ice. How did you learn to read a girl like Maud? His mother would have known exactly what she was up to; she didn't need to crack the code, she could read it effortlessly.

"Who is Nadia?"

"A friend from school."

"Why is she home?"

"Exeat weekend. You remember those? A weekend away from school. Lots of girls from my class are going to be there."

"Boys?"

"Don't be such an antediluvian, don't say 'boys' like the raptors are coming to tea. Boys don't do sleepovers, it's a girlie thing."

"Enlighten me."

Maud jumped down the last three stairs. "You take sleeping bags, listen to music, watch DVDs, talk, eat junk food, stay up most of the night, crash out in the early hours, get up late, hang about, listen to some more music. That kind of thing."

"What do Nadia's parents say about this? Are they there?"

" 'Course they are, they just shut themselves away. It's a big house, it isn't a problem."

"You didn't mention drink. You sip Dr Peppers, do you?"

"I do, because I don't drink, as you know, I don't like it. They'll have beer, cider, most likely, whatever anyone brings."

"Substances?"

"Oh, come on, Henry, when did you get so stuffy? And I don't do drugs, either, only I don't suppose you believe me."

"Would Mum let you go?"

Maud paused for a fraction of a second too long. " 'Course she would. She likes me spending time with my friends."

"The answer's I'll think about it. And don't start an argument, I'm not in the mood. Tell Nadia your horrible brother may not let you come, okay?"

She regarded him for a moment with an intensity that unnerved him. Then she shrugged. "Okay."

Their mother would definitely have said no, Henry was sure of that. How he wished Maud was safely at school, out of his jurisdiction, out of mischief. Who was this Nadia? Who were these friends — wasn't one of Maud's problems that she didn't make friends easily? "The other girls find her strange," her ex-headmistress had said. He'd worry about it later. "Where's Gina?"

"She went out for a walk. A while ago." Maud had her foot on the first step to go back upstairs, but she hesitated and came back into the hall. After a long pause she said, "You know how scared she is of that Livia woman? How she runs for cover at the mere thought of her?"

"Yes. And your point is?"

"I thought it was just fear of anyone in authority, but hey, she can deal with authority when she wants to. I didn't tell you about my music case, did I?"

"You threw a scene when you discovered you'd left it at school."

"Yeah, whatever. Anyhow, I rang up the music department, and that freaky secretary with a voice like a foghorn said I couldn't have it. She put me through to the main office, and they said nothing would be sent back until you'd settled any outstanding dues."

Henry ran his hand through his hair. "What?"

"I don't mind too much about my trunk, I've got lots of clothes here, they don't let me wear what I really like at school, so I don't take my favourite stuff. But I do mind about my music. I need it."

Henry looked at her intently. "Not so enraged about it anymore? Want me to give you some money to go out and buy some?"

"No need. Because I got a bit upset, on the phone, and Gina overheard me, and when I told her what was up, she took over. Blimey, I've never heard anything like it! She had them sorted out in about thirty seconds, asked to speak to someone more senior, and, believe it or not, they put her through to Mrs. Burgh."

"The head? Good God, that woman terrifies me."

"Not Gina. She didn't let Mrs. B. get a word in edgewise, just filled her in on unlawful retention of property, and guess what? They're sending my music back pronto!"

"Good for Gina," Henry said, momentarily stunned.

"So you see, she may be a scaredy-cat when it comes to literary life, but I'd pick her for my team in a crisis."

"Where did you say she is now?"

Maud shrugged. "Out is all I know. She's been drawing mind maps all morning, looks like a frenzied spider's been in the paint pot and whizzed all over the pages. You could put it up for the Turner art prize, I reckon. Said she was going cross-eyed and needed some fresh air. Odd, though, she said she'd only be gone an hour, and that was at two. I expect she's walking the plot, isn't that what writers do? Or maybe she's gone shopping."

"Has she got her phone with her? Give her a call."

"She took the SIM out, so that Livia and Dan and that Yolanda couldn't reach her.

And I don't think she's checking her emails."

Henry picked up his bag again. "When's dinner?"

"Half an hour. Some kind of Mughal dish, Anna found a new recipe."

"Tomorrow I'm going to get Gina a new SIM card, and then she can choose who has the number, and it needn't include her literary tormentors."

"Dementors, don't you think?"

"What's a dementor?"

"Sucks the joy out of you. Harry Potter."

"Damn Harry Potter. Well, if Gina isn't back in half an hour, I'll eat her share. She didn't say where she was going?"

"Out for fresh air, although that isn't so easy. I expect she went to the park."

Henry considered. It was one of the delights of living where he did that Regent's Park was within easy walking distance. Fifteen minutes max, then. "She can't be in the park now, it's dark."

"So it is. Perhaps she's been kidnapped."

TWENTY-ONE

Georgina hadn't made it to Regent's Park. In fact, she hadn't got anywhere near the park. She'd come out of the house and walked a few paces along the street, when a car drew into the curb beside her. A black car, big and glossy, with tinted windows. Gina, who wasn't interested in cars, had no idea what kind it was, but even to her ignorant eyes, it looked expensive. She would have walked on, but the driver rolled the window down and said he'd seen her come out of number seventeen, and was she by any chance Ms. Jackson.

Who was he? How did he know her name? What did he want?

The driver opened the door and stepped out on to the pavement. Georgina took a step or two back, although he didn't look in the least bit threatening, a young man with a pleasant open face, dressed in a blue button-down shirt and a dark jacket.

"I've come to pick up Georgina Jackson."

"There's some mistake," said Georgina. "That's me, and I didn't ask for any car."

Before she could take another breath, the driver was out of the car, the rear door was open, and with a swift, expert hand at her elbow, she found herself sitting in the back of the car. Two seconds later, and her kidnapper was behind the wheel again and the car was speeding away from the curb. It had all happened so quickly that she had no time to protest, but now she found her voice. "Stop this instant!" she shouted at the driver.

The car had paused at traffic lights, and Georgina, heedless of any traffic that might be coming, wrenched at the door. It remained firmly closed.

"It's locked," said the driver. "It's a safety precaution."

"Whose safety?"

"The safety of any passenger. It wouldn't be safe to jump out of a car while it was moving, or even while the engine was idling."

"In which case, please turn off the engine and let me get out. I don't know who you are, but I do know that I don't want to be in this car going wherever it is that you are taking me."

"You said you were Georgina Jackson."

"Who sent you?"

He didn't need to answer the question. Her nose had picked up a whiff of the fragrant cologne that Dan Vesey always wore. "This is Dan Vesey's car, isn't it?"

"That's right."

"You work for him. As a driver?"

"I'm his assistant. He usually drives himself, but sometimes he asks me to pick people up. Like you, for your meeting."

"Well, it's very courteous of Mr. Vesey to send a car to collect me, however, I don't have a meeting with Mr. Vesey or anyone else, so if you don't want me to call the police on my mobile phone this instant, you'd better stop and let me out."

"You don't have your mobile phone with you, Ms. Jackson."

That was perfectly true, but how the hell did he know that? He answered her unspoken question. "There are ways of tracing the location of a mobile phone. Yours is at present at number seventeen. You aren't. Ergo, you don't have your phone with you."

Georgina looked at the dashboard — more like something you'd find in the cockpit of a plane than in a car. "You've kidnapped me. You have coerced me into this car. That has to be illegal. Doesn't that

273

worry you?"

"Coercion? There was no coercion. A publisher sent his own car to pick up an author to come to a meeting."

"That's not my story."

"It's the story anyone will believe." The younger man took a neat left and did some zigzagging through residential streets. Did he have a name? Everyone had a name, but she didn't think she wanted to know his. She didn't really want to get on friendly terms with him.

"My name is Robert," he said in a kindly way. "I read your book."

Not, "I read your book and loved it." Or, "I really liked your book." No, just the ominous "I read your book."

She stopped thinking about Robert, and wondered how best to make a dash for it once they arrived outside the premises of Cadell & Davies. And then she stopped thinking about Robert, and the car, and the kidnap, and began to wonder why Dan Vesey had gone to these extraordinary lengths. How stupid to think that by not answering her phone, flagging all emails from Dan, Livia, or Yolanda as junk, that she was somehow out of reach; how absurd to think that the Vesey-Harkness brigade would leave her alone.

The car glided to a halt. This was her chance. Robert could hardly chase her down the street, particularly not if she yelled that she was being assaulted. Would they think that she wasn't prepared to make a scene? Oh, but she was, the thought of staring passers-by, or even an inquisitive policeman, was as nothing compared to facing Dan Vesey.

She heard a click as the door unlocked, but Robert stayed in the car. Another Robert, his clone, with darker hair, wider smile, but almost exactly the same shirt and jacket, was standing by the door. As she tumbled out of the car, he had her by the elbow and up the steps and inside the premises of Cadell & Davies before she could call out, let alone run for it.

She was hurried along like a piece of airport luggage on the conveyor belt, and before she could get her breath back, there she was in Dan Vesey's handsome office. And, in a realization of her worst fears, Dan Vesey was not alone. Seated at the table with him was, inevitably, Livia Harkness.

Not Yolanda, however; she must be grateful for that small mercy, although was she even now making her way through the thick of the London traffic?

Dan Vesey's greeting was all heartiness

and insincerity. He thanked her for sparing the time to join them, observing, "We know just how busy your schedule is right now. However, a progress meeting at this point seemed kind of essential."

Dan Vesey pulled out a chair for her, which meant that she was sitting directly opposite Livia, who was looking at her rather as a heron might survey a fish flapping in the water beneath its curved beak.

"Your behaviour has been extremely tiresome," she said without any preamble. "I'm used to authors who like to retreat while they are writing, but in this case, it is unhelpful and unnecessary." She was tapping on the table top with her cigarette holder. Was she the only woman in London who had a cigarette holder? One at least six inches long? And tortoiseshell, probably illegal. And, while she was thinking illegal, wasn't it illegal to smoke in an office? Any office?

As though to challenge her to say anything about the cigarette, Livia sent a perfectly formed smoke ring into the air, where it floated before wavering and disappearing.

The door opened, and a young woman came in. Tall, poised, polished, sleek from her shining black hair and silken olive skin to her gleaming patent leather boots.

Georgina had always had a hankering for a pair of patent leather boots. Of course, with the money in the bank, she could treat herself to a pair. After all, if her advance had to be paid back, what difference would the price of a pair of boots make? A few hours' work. Work as what? In a flash, Georgina saw herself serving burgers, waiting on tables in a sleazy joint somewhere in the Midwest, leaping through traffic to wash windscreens, standing on a freezing street corner handing out free papers to indifferent passers-by. Selling umbrellas in the rain . . .

Dan's voice snapped her out of this vivid and, she knew even as she had the thoughts, pointless, imaginative reverie. "Prue here is handling the publicity. Since you had to come into the office right now, it's a good opportunity for her to get to know you and liaise with you on the details. Prue?"

Prue leapt into action. Lights dimmed, a large rectangle of light appeared on the office wall, and a vivid jumble of faces, words and what seemed to be a large spear jazzed themselves on to the screen. The images faded, to be replaced by a copperplate signature: Jane Austen.

If Georgina had given it any thought, which she hadn't, she would have guessed that Dan Vesey would issue a press release announcing the momentous discovery, and that some reporters would pick up on it, it would be a minor news item, and then there would be a follow-up in the publishing press about the completed book. Higher-profile stuff would wait until publication approached, maybe she'd get an author tour, maybe she wouldn't.

She couldn't have been more wrong. Schedules, videos, internet action, websites flew across the screen. Press conferences, author visits, book festivals, television shows — in America, then the UK. "We have a star, a world-class celebrity," Prue announced. "Jane Austen. But Austen's dead, so she's no use to us. Therefore, Georgina has to be our action point." The lights went up, the pictures vanished and Prue advanced on Georgina.

"Stand up. Over there."

For a moment, Georgina thought that Dan, not content with kidnapping her, was going to march her off and lock her away, the key hidden until she emerged with a hundred thousand words under her belt.

Prue prowled round her. "Teeth okay, but whitening needs freshening up. Veneer would be best."

Georgina ran a nervous tongue along her

teeth, which had never been whitened, and certainly weren't going to be veneered. She knew all about veneering, which weakened your teeth and left you in thrall to your dentist for ever.

"Hair a disaster. It'll need the works, cut, colour. Skin not bad, nothing that a course of facials and a touch of Botox won't fix. Clothes — we need an appointment with a personal shopper. I'll brief her. And there's a lack of radiance, fitness will see to that, we'll arrange a personal trainer."

Enough was enough. "Lay off, if you don't mind. I'm a writer, not a freak show. I'll stay just the way I am, thank you."

"Read the contract," said Livia. "You agreed to all this stuff. These days, the way an author looks and behaves for the media is more important than how she writes."

"She?"

"No one gives a damn how male authors look. They just need to write well. Like newscasters: men have gravitas and know what they're talking about, women are there to look good. And take that prissy expression off your face, it's the way things are, get over it."

"That's not the way you run your business."

"You bet it isn't, or I'd be on the heap

inside a year. I'm not frontline, you are. Or you're going to be, as soon as you've finished this book. Talking of which, how many words have you done? How much have you sent to Yolanda?"

Why did she ask questions to which she knew the answers? Which were zero and zero. "I'm well into the first draft. I'm not sending anything to Yolanda until it's finished, that would be a waste of both our time. And I'm not spending hours at the dentist's having my teeth veneered nor going to the beauty parlour when I could be writing. I'm not a piece of furniture."

Dan, who had been talking in a loud voice to Prue, switched his attention back to Gina. "Did I hear *draft?* You haven't got time for drafts, just finish the goddam book, you should be nearly there by my reckoning. Send the stuff to us, and then we can start work on it. You need to get some moxie behind the book, Georgina, you really do. Once we've got it, then Prue's team will take over, like she said."

He stood up. The meeting was over.

"Do I get a lift back with Robert?"

Livia was now deep in conversation with Prue. Her eyes flicked in Georgina's direction. "You've got an Oyster card, use it. Tube, bus; up to you."

Twenty-Two

Henry was unsympathetic. "Kidnapped, indeed! Why did you get in the car? Why didn't you yell? You could be murdered and strewn across Epsom Forest by now, where's your sense of danger?"

"Obviously working quite well, since I wasn't in any danger. Physical danger, that is."

"Was he dashing, your abductor?" Maud asked. "Have some more rice, I've finished. Lovely food, Anna, how do you do it? Don't you ever get bored with cooking?"

"More chicken, Gina, you need protein for your brain."

Brain? What brain? She had never felt more witless. Or helpless, or feckless or a good few other *less*es.

"Did they just haul you in for a progress report?" Henry wanted to know. "Or was it something particular, the third degree from Dr. Yolanda, with you suspended by an inter-textuality or two?"

"She wasn't there. It was all about publicity."

"They must have asked how it was going," said Maud.

"They did."

"And you confessed all — or rather, nothing?"

"I lied."

"You need a routine," said Anna. "Perhaps you should go to work at the library, from nine until five, with a break for lunch."

Maud vetoed that. "All those books? She wouldn't write a word. Self-discipline is the virtue that takes you through life, self-discipline together with self-resilience will take you girls to the top."

Georgina felt she'd missed something. "You girls?"

"It's what my headmistress was always saying; yawn, yawn."

Henry was looking business-like. "Okay, let's get down to basics. Are you a lark or an owl?"

"Huh?"

"Do you work better in the morning or in the evening? I think you're a lark, you're compos mentis first thing and a bit slack after nine at night. So, you need to rise early and get stuck into your writing."

Anna was enthusiastic. "I rise early, I can wake you, with coffee, and then you write, and then you have breakfast, for half an hour, and then you write, and then you have another cup of coffee at eleven, and then you write, and then half an hour for a nutritious and balanced lunch, and then —"

"And then I write and write and write, great idea, only it doesn't quite work like that."

"It has to," said Henry. "No, don't have another glass of wine, you'll want a clear head. A chapter a day, you'll be through it in no time."

"Assuming always that the spiders walking through jungles approximate to a plot," said Maud. She got up, stretched and said she was going to go and play the oboe. "Slow movements of Baroque Concerti are what you want, Gina. It sets the brain humming at the right wavelength for creative endeavour."

Henry stared at his sister. "Wherever did you pick up that piece of nonsense?"

"It isn't nonsense, it happens to be true, and if you were a real scientist you'd check it out instead of dismissing my words of wisdom."

"She should be at school, quickly," said Anna. "She is bored and thinks too much."

Henry sighed. "God, I forgot, I'm taking her to look round one tomorrow. Which means I've got to get back to my desk, I've a heap of stuff to get through."

"Where are you going? Is it far?"

"Hampshire."

Maud's head came round the door. "Glad you remembered that. Gina had better postpone her routine for a day and come too, because it's Austen territory; only a few miles from Chawton."

"Chawton?" Henry said.

"Sharpen up, Jane Austen's house. We can go there after my interview. Gina gets inspired, you get some culture and I can cry in the room where she was ill. Oh, and we'll do Winchester Cathedral while we're about it, she's buried there, that's a must-see for Gina."

They were clear of London traffic and Henry was driving in his usual relaxed way, when his phone went off. He dug it out of his pocket and passed it to Georgina, who was sitting in the passenger seat at the front. "Answer it for me, would you?"

Georgina did so, and to her horror, the sharp, familiar tones of Livia Harkness's voice filled the car, making Henry sit up in alarm.

"Good God! Who the hell is that?"

"I recognize the voice," said Maud's voice from the back. "It's Georgina's friendly agent."

Georgina was holding the phone as though it were red hot. If it had been her phone, she would have let down the window and flung the offending object out into the hedge.

"Georgina? I know that's you. I can hear you breathing."

Georgina tried to hand the phone back to Henry, but he waved her away. "Can't talk while I'm driving," and then, in a whisper, "give it to Maud."

Georgina flicked the phone into the back, where Maud neatly caught it. She held the phone to her ear. "Hi, can I help? This is Henry Lefroy's phone, by the way. I am his sister. Who are you?"

"Put Georgina on. I know she's there."

"Georgina is presently at home. Sitting at her computer, writing furiously."

"She isn't. She's in the front seat of a silver VW Passat, driving out of London. Heading for the M3."

Twenty-Three

Henry had had enough. There was a parking place signed at the side of the road, and he braked and turned into it. He turned round and seized the phone from Maud. "Henry Lefroy here. Have you something to say to me?"

"I don't have time to waste. I want to speak to Georgina. Now."

"My sister told you that she is not here."

"She is. She was seen. Put her on."

Georgina and Henry looked at each other. Maud was hanging over the back of the front seats, pulling terrible faces in the direction of the phone. Georgina made miming gestures to Henry, urging him to turn the phone off. He did so, but two seconds later, it was vibrating into life. He passed it back to Maud. "Turn it off," he said. "Oh, and before you do, see if you can disable the voice mail. I don't want to have a string of messages from that woman ringing in my ears when I turn it back on again."

"How did they get hold of your number?" said Georgina. "And how on earth did they know I was in a silver car with you, heading to the M3?"

"I don't know about the telephone, although your Mr. Vesey does seem to have ways of getting telephone numbers, but I expect somebody who knows you saw you in the car," Maud said.

"I don't believe it," said Henry. "That would be a coincidence too far. It's much more likely that someone was keeping an eye on the house, saw you come out and set off after us."

"Robert, I expect," said Georgina. "Do you think I could sue Dan Vesey for harassment?"

Maud swung her head round and looked out the rear window. "Do you mean that someone is following us?"

They sat in the lay-by, watching the traffic. There was very little of it, as they were now on a country road, going cross-country. A lorry rumbled by, a man on a motorbike, a people carrier driven by a woman wearing sunglasses. Henry switched on the engine. "We aren't being followed."

"I'll send her a message," Georgina said a few miles later. She felt in her bag for her

287

phone. "No," and "Don't do that," came from Henry and Maud simultaneously.

"If you text her with that SIM, then she's got your new number," Maud pointed out.

"If I use Henry's, the minute I turn it on, she'll be there again."

"I doubt it," said Henry. "A snappy woman like that will have moved on, she'll try again later. Go on, you'll see I'm right."

Georgina read her message aloud. "Have gone to visit Jane Austen's house at Chawton. Back late. May contact you tomorrow." She quickly turned the phone off again, and handed it back to Henry.

"I predict a tirade of abuse about that one," said Henry.

"Are you really going to contact her tomorrow?" said Maud.

"No."

They turned off the road at a large sign which read: WARBURTON'S SCHOOL, INDEPENDENT DAY & BOARDING SCHOOL FOR GIRLS AGED 11–18.

Georgina said she'd stay in the car. "This looks scary, I'll keep my head down in here."

"We shan't be long," said Maud cheerily as she got out of the car. "I can tell at a glance that this isn't my kind of school."

"I wish you would make up your mind exactly what is your kind of school," said

Henry. "Then I needn't waste all this time traipsing around the countryside."

It was peaceful in the car. Henry had parked in the visitors' car park, which was a neat area surrounded by trees. Peering through a gap in the trees, Georgina could see what must be the gym block, with exercise bikes lined up behind a large expanse of plate glass. Birds sang, there was a faint sound of someone playing uncertain notes on a trombone, but otherwise the silence was only broken by the distant rumble of a tractor.

Georgina took out her notebook, turned the pages back, uncapped her pen and set to work making more wild diagrams. These continued for about ten minutes until a bell sounded, so loud that it made the air vibrate, and startled Georgina into dropping her pen. Suddenly the landscape was full of girls. A large group in sports gear trotted past the car park in one direction, another crowd with bags over their shoulders and files under their arms approached from the opposite direction.

Could she imagine Maud in all this mêlée? No, she could not. Henry had said that it was a big school, and there was a kind of determined purposefulness to these young women that made Georgina certain that

289

Maud wouldn't fit in. Certainly her appearance was all wrong, as these girls all had shining hair and make-up-free complexions.

A coach drew up, and another gaggle of girls, wearing grey skirts and navy blazers, poured out of a set of swing doors, each of them carrying a large musical instrument case. These were loaded into the luggage compartment of the coach, the girls clambered aboard and the coach drove off.

Silence descended once more. Georgina scrabbled under the rubber mat for her pen, but once she'd retrieved it, she found it impossible to concentrate on her plot. She let her mind drift, idly watching a squirrel run down from the tree and scamper over the tarmac and into the grass.

She got out of the car, wanting to stretch her legs, and went across to the other side of the little car park. The handsome building before her must be the main school building, and the modern parts she could see between the trees were later extensions. Once this had been a private house, with a fine Palladian façade and a roundel of grass in front of it. Just the kind of house where Jane Austen's family and friends might have lived and visited — at least, those who were wealthy enough to own a country estate. She sat down on a nearby tree stump and looked at the house, a golden colour in the autumn sunlight. She had to admit that there was something supremely pleasing about the classical proportions, the sash windows, the pediment and columns that marked the entrance. Somehow, this ordered elegance didn't go with those healthy cheerful girls in their sports clothes and their uniforms, with their trumpets and trombones and exercise machines.

Someone was coming out of the door behind the pillars. Maybe it was Henry and Maud. Could they have finished so quickly?

It wasn't. It was a man in strange clothes: breeches and a long, caped cloak. Faintly at first, then louder, came the sound of hooves, and she watched with disbelief as a carriage swept past her, two blinkered black horses moving in fine style. A man in a coat and a tall hat was perched in the driver's seat, holding a long whip. The carriage drew up in front of the house, a man in livery appeared and darted forward to let down the carriage steps as a woman in a striking hat adorned with feathers came out of the house and stepped into the coach. She was joined by the man in the cloak and as the carriage came back down the drive and swept past her, she could see the man and woman engaged in an animated conversation. As the carriage drew level with the tree stump, the man turned his head, smiled and lifted his gloved hand as though to acknowledge Georgina's presence.

The hooves faded into the distance. Bemused, Georgina rubbed her eyes and shook her head as though to brush the vision away. Then she saw a figure at a second-floor window of the house, and a minute later a rope made of sheets knotted together was lowered over the sill. Two seconds later, a bundle was thrown out of the window, followed by a girl in a straw bonnet who launched herself on to the sheets. As her feet touched the ground, Georgina heard hooves again, and a solitary horseman rode up to the house. He leapt off his horse and clasped the escapee in a passionate embrace, before heaving her up on to the horse and swinging back into the saddle behind her.

Horse, man and woman cantered towards her, and dissolved into nothingness before they reached her.

What was going on? Was she becoming subject to hallucinations? No, she must have drifted off into a doze while sitting on the tree stump, and fallen into one of those waking dreams which can seem more real than the world around you.

Or she could simply be losing her wits.

Perhaps what she needed was to take herself off smartly to a psychiatrist, and, there was a thought, if she were actually deranged, she couldn't possibly be expected to finish the book, could she?

Some people think all writers of fiction are crazy, said the clear, cold voice inside her head. *What's imagination but a form of derangement?*

"What's up, you look as though you'd seen a ghost," Henry said, when he returned to the car half an hour later, preceded by a cross-looking Maud.

Reluctant to talk about it, but needing to tell someone, she described what she'd seen. "It's not the first time, either," she added.

"You aren't deranged," said Henry calmly, as he drove through the school gates and on to the road. "You're just seeing things because your head is full of Jane Austen, and the book you've got to write is stressing you out."

Maud sat silently in the back. "I take it this wasn't the one?" Georgina asked, turning round to look at Maud.

"No way," said Maud. "And they won't want me. The person who interviewed me kept going on about team spirit. I don't do team spirit."

"Perhaps it's just as well," said Henry

cheerfully. "It's a fiendishly expensive school."

"I'm going to eat a huge lunch," announced Maud, "and forget what a failure I am. That woman had all my marks from St. Adelberta's, would you believe it? She asked me why my Latin results were so poor, and when I told her it was because I had an appalling teacher, she got quite cross. It's never the teacher's fault, you see, it has to be me. Oh, how I wish I lived in a different age, when I didn't have to go to school at all. I wish I could have a governess like Jane Eyre, all demure and grey."

"It would be very lonely," Georgina said. "Only think what it would be like to live in a place like that house in those days, just you and your family and the servants. No internet, no DVDs, no mobile phone. I don't think you'd like it a bit," Georgina said.

"I suppose not, once you've had those things you'd miss them. Still, if I'd lived two centuries ago I still think it would have been rather nice not to go to school and to have a governess. And go riding, and be expected to play the piano and sing."

"Only if you were rich and well-born."

"I take that as a given," said Maud. "And the trouble with that life was having to marry young and die in childbirth. I can't say I fancy that very much. How many schools left on our list, Henry?"

"Only one."

Georgina wasn't sure what she had been expecting of Jane Austen's house at Chawton, but she felt a strange sense of disappointment as she went round it.

"Tacky," observed Maud as they went in through the front door, and she saw the mouse mats and key rings showing Colin Firth in his TV role as Mr. Darcy. And then, to the woman who was dispensing tickets, "Where's the creaking door?"

The woman gave her a pitying look. "Ah, well, of course the creak hasn't lasted this long. And we aren't even sure which door it was. If you read the notices, it will tell you what you want to know."

Unabashed, Maud led the way out of the room into a tiny passage.

"What creaking door?" said Georgina.

Now it was Maud's turn to give a withering look. "One forgets how little you know about Jane Austen, which is unfortunate in the circumstances. Jane Austen used to write in the drawing room of this house, and the creaking door warned her when anyone was coming in, so that she could hide the pages of her manuscript under her embroidery, to keep people from seeing what she was writing. And," she continued as they went into the drawing room, "that's the table she wrote on."

The tiny table was the only thing in the house that stirred any emotion in Georgina. She stared down at it, a small round table set on a single shaft with three curved legs at its base. She couldn't have fitted her notebook on there, nor her laptop. And Jane Austen had sat here, listening to the creaking door, and had written one hundred and sixty thousand words of *Mansfield Park* and *Emma.*

She felt a sense of sadness as she looked at the polished wooden surface. How could Jane Austen have written in a public room? Couldn't she have had a room of her own?

It was a question that was answered when they went upstairs. The best room had belonged to Mrs. Austen, and across the passage from it was a small room, looking out the back into a small yard, which had been Jane and her sister Cassandra's room. But there were other rooms, why couldn't Jane have had a room of her own?

"She liked sharing with her sister," said Maud matter-of-factly. "It was the only company she had of her own age. They would have talked up here, where their mother couldn't hear them."

"That's fine for teenagers, but fancy sharing a room with your sister when you were forty. It's all very small and domestic, isn't it?"

The garden was probably charming in spring and summer, but it had an autumn melancholy to it. The sun which had shone so brilliantly while they were at the school had disappeared behind great clouds billowing high into the sky, and Georgina was glad to get back to the car.

"Useful for you?" said Henry. "You're very quiet."

"I liked the little table," Georgina said. "I shall never forget that, it wrung my heart."

Perhaps it was the anguish from Jane Austen's house that made the visit to Winchester Cathedral so poignant. It was dusk when they went through the West Door and the chilly hush settled about them.

"Jane Austen is buried in the south aisle," Maud said in a whisper. She'd made Henry stop at a florist, and carried a single red rose in her hand. Halfway down the aisle, she said, "Here it is," and plopped down on her knees, before brushing the gravestone with a gentle hand and then laying the rose on it.

Georgina saw the tears brimming in

Maud's eyes, and she felt a tell-tale prickle in her own. Henry came to her rescue.

"Let's stay for Evensong, shall we?"

They sat in the stall behind the choir of grown men and little boys wearing long red gowns with white collars and surplices. Henry leant over to whisper in Georgina's ear. "It's the same service Jane Austen would have heard, from *The Book of Common Prayer.* It's one of the few bits of the Anglican service they haven't rewritten in the style of a directive from the Inland Revenue."

As the choir sang the Nunc dimittis, Georgina thought of that quiet grave in the south aisle. *Lord, now lettest thou thy servant depart in peace.*

Twenty-Four

If Jane Austen could write a hundred-and-sixty-thousand-word novel on that tiny polished table, in the midst of family life, with a quill pen dipped into an inkstand, then she, Georgina Jackson, could turn out a hundred and twenty thousand words, in her own room, with the power of Apple and Microsoft at her elbow.

A hundred and twenty thousand words of what? Jane Austen wrote masterpieces. Had she gone on with *Love and Friendship,* it would have been another masterpiece. Jane Austen was a genius, Georgina Jackson wasn't. Why hadn't Jane Austen finished the book she'd started? What distracted her? Unhappiness at being in Bath, as received opinion had it? Or a busy social life there and in Southampton that made sitting down at a little table and scribbling away in her idle moments less attractive than friends and talk and theatre and gossip?

Perhaps her mother came down to break-fast every morning and said, "How's the new book going, Jane?" until her daughter was so full of rage she couldn't pen a word.

It didn't matter. This was idle speculation, and any speculation that was going to be done needed to be done on the page, here, with these characters.

Georgina had taken a dislike to Lady Carcenet. She was sly, manipulative, aware of a fading beauty, jealous of Susan's moral strength and youth and looks, all of which would be a reproach to a woman such as Lady C.

What if . . . ?

What if she went down to the kitchen and made a pot of coffee? That would wake up her brain, send some action round her grey cells. But first she would check out the American news. She was out of touch, time was she'd look at the *New York Times* every day; it was weeks since she'd done that. An article on baseball? That would be interesting.

She pulled herself up short. Baseball? When had she ever had any interest in baseball? This was procrastination, pure and simple. What was that site that had popped up in her mailbox, Procrastination 101? She might dip into that, it was bound to have a few useful tips.

Take your procrastination seriously. Here's today's task: sharpen some pencils. You don't have any pencils? Shame on you, that means you aren't taking advantage of the procrastinatory possibilities of Sudoku and other puzzles. Get your coat, and go to the stationer's. Find a proper shop, the supermarket won't do. Once at the stationer's, you can while away a good chunk of your morning's work time by stocking up on paper, notebooks, pens — all essentials for the active writer. Deliberate on your choice of pencils — HB, 2B, eraser on the end, red, yellow, blue? You'll need at least a dozen. Don't rush it. And don't forget to buy a sharpener.

Once back at your desk, they'll all need sharpening, and, with luck and perseverance, this can become part of

Henry knew the minute he came into the sitting room that Georgina hadn't written a word. It was the way she sat listening to Maud's scales that was the giveaway. It wasn't the capitulation of exhaustion, of a person worn out by a day's hard time at the keyboard. It was the defiant posture of one who intended to start tomorrow.

First thing.

Without fail.

He'd watched with dismay as Georgina hacked her way through endless versions of Chapter One of *The Sorrows of Jane Silver-smith*, persuading herself, day after day, that she'd cracked it, that tomorrow she would be on to Chapter Two and then she'd be on her way through the rest of the book.

Was *Love and Friendship* going to be another series of Chapter Ones? Disastrous, if so. Why didn't writers write? He had no idea. He was one of nature's Get-on-with-its. If something had to be done, do it. Yet he could appreciate that he had never had to stare at a blank page on the computer screen waiting for inspiration to strike and words to flow, one after another, sentence after sentence, paragraph after paragraph, chapter after chapter until, finally, miraculously, there was a pile of pages spilling out of the printer — a book.

And Georgina wasn't writing non-fiction. He was sure she'd have no problem researching, organizing and writing twenty or thirty coherent chapters on Victorian workhouses, or indeed Victorian workhorses or Victorian housework. Fiction was tougher. Facts and info in the end got you nowhere with a good story, although Georgina had buried herself in research for her previous books. Now she was on her own, and having to juggle characters convincingly; action ditto and purposeful; dialogue ditto and, in an attempt at the Jane Austenesque, also pithy and witty. His head reeled at the thought of it.

He would do some research of his own, find out a bit more about what made writers tick. Or not tick, as the case might be.

The next morning, his head whirling, Henry closed his computer and sat back in his chair. He flicked a pencil between his fingers, and looked at the textbook awaiting his attention. *Solar Astronomy in H-alpha.* What an ordered and simple world that was compared to the strange realm inhabited by writers, who seemed to suffer from all kinds of complaints, some of them obvious, like advanced sententiousness and chronic ego-inflation, some puzzling, such as only being able to write with your feet in a bucket of icy water, others dotty — why would dangling a crystal in front of your screen do anything for your writing?

His eyes fell on another book, *Foundations of Quantum Chromodynamics: An Introduction to Perturbative Methods in Gauge Theories.* No, he was wrong, there were stranger places than inside a writer's mind. Although maybe a writer's mind was a quantum computer; after all, Penrose said it might be. Seven plots, wasn't that the magic number? And presumably, any novel started in a particular way could end up with one of an infinite number of variations.

This was getting interesting. Assume a protagonist, an antagonist — what else? One of those sites he'd found had a useful analysis of what went into a novel. He flipped open his screen, made a quick retrace, and there it was. Protagonist, co-protagonist, antagonist, major characters, minor characters. Acts one, two, three. Opening, inciting incident, crisis, climax, ending. So, let the protagonist be *a,* the co-protagonist *b* and the antagonist *x,* and let there be seven plots, then . . . Did Georgina know all about this stuff? Were writers born knowing it, or did they sweat through it, as one might modules on fluid dynamics or magnetohydrodynamics?

He would ask her. He'd like to do that right away, but if she were writing today, it would be criminal to interrupt.

She wasn't at her computer, she was standing at the door. "I was going to have some coffee, how about you?"

"Anna is monitoring your caffeine intake."

"Anna isn't here."

"I think you'll find that Anna has hidden the coffee."

Georgina let out a wail and rubbed her hair with both hands. "My mind's a blank, I need to pep it up."

"Draw up that chair. Have a look at this, it's fascinating."

Georgina looked at the screen, blinked, shook her head, looked again. "Fascinating?"

"Yes. How does that structure work for Jane Austen's novels? If you can work that out, and if there's a pattern, then you have a template. Won't that make your job easier?"

"I don't need a template, I need a story."

Georgina slouched off to hunt for the hidden coffee, and Henry, knowing he should be doing his own work, went back to the structure of the novel. After a few minutes, he swung his chair round and got up. He went out of his study and called down from the landing for his sister. "Maud!"

"What?"

"Can you remember the plots of all Jane Austen's novels?"

"Why?"

"I want to analyze them, to help Georgina with her plot."

"You aren't talking plagiarism, are you?"

"Structure."

"Okay, what have you got?" Maud came jumping down the stairs and sat in Henry's chair. "We can't do this for all six books, that'd tax my brain too much. Let's do *Pride and Prejudice.* Or *Emma,* I don't mind."

"*Pride and Prejudice,* then. Protagonist, Elizabeth. Co-protagonist?"

"Mr. Darcy, of course. The romantic hero of all romantic heroes. He carries Elizabeth's missing happiness."

"What?"

"That's what the co-protagonist is for, I read about it. Opening? Easy, you get the whole set-up except for Mr. Darcy. The Bennets, the stranger arriving in their midst who's going to marry one of the daughters, the conflict between Mr. and Mrs. Bennet."

Georgina was back, holding a tray with a teapot and three mugs. "No coffee, so it's going to have to be a tea fix." She edged some books to one side and put the tray down on the table. "No chocolate biscuits, either; Anna must have a grudge against me. Why are you talking about the Bennets?"

"Because we're helping you," said Maud, not taking her eyes from the screen. "Look, here's an interactive chart for planning your novel. No wonder everybody in the world is writing a novel; sorry, Georgina. Inciting incident?"

"Elizabeth meets Darcy at the dance and is prejudiced against him," said Georgina. She poured the tea and handed a mug to Henry and one to Maud.

"What does the protagonist want?"

"To get away from her mother," said Georgina.

"To make a good marriage," said Henry.

"Obstacles?"

"Mr. Collins and Mr. Wickham, and her family, of course," said Georgina. "I shouldn't be doing this, I should be at my own computer, writing."

"You haven't got a plot," said Maud, without turning her head. "You've got a few pages of someone else's plot, that's all. Mind you, there are a lot of decisions you don't have to make."

"Such as?" said Henry.

"Genre. *Love and Friendship* isn't going to be another Harry Potter, or a Batman story, or a mediaeval time slip with a drippy modern heroine, or a tense thriller about shooting the president of the U.S.A., or a harrowing tale of paedophilia or whatever, is it? It's a romantic comedy. It's about love and happiness. And, given the title, about friendship, too. Come on, let's have the crisis."

"What crisis?"

"It says here it's what comes in about the middle of the book. That's easy, anyhow, it's Mr. Darcy's proposal. End of act two is next, that's got to be a downer, if you want to have a happy ending."

"Who says?" Georgina was intrigued, but also suspicious. "I never did any of this when I wrote my first book."

"Maybe you should have done," said Henry. "Downer — that's got to be where that idiotic Lydia runs off with Wickham."

"Ending — second proposal, happiness all round," Maud finished triumphantly. "There are sections here for sub-plots, but Georgina needs to think up a main plot before she goes haring off after the subs, so I won't put in Jane and Bingley or poor Charlotte's terrible fate. Now I'll print it, and voilà!"

"Voilà is all very well, and now we know how *Pride and Prejudice* works, but how does that help me?"

"It's a pattern. A model," said Henry. "How many pages do you have of the handwritten manuscript?"

"It comes to about three thousand words."

"And what happens? Come on, you've refused to tell us, but you have to if you want our help."

"Lady Carcenet is a widow who's summoned a cousin's young daughter, Susan, to come to Bath to be a companion to her."

"Is that it?" asked Maud.

"Isn't there a Susan in *Mansfield Park*?" said Henry.

"Futile Fanny's sister," said Maud. "At the end, she comes to take Fanny's place at *Mansfield Park*, and I tell you what, she'd have been a much more interesting heroine than Fanny Price. I hope you're going to have a lively heroine, Gina, and not one who's exhausted if she walks through the shrubbery. And don't forget the shrubbery, there are lots of shrubberies in Jane Austen."

"Never mind the shrubberies, Gina needs a storyline. Susan meets her match, that's a given. So what comes between them?"

"Lady Carcenet," said Maud promptly. "You can tell she's no good, not with a name like that. She'll be a spiteful old besom, a Lady Catherine all over again."

Henry was still thinking about *Pride and Prejudice.* "Could you tell from the opening chapter what was going to happen in the rest of the book?"

"No," said Georgina. "I'd say that Mr. Bingley was going to be the hero."

"You wouldn't," said Maud. "Think about it, you can't have a hero called Bingley."

"I haven't got a hero called anything," said Georgina. "But thank you very much, both of you. I'll take this page on *Pride and Prejudice;* who knows, it may inspire me."

"I'll lend you my Tom Lehrer CD if you like," said Maud. "You can listen to the Lobachevsky plagiarism song. And, remember, Shakespeare pinched most of his plots."

"Geniuses can do that, hacks can't."

Georgina took herself and her tea away. Maud made a tutting noise. "I don't think it's a good sign if a writer calls herself a hack."

"It does suggest a certain lack of confidence and self-esteem," Henry said.

TWENTY-FIVE

For the next week, Georgina spent hours every day at her desk. She plotted and planned and outlined, she drew up character biographies, and she produced ever more complicated diagrams with lines and coloured circles and arrows.

Sensing the futility of all this, she returned to the novels. She read the opening chapters and then flicked her way through the rest of the books, reminding herself of how the stories worked. She got up the site Maud and Henry had used to analyze *Pride and Prejudice,* and made an analysis of the other five novels.

How had Jane Austen planned and outlined her books? Georgina didn't know enough about literature to have any idea how nineteenth-century novelists wrote. A first draft, then worked over in painstaking detail, crossing out a word here, inserting a phrase there? How did those writers manage without a word processor? It would have been bad enough in the days of the type-writer, having to type the whole thing out again; just imagine having to copy out one hundred and sixty thousand words by hand with that quill pen, making the fair version which would go to the printer.

Come to that, imagine being a printer in the nineteenth century, working from hand-written manuscripts, setting every letter of the type by hand, making up the pages. Skilled work, a job rendered entirely super-fluous by modern technology. What she produced on her computer could, within seconds, emerge in a bookshop as a bound finished copy.

Only, at the rate she was going, the bound and finished copy would have an extent of about ten pages, since she hadn't managed to produce a single word of her own.

Henry, Maud and Anna treated her with the kind of tolerant gentleness that would be appropriate to an ill child or an injured pet. This annoyed Georgina intensely; she would much rather they had harangued and nagged her. Then she could have had an argument and felt the vitality of anger, instead of the strangling powerlessness and helplessness that overcame her as she sat there, hour after hour.

■ ■ ■ ■

Henry was concerned. Every day when he got back from college, he looked an enquiry at Maud, and she in turn shook her head. Anna went around with a frown on her face, endlessly cooking chicken broth and planning delicious meals to tempt Georgina, who had quite lost her appetite.

The three of them were sitting round the kitchen table, racking their brains as to what they could do to help Georgina, when the front doorbell rang. Maud ran upstairs to answer it, and a few minutes later came running back down the stairs, talking and laughing. Behind her was a young man of about Henry's age, a head shorter than him, with untidy brown hair and big brown eyes. Charles Grandison, Henry and Maud's country cousin.

Henry greeted him with a friendly slap on the shoulder. "Charlie, good to see you. What brings you to London?"

Charles lived in Kent, where he bred wild boar. "Visiting some of my best customers," he said. "Any chance of a bed for the night?"

Anna took out another glass and poured wine for Charles. He took no notice of Henry and paid no attention to Maud's

313

chatter, but was looking intently at Anna. "Aren't you going to introduce me, Henry?"

Henry was taken aback and stopped, "Haven't you met Anna before? Anna, I do apologize. This is Charlie Grandison, my cousin."

Anna gravely shook hands with him and then, her mind on practical matters, inquired if he would be dining with them.

Charles looked pleased. "If that's all right. If you have enough, as long as it isn't chops, or anything else that won't stretch."

Maud sniffed the air. A fragrant aroma, rich with garlic and spices, filled the kitchen. "Lamb, cooked for hours in wine with lots of garlic and onions. Am I right, Anna?"

"You're lucky, Charlie," Maud told him. "It would be a lean, mean fish night tonight normally, but at the moment Anna is trying to feed up Georgina, so there's plenty for one extra. You remember Georgina?"

"Your lodger," said Charles. "The writer, fearfully clever, frightened the wits out of me, I have to say."

Anna exclaimed at this. "It is true that she is clever, and works at the university, but how could she frighten anyone?"

"Writers are funny people, aren't they?" said Charles, still not taking his eyes off Anna as she moved around the kitchen. "A

314

head full of strange ideas, and you're never sure when you're with them that they aren't taking notes, and you'll find yourself in their next book, sounding like a perfect ass."

"Most writers say they never use real people in their books," said Maud severely. "They say real people are far too dull. And Georgina might say she finds you frightening because you work with wild boar. That's fairly formidable, don't you think?"

Anna came back to the table, face alight with interest. "Wild boar? What do you have to do with wild boar? Do you hunt them?"

Charles laughed. "No, I breed them. We raise them for food, not for hunting. I have hunted wild boar, in Germany, really just to see what it was like. I've never been so frightened in my life. They're vicious creatures, they go for you out of pure spite."

"The piglets are cute," said Maud. "I love their little stripes."

"They aren't cute when they grow up and weigh half a ton," said Charles. "But I respect them, and we mostly get on okay."

"I have an excellent recipe for wild boar," said Anna. "We have a lot of wild boar in Poland, which is where I come from."

"Poland?" said Charles, interested. "I've never been to Poland. Tell me about it."

Henry and Maud exchanged glances.

Henry got up from the table. "I'll leave you and Anna to talk about Poland and wild boar, Charlie. I've got a bit of work I want to do before dinner."

"And I don't want to hear about wild boar, in Poland or anywhere else," said Maud. "I know it'll get gory."

Upstairs, brother and sister looked at each other conspiratorially.

"He's smitten!" said Maud. "I never would have believed it, when you think of those fluffy dimbos he goes for."

"They never last."

"She's taller than him."

"He'll have to look up to her, that's all."

"He'll have to marry her if he sleeps with her," said Maud. "She has strong views on sex."

"He's only known her for five minutes, give them a chance. Even as we speak, they may have come to blows over a recipe for boar's head."

A dishevelled Georgina looked down from the upstairs landing. "What's going on? Why are you whispering on the stairs?"

"Don't get paranoid," said Maud, advancing up the next flight. "It's nothing to do with you. Charlie's here, Charles Grandison, you met him, our cousin. He's getting on like anything with Anna. A romance," she added hopefully. "Like in a book."

"Don't mention the word *romance,* or *book* if it comes to that. Maud, will you tell Anna not to bother with cooking for me, I don't feel like eating anything and I want to work."

"Okay," said Henry, before Maud could protest. And then, as Georgina's door shut behind her, he hissed at Maud, "Shut up, we'll haul her down when it's ready, and force-feed her if necessary. There's no point in arguing about it now."

"She isn't working. She's simply staring at a screen, or at sheets of paper covered in scribbles."

"That's the creative process."

Maud gave him a telling look. He retreated to the study, but instead of returning to solar physics, he went back to the sites he'd bookmarked about writers and writer's block. He read through several articles, clicked on links to other sites and then, finally, shut the lid of his computer. He leant back in his chair and stretched his long legs out under the desk. Then he flicked through the Page-A-Day desk diary — a "Far Side" one that Maud had given him. He counted the days, did a quick calculation in his head, frowned, sighed and turned to page 775 of *Quantum Chromodynamics.*

■ ■ ■ ■

Good wine, some excellent food and agreeable company cheered Georgina up, although she had started the meal in a sullen mood, angry with Maud for forcing her downstairs to the table. She would have made more of a fuss if Charles weren't there, but she didn't want to be rude in front of Henry's cousin, and guest.

Charles was passing on an invitation from his mother to spend the weekend at her country house.

"Invitation?" said Henry. "Does that mean I can say no?"

"Not if you value your skin. Rather a royal command, this one. Foxy's having a twenty-first, and she wants us all to go."

"God, is Foxy only twenty-one? The sophistication of today's young women is terrifying."

"Well, old man, you'll never hear the end of it if you don't come. Bring Sophie, you know Mum likes her."

"Oh God, I suppose I must say yes. I'll ring Sophie and see what her filming schedule is like, and whether she can get away for the weekend."

"I noticed that I'm not included in any

invitation," said Maud.

"Good God," said Henry. "I forgot to say, Charlie, Maud isn't here, okay?"

"If you say so. Where is she?"

"At school. St. Adelberta's."

Charles looked knowing. "Did they expel you, or did you run away?"

"Bit of both," said Maud.

"Risky, running away. I tried it once or twice, but I never got as far as the station before they hauled me back. Lack of planning," added Charles. "Should be quite easy if you time it right and have a good plan. Never did it myself, wouldn't have been welcomed back into the bosom of my family if I had, I can tell you. Why did you run away? I thought schools these days were all sweetness and light, people queuing up for places and crying when they have to go home at the end of term."

"Was your school like that?" Georgina asked.

Charles was taken aback. "Good Lord, no. Ghastly place, made a man of me. I'm not terribly clever, and I can't say I excelled at any sports, so they didn't think much of me. Not like Henry, he did okay at his school, he was bright, brilliant at maths and all that. Won prizes, even. Didn't bother me, really, I didn't want to go to university or anything like that. When I left school, I went to agricultural college. I never wanted to do anything but farming."

"The thing is," said Henry, bringing the conversation back to the matter in hand, "that I haven't told your mother about Maud."

"Which is wise," said Charles. "She'd probably drive straight here, scoop up Maud and take her back to St. Adelberta's."

"That would be a waste of time and effort," said Maud. "They wouldn't have me back."

Georgina looked thoughtfully at Maud.

Henry hated to see Georgina with those dark rings under her eyes, and he wished he could come up with a solution to her problems. He did have an idea or two, but he suspected that if he were to make any suggestion at this point, Georgina would simply turn on him. Or pack up her bags and go, since he had an idea that she was longing to make some dramatic gesture.

Ever since Maud had arrived unexpectedly from her school, Henry, Anna and Georgina had wondered what had induced her to run away — why then, as opposed to any other time. Henry had ventured a question or two, but Maud had given him her best blank look and said that it was a private matter.

Which was one of the reasons why it was proving so difficult to find her a new school. Without knowing what had been so terrible about St. Adelberta's, it was hard to make a sensible choice of a new one.

Now Georgina, tired and uncaring, came out with a straight question. "Maud, why did you run away?"

For a moment, Henry thought Maud was going to storm away from the table, reverting to the tantrums which had characterized her childhood. Instead, she rubbed at the side of her nose in a thoughtful way, and said, "This and that. Things like the bells."

"What bells?" Charles demanded. "Do you mean those damned things they ring at the end of every session? I must say they used to get on my nerves, although in the end you simply didn't hear them any more."

"All schools have those," said Maud with disdain. "I mean real bells, clanging ones in the church tower."

Henry looked at her in astonishment. "Do you mean to tell me that the ringing of church bells annoyed you so much that you felt you had to run away? I don't believe it."

"Not the ringing in the sense that you mean. Not the gentle peal of bells sounding across an idyllic English landscape. What I mean is actually pulling the bells. Standing there at the end of the rope and hauling it up and down, up and down. Bell ringing. Like Quasimodo. Compulsory for all music scholars at St. Adelberta's. It's called service to the community."

Charles was puzzled. "Come on, Maud. You're a musician, you should like bells."

She gave a withering glance. "Bells aren't music."

Georgina, filled with strange insight, went on, "The bell ringing was just representative, wasn't it? What you didn't like was all the direction. Do this, do that, be here, be there. And I don't suppose they gave you much choice, and I don't suppose they bothered whether you wanted to do it or not. Rebel," she added, in an undertone. "A rebellious little girl most likely grows up to be a rebellious woman."

"That's what schools are all about," said Charles. "I can't be doing with these places where everybody has an opinion, and everybody's feelings and thoughts have to be taken into consideration."

Anna turned round from the stove, holding the dish of lamb in padded gloves. She shut the oven door with her knee. "Good teachers take account of all this and do not

322

make unreasonable demands of their pupils," she said, placing the food on the table.

"Georgina's quite right," Maud said. "The bell ringing was the final straw, just another of the really stupid rules and obligations that they were always going on about. That's why they said I had a bad attitude, because when something was really pointless and stupid I said so. They don't like that. And the other girls in my class said I shouldn't argue with the teachers all the time."

"School certainly taught me to keep my mouth shut," said Charles cheerfully. "Best lesson I ever learned at school." He paused, thinking. "Probably the only lesson I learned at school. No point making a fuss about what you can't change. No point in giving your opinions about anything, you're bound to offend someone."

Long after midnight, an exhausted Georgina climbed into bed. She lay there, looking at the ceiling, until Maud came noisily out of the bathroom and, after a perfunctory knock, put her head round the door.

"Why are you lying there with the light on?"

"Just thinking," Georgina said. "Who's Foxy?"

"Oh, a wild cousin of Charlie's, on his

mother's side. No relation of ours. She fancies Henry. Goodnight."

Georgina turned over and switched out the light, but sleep eluded her. Desperate, she turned the light back on and reached for a book. *The Letters of Jane Austen.* She hadn't read any of them yet, she'd been too busy trying to find inspiration in the novels.

Anna came upstairs at seven the next morning, as requested by Georgina, and found her on her back, fast asleep, with the copy of Jane Austen's letters lying open on her chest, her hand hanging down at the side of the bed. On the floor by the bed was a notepad and a pen which must have fallen from her hand. Anna put down the coffee on the bedside table, and lifted the book off Georgina, who didn't stir. She picked up the notepad and pen and put the book on the desk. Scrawled on it were the words *Maud is more like Jane Austen than I am.*

Anna looked across at the sleeping figure. She called Georgina's name, quite softly, then rather more loudly. She gave her shoulder a shake. Georgina stirred, flung herself over and went back to sleep. Anna left the coffee where it was and went back downstairs.

Georgina woke at midday, emerging wild-eyed from a vivid dream in which she had, yet again, been pursued into dark realms of unfamiliar landscapes by Jane Austen, or at least by the woman in the portrait that adorned the cover of her edition of Jane Austen's letters. Sharp-eyed, plump-cheeked, this dream being had nothing of sweetness and light about her. This was a woman straight out of ancient Greece, cousin to the Furies, on nodding terms with Athene, a woman, moreover, who clearly dined merrily with Aristophanes.

How the unconscious mind distorted reality. She must get a grip. Jane Austen was the daughter of an English country vicar, a beloved daughter, sister, aunt, the author of some of the most life-enhancing novels ever written, stories with invariably happy endings.

And an author who penned some of the wittiest and sharpest lines ever written.

"That's the real problem," she told Henry, when he came in looking shocked after a lecture on P-mode helioseismology.

"What is?" Henry stretched out in his favourite armchair in the sitting room and took a gulp of the reviving mug of tea that Anna thoughtfully provided.

Georgina had given up on her computer and desk, and had been out most of the day walking the plot. Or rather, brooding on the enigma that was Jane Austen.

"The problem is that Jane Austen is a comic writer," she said. "She wrote comedies. She can make you laugh out loud, and she created some of the most preposterous and outrageous comic figures ever. Think of Mr. Collins."

Maud, who was sitting on the piano stool, chimed in, "Or Mrs. Norris, who is so horrible, but she's funny at the same time. And, talking of Jane Austen, which is a subject that dominates the conversation around here, at least when it's not about wild boar, why did you write that I'm more like Jane Austen than you are?"

"Have you been snooping?"

"Nope. Anna told me. You'd written it in letters an inch high, nothing secret about it."

"I don't remember writing that — yes, I do. It was those letters. Gossip, family news, a dress length, and then bang, one of her devastating remarks. It reminded me of you, direct, clear-minded, cutting through all the niceties and getting to the heart of the matter. Telling it like it is."

Henry agreed. "A mind clear of cant, Samuel Johnson would have said. That's what an eighteenth-century upbringing in the hands of a scholarly father did for her."

"Is that complimentary, what you just said about me?" Maud asked. "It doesn't sound like a life skill that I need. I tell you what, Jane Austen wasn't at all PC."

"Lucky her, living in a time when she didn't have to be."

His tea drunk, and the memory of p-modes and convection cells receding, Henry's mind was sharpened. "Maud mentioned plagiarism yesterday. It's an idea. Take stuff from her novels and letters and tweak them, different context, different characters. It would give an authentic flavour to your book, wouldn't it?"

"Yolanda Vesey would sniff out my thefts in a second."

"So what? Isn't it in her interest as much as yours and everyone else's for you to get the book written? You've got an impossible deadline, you have to cut corners somewhere. At least, if you have scruples about pinching words, can't you make up a plot which is an amalgam of her novels? Especially of *Mansfield Park* and *Emma,* because those were the next two she wrote, you could justify that, surely."

"Don't think I haven't tried." Georgina prowled up and down as she spoke. "It's no good, it doesn't gel, it doesn't come out as a coherent story at all. And one thing I am sure of, there's no way I can wing it through this. I've got to have a detailed outline, everything in place. Only every time I start, it falls apart. I've had a go at just picking up from the last words of her opening pages of *Love and Friendship* and plunging in."

She was silent, and Maud, looking at her expectantly, said, "Go on, what happens?"

"Rubbish happens. It's no good, there are writers who are quick, and writers who are —"

"Dead," Maud put in. "In a literary if not a literal sense. Lots of writers and composers, too, turn out good stuff in no time at all. Look at Mozart."

"If I were Mozart, or if I had one percent of Mozart's genius, I wouldn't be in this fix."

"If you were Mozart, you'd be in a place where Livia Harkness couldn't get at you, and as for one percent, hooey. I read that nobody ever uses more than ten percent of their potential. Perhaps you should sign up for one of these self-improvement courses. You know, you visualize it, and poof! It's done."

"All I can visualize is Livia Harkness in a mood, and Dan Vesey on the phone to his lawyers."

"Okay, let's be practical," Henry said.

"Shut up, Maud, Georgina doesn't need arguments, she needs help."

Twenty-Six

Henry didn't have to go in to college that week, and was contemplating a day's work in his study. The sun didn't reach in there at this time of year, and he looked round the untidy room with a sense of dissatisfaction. Normally, he wasn't much bothered by his surroundings, but today the cluttered desk annoyed him, so he heaved a pile of books off the desk and on to the floor. He looked at the papers spread over what space remained on the surface, considered sorting them out and decided it was a moment to decamp from the battlefield. Like Wellington, he could be masterly in retreat.

The kitchen would be empty: Gina was in her garret, writing, one hoped; Maud was in her room doing God knew what, and Anna was out, he had heard her singing as she went up the basement steps. Using his laptop as a tray, he laid a textbook on it, a pad of paper, two pencils, a ruler, a pen, a calculator and his iPod.

Pleased with his sense of balance, he went down the stairs to the kitchen, missed the bottom step and by means of a juggling motion worthy of a talented Auguste, just saved his laptop from destruction. He reassembled his possessions, laid them out on the kitchen table and plugged in his computer. Since he was down here, he might as well have a beer. He opened the fridge, took out a bottle, helped himself to a few grapes and settled down to work.

For ten minutes. Footsteps, and there was Georgina, even darker circles under her eyes, looking harassed. "Hungry? Thirsty?" he enquired. "Have a beer, how's it going?"

Georgina sat down on the other side of the table, running her fingers through her hair and giving herself the appearance of something wild in a Greek play. "Going? It isn't. Or you could say, it's going nowhere." She got up and wandered around the kitchen. "Sorry, I'm disturbing you."

"I hadn't really started."

"I envy you, you know that? You work for hours on end, you open a book or your computer and there you are, deep in whatever you need to be deep in, and when you look up, there's a mass of work done. I used to be like that. I used to put in long sessions like that in the library, thinking nothing of it, and satisfied at the end of the day that I'd achieved something. Same when I wrote *Magdalene Crib.* I had a schedule, I had my notes, I had all my research done, and I did it. What's gone wrong?" She opened a drawer in the dresser, investigated the contents and then pulled the drawer right out. She laid it on the table and began to remove its contents one by one. "This drawer's a mess."

"It's meant to be. It's the odds and ends drawer. No one ever tidies that drawer."

Georgina wound a piece of string round her fingers and tucked the ends in.

Someone was singing, or rather chanting, a descending scale. Maud was coming down the stairs. "I heard voices," she said. "Move along a bit, Georgina. What's all this stuff? Heavens, you aren't tidying drawers, are you? Isn't that what writers do when they really are stuck? Do you think you've got writer's block? It can go on for years and years, you know."

"Thanks. I haven't got writer's block. I've got writer's funk. In fact, I'm not a writer. I'm an ex-writer, or possibly an unwriter, and I've got unwriter's frozen fingers and jellied brains syndrome."

"Did Jane Austen ever suffer from writer's

block?" asked Maud.

"She wouldn't have called it that, people like Jane Austen didn't dwell on their psychological state. Look how Mr. Bennet mocks Mrs. Bennet for her 'nerves.' Now she'd tell all about her nerves in a newspaper, and say what Mr. B. was like in bed." Georgina rubbed her eyes. "I'm becoming obsessed by this woman, I'm starting to think that her moral values might be good ones, how sad is that? A clergyman's daughter from two centuries back?"

"You're skirting around the subject of writer's block," Maud said, giving Georgina a severe look. "Concentrate. All those years she didn't write anything, maybe that's why."

"Who knows why she didn't write? I wish she had, I wish with all my heart she'd sat down and finished *Love and Friendship,* and then I wouldn't have this problem."

"No, but you'd be on the plane back to America," Henry said. Was what he wanted to say going to be any use to Georgina, or simply panic her more? "I've been doing a bit of research on writer's block. Seems to have umpteen causes, but the one that fits your case is a stinker. It's caused by not wanting to write the book you are writing."

Maud was sucking at her reed. She blew

into it, making a fearsome squawk. "That's stupid. How often does that happen, people writing books they don't want to write. I mean, who makes them? Like there aren't enough books out there?"

"Livia Harkness, that's who," said Georgina. "She's got another author who has to turn out soft porn to make ends meet. Under a pseudonym, of course — she's got a reputation as a serious writer. She hates doing it, even though she's very good at it, and Livia won't let her stop, because of all the money it brings in."

"How do you know about her?" asked Henry. "Does Livia H. gossip about her clients?"

"Hell, no. Gossip? Idle chatter? The chitchat, the give-and-take of daily conversation? Not Livia. She uses words like every one of them has to earn its living."

"Is there a Mr. Harkness?"

"Not that I know of, and I begin to doubt that there ever were a Mr. and Mrs. Harkness, her progenitors; I reckon Livia sprang fully formed from some alien's head."

"So how did you find out about the soft porn?" Maud sat down and propped her elbows on the kitchen table. "Do tell, fascinating insights into the literary world are much more fun than your writer's block."

Georgina picked up a scrum of metal paper clips and began to separate them. "It was at a writer's conference. Livia Harkness's clients tend to get in a gaggle and bitch about her, it's because we're all terrified of her."

"You have to stand up to bullies, and then they crumple."

"Not Livia Harkness. She doesn't do crumpling, believe me."

"Then why don't they go to other agents?" Henry said.

"Because she's so damn good at what she does, and she gets her authors good deals and fights like a terrier for them when publishers get high-handed and mean with the advances."

"She hasn't done much fighting on your behalf, she's not exactly fending off that Dan person."

"She got Georgina a fat advance," Henry pointed out. "Which she'll have to repay if she doesn't get a move on and write that book, and honestly, Gina, I don't think you can."

Georgina tugged at a clip and bent it so fiercely that it snapped, in the process jabbing her in the finger and drawing blood.

"What is it with paper clips, why are they so vicious?" she said, running the wounded digit under the cold tap. She had her back to Henry and Maud, so they couldn't see her face. "Thanks for that, Henry, it's so helpful to have it laid out in such clear terms. Basically, I'm screwed, is what you're saying."

More footsteps, from outside this time. Anna paused at the door to remove the cigarette from her mouth and stubbed it into the flowerpot full of sand which she kept outside the back door for the purpose. She shook out her umbrella, and backed into the kitchen.

"I go out, I leave the kitchen empty and completely clean and tidy. I come back, only two hours later, and it is like a camp here. Books and papers, the tin of silver polish and a horrid rag, and this drawer open with its contents everywhere. What is all this for?"

"Council of war," Henry said. "Don't fuss about the mess, sit down and join in. Gina isn't writing, or not to any effect, and we're getting to the bottom of it."

Anna sat. "The best way to get anything done is to know that you starve if you don't do it. It concentrates the mind."

"Gina is an artist, Anna. She has to write a book she doesn't want to write, it's out of her area of expertise."

"Tessitura," Maud said. "All cracked notes below, and can't reach the high ones."

"Gina is a novelist, this is a novel, no one is asking her to write one of Henry's science textbooks," Anna said.

"There are novels and novels," said Henry. "And she's having to write in someone else's voice. I suppose there are authors with a gift for pastiche, but it looks like Gina isn't one of them."

"Then what is to be done?"

"I just told her I've been doing some research about the literary world. I think she needs a ghost."

Anna let out an exclamation of dismay. "Ghost? You're crazy! A spirit summoned from other realms? The Catholic church is completely opposed to such practices, they are extremely dangerous. And how would a spirit help?"

"Not a spook, a ghostwriter, Anna. Perfectly harmless."

"Harmless? This is what happens in a country where everybody is an atheist. Gina cannot risk her immortal soul for the sake of a book! And besides, it's impractical. How can you summon a ghostwriter? How do you know that the ghost of Jane Austen will speak in her ear? It could be Dostoevsky, and then where would she be, with a story in Russian about doom and despair? You are not sensible, Henry."

Georgina laughed as she hadn't done for a long time. "Oh, if only I could summon up the spirit of Jane Austen! Never mind my immortal soul, I'd do it."

"There was a woman who said she was getting music from Chopin," said Maud. "Some of it wasn't bad, but I thought, why Chopin? Why not Mozart?"

Anna was frowning and pursing her lips. "This is not a subject for jokes and laughter."

"It's all right, Anna. It's nothing to do with spirits and eternal realms. It's completely down-to-earth, ghostwriters are just writers who write books for people who can't write them themselves. I'll show you."

Georgina ran up the stairs to her room, and came back with some magazines. "Here are some copies of *The Author,* they always have ads for ghosts at the back."

"Who employs these ghostwriters?"

"People who've got a story to tell, but who can't write. Victims of child abuse, for instance; publishers pay a fortune for those, only it needs a professional writer to put the terrible details into shape so that mums can buy the paperback at the supermarket

338

and drool over the kiddie sex, while exclaiming how dreadful it all is — don't ask me why. Celebrities who are commissioned to write novels nearly always use ghosts. They get huge advances because they're famous, only most of them can't even spell their own names, let alone write a book. Ex–prime ministers, of course there aren't too many of those, but they're offered millions for their memoirs or autobiographies. They might be able to turn out a paragraph or two, but they're mostly too busy making money in other ways to actually put their fingers on the keys."

Georgina could see that although Anna was relieved on a spiritual level, she was now disturbed on the moral front.

"So I buy a book which has an author's name on the cover, and that person didn't write the book?"

"Exactly. And publishers use ghosts when they've got a really rotten book by an author they think is promotable — young, sexy, right ethnic origin, only can't write for toffee. Give their hopeless manuscript to a ghost, and there you are, a bestseller."

"Don't worry about it, Anna," said Maud. "It's a wicked place, the literary world, there's no point getting sentimental about it. Come on, Henry, how would a ghost help

339

Georgina?"

"That's obvious, Maud, he or she would write the book for me."

"Problem solved. It'll cost you, I suppose, but you've got all that lovely money from Cadell and Davies, haven't you? Isn't it worth spending some of that to get the book written?"

For a moment, Georgina was tempted. The relief of handing over her notes to a real writer, a person who sat down at her or his computer every morning and produced the requisite number of words. Could she find a ghost who could write in the style of Jane Austen? In the time? She flipped open another copy of *The Author* and began to read the ghost ads with closer attention.

"What about the non-disclosure clause Livia Harkness got you to sign?" Henry said. "Could you do it without telling her what you were doing?"

The mention of Livia's name brought Georgina back to earth and reality with a swift bump, and an abandonment of the straw she had been about to clutch.

"Of course I can't do it. I'm a writer, not an illiterate celeb or a lying politician. Anna's right, I can't put my name on something I haven't written. It would be so dishonest. And I'd have to tell the ghost why

I needed it done, and . . . No, it's a non-starter. Sorry Henry, nice idea, but it won't work."

Why was she sitting here picking at paper clips and unknotting twine, when she should be at her keyboard, clocking up the paragraphs? "I'd better get back to it," she said without enthusiasm.

She went up the stairs a good deal more slowly than she'd come down them, no coffee or untidy drawers to distract her. Not that she didn't have drawers in her room, but every one of them had already been tidied into rigid order. Her books had been rearranged, and her CDs sorted out, with missing tracks added to her iPod. As for her computer files, everything was in its place, old stuff deleted, updates checked.

Short of painting the walls and ceiling, or buying a sewing machine and setting about making cushion covers, there was nothing for Georgina to do in there.

Except sit and write.

Or waste hours on the internet, but even that was now impossible, at least until seven o'clock that evening. She'd found a program on the Procrastination site, called *The Writer's Little Helper, a Personal Training Program.* It kicked in at 7 a.m., loaded a day's schedule, and then severed her internet access for the day. Not even turning the computer off and restarting would restore the connection.

She shouldn't have done that, she'd have to work out a way to remove the program. She sat down at her computer.

The Little Helper was wise to that. Of course she could remove the files and trash them, but why would she want to do that? Did she want to waste time on the computer more than she wanted to write a book? Yes? Was she pretending it was research? Here was advice from her Writer's Mentor.

It made sense. Routine was the writer's ally. Butt on seat, fingers on keys was how books got written. No more, no less. Self-discipline, willpower, ambition: those were the qualities that would drive a writer to her goal.

Georgina looked around the room as though a ghostwriter might have materialized in her absence, perched on the shelf above the door, perhaps, or skulking in the corner.

And finally, with the sharp words of the Writer's Little Helper ringing in her ears, something went ping in her brain. She could do it, and she was going to do it. Self-discipline? Yes. Willpower? Tick. Ambition? Sort of.

A fresh page, the magic words, *Chapter Two,* and she was off.

Twenty-Seven

Routine was to be her friend, and the routine that Georgina adopted was rigorous. Up at seven, shower, fifteen-minute brisk walk along the street and back down the other side. Breakfast, nourishing, with coffee, and a thermos of coffee to take up to her room with her, despite Anna's protests that coffee in a thermos was:

a) unhealthy
b) not at the right temperature
c) terrible tasting
d) uncivilized

"I don't want to speak to a soul all day," Georgina said, as she put in a request for a packed lunch, like Henry's.

"Eating in your room is definitely not civilized."

"Too bad." No, she wasn't going to sit at her desk all day long and numb her legs. "I shall take regular walks. And in the evening, with all those hours under my belt, and all those words on the page, I shall come down to be sociable and eat a proper meal."

It was hard, grinding work, but for Georgina at this time, hard was easy. She liked her daily schedule, and when she took the twenty minutes off three times a day, midmorning, after lunch, and midafternoon, she walked with her earphones on and listened to the recordings of the Jane Austen novels that she'd downloaded.

Every five hundred words, she came to the end of whichever paragraph she was writing, and set about revising and editing what she had written, paying careful attention to sentence length, vocabulary, syntax and punctuation, slavishly following the way that Jane Austin had crafted her sentences.

She had access to the complete *Oxford English Dictionary,* and set about methodically checking the etymology of any word about which she had a doubt. When was it first used, was it too modern, too slangy?

With this method, she managed to achieve about two thousand words each day. It was going to be a close-run thing, but for the first time she felt that she was going to turn out a passable manuscript, correctly written in the style of Jane Austen. It might not be literature, but, closely modelled on the six novels, it would do.

She used the novels as templates. From *Emma,* she took a querulous old man, turning him into Susan's grandfather. From *Pride and Prejudice* she took a sub-plot of a plain woman, no longer young, quite happy to forego any real chance of happiness in a marriage for the sake of having her own establishment. Fanny Price provided a degree of victimhood to Susan, while Mrs. Norris was an excellent prototype of a Lady Carcenet. *Northanger Abbey* gave Susan a rather silly younger sister, while Willoughby, with a dash of Wickham, made for a good villain.

She added an ill-fated attachment, an elopement, family dissension and a setting that moved between an elegant town house in Bath and a fine country seat, a mixture of Mansfield Park and Lacock Abbey.

Shrubberies abounded, as did some pleasing walks in Dorset, a seaside scene and various carriage rides. Susan took a muddy walk in the style of Elizabeth Bennet, and she had an untrustworthy friend, a mixture of Isabella Thorpe, Lucy Steele, and Maria Crawford.

The hero wasn't difficult at all. He had to be tall, dark and handsome, proud, rich and possessed of a very fine house and estate.

An unpleasant clergyman, a few servants in the background, a dance, a dinner party and the mixture was complete.

By the third day of this regime, Henry could tell that things were going well for Georgina, and he heaved a sigh of relief before plunging back into his studies, urgent now, as the deadline for a complex piece of coursework loomed. His own emotional life was on hold, since Sophie was proving distinctly elusive. Phone calls went un-returned, text messages ignored and emails went unanswered. This, he told himself, was because Sophie was on location, working hard, and probably out of reach of these kinds of messages. He hoped that she would pick up one or other of his missives, and told his aunt he was sure that Sophie would be coming with him for the weekend.

She replied in her acerbic way that Sophie had better, as otherwise they would sit down thirteen to dinner, which she wouldn't countenance.

Email from
Henry@seaofcrises.co.uk

Suggest teddy bear for four-teenth seat if Sophie can't

347

make it.

Love Henry

Email from
Pamela@grandison.co.uk

I don't do bears.

Henry and Maud visited another school, which Maud gave a swift thumbs-down. "The music department isn't up to much, and I don't think that the headmaster was too keen on my purple hair."

"I don't like it either," said Henry "I hope it washes out."

"I told you it does. Don't be so stuffy."

Georgina worked like a fiend for ten days without a break. She worked all through Saturday and Sunday, ignoring all suggestions that she should take some time off, and triumphantly looking at her word count as it reached and passed the twenty thousand figure.

She only needed to keep this up for another fifty days, and with a few days' grace she would be at the required word length, with a polished manuscript. She knew many writers preferred to do a first draft at speed, and then to take the time to revise it afterwards. They asserted that it was better to write without employing your critical faculty, but Georgina knew that in her case this would make for a disastrous book, which would in no way correspond to what she had been commissioned to write.

She felt a sense of elation and triumph. She'd cracked it. Hard work was the secret, as always. She was going to get *Love and Friendship* written and delivered on time.

Stretching after a long session at the keyboard, she padded down to the kitchen to hunt for a biscuit. Maud was down there, helping Anna make a ginger cake.

"Henry's favourite," she said. "Anna reckons he needs feeding up, he's working so hard at the moment. That's what happens when you put off work until the last minute," she added primly as she dipped a finger into the mixture and tasted it. "It needs a bit more ginger, Anna."

"It does not." As Anna took the bowl away, the doorbell sounded, a demanding, repeating peal.

"Who on earth is that?" Georgina said.

Maud licked her finger and went over to the window to peer up into the street. "There's quite a crowd up there. A couple of people with cameras, what's going on?"

"I'll go and see," said Georgina. "They'll

disturb Henry if they go on like that, what the hell do they think they're doing?"

She went out of the basement door into the little yard, and bounded up the steps to street level. An astonishing scene met her eyes, as four or five men and women were clustered around the entrance to the house. As Maud had said, three of them were holding large cameras.

"Can I help you?" she said. "And please don't ring the doorbell like that, it's very antisocial."

A flash went off, and she recoiled for a brief second, gathering her wits. "Cut that out. What are you doing here?" Gina had some familiarity with the paparazzi from when the second of her stepmothers had been discovered in flagrante with the host of a popular TV show. These were the English variety, but brothers and sisters under the skin.

"We just want a word with Sophie Fanshawe."

Sophie? What was going on?

"Sophie Fanshawe isn't here."

"This is where she stays in London, isn't it? This guy Henry Lefroy's her boyfriend. Is he in?"

"No, he isn't."

"Who are you?"

Georgina's mind was working swiftly. "I'm house-sitting for Mr. Lefroy. And," she added as Maud came up the steps, eyes round with curiosity and interest, "keeping his sister company."

Maud had managed to get a good deal of flour on her clothes, and the white patches on her black garments, combined with her purple hair, made-up pallor and dark-rimmed eyes, gave her a very strange appearance.

Nonplussed, the representatives of the press stared at her. She blinked back at them. "If you want Sophie, you've come to the wrong place, she isn't here," she said in a bored voice. "She's down in the country with my brother."

"Where in the country?"

"Like I'm going to give you their address?"

"Are you sure she's with this Henry guy and not with Chris Denby?"

"What's your view on the role Sophie's landed for herself in Hollywood?"

"Will your brother be joining her out there?"

"None of your business," Georgina said. "Now, go."

One of the journalists, a woman with bright red hair and sunglasses, looked intently at Georgina. "You sure you're just house-sitting? You sure Henry isn't two-timing Sophie?"

Georgina laughed. "What, me instead of Sophie? Please!"

Maud whipped down the basement steps in front of Georgina and vanished through the kitchen. As Georgina sank into a chair, Maud reappeared, saying she'd disconnected the doorbell. "So if any of them come back, they won't bother us."

"What if Henry goes out?" said Anna. "Shouldn't we tell him about these people?"

"Absolutely not," Georgina said. "He needs to concentrate, not worry about the press and Sophie. I wonder what all that was about?"

"Sophie's been offered a big part in an American TV series," Maud said. "I read about it this morning. Google Sophie's name and you'll see. Two English actors, her and a guy called Chris Denby. There's a pic of them together, looking rather cosy, I must say, but that's actors for you, smooch when on show, not on speaking terms when the publicity lights go off."

Chris Denby? Wasn't he the actor in breeches? When Sophie had been in Lacock, instead of Ireland?

"She will have told Henry this news,"

352

Anna said.

"Yeah," said Maud. "I suppose."

"And if not, he can catch up with her news at the weekend, when they're going to stay with your aunt," Georgina said.

Anna and Maud exchanged glances.

"Whatever," Maud said.

Twenty-Eight

Georgina awoke on the morning of the eleventh day with a strange numbness in one hand. She must have slept on it. She had a pain in her neck as well, further proof that she had slept awkwardly. She went for a brisk walk, came back to her computer and was surprised to find as she opened it that her fingers were rather painful. Stiff, that was all, the weather had been damp and maybe she had a touch of premature rheumatism. After all, wasn't that the price you paid for living in England?

As she put her fingers to the keys a stab of pain went from her elbow up to her neck. She waited a few minutes and then tried again. An even worse pain surged through her fingers and travelled via wrist, elbow and shoulder to her neck, where her head felt as though it had been spun round several times in its socket before being replaced at a strange angle.

What the hell was the matter with her?

She began to feel anxious. Twenty minutes of her writing time gone, and she hadn't produced a single word. She went into the bathroom, opened the white cabinet and fished around for the extra-strong aspirin that she knew were there. Ignoring the instructions on the packet, she dissolved two of them in a glass of water, swallowed them and waited impatiently for them to take effect. Ten minutes later, with half an hour's good work time wasted, she tentatively tapped at the keyboard. Tender, yes; agonizing, no. It was obviously a kind of stiffness, and she would work through it, wasn't that what athletes did?

An hour later, she admitted defeat. Clearly aspirin was not the answer. Glancing at her watch with a worried frown, she bundled herself into a jacket and scarf, ran down the stairs and flew out of the house, without pausing to answer Maud's startled query as to why she'd left her desk.

Whatever was wrong with her didn't seem to have reached her back or her legs, so perhaps she didn't face total paralysis after all. The doctor's surgery was at the end of their road. Georgina went in and stood impatiently behind a tall blonde woman holding the hand of a child whose face appeared to be covered with spots. That was all she needed, she would get over this stiffness to go down with some kind of London plague.

Finally the woman completed her interminable description of what was wrong with little Finola, as if anybody couldn't see what was wrong with the child, and Georgina took her place at the counter.

"Two weeks? I have to wait for two weeks to see a doctor?"

"Well, you can walk, can't you? And your speech isn't slurred, and from your description of what is wrong with you I have to say I can't count it as an emergency. I can ring you if we get a cancellation, but I have to tell you there's a waiting list at the moment of fifty-six people awaiting cancellations, so I don't rate your chances very highly."

"That child got to see a doctor right away."

"Children have priority. Finola comes out in a rash when she eats too many green apples, but it is the rule of the practice that any rash must be investigated. So she has to see the doctor. Meanwhile —"

"Meanwhile I can't work, I'm in pain and you can't do anything for me."

"We only have your word for it that you are in pain." She looked at Georgina, clearly wondering if this patient might be going to

356

get violent. She hesitated. "We have Dr. Perry here this morning. He is qualified, but hasn't finished his general practitioner training, so he can't do a formal diagnosis or prescribe anything except under the direction of one of our regular doctors. But I'm sure he'll be able to explain to you why there is nothing wrong with you."

Georgina wasn't sure that she really wanted to see Dr. Perry, but she was desperate. If he couldn't prescribe officially, perhaps he could recommend something she could buy over the counter at the pharmacy.

Dr. Perry was young and pink, with a round head and an engaging smile. He listened to what Georgina had to say, asked her about her work routine, felt her elbow — agony, twisted her head — excruciating, and flexed her fingers; Georgina thought she might be going to pass out.

"Nothing serious at all," he said with great satisfaction. "I expect you've been imagining all kinds of things that might be wrong with you. Cheer up, it's nothing that time and rest won't solve, although I think you'll have to change your working habits. No typing for a great many weeks."

Georgina stared at him. "What on earth do you mean?"

"You have a repetitive stress injury. Caused by poor posture and too much typing. Writers didn't get it in the days of manual typewriters, because having to stop at the end of every line and move the carriage back, and then having to roll the paper in at the end of every page meant that their actions were never as repetitive as they are now on the computer when you just carry on typing."

RSI. Of course. But RSI was something that happened to tennis players, secretaries, musicians. In effect, other people.

A stunned Georgina came out of the surgery with her arm in a sling and a prescription for a painkiller written out by Dr. Perry and signed, after a further half-hour wait, by another doctor. She had an appointment in three weeks' time with the practice physiotherapist, and friendly final advice from Dr. Perry that of course she could use the mouse and type with her left hand, but the chances were if she did that exactly the same thing would happen to that one.

Maud turned out to know a good deal about RSI. "All young musicians these days are supposed to see Alexander practitioners," she announced. "That's probably what you need to do. They readjust your body, and you learn how you do things, and how to do it better and you don't put any stress on yourself. Only by the time it's got as bad as it has with you, I'm not sure there's much anybody can do about it. Except to stop doing whatever it is that's given it to you. We had a pianist at school who had to stop playing for two years."

"Two years?"

Henry, brought up-to-date on the situation, was more sanguine. "All these doctors are alarmist, and I expect a newly qualified one is even worse than most of them. You'll simply have to take two or three days off, don't go near the keyboard, and then I'm sure you'll find it'll wear off and you'll be perfectly all right."

Maud agreed. "It'll do you good anyway to have a pause. Otherwise I'm sure you'll run out of things to write. Filling the well of inspiration and all that."

Inspiration? She wasn't relying on anything as tricky as inspiration, it was hard work that was turning out the pages. Georgina retreated to her room, and taking a double dose of the painkiller that the doctor had given her, set about trying to use the mouse with her left hand. It was clumsy, but with perseverance she would get the hang of it. Left-handed children used to be made to write with their right hands, and they managed it. What was using a mouse compared to that?

She had many lost hours of writing to make up, so she worked through the afternoon and evening, refusing to leave her room or her computer. "It's much slower just using my left hand," she explained to Anna, who came up clucking with disapproval, but bringing with her a wonderful steak sandwich. "I'm sure it will get faster as I practice, and if I leave my other arm in a sling for a couple of days, I'm certain the whole thing will just wear off, as Henry says."

Anna shook her head, and went back into the kitchen. She tidied up, and then went outside with her phone and a cigarette to have a long conversation with Charles.

The next morning, Georgina's right arm was no better, and there was an ominous tingling in her left hand, and a pain in her left elbow. She took some more painkillers, and went back to work.

Henry let himself in, and was greeted by an anxious Maud. "I think Georgina is having some kind of a breakdown," she announced in extravagant tones. "There have been all sorts of funny noises coming out of her room; of course she could be listening to some band that I'd never heard of, but I think she's either in a temper or in pain. Possibly both."

Henry went up the stairs two at a time, gave a perfunctory knock on Georgina's door and went in. Georgina was slumped over her keyboard, a pencil held between her teeth.

Henry took the pencil out of her mouth. "You'll do yourself a serious injury if you do that," he said calmly. "Either you'll ram the pencil into the roof of your mouth, which could be nasty, or you'll break it together with a tooth or two. Give yourself a rest, for heaven's sake. I take it that your left arm now has tennis elbow, or whatever the up-to-date terminology for it is. I've got a suggestion," he went on. "I finally heard back from Sophie, and she can't make it this weekend. My aunt will be livid if I turn up by myself, so why don't you come with me?"

"A fine guest I'd be, when I can't use a knife, and if this goes on I doubt if I'd even be able to use a fork."

"I'll sit next to you and cut your food up for you. You'll be doing me a favour, it will do you good to get away, the food is always excellent there and you can probably pick up an oddity or two to add to your character list."

Georgina looked in despair at the pile of paper. She had drawn up a large chart which was pinned on the wall, and she pointed out to Henry how much she was falling behind.

"What you need is a rest from the keyboard. If you don't come with me, I'll probably come back to find you're trying to type with your toes."

Twenty-Nine

"How convenient is that?" said Maud. "You're off to Motley Manor, and my friend Nadia's house is only about five miles from there, so you can drop me off."

Maud's nagging had been too much for Henry, who had reluctantly said she could stay with Nadia.

Maud tried to persuade Georgina that she would be much more comfortable in the back of the car — "No chance of your arm knocking against anything there, far more room" — but was put in her place, which was in the back, by Henry.

"Get in, before I change my mind about giving you a lift, and instead deposit you at the Tube station to make your own way."

Motley Manor was in Kent. "Good thing we're not going there in the depths of winter," said Maud. "It snows a lot in Kent." She then hooked herself up to her earphones and subsided into happy silence.

"Kent is one of Jane Austen's counties," said Henry as they made their slow way through the southern outskirts of London. "Hunsford, which is where Rosings is, was in Kent. Elizabeth went to stay with the Collinses there; quite a journey in those days, from Hertfordshire to Kent."

"Didn't Jane Austen's brother, the rich one who was adopted, have a house in Kent?"

"Godmersham."

"From the letters, it looked like she visited him a lot. I suppose it might be the model for Rosings. I wonder if there was a formidable old aunt in residence there, like Lady Catherine de Bourgh."

"You know how in films and on TV they always portray Lady Catherine as being a grande dame, a kind of archetypal great-aunt? It's completely wrong," said Henry.

He braked abruptly as a mad pedestrian launched herself on to a crossing when his wheels were nearly on it. He waited patiently until the elderly woman had made her away across, ignoring her rude gesture.

"Wrong?"

"She can't have been more than forty-something."

"Why?"

"Think about it, she has a daughter, Anne.

A young woman who's not yet married and whom she wants to marry her cousin, Mr. Darcy. Lady Catherine might have had a baby when she was past forty, but it's much more likely that she would have had her when she was in her early twenties. It's the same with Mrs. Bennet. She's always played as being well past middle age, and yet she can't be. Do the arithmetic."

Georgina thought about the ages of the Bennet family. "Forty then was much older than forty now. Teeth and health and things like that."

"Even so, there's no way that Lady Catherine would be a grey-haired wrinkly. If I were casting a film, I think I'd have Kristin Scott Thomas play her."

Maud spoke up from the back. "That's an old game, casting Jane Austen adaptations. Like, who for Mr. Darcy?"

It was a mystery to Georgina how Maud could have her ears full of earphones, and be listening to music, and yet hear what she and Henry were saying. Maud removed her earphones. "I'll begin," she said. "I'm very good at this, we did it a lot at school."

"Do you know," Georgina said, "I'd much rather not talk or think about Jane Austen at all. Not now, and not for the next two days. I'm starting to hate the very sound of her name."

"Over-exposure leading to an over-loaded system," said Maud, stuffing her earphones back in place. "In your mind, that is. All the little neurons working overtime." She whistled a few bars of music. "I really love this bit."

Nadia's house was about half a mile out of a small town, set well back from the road. It was a modern house, quite large and totally characterless. Maud was out of the car and round to the back to get her bag out almost before Henry had put the brakes on. "No, don't get out," she said. "I'm not a child being delivered to a party, I can manage perfectly well on my own, thank you. Goodbye, don't give my love to Aunt Pamela, since that would give the game away, but have a wonderful weekend." She went up to the front door, and stood there, clearly not intending to ring the bell until Henry had driven away.

He turned the car and headed off back down the short drive to the main road. He was frowning. "I don't like just leaving her here."

Georgina twisted round in her seat and looked back at the house. "It's okay, the door's opened and she's gone in. She's got money, she's got a mobile phone and you know where she is. What can possibly go wrong? Would your mum be worried about her?"

"I have an uneasy feeling my mother wouldn't have let her come."

"So why did you agree?"

"She doesn't have many friends, and she was keen, and she's having a hard time of it, trying to find a school she likes which will take her." He paused and shook his head, adding in exasperation, "I'm not cut out for all this responsibility, damn it."

"Speaking as one who was once a fourteen-year-old girl, I think you're doing just fine."

Soon after dropping off Maud, Henry turned off on to a side road. The light was fading, and the trees and hedges were stark against the twilight sky. The winding road narrowed, and Henry slowed down, taking his car carefully round muddy corners, once only just avoiding collision with a tractor with no lights coming in the other direction.

The stillness and solitude soothed Georgina. "All of England must have been like this in Jane Austen's day."

"I thought Jane Austen was on the banned list."

The gates to Motley Manor were wrought iron and imposing, and the heraldic dragons, clasping shields in giant claws, looked down from supercilious snouts. In days gone by, the gate would have been opened by a lodge-keeper, who would have greeted the arrivals with "Good to see you, Mr. Henry," or a lodge-keeper's wife, in service with the family since she was in her cradle, dropping a curtsey and smiling fondly at a young member of the family.

"It's electronically controlled," Henry explained, as the gates swung open and he drove through them. "CCTV, with screens here and there so that they can let visitors in."

"Not very Jane Austen."

The drive to the house was up an incline. It was long and straight, with lime trees marching alongside. "The original entrance was further round, but it was altered when the park was landscaped in 1750."

"By Capability Brown?" asked Georgina.

"Naturally."

Georgina was beginning to feel alarmed. "Henry, I get the feeling that your family is seriously rich."

"No such luck," said Henry. "My aunt is rich, but she's only my aunt by marriage. This is her house, it's been in her family for generations. Her grandfather won a fortune on the Irish sweep or some lottery, and invested it surprisingly well, and once you get to a certain level of wealth, it's quite easy to hang on to it. They need it, because these days a house like this costs a fortune to maintain and run."

"Where do the wild boar come into it? Are they kept round the back someplace?"

"Good God, no. My aunt wouldn't have anything as unruly as wild boar on the premises. No, that's entirely Charlie's business, and his place is about twenty miles from here. Look, there's the manor."

It was a manor house out of a picture book, or out of a BBC cosy crime dramatization. Its mellow brick façade glowed slightly pink in the last light of the day, and Georgina was enchanted by its pleasing proportions, the numerous sash windows with white surrounds, and the vigorous rose, still bearing some blooms, which spread over the handsome doorway and along the front of the house. It looked like a house to live in, not to impress.

"It was a fortified manor house, originally," said Henry. "Then it got smartened up in the eighteenth century, but it still has a great hall from its original manorial days, you'll see when we get inside." As he drew up, the big front door opened. "There's my aunt. Oh, and she isn't Mrs. Grandison, by the way, she's Lady Pamela, although she'll tell you to call her Pam."

Lady Pamela? Henry hadn't said anything about a title. "Does that make your uncle a lord?"

"Definitely not. It's my aunt's title, because her father's an earl."

Georgina had somehow expected Pamela Grandison — Lady Pamela, for God's sake — to be a comfortable body in tweeds, like a character from an Agatha Christie novel, or one of Bertie Wooster's aunts. Not so. Lady Pamela was aloof and elegant. Sleek platinum hair, a beautifully made-up face, and a cashmere sweater and tailored pants that looked as though they had been made for her. Hooded eyes, a modulated, authoritative voice, and Georgina felt the complete hick.

"Henry," Lady Pamela said, presenting a cheek to her nephew. "This is Georgina, I take it." She held out her hand. "How do you do? Welcome to Motley Manor, we're glad you could come."

Georgina raised her arm in its sling, and extended her left hand, which her hostess ignored. "How did you hurt your arm, did you have a fall?" She didn't wait for a reply, but said sharply, "Wickham, come here at once."

As she spoke Georgina heard a snarl, and looked down to find a small dog at her feet, his teeth buried in the calf of her new patent leather boot.

Henry bent down to pull the dog away, taking care, Georgina noticed, to keep his hands away from the action end of the little creature. Bulbous eyes looked furiously up at her. "Pam's pug. Meet Wickham," Henry said.

Georgina didn't know whether to be glad that she was wearing leather boots, thus saving her leg from a vicious wound, or sorry, because she suspected that when she looked at the boot, she would find tooth marks imprinted on the glossy leather.

"He likes you," said Lady Pamela. "He only goes for people he likes, take it as a compliment."

It was a compliment Georgina felt she could do without, and she kept a wary distance from the still-growling pug as she and Henry followed his aunt into the house.

Georgina, amazed, at once forgot all about the pug and her boot. The hall, the one that Henry had said was the original great hall of the manor, rose to a height of about twenty feet. A gallery ran around three of the walls at first floor level, and a carved oak staircase led up to it. The floor had broad polished floorboards, more oak, with some beautiful Oriental rugs on them. On the wall opposite was a large stone fireplace set beneath a wide arch and in front of it were a bulgy sofa in faded red velvet and a couple of armchairs. On the walls of the gallery, Georgina made out a line of pictures, large, gloomy canvases in massive gilt frames: ships on stormy seas, lines of soldiers and guns puffing out little balls of white smoke, portraits of men in uniform, scarlet with swords, blue with cocked hats and telescopes.

Georgina realized she was gaping and gawping as she drew her gaze away from the hall and paintings to find that Lady Pamela was speaking to her. Before she could apologize and ask her to repeat what she'd said, her hostess was halfway to the stairs, talking to Henry.

"You're in the Tulip Room as usual. I've put Georgina in the Rose Room. She doesn't seem terribly bright, I must say, I thought you said she held a university position and had written a book. It is extraordinary how people get on these days. But of course she's American."

As though that explained it all. Georgina

wished she were a pug, and could sink her teeth into a well-turned ankle or two.

Lady Pamela led the way along a landing and into a wide corridor, lined with prints of bucolic scenes. She turned her head to address Henry, keeping step with Georgina a few paces behind. "Who is this girl Charles is bringing for the weekend? He was very unforthcoming when I asked him about her. I told him to invite Hermione, but he says he and Hermione aren't on speaking terms any more."

"Hermione's become a vegetarian."

"How tiresome of her. Well, I hope this girl's presentable, whoever she is. Charles should stop dating so many different girls and settle down. You too, Henry. It's high time you were married." She paused in front of a cream door with a tiny rose painted on the central panel, opened it, and gestured for Georgina to go in, expressing the hope that the room would be to her liking.

In the Rose Room, with the door firmly shut, Georgina sank down on the bed. It had a wooden frame, a kind of miniature four-poster, and the mattress was plump and well-sprung with a chintz cover in a rose and cream pattern. The drapes matched the cover, the carpet was rose pink, and Georgina knew without looking that the adjoining bathroom would have fluffy pink towels.

She slid off the bed and began to unpack her bag, a tricky task to accomplish single-handed. She carefully eased her right arm out of its sling, and tentatively reached into the bag for the sponge bag. A stab of pain ran through her fingers, savaged her elbow and continued to her shoulder and neck. She put her arm back in the sling, and by using her left hand and teeth, managed to put her things away.

"Take the weekend off entirely, get away from the keyboard and rest your wrists," Henry had advised. She'd had an acute sense of guilt when she closed her bedroom door, her computer shut on her desk, and she felt an obscure relief at the stab of pain in her hand and shoulder, which seemed to justify her decision to leave her laptop behind in London.

Now what? She hadn't paid much attention on the way up here, and she had a suspicion that she was going to have trouble finding her way down stairs to the right room. And what was the right room? Didn't people in English houses have tea around this time? Although Pamela Grandison's slim figure was not indicative of a person who had anything more than a cup of Earl

Grey, possibly with a daring slice of lemon in it.

She was saved by Henry, who knocked on the door and then came in to enquire how she had managed with her unpacking. "Thoughtless of me, it must be difficult to do with only one hand. Still, I see you've managed. Do you want tea? I don't; Pam's dinners are excellent, and better attempted on an empty stomach. Let's go and play billiards until it's time to change for dinner."

"I feel when it's time to change I'm going to be escorted up to my room by a maid in a mob cap bearing an oil lamp, or possibly a branch of candles, to have my stays fastened and my hair put up. And I can't play billiards with one arm, even if I knew how to play it at all, which I don't."

"Can you play pool? Yes? Then you won't have any trouble with billiards, it's just a bit more stately. You can use a rest, and we'll both play one-handed. The only rule is, don't rip the baize. The billiard room is at the front, so we can keep an eye out for Charlie."

Georgina looked around the panelled billiard room with interest. Henry switched on the main light, which hung over the billiard table, a symphony of mahogany and green baize supported on eight stout legs, which stood in the centre of the room. "I know I don't want to think about Jane Austen, but this must have been the kind of room where they put on *Lover's Vows* in *Mansfield Park,* I'm sure they set up the theatre in Sir Thomas Bertram's billiard room. How ever did they get the table out? It's massive."

Henry was chalking a cue for Georgina. "Three balls, two white, one red, and I'll tell you how to play as we go along."

Georgina found the dark room, silent except for the soft thunk of cue against ball and the louder clunks as the billiard balls collided, very peaceful. Henry was an extraordinarily calm man. Not placid, not lacking in energy, just with a calm nature. Maybe that was what spending your time pondering the sun did for you. Not that the sun was calm; Henry had shown her photos of solar storms and flares, unnervingly active. Henry had nice hands. She didn't like stubby fingers, but Henry's hand, set on the green baize with the cue aligned between thumb and forefinger, was just right. His voice suited the room, too, neither too deep nor too sharp, but resonant and definite.

Concentrate, how could she have missed that? Her ball whizzed to the other side of the table and plopped into the netted pocket. Henry went round to get it out, and paused at the sound of a car approaching.

"That's Charlie." He went to the window and drew back the heavy red velvet curtain. "Yes, here he is."

Georgina joined him at the window just as the car drew up. Charlie got out and went round to the other side to let out his passenger.

"Good heavens," said Henry. "That's possibly not the wisest thing Charlie's done."

THIRTY

Georgina couldn't believe her eyes. Standing in the circle of light cast by the lamp above the front door was Anna, looking absurdly fair and pretty in a voluminous fur jacket she'd been delighted to find in a thrift shop.

"Wait here while I park the car," Charlie called out to her.

"Come on," Henry said to Georgina, letting the curtain drop. "We can finish our game another time."

They arrived in the hall to find Lady Pamela already at the front door, looking Anna up and down.

"Who are you?"

"I am Anna Bednarska."

"What are you doing here? You're Polish, of course, one of the catering team, don't you know to go round to the back, to the kitchen? And you're late, all the others have been here for hours."

Charles emerged out of the darkness. "What's going on?"

"Charles, I expected you earlier. You haven't come alone, have you? You know I won't sit down thirteen to dinner."

"What are you talking about? Of course I'm not alone, you can see I'm not, with Anna standing here in front of you."

"This person? She's a Pole, with the caterers. I've told her to go round to the kitchen."

"You've put your foot in it," said Charles crossly. "Honestly, Mum, you really have mislaid your manners. This is Anna, who's a guest. My guest, your guest. Kitchen, indeed! Anna, welcome to Motley Manor. Hi, Henry, Georgina." He gave his mother a vexed look. "Do you mind if we come in? It's cold out here."

Drinks were served in the hall, and Georgina, looking down at the gathering from the gallery, was intimidated. She hated meeting a large number of strangers, and a familiar feeling of shyness, helplessness and irritation at herself for not having grown out of it came over her, despite the fact she was wearing her morale-boosting dress, a velvet Jean Muir she'd found in a charity shop. She didn't want to go down those stairs and join the group of loud, confident people, standing with drinks in their hands, all of whom seemed to know one another. Although there was Anna, who certainly didn't know anyone except Charlie, smiling and chatting with a thin-lipped woman in an expensive-looking green dress.

"Come on," said Henry. "Down we go." He followed her down the stairs, and then guided her across to meet his uncle, a fresh-faced, tall man who seemed to have a much milder temperament than his wife, and then, in rapid succession, Georgina was introduced to a jolly man who turned out to be a senior judge — Henry whispered in her ear that in the bad old days he would most certainly have been a hanging judge, despite his amiable appearance — and a woman with several chins who bred Shetland ponies.

All of them asked Georgina how she had injured her arm, and all of them had remedies to suggest. Some made a kind of sense, such as that far too many people wrote and published books these days, so one the less was all to the good; others were less practical, one coming up with a gruesome account of how a niece had crushed various ligaments and had been cured by alternating compresses of ice and extreme heat.

Georgina was beginning to feel that possibly these were not her kind of people. Most of them seemed to know each other very well, and they were exchanging gossip and news about other people that Georgina didn't know, and by the sound of it wouldn't want to know. Her only consolation was that Henry was looking distinctly bored.

"Is this why Sophie wriggled out of the invitation?" she asked Henry, sotto voce, nodding at the other guests.

"Actually, Sophie gets on very well with my aunt and her friends. The one thing all these people have in common, in case you haven't noticed, is horses. My aunt breeds horses, didn't I tell you? Sophie loves horses, and rides whenever she can."

"You too?"

"I do ride, and I like horses. That's how Sophie and I first met, when I was riding in Richmond Park, and she'd come off her horse. But I'm not fanatical."

Pamela Grandison shimmered towards them and addressed Henry. "Talk to Christian, he wants to know how you're getting on. Charm him, he's going to buy one of my Arabs." Without waiting for a reply, she flashed a smile and headed off to another cluster of guests.

"Arabs?" asked Georgina.

"Horses. Arabian horses."

"Big eyes and little ears with sweeping manes and tails, that zip along at high speed?"

"Those are the ones. Pam breeds them."

"What does your uncle do? Is he a horse-breeder as well?"

"No, he's a banker. That's how I got into banking."

"Has he been made redundant?"

Henry shook his head. "He doesn't do dangerous banking. He works for the family bank, not my family, I hasten to add, Pam's family. It's a private bank, been going since the year dot, all very staid and unadventurous, luckily for Rupert. I think he'd be hard put to explain what a credit derivative swap is. Although so would I, that's a lesson I learned the hard way, never invest in anything a bright ten-year-old couldn't understand."

Christian turned out to be a formidably tall man with a bald head and bristly eyebrows. He boomed at Henry, and said he was wasting his time with solar physics, he'd be back in a bank where he belonged as soon as this present little spot of trouble was behind them. He enquired what Georgina did, and discovering that she was a writer, announced with triumph that he hadn't read a book for twenty years.

"A publisher's delight," Henry murmured in Georgina's ear.

"He is," said Georgina. "Publishers always want to sell their books to people who don't read. They reckon it's an untapped market, one with the greatest potential for growth."

Georgina was drinking champagne, and the bubbles were making her want to sneeze. She put her glass down and pressed at her nose, while her eyes watered. At that moment a vision in a flame-coloured dress moulded on to an exquisite figure slid out from the other guests and wrapped herself around Henry.

"Hello, Foxy," Henry said, rescuing his glass and disentangling himself.

Georgina could see why she was nicknamed Foxy. Her flaming red hair was the giveaway.

"No Sophie, I was so delighted when Charlie told me that she couldn't come." She turned big green eyes on Georgina. "You must be Georgina, Henry's lodger. Charlie told me that Henry was bringing his resident author. Anyone is better than Sophie," she added, giving Henry a languishing look. "I've adored Henry ever since I had a crush on him at the age of thirteen, and he never casts a single glance in my direction. I'm so pleased that you're hardly seeing anything of Sophie these days."

"Behave, Foxy," said Henry, for once looking rather put out. "Sophie is away filming, she's very sorry to have to miss your birthday party, but work comes first."

"That's not what I heard. Never mind, at least you're here, and I'm sure you're going to look wonderfully glamorous and sexy in your costume tomorrow."

"Costume?"

"Didn't you read the invitation, Henry?"

"Not from cover to cover, no."

"Your bad, then. Because it said 'Costume' quite clearly on the invitation, which also, incidentally, was designed in a Regency style."

Foxy drifted off to find other prey, leaving Henry saying rude things under his breath. "Costume! Fancy dress. Why the devil didn't Charlie warn me? If I'd known, I certainly wouldn't be here."

Nor would I, Georgina said, but to herself, not wanting to fuel Henry's temper.

"No good blaming me," said Charles, when Henry buttonholed him a few moments later. "I didn't spot that either, got a bit of a shock when Foxy mentioned it to me just now. Could have guessed she'd pull something like that, you know how she's always loved to dress up, and she has a thing about the Regency. She's going as Lady Caroline Lamb, whoever she was, sounds like a slut from what she told me."

"What, we have to go as historical characters, isn't it enough to blackmail us into pantaloons?"

"Silk stockings, to be correct. So Foxy informed me."

The two men looked at one another, gloom written on their faces.

"What about you, Anna, what are you going to wear?" Georgina asked. "I've brought my sole evening dress, and it's completely twenty-first-century."

"I have a vintage dress I bought at a church sale, which is from the nineteen seventies."

"Cheer up," said Charles. "Meet me tomorrow morning at the dressing-up box."

Henry sighed. "Has it come to that?"

"Dressing-up box?" Georgina said. "Tutus with fairy wings and cowboy outfits?"

"Not quite," said Henry. "Pam's family went in a lot for amateur theatricals, and so they've got quite a collection. What a waste of time, and what a sight we'll look."

A waiter came past, collecting their glasses. He was a tall young man, with very pale hair, and Anna gave a shriek of delight as she saw him, and broke into a flood of what Georgina supposed must be Polish.

Ill timing, since at that moment Lady Pamela came over to talk to Charles. "A friend of yours?" she asked Anna.

"A friend? No, he is my cousin, Stefan. What joy!"

Lady Pamela looked far from joyful. "I'm sure you can continue your conversation later on, but meanwhile perhaps he can continue with his duties."

Charles, anxious to draw his mother's attention away from Anna, whom she was looking at with narrowed eyes, asked if all the guests were there. "I'm feeling peckish."

"Three more to come. The Palmers rang, James was held up at the House. Ah, I think I hear them now."

"Palmers?" said Georgina apprehensively. Of course, it was a common enough name.

"James Palmer and his wife, Charlotte," said Charles. "He's an MP, strange chap, prone to look on the dark side of things, don't know how he ever got elected."

Well, her James Palmer was a critic and a dissolutionist, if there were such a thing; it couldn't be the same man.

It was. With a pretty wife, who had a cloud of dark hair, a delighted laugh and was quite heavily pregnant. "James is so droll," she was saying as they came into the hall.

The evening wasn't going well for Georgina. The champagne disagreed with her, she didn't care for Foxy, she was hungry, the thought of the dressing-up box appalled her, Lady Pamela's dislike of Anna annoyed her and now James Palmer had appeared. Oh well, things couldn't get much worse.

"Thank God," said Charles, as Rupert went to open the front door to admit the final arrival. "Now we can eat. Didn't know the parents had invited him, but this chap will be company for you, Gina, a fellow American, and I believe he works in your biz."

It had just turned into the dinner party from hell, as Dan Vesey removed his elegant cashmere coat and handed it to a hovering Pole.

THIRTY-ONE

Shades of Jane Austen gathered round Georgina as she went into the dining room. It was a perfect room and, as Henry told her, virtually unchanged for two centuries. The shining mahogany table was set with plain, heavy silver and austere glasses, all of which gleamed in the light from several candelabra. The floor was wooden, with yet another Oriental rug, and on the elegant sideboard was a silver rose bowl filled with dusky roses that matched the walls. The chairs had graceful Regency curves, and the portraits that hung around the walls were of men and women in the clothes of the late eighteenth and early nineteenth century.

"One can imagine Mr. and Mrs. Bennet presiding over the dinner party they gave for Mr. Bingley, and hoping Mr. Darcy appreciated the fat haunch of venison," Henry said, as he pushed her chair in for her.

Georgina was as glad to find Henry on

one side of her, as she was alarmed to find James Palmer on the other, but at least Dan Vesey was as far away from her as it was possible to be. "What have you done to your arm?" James Palmer asked. "Had a fall? Thought not, you don't look one of the horsey set. Tripped down the stairs, one too many, I dare say."

"RSI," said Georgina.

"They say once you get that it never goes away. Everyone will have it sooner or later, it's computers that cause it. I don't use one these days, I dictate to my secretary."

"I gather you're a member of Parliament."

"Yes, I didn't mention it when we met. Puts people off, fat cats, snouts in trough, all that kind of stuff. And don't give me that look of moral disapproval, I told you no lies. I did review your book, I do detest Jane Austen and I am gathering material for a documentary on the dissolution of the monasteries. Can't live on an MP's salary, not these days, not now they're keeping tabs on all one's expenses. That's my wife," he added, nodding down the table to where Charlotte Palmer was laughing at some remark made by the tall balding man. "Don't get married, take my advice, causes nothing but trouble. Of course, if you're in my job and you don't have a wife and

389

preferably children, everyone assumes you're gay."

"Does that matter? Who cares, these days?"

"Some do, some don't. I couldn't give a damn, I went to an all-boys public school, nothing in the buggery line bothers me. But my constituents are a lot prissier than I am, and they like a family man."

Georgina leaned back in her seat to allow a plate to be put in front of her.

"I warn you," said Henry, "there will be at least five courses, and you'll rise from the table feeling like a python. All perfectly delicious, but Pam has these rushes of blood to the head, and re-creates meals from some old recipe which belonged to an ancestor of hers. Good research for you, since it's probably the kind of food they ate at Mansfield Park."

Another nimble waiter had poured champagne into her glass. One of her glasses; she wondered how many wines were going to be served during the course of the meal. Lady Pamela's voice came commandingly down from the foot of the table, "You won't have any trouble with this, Georgina, because you can eat it with a fork. When you need to use a knife, I told one of the boys to cut your food up for you."

Having thus drawn the attention of the entire table to Georgina's sling, she turned back to the guests on her right, a dark middle-aged man with a five-o'clock shadow, wearing a soutane with a lavender sash.

"That's Pam's pet cleric," Henry whispered informatively. "You didn't meet him before dinner, because he only arrived about ten minutes ago. He's just flown in from Rome, he's one of your nomadic priests, always off somewhere for meetings and consultations."

"Is Lady Pamela Catholic?" asked Georgina. She knew that the English didn't consider religion a suitable topic for the dinner table, but she was curious.

"She is, Rupert isn't. Charlie and the others were all brought up as Catholics, that was the deal when they got married."

"So she can't object to Anna on religious grounds."

"True, but I think she'll find plenty of other things that she doesn't like about Anna."

Lady Pamela might find a lot she didn't like about Anna; Dan Vesey eyed Georgina as though she were Lucifer putting his head through the tent flaps.

"Holy shit, what are you doing here?" was

391

his friendly greeting over coffee in the drawing room. It was an enchanting room of chintz and velvet; at least enchanting until Dan Vesey came over and joined her on a sofa. "You haven't got time to hang around the English social circuit, you've got a book to write. I've got a lot riding on this book, and here you are, out in the sticks with your arm in a sling. What the hell do you think you're up to?"

"Nice to see you, Dan."

"Don't give me that. Yolanda says she's had nothing more from you, you don't answer emails or the phone, all you do is go out for goddamn walks every couple of hours."

So he was still spying on her. "Actually, I'm getting on fine. Don't worry about my arm, I hurt it, but it doesn't matter. Typing's so last century; I use voice recognition."

"Well, good for you, top marks, take a gold star, but where are the words?"

Thirty-Two

Georgina loved the kitchen at Motley Manor, where she found herself at midnight. It was old-fashioned, comfortable and functional, with dressers and wall cupboards with drawers and shelves and hooks, a beamed ceiling from which utensils, herbs and a ham hung, a pantry with marble slabs, a utility called a scullery, with a huge porcelain sink, and a large scrubbed wooden table in the centre of the room.

The cooking equipment was modern enough, but the kitchen was essentially the same as when he came to stay as a child, Henry told her. "I spent a lot of time in here, it was always my favourite place. Thank God Pam and Rupert have never gone in for granite work surfaces and all that stuff, this is how a kitchen should be."

It was a merry crowd there, much better company than in the dining room and drawing room, and Georgina, still recovering from her bruising encounter with Dan Vesey, began to relax. Henry had rescued her from Dan's cross-examination about her progress on the book, when he materialized like a guardian angel and smoothly took her away to the other side of the room. "You will excuse me if I borrow Georgina for a moment, the Monsignor wants to meet her."

Anna's cousin leapt to his feet and gave Georgina his chair. Anna and Charles were already sitting at the table, Anna talking a mixture of Polish and English, and Charles talking venison and wild boar recipes with a lanky, dark Pole called Ladislaw, who was the chef.

"My mother thinks Ladislaw should open a restaurant," said Charles. "She's offered to back him."

"Restaurants close faster than they open," said Ladislaw. "I like doing it this way, going into people's houses, cooking for them. No overheads, employ friends and relations for the night, no hassle. Even if I have to cook from strange recipes of two hundred years ago."

Henry had discovered that Anna's cousin, Stefan, the waiter, was doing a physics doctorate at Imperial College, and was enjoying an intense conversation about quarks.

Georgina sat in a happy haze. Dan Vesey must be off the premises now, as well as the Palmers, and she could put up with any amount of horse talk with any other guests still around. Tomorrow's evil, the Regency dance, was sufficient unto the day, and as for Monday and her arm and the book, that was in another time. Besides, surely her arm was hurting less. A couple of days off, and she'd be fine.

A wail rent the air.

Charles knew at once what it was. "Someone at the gate, I suppose some guests just discovered they left something behind." He got to his feet and went over to the door to look at the video screen.

Henry gave it a casual glance, then sprang to his feet. "That's Maud!" He was out of the kitchen door two seconds later. Charles pressed the button to open the gates, and then followed Henry at a run.

Georgina stared at the bedraggled figure on the screen. What was Maud doing out there, soaking wet, at this time of night?

She and Anna flew to the front door, and opened it. Lady Pamela's voice came out of the gloom of the gallery. "What's going on?"

Georgina looked up. "Maud's at the gate."

"Where's Charles? Henry?"

"They're on their way to the gate."

"On foot, I suppose, doing the hundred-yard dash." Lady Pamela swept past them, and two minutes later, the headlights of a car showed in front of the house before it headed off down the drive.

In no time at all, the car was back in front of the house, and Henry was bundling Maud out of the back seat and into the hall, where she sat pale-faced and sodden, her eyes panda-like from streaked mascara. "I'm perfectly all right," she said defiantly.

"How the hell did you get here? And why?" demanded Henry.

"I walked, okay? And I had to, because I was locked out. My phone and money and everything else were in the house. So I walked here."

"But it's five miles!"

"So?"

"On the road? In the dark?" said Henry furiously. "It's a miracle you weren't knocked down."

"No, it isn't. It isn't exactly a main road, is it? Whenever I heard a car, I just jumped in the ditch or hid in the hedge. I thought of hitching, but it didn't seem like a good idea. Besides, most of the cars were going the other way. Is there anything to eat?"

"Never mind that," said Henry. "I want to get to the bottom of this. Where was Nadia,

where were all your other friends? Why
didn't you just ring on the doorbell and get
let in?"

"They weren't there. Can I have something to eat, please? I haven't had anything
since lunch."

Lady Pamela came in through the front
door. She gave Maud one look, raised her
eyebrows in exasperation and took charge.

Breakfast at Motley Manor was an informal
affair, Georgina discovered when she came
down the next morning. After the large dinner, she'd felt she would never be hungry
again, but finding a sideboard laden with
bacon, eggs, sausages, and various other
goodies, she decided that the cup of coffee
which was all she'd planned she would have,
was not enough.

Henry, Charles and Anna were already in
the dining room. Maud, Henry informed
her, was fast asleep.

"Did you discover what happened to her?"
asked Georgina.

"My mother got it out of her," said
Charles. "Maud held out against her questioning for about thirty seconds, I gather,
and then tried a bundle of fibs for another
thirty seconds before she came up with the
truth."

"Which was," continued Henry, "that the sleepover didn't happen. And Nadia, who sounds a nasty piece of work, had only invited Maud as a stooge. She planned to spend the weekend with her boyfriend, and wanted Maud in the house to answer the phone if her mother rang, so that her mother would believe that she had friends there. One suspects that her mother doesn't entirely trust daughter Nadia."

"Such a mother, with such a daughter, is irresponsible," said Anna. "She was very foolish to go away and leave her daughter in the house, with or without friends. My mother would never have made such a silly mistake."

"But how did Maud come to be shut out?" Georgina asked.

"Nadia wasn't intending to have her boyfriend in the house for the weekend. Instead, they were flying off to Barcelona, no less, leaving Maud in the house. When she realized they were going and leaving her alone there, she rushed out of the house, the door locked behind her, all her things inside, while the boyfriend's car was driving away at high speed."

"Mum's furious," said Charles. "Further questioning elicited the information that Nadia is the same age as Maud. The boyfriend, according to Maud, must be in his twenties. So she's been on the phone, trying to track down one or other of Nadia's parents, the school and the police. Maud says that she doesn't think Nadia was planning to go back to school after the weekend."

"Sounds to me as though Maud might have made a good decision in taking herself out of that school of hers," said Georgina.

Lady Pamela walked into the kitchen. "Henry, we need to talk about Maud," she said without preamble.

"Good morning," said Charles.

His mother looked around as though she had only just noticed that he and the others were there. "Good morning, Charles, everyone," and, speaking in the general direction of Georgina and Anna, she expressed a hope that they had slept well. Charles pulled out a chair for her, and silently placed a cup of coffee in front of her. "You may as well say what you have to say about Maud here and now," said Charles. "Since Anna and Georgina live in Henry's house, and have seen a lot of Maud, they probably have some sensible ideas."

"It seems extraordinary to me that with three adults in the house, Maud has been allowed to get away with what she has.

Henry, why didn't you tell me she'd run away from St. Adelberta's? She says they won't have her back, but that's nonsense. I can make a phone call this morning, and she can return there this afternoon."

"She'd only run away again, Pam," said Henry. "And, judging by what we've heard about Nadia, I'm not sure that the company there is what I'd want for Maud."

"Every school has its problem girls," said his aunt.

"And it appears that Maud is one of them."

"I blame your parents. They've brought Maud up extraordinarily badly; they may be eccentrics, but they shouldn't make her into one, it simply isn't fair on the girl. They have no business to go away for six months at a stretch, and to such a ridiculous place. You must get in touch with your mother directly, Henry, and tell her she has to come home at once and sort Maud out."

"No can do," said Henry. "They were taken out there on one of the Antarctic survey ships, and it won't call again for weeks yet, when it'll take them off again. If it were a full-scale emergency, a medical matter, something like that, then they might launch a special operation to get them out of the Antarctic. But I'm afraid Maud running away from school doesn't count. She's my responsibility while they're there, and I say she isn't going back to that school. I've done my best to find a new one, but with no luck so far. It's just a matter of time, though."

"It's a pity she isn't a Catholic," said Charles. "Then she could go to Ampleforth. Very few students run away from there, as far as I know. The monks would soon sort her out."

"Monks," exclaimed Anna. "You can't be serious, she can't go into a monastery."

"Calm down," said Charles. "It isn't a monastery, well, not exactly. It's a boarding school, where I went, actually, only these days they take girls as well. In my day it was only boys."

"Well, we aren't Catholics," said Henry. "And my mother doesn't want Maud to go to a co-ed school. She'll consider it when Maud gets to the sixth form, but until then she thinks girls are better off in single-sex schools."

"I agree with her," said Lady Pamela. "But in the circumstances, Henry, I think you're going to have to consider a co-ed school. I suggest Hartbury. I'm a governor there. It's an unusual school, and they very often have a lot of success with children who haven't fitted in elsewhere."

"I've heard of it, of course," said Henry doubtfully.

"I suppose Maud still plays the oboe? They might give her a music scholarship. For myself, I think all this music does a girl no good at all. Much better to be good at sport, then you fit in at any school. Foxy never had any problems at St. Adelberta's, and she can't tell one note from another."

"Maud does need to be at school, and soon, I agree," said Henry.

"I'll give the headmaster of Hartbury a ring this morning," said Lady Pamela. "She may be able to start after half term, if they have a place."

She finished her coffee and left, leaving the others feeling rather as though a hurricane had passed through.

"An exhausting woman, my mother," said Charles, reaching out and taking Anna's hand. "But her heart's in the right place."

Georgina had her doubts about that.

Charles got up. "Come on, dressing-up time."

THIRTY-THREE

Foxy's dance was being held in a stately home not far from Motley Manor. "The house used to belong to Pam's family," said Henry as they drove up a straight drive, torches glowing on either side. "It fell into rack and ruin after the war, and it was far too big for the family to keep up. Then, about ten years ago, a millionaire bought it and restored it to its original glory. He's rarely there, but it's used for filming, and he's let Foxy have it for her party, because she's his goddaughter."

The Palladian façade of the house was lit up, and, to Georgina's amazement, there were two white-breeched footmen in powdered wigs standing one on either side of the open door to greet the guests.

Charles was rather pleased with the outfit he'd discovered in the dressing-up box, which was a blue coat that didn't fit him too badly, and a pair of pantaloons. Henry had gone for black, saying that if he had to dress up and look like a fool, at least he could be inconspicuous. Privately, Georgina thought he looked very handsome in the long jacket, white shirt and a stock which his aunt had tied for him with ruthless efficiency.

Anna had found the perfect dress, falling on it with little cries of delight. It was pale blue, which went with her eyes and her fair prettiness, floating muslin with a satin sash. Georgina hadn't been so lucky. The only dress that fitted her made her feel like a piece of furniture that had been reupholstered. "I'm sure brocade is completely wrong for the period, and I know I saw a cushion here at Motley Manor in exactly this fabric."

"You probably did," said Charles. "A lot of these costumes were run up in the days when there was always a servant who could sew, using whatever material came to hand. Still, I think it suits you."

Looking at the glorious costumes on many of the other guests, Georgina could at least feel sure that nobody would look twice at hers.

Foxy greeted them with joyful cries. She was wearing an almost transparent gauze dress, with a spangled rust-coloured gossamer shawl draped over her elbows. She looked sensational, and Henry told her so, earning himself a lingering kiss on the mouth.

A string quartet was playing in the entrance hall, and as they moved with the throng towards the ballroom, they heard more music wafting out from there. The musicians, all in costume, were seated on a small balcony overlooking the ballroom.

"I can't think what Foxy is up to," said Charles. "It's all very well having those people up there, scraping and bowing away, but she's mad if she thinks anyone is going to be able to dance to that."

Foxy appeared beside him, as though by magic. "Oh, yes, they are, Charlie. Trust me. This is no ordinary dance, it is a re-creation of a past lifestyle; it's an experience."

"An experience of what?" said Henry suspiciously.

"Of a Regency ball."

"Good for you, anyhow, Georgina," said Henry. "You'll be able to pick up plenty of local colour. Only if Foxy reckons this lot are going to dance, she's wrong."

He had underestimated Foxy's ingenuity. Not only had she employed the musicians, but she had arranged for a teacher of historic dance to attend, together with some of her team of professional dancers. "In no time at all," she said, "we'll all be dancing minuets, Janine says it's terribly easy, and later on, there's even going to be a quadrille."

Henry closed his eyes, a pained expression on his face. Georgina felt no happier about it than he did, not because she wasn't interested in minuets, but because it reminded her of the book she should, even now, be writing. Although, with her arm hurting the way it did, she couldn't write or dance.

"I expect it only hurts if people jolt it," said Foxy, "I shall warn everyone to be extra careful. Don't think you can get out of dancing, everyone here tonight is going to dance."

Georgina found herself standing next to Rupert Grandison. He looked extremely distinguished in what appeared to be a very well fitting nineteenth-century evening dress. He noticed her looking him up and down. "Lucky thing, there was a time in the nineteen thirties when costume parties were all the rage. My father-in-law had this made by his tailor and fortunately it fits me pretty well. Pam is wearing a costume of her mother's from the same time."

Georgina thought that Lady Pamela's

costume was extraordinary, consisting as it did of a puce satin high-waisted dress beaded with brilliants, and a matching turban which sported an immense feather held in place with a large diamond, which Georgina suspected was genuine. She carried a fan, and, unlike many of the guests, appeared completely unselfconscious about her appearance.

Foxy was right about everyone dancing, but wrong about Georgina taking part. She tried but found her movements awkward and clumsy because of the sling, and after being jostled once or twice by other dancers, she retreated to sit on the gilt chair and watch the proceedings.

In fact, she was happy to do so, and after a while she removed herself from the ballroom and made her way upstairs to the musicians' gallery. She stood at the back and looked down at the dancers. For the first time she could see why dancing was so central to Jane Austen's novels. She watched the couples dancing side by side, moving forward, backward and then to the left and to the right, hands linked in a high, graceful hold.

The first strong beat was followed by the light, tripping second and third beats, and the elegant, graceful movements were strangely sexy. And, even though many of the dancers were having to concentrate on the steps, they also found time to talk to one another.

Henry took Georgina in to supper, and they sat at a table with Charles and Anna and some other lively, noisy people whom Charles and Henry knew but she and Anna didn't. Anna was completely self-possessed, not at all uncomfortable at being among a group of strangers, and said that she liked the dancing very much indeed. "It is exhilarating, it is a shame that you can't join in."

"Did you see her?" Charles asked Georgina. "She picked it up at once, she's a terrific dancer, light on her feet and looks wonderful doing it."

Georgina liked the pride with which he praised Anna. She also thought that Henry danced rather well, although the sight of him going down the dance with Foxy, laughing and talking, had rather irritated her.

After supper the dancing resumed, and Georgina went back to a corner of the ballroom to watch. Here she was joined after a few minutes by a pink-faced girl wearing an ornate gown with lots of ruffles around the bottom. She plumped herself down besides Georgina, and let out a fat sigh.

"I've got a bad toe," she announced. "Ali Baba stood on it a while ago, he's my horse, you know, and I'm losing the nail. My toe's hurting like mad, and although I tried dancing in my stockings, it's just too painful. Does your arm hurt much? Have you broken it?"

Georgina explained.

"Well, a writer!" said the girl. "I always thought I'd like to write a book, but I'm too dim. I like reading, though; what's the title of yours? I'll look out for it."

Georgina had an idea that *Magdalene Crib* might not be the kind of book that her companion liked to read.

"I'm Lally, by the way," the girl said. "Lally Rushworth. You came with Henry, didn't you? Is he rather cut up about Sophie?"

"Why should he be?"

"Well, they aren't together any more, are they?"

"They are, as far as I know."

"I heard she'd taken up with one of her fellow actors, or perhaps there was nothing in it. People are such gossips. Do you know many people here?"

"Practically nobody."

"Well, I know everyone. I can tell you all about them." She followed the direction of

Georgina's eyes. Georgina was gazing at one of the most attractive men she had ever seen. He was standing out of the dance, and talking to an equally attractive young woman, with lively, laughing eyes. She was looking up at him with a smile on her lips, and he was bending slightly forward, with such a look of affection on his face that it quite took her breath away.

"That's Fitzwilliam, gorgeous, isn't he? No good casting your eyes in that direction, though, he doesn't have eyes for anyone except Liz. They're getting married before Christmas. Lucky her, I say."

Georgina turned her attention away from the couple whose delight in each other brought a lump to her throat, and found herself looking at a dark man with a sensuous mouth and a rakish air.

"That's Willoughby, and that long-necked woman beside him is Caroline, Caroline Grey, they're getting married soon, too. He's marrying her for her money, she's a lawyer who does something called intellectual property, makes about a million a year. He's terribly expensive and doesn't earn much himself. He went around for ages with Marianne, and she's still awfully cut up about him."

Georgina closed her eyes, wondering if

she had had too much wine with her supper. She must be mishearing what this girl was saying. This whole Jane Austen thing was becoming a fixation and unbalancing her mind.

Lally was still talking. "That's Sir Thomas over there, Sir Thomas Bertram. He's quite ancient and a bit stately, but rather a sweetie really. His wife is the most indolent woman I've ever met, I'm terribly surprised he managed to get her here tonight."

This was too much. Making an excuse, Georgina left Lally to her own devices and walked over to the other side of the room. There after a few minutes, she was joined by Henry, breathless after his attempts at the quadrille.

"You know, this dancing has got something. Foxy says they're going to do a waltz next, do you think you could grit your teeth and dance with me?"

Georgina knew it would be painful, but on the other hand she wanted to waltz with Henry. "I've been having the strangest conversation with that girl sitting over there," she told him as he led her on to the floor. "She was telling me about people here, and I had the strangest fancy that they all were characters out of Jane Austen's novels. I think I need to see a shrink."

"What girl? I didn't see anyone with you."

Georgina gave up. She shut her eyes for a moment, opened them, and then with Henry's strong arm around her waist, and his count of one, two, three sounding in her ears, began to waltz.

It was at that moment she was struck by three revelations, which reached her consciousness almost simultaneously.

Here, at the ball, for the first time, she appreciated how the world of Jane Austen's novels had intruded into her everyday life in such a mysterious way, nudging her into an acceptance of the vitality and existence the characters of a master storyteller could take on. Plot is incidental, characters live, she muttered to herself as Henry, holding her with kind care, swung her round.

"What did you say?" he asked.

"Nothing."

What about those people who'd drifted in and out of her sight, apparently from the nineteenth century? They weren't characters from Jane Austen, nor were they characters from her version of *Love and Friendship.* Whoever they were, they weren't Susan or Lady Carcenet or anyone from their circle. Whoever they were, they had a message for her, and it was time she paid attention to what it might be.

Thirdly, and this disturbed her more than all the rest, she realized she was falling in love with Henry.

Thirty-Four

It was some while since Georgina had felt so depressed on a Monday morning. In general, Monday mornings held no threat for her, she was usually happy that a new week was beginning and inclined to look forward to what the following days would bring.

Not this Monday. This Monday she woke up with a feeling of oppression. Outside her window, the weather had reverted to that state of grey sky and drizzle where she couldn't tell where the clouds ended and the rain began. She had a nagging headache. A hangover? No, this was a headache of foreboding, a headache brought on not by what was past, but what was to come, and by the shadow that lurked at the back of her mind, the shadow of her impending departure from Henry's house and Henry's life.

As soon as the book was finished, she'd

have to move. It would be too painful being here, seeing Henry every day, and, worst of all, seeing him and Sophie together, when Sophie deigned finally to appear. For a moment she hated Sophie — how could she treat Henry in so cavalier a fashion? But she didn't really hate Sophie, she was simply jealous of her. And jealousy, Georgina was very well aware, was about the most destructive emotion going, and one she wanted nothing to do with.

Work was the answer, work would be her immediate refuge. If it didn't bring her heartsease, it could provide a distraction, and some solace. An occupied mind shut out emotion, she'd learned that as a girl.

She swallowed a couple of painkillers and turned on her computer. An email from Yolanda Vesey. She had sent twenty thousand words to her before going off for the weekend. Yolanda Vesey was evidently an eager beaver, a woman who worked on weekends. Georgina heaved a sigh of relief as she read the email. Yolanda Vesey was surprisingly complimentary. Her first analysis showed that sentence length, grammatical constructions, word length, and vocabulary choice were well within the parameters that she had set out. She would await the next twenty thousand words by the end of the week.

Georgina gingerly tapped a key or two with her right hand, and wished she hadn't. When she applied her left-hand fingers to the key she had an ominous tingling sensation again.

It was Maud who came up with a plan. "Even if the school takes me, and Aunt Pamela thinks they will, I shan't be starting until after half term. Henry is going to take me down later in the week to look at it, but apart from that I've got plenty of time. Why don't you dictate the book into a tape recorder, and then I'll key it into the computer for you? It can't be too difficult, typists used to do it all the time."

Clutching at straws, Georgina said to herself, but she didn't have much else to cling to.

"Print out what you've done so far, so I know where the story is going, and then you get dictating, and I'll get typing. Henry's got a little mike that plugs into his iPod, you can borrow that."

Every fibre of Georgina's being told her that this wasn't going to work. She wrote with her hands, not with her voice. There were people, she knew, who wrote books by dictation, as she had discovered when she read about Walter Scott and his secretaries.

Maud was more sanguine. As she carried the pages off, she said airily that it was simply a matter of trusting yourself. She had a good book about how the left brain and right brain meshed, or didn't mesh, maybe Georgina would like to look at it while she was waiting for Maud to finish reading the manuscript. "You should be able to dictate much more quickly than you type," Maud pointed out helpfully. "So this way you might actually get the book finished in time."

Georgina plugged the microphone into the iPod, shut her eyes and tried to think of something to say. Her mind was a blank. Okay, she'd read something into it, just to get the hang of it. A minute later she was reading the headlines from the news off the screen. It didn't seem so very difficult, and when she played it back it sounded quite good. So she could begin. "Chapter Eight," she said, and then pressed the pause button. She couldn't think of anything to say, maybe she needed to get the imaginative side of her mind running. Maybe if she played a game for a while, nothing too hard on the hand, it would do the trick.

A bang on the door, and Georgina looked up, realizing that half the morning had gone. Maud, a wild look in her eyes, was standing at the door clutching the manuscript.

Georgina started guiltily. "Are you waiting to begin? I haven't got very far yet, it's going to take some getting used to."

"Just as well," said Maud.

"Have you read it? Yolanda Vesey has and she says it's absolutely right for Jane Austen's style."

"I don't know about style, I mean I recognize words and phrases here and how Jane Austen might have used them, but really, what I've got to say, is — well, not to wrap up the truth, it's unreadable."

Georgina's first reaction was one of fury. She snatched the script out of Maud's hands. "Maud, really, I knew it was a mistake, one should never give a draft to other people to read. It's impossible for anyone else to understand what a writer's trying to do."

"Come off it, Georgina. That's not a draft, I never saw anything so polished. The trouble is, it isn't Jane Austen, because what it is, is dull. Jane Austen is never dull. I had to force myself to read past the first twenty pages or so, I could tell to a sentence, even if I didn't know, where Jane Austen left off and you started."

"That's a sweeping condemnation."

"Well, there's no point you going on writing another hundred thousand words that nobody will ever want to read. It's no more Jane Austen than the Highway Code. It's all there, the names and characters and situations and all that, but all the people in it are as dead as dodos. Lifeless. Unquick. It's like Henry said, your heart isn't in it."

With those words, and darting a quick look at Georgina's drained face, Maud whisked herself out of the room, for once not shutting the door with a bang.

Life hadn't been a bundle of joy recently, but that Monday would go down in Georgina's memory as the worst day in a long time. At least before, she had the feeling that once she got started, she could probably do it. Now she knew that she couldn't. She'd given it her best try, and, she had to admit Maud was perfectly right, it was terrible. Leaden hardly began to describe it.

Georgina took some faint satisfaction in slowly ripping the manuscript into tiny pieces and throwing the fragments into her wastepaper basket, and a kind of catharsis in dumping the document and its backup copies into the trash and emptying it. Of course it still existed out in cyberspace, since Yolanda had a copy; she just prayed that she didn't show it to her brother. Or perhaps Dan Vesey neither knew nor cared that it was so dreary.

Livia would.

Maud, with rare tact, took herself off for the afternoon. Anna was out, and Georgina had the house to herself. She prowled about unhappily, turned the television on and off, thought of getting lost in a computer game again, decided against it, made herself cups of coffee which she didn't drink and a sandwich that she didn't eat. She turned the radio on. It was a book programme, and they were discussing adaptations of Jane Austen's novels for television and film. She contemplated hurling the radio into the yard, but didn't have the energy nor the use of her right arm to make it an effective gesture.

Finally, she could stand being in the house no longer. She put on a shabby old jacket, which she had been meaning to throw away, but which suited her mood, rammed her beret on her head and, eyes down and shoulders hunched, went out to go for a long walk in the rain.

Henry was staying late at college for an evening lecture. Anna and Maud were so sympathetic that Georgina wanted to scream at them. The fish pie tasted like cotton wool with bits in it, and soon after eating Georgina went up to her room, had a bath and went to bed.

Music woke her out of her sleep, startling her. Bemused by the sound, she sat up; was she dreaming? Then the bedroom door swung open, to reveal Maud standing there with her oboe, playing "Happy Birthday to You." It was Georgina's twenty-eighth birthday, and she had forgotten all about it.

THIRTY-FIVE

Not so the others. Anna had knitted her an exquisite jumper in dark green and scarlet, in a mixture of mohair and scraps of silk; it was a work of art, and Georgina loved it. Maud had bought her a brooch. "It's only costume jewellery, but when I saw it I thought you'd really like it." Georgina, knowing that Maud had very little money, was touched; she just hoped that Maud hadn't spent too much on it, but Anna reassured her. "She spent hours looking for it, going round all the charity shops until she found just what she wanted. I don't think it cost a lot, but I told her that it was a gift that you would appreciate very much."

Henry had gone out early, Anna said. He was going to be back in good time, and there was to be a special meal to celebrate her birthday. Charlie was coming up from the country, she added, saying his name with a warmth that made Maud and Georgina exchange knowing looks.

Henry's present was downstairs on the kitchen table. Attached to it was a large label, OPEN NOW. Georgina unwrapped the parcel, and felt a stab of disappointment as she took out a set of headphones with a microphone attached, and an item of computer software. DICTATE, it said on the box in large letters. Henry had written on a Post-it in his clear handwriting, "I think this is what you need."

Maud pulled a face. "Henry wouldn't say what he'd got you, but I can't say it looks very exciting. What is it? A game?"

Georgina was reading the leaflet that accompanied it. "No, it's a voice recognition program. You talk into it, and it comes up on your computer as text. Or that's the theory; I've heard that these programs don't ever work. Well, it's kind of him to think of it," she said unenthusiastically.

"Open the card," said Maud.

It was a big card, in a thick envelope. She took it out and opened it and a mellifluous voice filled the kitchen:

Loving in truth, and fain in verse my love
    to show,
That the dear she might take some
    pleasure of my pain,

Pleasure might cause her read, reading
  might make her know,
Knowledge might pity win, and pity grace
  obtain. . . .

Startled, Georgina shut the card, then slowly opened it again for a second or two before closing it and putting it back in the envelope.

"It's kind of a reverse howler, sweet words instead of shrieks and nags. I love those talking cards," said Maud. "That's by Sir Philip Sidney, he wrote some good lyrics." Humming to herself, she clomped out of the room. Georgina sat down at the table, across from Anna, who was looking at some papers with a worried expression.

"Homework?" said Georgina. "Need any help?"

Anna pursed her lips. "No, not homework. This is a form that Stefan has to fill in, for the university. It is to do with what happens to him next year, when he has finished his doctorate. His English is good, but he finds official language difficult, and so he asked me to read the form and the documentation through for him. Only I don't understand it at all."

"May I see?" Georgina said.

Anna passed the folder over, and Georgina

began to read. She looked up at Anna. "Has he gone to the Administration Office about this?"

"Yes, but they didn't help him."

"It's a muddle, that's all. Some of this is relevant to him, and some of it won't be." Georgina looked at Anna's troubled face. She reached out and touched her hand. "Look, why don't you let me deal with this for Stefan? I'm used to this stuff, and I've a friend on the admin side at my college who'll know the people at Imperial. Between us, I'm sure we can sort it out for your cousin. If he won't mind my helping, that is. I don't want to interfere."

Anna's smile lit up the room. "Of course he will not mind. But this is too big a kindness, you don't have time, you need every minute for your book."

"No, I don't, not any more, not at the moment. And as for kindness, look at all you do for me."

Georgina took the folder and her presents back to her room. After a swift burst of activity, going through Stefan's forms before phoning her friend at college and bundling up the paperwork to post to her, she sank into inertia, utterly at a loose end, as though she were waiting for something to happen.

Like what?

Well, she had better try out the program that Henry had given her, so that she could say thank you nicely when he came back at the end of the day. "Only takes minutes to train," it said on the box. She was sceptical. However, she put on the headset, plugged herself in and methodically read through the training texts. So far so good. She could try it out, but she had no enthusiasm for it, and she'd had enough of reading out loud for the moment. She took off the headset, switched off the programme and picked up a book, which turned out to be *The Letters of Jane Austen.* No, she couldn't cope with them right now.

Well, she'd better have another go with this dictation thing. At least the computer software wouldn't read what she'd written and tell her it was dull. She opened a new document, and after a moment's hesitation spoke into the microphone.

"It is a truth universally acknowledged, that a single man in possession of good fortune, must be in want of a wife."

On the screen appeared *That you; as a single man Thresher good fortune must be in want of a wife.*

Gobbledygook. She adjusted the headset, and tried again.

A pause and then up came the words, *It is*

not a single possession of auction asked me.

Gibberish.

She studied the diagram in the leaflet intently, manoeuvred the microphone into what must be the right position and tried again.

It is acknowledged the station book must be in want of a knife.

What was that computer phrase? GIGO: Garbage In, Garbage Out. This was something different, this was GPIGO: great prose in, garbage out.

Of course, what she really needed was a program to work the other way: garbage in, great prose out.

She gave up, removed the headset and abandoned the program. Whatever might be the solution to her writing problems, this wasn't it.

Henry would understand, he must have had to deal with duff software in his time. Thinking of Henry, she realized that she hadn't listened to his card all the way through. She sat in her armchair, and opened it. The voice of the man reading the poem was beautiful, and the lyrical words flowed over her, sending tingles up and down her spine, as she listened to the heart of a poet seeking to express his love.

As though her senses were suddenly sharpened, the next lines sang out in her head.

I sought fit words to paint the blackest
    face of woe:
Studying inventions fine, her wits to
    entertain,
Oft turning others' leaves, to see if thence
    would flow
Some fresh and fruitful showers upon my
    sunburned brain.
But words came halting forth, wanting
    Invention's stay;
Invention, Nature's child, fled stepdame
    Study's blows;
And others' feet still seemed but
    strangers in my way.
Thus, great with child to speak, and
    helpless in my throes,
Biting my truant pen, beating myself for
    spite:
"Fool," said my Muse to me, "look in thy
    heart, and write."

She listened again. And again, silently speaking the words with the reader.

Look in thy heart, and write.

She shot out of her chair as though impelled by some unknown force, sat down at her desk, tugged the headset into position, and willing it to work, began to speak.

It came out as gibberish. Random words, half sentences, nonsense, which left Georgina voiceless and frustrated. She picked up the microphone stand, ready to hurl it across the room, when she noticed a little glowing red light.

Perhaps if she switched the microphone on, she might get better results.

For the next few weeks, Georgina lived in two separate worlds, and time-travelled between them. World One was *Love and Friendship,* an early-nineteenth-century world inhabited by a vigorous, spirited and independent-minded Susan, by her aunt, the vicious, scheming, depraved Lady Carcenet, by her suitors, a world of horses and carriages and candles and oil lamps, and a world alive with love and passion.

World Two was a twenty-first-century world in which, strangely detached, and with a sense of unreality, she spent the hours of her days and nights when she wasn't writing or thinking about Susan and her destiny.

The detachment allowed her to put aside, as though in a shut-off compartment, her feelings for Henry, and, more practically, made her fearless in dealing with Livia

Harkness and Dan and Yolanda Vesey. When they emailed her, they received short, sharp, noncommittal replies. Her writing was going well, she'd be in touch in due course. She ignored their text messages, deleted their voice mail messages and refused to speak to anyone on the landline.

In this world, she was pleased when Maud was given a place at Hartbury. "Wonder how many favours Aunt Pam had to call in to pull that off," Maud said when she came in to say goodbye before Henry drove her down to Hartbury for the second half of term. She threw her arms around Georgina and hugged her, a display of affection so uncharacteristic from reserved Maud that Georgina quite forgave her the spasm of pain it caused her arm.

She listened, as though hearing news from another planet, when Henry, relieved to have his sister back at school, but worried that she might not settle down, told her that he'd heard from Maud who said it wasn't too bad, although the food was foul. "She's doing an oboe solo at the end-of-term concert, we could go down."

Georgina borrowed Maud's recording of Mozart oboe sonatas, which she listened to while she walked her story, wrapped up against the blasts of an early and spiteful winter, occasionally looking up at a redbrick façade of an eighteenth-century house and mentally placing a scene inside, setting her characters in a first-floor drawing room lit by the glow of candlelight.

Henry and Anna treated her with a tact and sensitivity that, had she given it a moment's thought, would have amazed her. She worked solidly every morning, and after a few days, when she realized that the text, although readable, needed a lot of correction that she couldn't possibly attempt, given the amount of mouse work involved, Henry came up with an immediate and practical solution.

"Send your work to someone who can sort out the errors and send you back a clean text." He found just the person, a housebound young mother with an eye for detail and copy editing experience. "Damn the expense," he said. "Money won't be a problem if you can get the book written. Here's Marcia's email address, she's waiting to hear from you, and she knows it's urgent."

In the afternoons, Georgina read through what Marcia sent back, and dictated bubble comments to the script for later revision. In the evenings, Anna cooked wonderful food for her, and afterwards she would sit wrapped in a silent dream in the drawing room, listening to Anna playing the piano. Henry often joined them, stretching his long legs out in front of the fire with one of his heavy textbooks on his knee.

Thirty-Six

One Tuesday morning, Georgina was at her desk as usual. Outside, a pale, wintry sun was making the last remnants of frost twinkle on the leaves. Inside, snug in a scarlet cashmere jersey, she was far away from modern-day Marylebone. It was ten o'clock in London, but to her it was a summer evening, and Susan, wearing a pale green flounced gown, was making her entrance into a room full of fashionable people, with hundreds of candles shedding a warm glow over the throng.

A tap on the door. Georgina ignored it; she knew that neither Henry nor Anna would dream of disturbing her when she was working.

She was wrong, Henry had done the unforgivable and intruded into her other world. He stood at her door, looking unusually elegant in a charcoal banker's suit.

Georgina paused her speech programme,

and looked round, savage at being inter-rupted. "Is there an emergency? Is the house on fire?"

"No," said Henry, coming into the room. "But you have to come out of your fictive trance, just for today. Put on some glad rags, we're going to a wedding."

Georgina stared at him. "Wedding? Whose wedding?"

"Anna's wedding."

Georgina blinked, dragging her mind back into the present day. She had a character called Anna in her book, and that Anna had a wedding scheduled for around Chapter Forty-eight. But Henry couldn't be talking about her Anna. "Anna? What do you mean, Anna's wedding?"

Henry spoke slowly and clearly. "Anna and Charlie are getting married today. They've kept completely quiet about it, and only let friends and relatives know this morning. Mind you, anyone could have seen it coming."

Georgina, the world of her book now receding, was troubled. She had been so wrapped up in her writing that she hadn't noticed what was happening around her. Yes, Charlie had been at the house rather a lot, but he had explained his frequent visits by saying that he was doing a lot of promotional work in London at the moment. She was ashamed not to have noticed that Anna and Charlie were so much in love that they were going to get married. And what would Lady Pamela have to say about it?

"Pam is furious," said Henry. "I've had her on the phone for half an hour, telling me I've got to put a stop to it."

"What exactly does she have against Anna, apart from her being Polish?"

"I don't have the time to tell you. Come on, get a move on, or we'll arrive after the bride."

Georgina got up and headed for her cupboard. She spoke over her shoulder, "Where are they getting married, at the register office?"

"Anna, at a register office? Don't be ridiculous, the ceremony is at St. Stephen's, it's a Catholic church with a Polish priest, and a largely Polish congregation. For all I know, the service will be in Polish."

"That certainly won't please Lady Pamela, or isn't she coming? Turn your back while I get changed."

"I'm not sure. It sounded like she was planning a boycott, but then I spoke to Rupert and he said he would make sure she would be there. He's rather pleased, he's got a romantic streak, the old devil."

Ten minutes later, clad in an elegant claret-coloured suit, and with her make-up bag in her hand, Georgina followed Henry out of the house.

He hailed a taxi. "I'll never find anywhere to park near the church," he said, holding the door open for Georgina. As the taxi rumbled towards the church, Georgina applied her make-up, and then put on the earrings she'd snatched up as she left her room.

Georgina had left love and romance on the page only to find herself face-to-face with the real thing. The church was Victorian and gloomy, but the altar was heaped with lilies, and huge wax candles enclosed Anna and Charlie in a soft circle of light as they stood in front of the priest, bathed in fragrant incense. Georgina sat completely still while Anna and Charlie exchanged their vows in clear, certain voices. The way Charlie looked at Anna as he came back down the aisle from the altar with his bride on his arm made her heart turn over.

Anna, radiantly lovely in a cream silk dress she had made herself, was aglow with happiness. Next to Henry, Rupert Grandison was audibly sniffing. Lady Pamela had remained stony-faced throughout the service, and after the ceremony was over, although she condescended to give Anna a peck on the cheek, was clearly set to refuse to join the bride and groom and their friends for lunch at a Polish restaurant in Soho.

Rupert wasn't having any of it. Georgina overheard him having it out with his wife. "Charles is our son. Anna is now our daughter-in-law. They are man and wife, married in church, by a priest, so you can't pretend it hasn't happened. There's nothing you can do about it, other than accept it with a good grace. And, speaking for myself, I would far rather have Anna as a daughter-in-law than Hermione or any other of Charles's past girlfriends. Besides, I like Polish food, and I'm going to this lunch, with or without you."

It was a wonderful meal, lasting far into the afternoon, made even more enjoyable by the lively presence of Anna's Polish friends and relations and a posse of friends of Charlie's, who had abandoned desks at banks, law offices, and in the case of an Olympic rower, a training schedule on the choppy waters of the Thames, to come to the wedding.

Henry refused to let Georgina go back to her desk. "For one thing, you're tipsy, and anything you wrote would have to be rewritten in the clear light of day tomorrow, and for another, I shall feel desolate if I have to sit downstairs by myself. I'm going to take you out to a film."

Put like that, it would have been churlish to lock herself away upstairs again, and besides, Henry was right; she was in no state to write anything that would make sense. "We shall miss Anna," she said to Henry as they walked back from the cinema. "It'll be nothing but takeaways from now on."

"Don't you be so sure," said Henry cryptically.

"Are you planning to go on a cookery course?"

Henry didn't reply, but gave her a sardonic look as he opened the front door and stood back to let her go in.

When Georgina came downstairs into the kitchen the day after the wedding, feeling distinctly the worse for wear, she discovered why Henry hadn't been bothered by the prospect of takeaways. Anna, mindful of the gap her disappearance into the country to raise wild boar with Charlie would leave in Henry's household, had thoughtfully provided a replacement, and there was the lanky Pole whom Georgina had last seen in the kitchen at Motley Manor, with a long apron tied around his waist, making coffee.

"Hi, you remember me? I'm Stefan."

"You're the one doing physics at Imperial."

"That's right, and I've taken over from Anna. This is much better than the digs I've been in, I'm very grateful to Henry and Anna for fixing me up. You are a writer, Anna told me all about you, and how you have to spend all day and every day working. And you sorted out my application and funding papers for me, and I am grateful. So I make you a nourishing breakfast, and then you get back to work, okay?"

Stefan was also a pianist, although his repertoire was different from Anna's, and his playing was often interrupted by a question from Henry. Georgina would slip away as the two men settled down to an interesting discussion about strangelets, the Higgs boson and other mysterious particles.

THIRTY-SEVEN

Henry was thankful that Georgina seemed to be coming up with the goods, although he found her a strange companion during these weeks; distant, and often, as his Scottish cousin would have said, away with the fairies.

And he was slightly disturbed by the brightly coloured Post-it notes Georgina was in the habit of leaving about the house attached to doors, the banister rail, mirrors, pictures and even, once, on the keyboard of the piano — Stefan took that one off with a tsk of disapproval, and carefully polished the keys to remove any trace of stickiness. Henry ventured to ask what they were, and she looked at him with vague eyes.

"The notes? They're just to remind me of things I need to research. Not in any great depth, I haven't got time to do that. Wikipedia and Google give me most of what I need."

That was all very well, but Henry couldn't help wondering why she needed to research these particular subjects.

The Peninsular War
Coach travel over the Alps
DUELLING — swords or pistols
Elopement — affairs — taboos
Men's underwear — ring costume museum
BROTHELS in St. James's Street & Paris
The third sex in 18th-century England

The third sex? Brothels? Paris? In a Jane Austen novel?

He didn't dare make further enquiries about the notes, because he appreciated that the last thing she wanted at the moment was to talk about anything to do with the book. Writers worked in strange ways, he supposed she needed background information which she wouldn't ever actually use in her writing.

Jane Austen might never have written about the war with Napoleon, or about the sexual habits of the wider world in which she lived, but she certainly knew what was going on in that world. She could hardly help but know about the war, with her cousin being married to a man who was beheaded by the French, and her two brothers serving in the Navy, while the newspapers of that time, which she would undoubtedly have read, weren't at all mealy-mouthed about scandals, sexual or otherwise.

Clearly, Georgina was immersing herself in the social and political milieu of the time, and he found that impressive.

Georgina's writing habits had another benefit for him; with her working so hard, it was easier for him to concentrate on his studies, a definite plus since he was at a very demanding stage of his course. He had been heartened to have a response, after some time, from his parents, approving of the decision to send Maud to Hartbury. She sent him emails, grumbling about the sport — "Lacrosse, I ask you" — and the awfulness of the food and the oppressiveness of some master who insisted that she comply with the dress code — she probably had to dispense with purple hair, then — but he could tell that even if not happy, she certainly wasn't unhappy.

He was amused to learn that Pam had been down one Sunday to see her and take her out to lunch. She reported back in an astringent phone call that she had been right in the judgement that the school would suit

Maud. She looked well, was eating like a horse and seemed to think that she might be able to take a music scholarship in the new year, which would take some of the strain off his parents' finances.

It was very early on a Monday morning, the first day of December, a day that dawned sparkling with a magical frost, when Georgina finally pronounced the magic words,

THE END

She felt no sense of achievement, no joy at what she had done, just numbness. She'd bought herself a fast printer, having despaired at the reluctance of her original one to print more than twenty pages without throwing a fit, and now she watched, mesmerized, as four hundred and seventy-five pages flew out of the printer.

She printed out four copies. One she took down and laid on Henry's desk, with a Post-it saying, READ ME. She tucked the next two into Jiffy bags and walked to the post office, dispatching one to Maud and the other to Anna.

Alone in the house, she sat in the drawing room looking out the window, feeling quite empty. Stefan discovered her there a little later, and finding she was literally empty, insisted that she eat a large English breakfast, something he adored cooking. While she ate it, he planned her day for her.

"When one has achieved a big intellectual and emotional task, such as you have, one needs mental and spiritual refreshment. You must go to a spa, and have a massage, and swim and be wrapped in algae. This will make you feel much better, and restore you to yourself."

Georgina blinked at him. "Spa?" She thought of Aix-les-Bains, or possibly Baden-Baden, what an absurd suggestion, but Stefan explained he meant somewhere nearer home and put her into a taxi to Covent Garden.

There, smothered in Dead Sea mud, massaged, manicured, pedicured and slapped about in a deep-cleansing routine, Georgina slowly began to come back to life.

Back home, she retreated into her room once more, closed the door, sat herself down in the armchair, picked up her manuscript and began to read.

Thirty-Eight

Email from
mlefroy666@hartbury.sch.uk
To georgina@seaofcrises.co.uk
SUBJECT Book

Hi Gina

I skived off double physics this am (don't tell Henry) to go and read your book in the loo, where they can't get at you. I hope you appreciate my sacrifice — it means I get detention for skipping lessons.

I don't mind, I LOVE the book — it's fantastic — a GREAT read — I raced through it, even missed break to finish it.

Only — it isn't Jane Austen, is it?

Maud x

Georgina read the email, which didn't surprise her. Maud, as usual, had gone straight to the heart of the matter. Her own heart was down in her leopard-patterned ballerinas as she turned off her computer and went out of her room.

Stefan and Henry were in the kitchen, Stefan loading the dishwasher, and Henry sitting at the table, the typed pile of *Love and Friendship* in front of him.

He jumped to his feet, took hold of Georgina, hugged her fiercely, swinging her off her feet and round in a circle before putting her down.

"Watch out for my arm," she cried, hurting, but loving the hug.

"Never mind your arm. What an amazing, brilliant book. I had no idea you could write like that."

His praise instantly raised her spirits; yes, she was in a fix, but at least Henry and Maud liked the book.

"If only I'd known that yesterday was going to be The End day, I'd have been back earlier. You were in bed by the time I got in, and I sat down and read your book until three this morning. I couldn't bear to put it down." His face grew suddenly sombre. "The only trouble is —"

"You don't have to tell me."

"It isn't exactly Jane Austen."

"No."

"What happened?"

Georgina sat down at the table, and dropped her head into her hands. "You tell me," she said in a muffled voice. She raised her head and gave him a direct look. "No, don't, you don't need to because I know perfectly well what happened. I wrote the book I wanted to write. Not the book I ought to have written, or the kind of book I thought I would like to write, this came from somewhere quite different. I never imagined I could write a book like this, not in a thousand years."

"Good for you," said Henry.

Georgina's voice was anguished. "What really throws me is that all the time I was writing and sending chapters off to Marcia and getting them back and reading them through and then editing what I'd written, I never for one moment noticed that what I was writing wasn't remotely like Jane Austen. How could I have been so stupid?"

"Didn't your scenes give you a clue? That one in a brothel in Paris; very sexy, very graphic, I liked that a lot, or the pistols at dawn scene, with a pair of whores quarrelling behind a tree? What about the bit where Susan is taken for a French spy, and barely escapes with her life? She's a great heroine, by the way, I fell in love with her. Only there's no way you or anyone else can dress this up as a Jane Austen novel. Let alone one called *Love and Friendship*."

"I know, I know. I simply took leave of my senses and wrote without thinking what I was doing. What am I going to do now?"

The telephone rang, and Henry went over to the wall to pick up. He put his hand over it. "It's Anna. She's read your book." He listened intently a few minutes, nodding in agreement, then said goodbye. "I didn't think you'd want to talk to her at the moment. She adored it, every word of it, only she says she doesn't think it's like anything that Jane Austen could ever have written."

Henry and Georgina sat and looked at one another. Stefan, much intrigued by what was going on, joined them at the table and demanded to hear the entire story, with all the facts and particulars in their proper order. "Clearly, you have a problem. The only way to work through a problem is to write it down, with all its elements and then, rationally, set about solving it. Henry will agree with me on this."

He took out a notebook and a pen, and listened intently to the story of how Georgina came to be writing *Love and Friendship* in the first place, and how it had in various ways gone so wrong. He sat in silent thought for some time before he spoke.

"Every problem has a solution," he announced. "Yet I think what you have here is a solution without a problem."

Georgina looked at him, mystified. "In a parallel universe, perhaps?"

"Your problem is not essentially the writing of a book by Jane Austen called *Love and Friendship*. Your problem is that you need to write a book so you do not have to go back to America, and so you can make enough money to stay in England and to pay rent to Henry. Is that right?"

"It's a good way to look at it," said Henry, interested. "Go on."

"I haven't read the book, and if I did I would not be able to judge it, I know nothing about Jane Austen. But Henry and Anna and Henry's sister have read it, and say that it's a good book."

"A page turner," said Henry.

"Exactly. What is called a compulsive read. And books like this sell, readers like such books, and so it will make a lot of money for Georgina."

"That's all fine and dandy," Georgina said. "Only I don't have a contract for the book I've actually written, I have a contract for a book I haven't written. The delivery deadline for which is next Monday. I've blown it. I've let my agent and my publisher down, and I've let myself down, and I got a chunk of money that I'll have to pay back, and I don't know how I'll ever be able to do that."

Henry was thinking. "If this book is as good as we all think it is, then surely someone will want to publish it. That would bring you some money, as Stefan pointed out."

For a moment, Georgina felt a surge of hope, then the words of the contract came into her mind. "No. Since I haven't written the book that Cadell and Davies want, they'll reject it, and if another publisher picked it up and wanted to publish it, anything they were prepared to offer would have to go back to Cadell and Davies."

"In this case," Stefan said, "an alternative way is for you to persuade Cadell and Davies that this is a book that they want to publish in any case. Why does it have to be a Jane Austen? Does there need to be another Jane Austen novel, aren't there enough?"

"If they don't have this Jane Austen look-alike from me, it means that when they release the details of their discovery, some other publisher will come out with a finished book. That's why they wanted it done so quickly."

"Can Livia Harkness give you any advice about this?" asked Henry. "I assume you sent it to her."

"No, I didn't. I wanted all of you to read it first. I was planning to send it to her at the end of the week. Only as soon as I read it through myself yesterday, when I wasn't any longer in the peculiar state I have been in these last few weeks, I knew at once it was hopeless. Livia will be incandescent with fury, and I think we can take it that, as of now, I no longer have an agent."

The phone went again, and Henry got up to answer it.

Georgina knew with utter certainty that it was Livia on the other end of the line. She pushed her chair back and stood up as Henry picked up the receiver. Livia Harkness's sharp tones rang out into the kitchen. Henry held the phone away from his ear and raised his eyebrows enquiringly at Georgina.

She winced, and shook her head, and then, as the word *coward* sounded in her ears, she reached out for the phone.

"Are you sure?" he hissed. "I know you'll have to face her sooner or later, but do you want to do it now?"

She took hold of the phone, shut her eyes, took a deep breath and said, "Georgina here."

"Didn't you get my email? I want you here, now." And the phone went dead.

Georgina looked despairingly at Henry. "She's a mind reader. Or maybe Dan Vesey's stooge down the road has been reading the manuscript through my window with a telescope, and knows just how wrong it is."

"What are you going to do?" said Henry.

"What would you do?"

"I've never had to deal face-to-face with your agent. She scares me witless on the phone, so I don't think I'd care to."

Of all the things that she might like to do that day, bottom of the list was an encounter with Livia. She didn't have to go, she didn't have to be at Livia's beck and call. A brief tussle with cowardice, and she was heading for the door. "Better get it over with."

She wore her patent leather boots to give her confidence; much polishing had moved most of the traces of Wickham's tooth marks, and at least Livia couldn't think they'd come from the thrift shop.

She took a taxi to the offices of Harkness and Philby. The words sang in her head,

Harkness and Philby Literary Agency. Had there ever been a Philby? Perhaps the agency had been founded back in the bad old days when England was riddled with spies, and it had something to do with the most famous of the Cambridge bunch, Kim Philby. Or perhaps Philby ran the financial side of things, working away at accounts of the top of the house.

Too soon, the taxi drew up. Georgina paid the driver, giving him an extravagant tip — what was a pound or so given the financial state she'd now be in? She climbed the steps, pushed the door open and went in.

Tish had new spectacles, tinted a rosy pink, which might improve her view of life but gave her an oddly rodent-like appearance. She looked at Georgina, took in the boots, made a moue of what might have been approval and gestured at the stairs. "She's expecting you, go on up."

Georgina paused at Livia's door, summoning her courage, knocked and turned the handle. "Good morning, Livia."

Livia's eyes were fastened on the parcel under Georgina's arm.

"Is that the book? Why is your arm in a sling?"

"I've got RSI. And yes, this is the book."

"The book. Yes. That's why I wanted you

here. Sit down, although this won't take long, bad news never does. Have you ever heard of a Professor Windlesham?"

Georgina nearly slipped off her chair; as usual, she was perched on the edge of it. Of all the openings she had expected from Livia, none involved Rollo Windlesham. "I know Rollo Windlesham, yes."

"It's of no importance whether you know him or not. The thing is that the man has dropped a bombshell, and it affects you and me and Dan Vesey. How much of that novel have you actually written?"

"All of it," said Georgina.

"First draft?"

"No. This is the final version."

"Well, I hope you enjoyed writing it, because nobody is going to be reading it."

Georgina stared at her. Livia Harkness knew; she knew that Georgina had written the wrong book. Goddammit, how?

"This Professor Windlesham, I suppose he is genuine, he is what he purports to be?"

"It depends what he says he is."

"Don't get cute with me. The guy is some kind of an authority on English literature, right?"

"Right. He has a chair at Oxford."

"Turns out he knows all about the opening chapter of *Love and Friendship*. He

454

heard a rumour about what was going on at Cadell and Davies, went through his filing cabinets and came up with a letter from one Dennis Partridge."

Dennis Partridge? Georgina frowned, trying to make sense of Livia's bizarre pronouncements. What on earth was Livia talking about? Who was Dennis Partridge? What did he have to do with *Love and Friendship?*

"It turns out that this guy Partridge wrote that opening chapter of *Love and Friendship.*"

The words shot around in Georgina's head before they made any sense. "Wrote the opening chapter of *Love and Friendship?* But it's in Jane Austen's handwriting, it's been in the cupboard at Cadell and Davies for two hundred years."

"One hundred years, in fact. Partridge, who seems to have been a master of pastiche, I wouldn't mind having him on my list, set out to write a new Jane Austen book called *Love and Friendship.*"

"So where's the rest of it?"

"That's all he wrote. It was 1914, and he went and signed up, the fool, and died three weeks later."

"But the handwriting experts said it was Jane Austen's own handwriting."

"Partridge was an all-round forger, and it

turns out he taught himself to write in Jane Austen's hand. He planned to produce a whole manuscript, and then sell it as the real thing."

"And no one knew, except Rollo?"

"Windlesham says it's a forgotten footnote in the history of forged manuscripts and Jane Austen sequels, and of little interest to anyone. He thinks it's an immense joke that Dan Vesey was taken in by it."

"What does Dan Vesey think?"

"He doesn't see the joke."

Oh, but Rollo would be relishing it, and not least because of the fact that Georgina had been caught up in it. Georgina was prepared to bet that Professor Windlesham had heard that rumour way back, before she'd written a word, and had bided his time, moving in to quash Dan's grandiose plans at precisely the right moment.

Livia had lit a cigarette while she was talking, and tendrils of smoke wafted towards Georgina.

"I really wish you wouldn't smoke while I'm here. It makes my eyes water."

"Like I care about your eyes. Right, we have to discuss where this leaves you. You'll get to keep the signature advance, there's no way I'm letting Dan Vesey have that back. You can kiss goodbye to the rest of it.

Leave that manuscript with me. Is it any good?"

Georgina hesitated. "You can be the judge of that."

"I'll be in touch. Or not, as the case may be."

Dazed, unable to grasp the full meaning of what Livia had just told her, Georgina went slowly down the steps to the street. She felt reborn as the guilt and apprehension rolled off her shoulders. She wasn't ruined, she hadn't let anyone down, and, whether Livia liked it or not, she'd discovered what a joy writing could be.

She danced back to Marylebone, feeling happier than she had done for a long while. She stopped at the flower stall at the corner of the street, and bought a large red cyclamen in a pot.

Henry, who'd been in his study, unable to work, and constantly going over to the window to see if Gina was coming, was at the door when she got there, a tall, insouciant figure, whose presence gave Georgina a burst of joy.

"Well? Did you survive your trip into the lion's den? Did Livia give you a plant?"

Georgina put the cyclamen down beside her, stood on tiptoe and gave Henry an even more lingering kiss than Foxy's had been. Henry looked taken aback, then drew her into the hall to continue the good work. Georgina emerged, breathless and even happier, if that were possible, and she and Henry looked at one another. His mouth twitched. "Charlie rang."

"Don't tell me he's read the book."

"Good Lord, no. Charlie hasn't read a book in years, if ever." He went out on to the step and retrieved the plant. "No," he went on, shutting the door behind him, "his girl in the office down there gets the gossip rags, which of course Charlie reads from cover to cover. It appears that Sophie is all over one of them this week, wearing practically nothing in a Caribbean hideout with a celebrated actor, one Chris Denby."

Georgina was torn, half wanting to murder Sophie for daring to let Henry down, half overwhelmed with delight that Sophie had found other fish to fry. How could she prefer a man like that to Henry?

Madness.

"Do you mind?"

Henry looked down at her, smiling, amused, quizzical. "Not at all. Relieved, in fact. As far as I'm concerned, romance starts right here."

Epilogue

A week later
Email from
livia.harkness@hplitagency.co.uk
To georgina@seaofcrises.co.uk

Ring me.
Now.

Ten months later
BESTSELLERS — FICTION
Love Is a Frenzy
Georgina Jackson
Cadell & Davies, £14.99, 506pp

This autumn's must-read is Georgina Jackson's stunning **Love Is a Frenzy,** the best historical I've read all year. It's racy, pacy and splices high drama with moments of pure comedy. Susan is a sparkling heroine with attitude, while the dashing Wriothesley is as sexy a hero as ever wore breeches. Sex and scandal, lust and passion, intrigue and treachery and luscious settings in London and Paris combine to make a story you can't put down. Buy!

A year later
AUTHOR WEDS
Bestselling novelist Georgina Jackson, author of the hugely successful **Love Is a Frenzy,** and physicist Henry Lefroy, nephew of Lady Pamela Grandison, were married yesterday in a ceremony in Winchester Cathedral. They are off to New York for a combined honeymoon and book tour.

ACKNOWLEDGMENTS

Thank you, Teresa Chris, Trish Grader, Sam Gurney, Patricia Moosbrugger, Amanda Patten and Michael Weare.

■ ■ ■ ■

TOUCHSTONE
READING
GROUP GUIDE
WRITING JANE AUSTEN

ELIZABETH ASTON

■ ■ ■ ■

FOR DISCUSSION

1. When Georgina takes the Jane Austen tour in Bath, she's startled to learn one tourist's opinion of the original books and the written word in general: "Never read it, and don't want to," said Dot. "Haven't got time for that, and reading's passé, no one reads these days, books and all that are finished" (page 123). Do you agree? What do you think of the disparity among the fans on the tour?

2. Early on, Georgina resists Austen's style and subjects. "That's why this fascination with Jane Austen is so damaging, people harking back to a time when people were seriously oppressed, and pretending it was some kind of golden age" (page 124). Do you identify with the subject matter of Jane Austen's novels or do you find them alienating?

3. Were you surprised by Georgina's first reaction to finishing the chapter of Jane Austen's novel, *Love and Friendship*? Why do you think Georgina so fervently resists this job at first, and later is so reluctant to read the original novels? She cites Charlotte Brontë's opinion: *"The Passions are perfectly unknown to her; she rejects even a speaking acquaintance with that stormy Sisterhood; even to the Feelings she vouchsafes no more than an occasional graceful but distant recognition"* (page 146). Do you agree or disagree with Charlotte Brontë (and Georgina)?

4. What do you think of Livia's, Yolanda's, and Dan Vesey's behavior toward Georgina? How could they have handled the task at hand differently? When she finally does break down and starts reading Jane Austen, she goes on a reading binge that lasts for days, only coming up for the occasional meal. Have you ever been lost in a book like that?

5. Georgina's friend Bel, an Austen enthusiast, believes Jane Austen was the "ultimate realist": "Nostalgia, dreams for a past that never existed. Isn't that what all this is about? Aren't you selling a dream? . . . So

was Jane Austen with her vision of marriage between two equals — how often does that ever happen? Isn't that what all fiction is? Some good dreams, some nightmares" (page 165–166). Who do you think is more of a realist — Jane Austen, Bel or Georgina?

6. Once Georgina starts drafting outlines for her narrative, she reminds herself: "Of course the storyline didn't have to be stunningly original or even complex. The power of Jane Austen's storytelling lay in a perfect depiction of the characters and the creation of the lives they lived, not in startling events or thrilling about-turns" (page 260). Do you agree with this assessment of Austen's work?

7. What roles do Henry, Maud and even Anna play in the creation of *Love and Friendship*? How important is their input to Georgina and why?

8. Why do you think Georgina says of Maud, "She's more like Jane Austen than I am?"

9. Henry gets frustrated with Georgina's procrastination and tries to approach it

from a scientific point of view. What advice would you have offered her? Writing her first novel, *Magdalene Crib,* was a very orderly experience. Why do you think she's struggling with this assignment?

10. Were you surprised by Georgina's reaction to the news about Rollo Windlesham, her old professor, and Dennis Partridge and their involvement with the original text? What did you think of the ending? Does it feel satisfying?

11. How are the characters in *Writing Jane Austen* similar to characters one would find in an actual Jane Austen novel? How is the book similar?

A CONVERSATION WITH ELIZABETH ASTON

You've written many Austen-themed novels, including *Mr. Darcy's Dream* and *Mr. Darcy's Daughters*. What made you want to write a contemporary story? How is it different from writing a period novel?

The great delight of Jane Austen's novels is that they're as fresh today as when they were written, and in some ways, we read her as though she were a contemporary novelist writing historical novels. But of course, she was a contemporary novelist, writing about her times and mores. I'm a twenty-first-century novelist, whether I write historicals or contemporary fiction, and I thought it would be fun to write a novel set in the present day, but with Jane Austen books as a central theme.

The secret of good novels is the same across time and genre: characters that jump off the page, whether they're likeable or not, and a lively plot which keeps the reader guessing. With historicals there has to be a strongly researched background and a linguistic style which echoes the language of the period, whereas contemporaries need to capture life and language of today.

Your previous books about Jane Austen have been very successful. Why do you think Jane Austen has such appeal? How is she relatable in the modern-day world?

Jane Austen's appeal is the same as that of Mozart — she was a genius, whose writing speaks to the soul while it enchants and delights. Her characters spring from the page, and have an integrity and reality that make them our friends (and foes — think of Mrs. Norris in Mansfield Park!). Because of her deep understanding of human nature, and her portrayal of the *comédie humaine,* she transcends the gap of two centuries between then and now.

You studied Jane Austen at Oxford, including with her biographer Lord David Cecil. How has that helped you in writing your novels?

The rigour of those studies of the novels, the language and the background, have been tremendously useful. As has the study of Jane Austen's contemporaries and the familiarity with the cultural, intellectual and social milieu of her life.

Could you relate to Georgina's desperation over attempting such a daunting task? Have you ever suffered from writer's block?

Writing any book in that kind of time frame is difficult. It's possible when it's the culmination of months or years of brooding over characters and plot, but from scratch? Very hard! And in another writer's style is even harder.

Like many writers, I procrastinate. I might call it writer's block to gain sympathy from friends and family, but they don't believe a word of it!

How long does it take you to complete a novel from start to finish? How much research do you do for each book?

Some books have been rattling round in my head for years, others a few months. At any time I have about six ideas on the go. Getting words down on the page for a first draft is something I like to do at speed, and that takes weeks, not months. Then comes the hard work of revising and rewriting and editing. With a historical set in the early nineteenth century, I have years of general research and knowledge behind me, so I write the book first and then research all the extra facts and details and background I need.

Which Austen novel is your personal favorite?

Whichever one I read most recently! But I have a special affection for *Pride and Prejudice.*

Would you ever accept the task that Georgina has been charged with, and finish a Jane Austen novel?

No!

Apart from Jane Austen, what other writers do you read and admire?

That's a very long list indeed, as I'm a voracious reader in all kinds of genres, fiction and non-fiction. As a writer and reader and Jane Austen enthusiast, I'm a huge fan of the historical novelist Patrick O'Brian — and Jane Austen was the author he most admired.

ABOUT THE AUTHOR

Elizabeth Aston is a passionate Jane Austen fan who studied with Austen biographer Lord David Cecil at Oxford. The author of numerous novels, she lives in Malta and Italy. Visit her at Elizabeth-Aston.com.

The employees of Thorndike Press hope you have enjoyed this Large Print book. All our Thorndike, Wheeler, and Kennebec Large Print titles are designed for easy reading, and all our books are made to last. Other Thorndike Press Large Print books are available at your library, through selected bookstores, or directly from us.

For information about titles, please call:
  (800) 223-1244

or visit our Web site at:
  http://gale.cengage.com/thorndike

To share your comments, please write:
Publisher
Thorndike Press
295 Kennedy Memorial Drive
Waterville, ME 04901